D1483705

To Bob

For all his love, support, and many kindnesses
during a very difficult time

ACKNOWLEDGMENTS

My deepest thanks go to the following people for giving so freely of their time and energy in the evolution of this book and its story line. The book would've been much less authentic without their input, and any errors that are found are mine, not theirs.

For research help in the Kirkland/Bellevue Area:

Gloria Bickley, Tucson, Arizona; formerly of Kirkland, Washington
Jo Dooley, Smokie Jo's, Kirkland, Washington
Betsey Greenbaum, Bellevue, Washington
Mary Welborn, Park Ranger, Bridle Trails State Park, Kirkland, Washington

For help in establishing a fictional church and its accompanying structure, administration and philosophy:

Michael and Susan Gilpatrick, Clovis, California
Bill Wippel, Director of Community Relations, Gospel Mission, Seattle, Washington
Clovis Christian Church, Clovis, California

For help in founding and developing a philosophy for a religious school:

Linda and Mark Bedford, Santa Cruz, California
David and Marjaneh Gilpatrick, Gilbert, Arizona
Sandra and David Reese, Dixon, California

For general research help:
Shirley Brusius, Van Dyne, Wisconsin
Kay Conrad, Research librarian, Fond du Lac Public Library, Fond du Lac, Wisconsin
Leslyn Shires, Director, Fond du Lac Public Library, Fond du Lac, Wisconsin

For loving guidance and a writing table in her spare bedroom:
Debra Jeanne Gilpatrick, no longer with us.

Yea, though I walk through the
valley of the shadow of death . . .
Psalms 23:4

The righteous . . . shall wash his feet
in the blood of the wicked.
Psalms 58:10

SHADOW OF DEATH

Chapter One

Kate MacLean emerged from the dimness of the King County courthouse into the brilliant May sunshine flooding downtown Seattle, stepped out of the stream of foot traffic at the top of the broad courthouse stairs and blinked rapidly against the glare of the sudden harsh daylight. The courthouse was situated a few blocks east of the city's waterfront, well up the slope toward Capitol Hill, and through narrow slits between neighboring skyscrapers she could see Elliot Bay shimmering at her feet. A sleek white ferry glided across the slender needle of the visual space, headed for an island in the Sound. Bainbridge, possibly? Vashon? Watching the smooth motion of the ferry, she envied the passengers. No clogged bridges between them and home. No traffic clots. No fighting for every inch of freeway space. Just drive abroad and drift on home.

She glanced at her watch, two-thirty, then at the man who'd stepped out of the traffic stream with her. Sam Morrison, too, was staring at the bay below them, a dark, brooding look on his swarthy face. They'd lost, he and she. The jury had acquitted the slime accused of a drive-by shooting, choosing to believe the fairy-tale alibis provided by other fellow slimes rather than trust in the hard physical evidence of guns, bullets, fingerprints and ballistics tests. And after all the work she and Sam had done on the case. The crime scene details, the interviews, the careful documentation of means, motive and opportunity. How could twelve people simply toss it all aside? Granted, she and Sam hadn't found an eyewitness to the shooting. The victim, a motel clerk on a late-night, after-work stroll, had been walking alone, the residential street deserted. But even so, the bullets matched the gun, the fingerprints on the gun matched the accused. How could twelve supposedly rational, supposedly intelligent people so casually and willfully dump all that official testimony overboard and choose instead to believe the parade of sullen-eyed punks who'd lied through their teeth? All-night rap session indeed. How could the jury not see through it? How could they turn that animal loose to kill again? How could they!

A slight touch on her arm brought her back to the present. "You okay?" Sam asked.

She became aware of just how tightly her fists were clenched then. She drew in a deep breath and with an effort, forced her muscles to relax. "Yeah, I'm fine. Just mulling over the joys of being a cop."

Then she really was all right. You chalk one up for the bad guys, then let it go and move on. Sooner or later, the punk'd kill again. Sooner or later, the cops would get him. You let this one go and move on.

The sun passed into the western half of the sky, and it poured its warmth over her. She raised her face up to it, closing her eyes, ignoring the sounds of a city droning around her, and let the warmth penetrate the pores of her skin. The image of the sleek white ferry came to mind. The thought of taking an impromptu ride on one was appealing. They could park their cars down at the terminal and catch the next boat out to one of the islands, any island, she didn't care. Just let the calm and peace of water and sky wash away months of tense cophood, the only screams those of the seagulls.

She stood a moment, ignoring the powerful surge of the crowds leaving the courtroom flowing down the courthouse steps, and gazed out over the Sound into a vision of a cleaner, better world out there somewhere. Two-thirty. By the time they fought the clog across the bridge to the Eastside, they'd be off-shift. Well, almost. Then she grinned to herself. Talk about rationalizing . . . "Let's play hooky," she said, pointing toward the ferry.

He was staring at his own slice of the Sound, and that dark, brooding look he'd been wearing the last few weeks was back again. At forty, the raw bones of youth were buried beneath a comfortable layer of flesh stretched over a six-foot frame. His shoulders were broad and strong, his stomach only slightly thickened around the middle, and his forearms were made of steel. He looked like he could manhandle a gorilla with each hand and never miss a breath. It was a typical cop's body, well trained, well hewn, intimidating when he wanted it to be, comfortable when he relaxed.

But it was his face that always fascinated her. Lean and long, with the start of middle-aged dewlaps at the side of the jaw, he looked like a basset hound who'd just lost his bone. Especially with those warm brown eyes slanting downward at the outer edges. They seemed to view the world with a gentle reflection that took it all in. But he couldn't quite hide the sadness that seemed to be underneath the preoccupied air surrounding him.

Still staring at the Sound, his expression unreadable, he didn't answer right away. He seemed to be wrestling with some decision that needed to be made, his forthrightness gone for the moment. He'd become aloof and remote, about as much company as a corpse. And sad, she thought. Unalterably sad.

His lips tightening, he gripped her arm, decision made. "Let's just go have some coffee. I'll drive, then we'll come back for your car."

Down at the waterfront, he found a parking space under the viaduct, across the street from the Sound, and guided her across Alaskan Way to the broad promenade. Walking briskly, working his way around the knots and tangles of brightly clothed tourists busy with their cameras, he led her to Ivar's, waited in line for their coffees at a walk-up window, then found an empty, semi-isolated bench facing the water some ways out on the wharf. Instantly, a dozen seagulls sailed in and landed on the dock railing in front of them, ogling the Styrofoam coffee cups with cockeyed optimism.

She tried to read his expression, but it was impossible, he was too self-contained. Suddenly she didn't want to know what the problem was, and she turned away from him, overwhelmed by a powerful urge to go home, climb into bed and pull the covers over her head.

An Andrew Lloyd Webber song, "Tell Me on a Sunday," suddenly ran through her mind. The fellow had found a new love and was about ready to break up with his current girl, and the girl, sensing the breakup coming, sings her wishes for the where and when of it to happen. She wanted to be told in a park on a Sunday afternoon. Well, this wasn't quite a park. Just one of the world's more interesting waterfronts. And it wasn't a Sunday. It was just another Wednesday. And she certainly wasn't Sam's girl. All they'd been were partners. And good friends. An after-work drink or two. A pool game now and then. A Mexican dinner, often. Sam loved Mexican.

And yet . . .

Kate gathered her weary muscles together in preparation for whatever was coming and raised the Styrofoam coffee cup. "Cheers." She took a strong swallow.

Sam didn't respond to the toast. He simply twisted his cup around and around in his hand, staring down into the muddy liquid. Finally, his eyes still glued to the cup, he said, "I've asked the Captain for a transfer. To the Duty desk. Day shift."

Kate froze, staring at him.

"It'll give me regular hours," he said lightly. "A forty-hour week, no overtime, and no crisis calls. I walk in, put in my shift, and walk out again. Sounds pretty neat, doesn't it?"

He raised his cup and took a swallow, giving her plenty of time to respond. When she continued to remain silent, he finally glanced over at her and gave a mocking smile. "You might at least ask why," he said. "Help me out a little here."

She said nothing.

He gave it up then. Gave up all pretense of lightness, gave up all pretense of humor, and for the first time, real emotion showed through. Misery. Pure and simple misery. He looked back down at his coffee. "I'm reconciling with Janet," he said quietly.

And there it was.

She looked down at her own coffee. "I see," she murmured.

For some reason, her response made him angry. "No, you don't see," he snapped, flushing. "How can you possibly see?" He got up, crossed the two spaces to the wharf railing, scaring the seagulls away, and leaned back against it and stared at her, intent now on getting it all out. "She came to me a few weeks ago. She told me that for the last couple of years, she's been undergoing therapy. And she said that once she stopped making my work the focus for all of her unhappiness, all the old resentments went away and she realized how important it was to give the marriage another chance." He paused a moment before continuing on, his eyes begging Kate, pleading with her for understanding.

She stared out at the scene in front of her as she listened to him describe the series of meetings held between the two of them. She watched as the startled seagulls resettled on the railings a safe distance away and began scolding them both. Beyond, the deep blue waters of the Sound formed the perfect backdrop for their soft gray-and-white bodies. As Sam continued to describe how he'd finally reached the decision to try once more, she idly watched the freighter traffic from the Orient moving up and down the Sound. Then one of the pristine white ferries hove into view, drifting into the terminal with a tumultuous blast of its horn to announce its arrival. Beyond the boat traffic, the vast snow-covered Olympic Mountain Range rolled away into the distant sky. The romance of the sea, all rolled up into one picturesque waterfront. She drowned herself in it.

Then Sam's voice took on an urgency that cut through the haze. "Janet and I spent ten years together, Katie," he said in a voice that was half pleading, half angry. "Ten years of shared history. You just don't throw that overboard. You just don't give up on it lightly. Not if there's a snowball's chance in hell it can be made to work." He paused. "You can see that, can't you Katie?" You can see it's the only fair thing to do, can't you, Katie?" He stared at her, waiting, pleading, until suddenly his frustration at her total lack of response swelled and he slapped the rail, startling the seagulls again. "Goddammit, Katie, say something!"

What was she going to say? You look like hell, Sam? You're the most miserable-looking, unhappy reconciling husband I've ever seen?

She dropped her gaze to her own coffee cup. There was still a good half-cup of coffee left. A coat of slick drifted over the top of the black liquid, like the rainbowed oil slicks drifting around the pier pilings, and her stomach suddenly turned sour and she shivered.

A shadow fell over the cup, and she glanced up. Sam was standing directly in front of her, the dark hair glowing in the sunrays flowing in behind him. The anger was gone now, and only sadness was left. He reached down and stroked the forward curl of her hair. His voice was soft and gentle as he spoke the one word, "Katie . . . "

She dropped her gaze back down again feeling the gentleness of his touch as he followed the strand of hair down to her shoulders and lifted the single curl gently in his hand.

They formed a tableau for a long moment, with her seated, her head bowed, and him standing over her, his hand holding the one curl tucked into the palm of his hand.

Once sure of her control, she looked up at him and managed an almost-smile from somewhere. "I think it's time to go, Sam. I think I'd like to go now."

They rode back to her car in silence. When he swung in next to it, he gripped her arm, forestalling her from leaving. "Katie . . . "

She turned then, and looked him square in the eye. "Good luck, Sam," she said softly, the almost-smile still in place. "God bless you both." Before he could respond, she was out of his car and into her own.

His shoulders sagged for a second and he ran a weary hand down the length of his face. Then he straightened and put his car in gear. His face once again unreadable, he gave her a farewell nod and drove away.

She let him get well ahead of her, then started to maneuver along the hillside streets of the city to the freeway on-ramp. With some judicious cutting in, she made the four-lane jog across I-5 to get over into the far right lane for the turnoff to Lake Washington and the Evergreen Bridge, then took her place in the creep-crawl that passed for traffic flow these days. The hell with work, she decided. She was going home.

Home was an old, small two-bedroom Cape Cod, with white clapboard siding and a steeply pitched roof, set on a large corner lot in an old residential section of Kirkland, west of Market and a couple of blocks up from Lake Washington. Definitely, the low-rent district. Which had made it affordable. She'd bought it just before the big upsurge in real estate prices a few years back, and had counted her blessings. How large those blessings actually were was shocking. Nothing about the place was fancy. Not the house, not the landscaping, not the decor. But with its proximity to the lake, the modest little cottage had almost quadrupled in value. The Californians flooding the area, she'd been told, would kill for a location like hers.

She climbed the old-fashioned front veranda to pick up the mail from the wall box, riffling through the pile as she unlocked the door. Circulars, a catalog and a utility bill. She gave the living room off to the right a typical homecoming once-over, then veered left from the tiny foyer into her den and dumped the mail on her desk. The red light glowed steadily on the answering machine. No messages. She took a moment to call in to the station. She was told that all was still quiet, as it had been for the last few weeks, so she could take a couple of comp hours off. But she was also reminded that she was next up in rotation. She hung up and dug her pager out, then continued on down the hall to the back bedroom.

Within minutes, she'd stripped off her good go-to-court suit and pulled on a pair of old shorts and a T-shirt. She dragged her rattiest pair of canvas shoes from out of the closet, white ones gone black with grime, with holes in the toes and unraveling threads at the heel, grabbed her pager and headed for the backyard.

Her last major project inside the house was painting the grung-awful laundry room. But instead of getting the paint on her way home, she'd stopped at a nursery and popped for a few flats of annuals—geraniums, petunias, Sweet William, alyssum—a cheerful mixture of scarlets and pinks and corals and yellows. More than she'd ever need, more than she'd ever plant. She didn't care. They were her equivalent of comfort food. She gathered her gardening tools from the garage, loaded the flats into a wheelbarrow, then headed for the far side of the house.

After the first few probes of the trowel into the soft loam, the tension in her shoulder began to ease a little. She dug a deep hole for three brilliant scarlet geraniums, then surrounded them with white petunias. Several Sweet Williams formed their own triangle, then another grouping of geraniums and petunias. The alyssum would edge the length of the garden.

The sun, dropping down now into the western sky, was warm on her bare arms as she worked, and as the heat soaked into her body, her mind loosened its strict control, and she mulled over what Sam had said.

Poor Sam. The obvious question that she had *not* voiced to him concerned this newfound maturity of Janet's. If she was suddenly so all-fired understanding about his work, then why did he have to transfer to the Duty desk and to regular hours like a factory worker clocking in at eight and clocking back out at four? If Janet had truly undergone a transformation, wouldn't she accept his work in the Detective division, with all its uncertainties and chaotic hours?

And what did this do to his candidacy for lieutenant? The Captain had finally gotten funding to fill some of the slots beneath him, and the jockeying for positions had begun. There were only two candidates for the Homicide slot—Sam and Goddard. And Goddard was running a heavy lobbying campaign with the high brass, with the Chief coming down on all fours in his corner. If Sam backed out, Goddard would inevitably head up Homicide. God help them all if that happened. Particularly her. In fact, her job would be in jeopardy if Goddard was in charge. He'd put together a file on her, document even the smallest error she made, and eventually oust her. And why would a supposedly newly matured Janet force Sam to give up a promotion, too? The lady's actions were at odds with her words. Couldn't Sam see that?

Third grouping planted now, Katie sat back on her heels and swiped some sweat off her forehead with a forearm, shaking her head at the contradictions inherent in the Sam/Janet reconciliation. Unless Sam gave way to Janet's will entirely, it was doomed to die again. And all that pain, all that struggle . . .

The beep of the pager interrupted her thoughts. She hadn't even been in the garden for an hour. So much for peace and quiet. She rose and brushed loose soil off her knees. The pager beeped again. Hang on, she muttered, I'm coming. She switched it off and put on a burst of speed to get to her phone.

She listened as the Duty sergeant described the call, making notes, then headed toward her bedroom to change. A new case. A body at Bridle Trails State Park. Jeans and boots, then. She put on the clothes, grabbed the shoulder holster to strap on over her top, then pulled a light denim jacket on to hide the holster. She checked her new small .38 automatic, shoved it into place and buttoned up her jacket.

A new case, she thought again. And suddenly her spirits began to climb.

Chapter Two

Bridle Trails State Park was a square mile of heavy forest set in the middle of subdivisions, up the hill and across the 405 freeway from the main downtown part of Kirkland. Originally situated admist sprawling horse farms, developers had bought up most of the surrounding acreage, bulldozed woods and farms into barren ground and jammed the land with condo units and houses standing elbow to elbow. A few farms did remain, however, refreshing patches of quiet pastures among the bulldozed scabs, with horses grazing peacefully along the wood-rail fences. As Kate approached the northernmost boundary of the park, the last of the horse farms and housing developments slid past and she was engulfed by high canyon walls of evergreen forest, dim and shadowed in the late afternoon sun.

The main entrance to the park lay near its southern end. A couple of squad cars guarded each side of the entrance like a pair of estate lions, leaving a single lane free for access into the park itself. The media hadn't arrived yet, and there were no houses close enough to the entrance to draw any of the curious. The few passing cars that did slow were waved on their way by one of the uniformed cops. Driving her old Honda Civic, Kate had to show her ID. "Detective, Homicide," she said to the young patrol cop.

He looked chagrined, as if he should've known that, and motioned her on in.

A hard-packed dirt road led through a narrowed gap of tall evergreens into a parking area broad and deep enough to turn horse trailers around in one easy swing. A small tan trailer pulled by a GMC pickup was parked on the far side of the oval, its nose headed back out. A magnificent brown mare was hitched to a ring on the side of the trailer and with a mild, calm gaze, she watched Kate drive in and park. Two more squad cars were angled in against a wall of evergreens, and a small four-wheel drive utility jeep was pulled up in front of a white wooden swing gate that barred vehicle access to the northern areas of the park. A patrol officer stood guard at that gate, and opposite him, across the roadway, an older uniformed cop, George Leffick, guarded a narrow trail leading into the woods to the south. As Kate walked up to him, he eyed her with the same patient gaze as the mare.

Hands jammed into her jacket pocket, Kate listened as George told her the little he knew. A female horseback rider had come upon the dead body of a young woman in a clearing off the southern trail. The rider had hunted up the ranger and the ranger had called the police.

"Where's the rider now?" Kate asked.

He nodded toward the northern vehicle-access road, where the other uniformed cop stood guard. "There's a riding ring and some picnic tables back there among the trees. The ranger's keeping her up there."

"Is she all right?"

"Seems to be. She's an elderly lady, one of those tough old gals who keep their heads in the worst of times."

"And the body? Did they disturb it at all?"

He shook his head, no. "The old woman knows dead when she sees it. When she spotted it, she simply turned the horse and galloped off for the ranger."

"Any visible wounds on the victim?"

"Nope. It's like she just laid down and went to sleep."

That was enough. Kate didn't want her own first view of the scene tainted by secondhand impressions. "Okay, thanks, George. I'll check the body out first. Keep the rider and ranger up there until I get back."

The trail was clear and firm, winding in and around wild mixtures of fir, hemlock, alder and madrona, rising and dipping as it followed the contours of the earth. Generous amounts of sand had been spread to soak up rain and keep mud to a minimum, and over time, numerous hooves had packed it down into a hard surface that made walking as easy as a stroll on a city sidewalk. The trailside had been shorn of protruding branches to prevent harm to horse and riders. Beyond the manicured wall, the forest wilderness was intact, the smell of damp moss and molding leaves combining in a rich earthy blend that was sharp yet not unpleasant to breathe in. The noises of civilization faded away, muffled by the thick undergrowth, and a deep silence permeated the woods with just the faintest sound of freeway traffic humming in the distance. Around the third bend, a small natural clearing lay to one side of the trail, surrounded by a wall of salal bushes and evergreen trees. The body lay in the center of a large patch of lady ferns filling the clearing.

She was young, eighteen, nineteen at the most. A beautiful girl, with even features, a softly rounded chin, thick dark eyebrows shaped in a natural arch, and deep brown hair brushed smoothly back from a low forehead, pillowing her head in soft, thick waves. She wore a gray granny-style jumper, wool from the look of it, over a long-sleeved white blouse primly buttoned up to the collar, with a thin black ribbon tied in a bow at the neck. There were no visible wounds, and no disarray of clothing. Her legs were stretched out flat, the jumper skirt smoothed down over her knees in a proper fashion, and her hands were loosely crossed on her breast. Her fingers were long, slender and ringless, her nails unpainted, cut short and blunt. Kate couldn't detect any makeup. The simple black bow at the neck was the only decorative touch the girl wore. It was an austere getup for a young girl, almost like a uniform.

She had such a look of innocence, Kate thought. There was no expression of death pain to spoil the utter beauty of her stillness. The gently rounded face was placid, at ease, and the mouth had a sweet up-curve at the corners. She gave the impression of a gentle, trusting soul who wouldn't be looking for harm to befall her in any way. As George had said, she looked like she'd simply lain down and gone to sleep.

Kate left the visual body inspection a moment and scanned the area. The perimeter of the clearing was a solid wall of forest, with a mixture of trees, salal bushes, and scrubby undergrowth edged by tangles of fallen branches and rotting logs. The wild bracken and ferns cradled the body like a feather bed, and from where she stood on the trail, there were no obvious signs of any human imprint other than the victim herself. It was as if a group of sprites had carried the prone girl out into the center of the glen and laid her flat on the rich bower of greens, then had vanished, leaving no telltale traces of their presence. There was no purse, no schoolbook, nothing around that could identify the victim other than the body itself.

She turned her attention back to the girl. Life lost at the very threshold of adulthood seemed almost unbearably poignant. The girl surely had had her hopes and dreams. College, possibly, a career of some kind. Love, a husband, children. All the potential of a rich, productive, fertile life had lain ahead of her. Now brought to nought. Why? And by whom? Kate took her notebook out of her purse and began sketching the scene and body location, making notes as they occurred to her.

Most of the official crime scene personnel had arrived by the time she got back to the parking area. Men were setting up wooden barriers across the driveway entrance and marking off the park with the yellow crime scene tape. A forensic photographer was eyeing the deep woods and peering up at the fading daylight, then plying through an assortment of lenses in his case. Technicians were checking the contents of their evidence cases at the rear of the crime van, refilling supplies as needed. The M.E. stood to one side, talking to a man Kate didn't recognize.

Sam had arrived and was huddled with George. He'd already spotted her and as he listened to George, they stared at each other for a long moment across the span of the parking lot. As usual, when he chose it to be, his face was unreadable. Then she broke her gaze free and instead of joining him, she walked over to the M.E.

"You been poking around in there, Katie?" The M.E. gestured toward the woods. He was a small man, crusty and autocratic at his crime scenes, given to scowls and grumps. "Hope you didn't spoil things."

"All intact," she assured him. She raised an eyebrow in question at the tall, lanky stranger standing next to him.

The M.E. caught the look. "Sorry," he grumped. "Katie MacLean, Len Franklin. Len's out here from the cornfields of the Midwest for a couple of months, learning how his big-city cousins do things. He'll be taking charge of this one."

Kate gave Len a curious going-over. He was a bit younger than Sam, in his mid-thirties, she guessed, six foot one or two, with a broad-shouldered, solid build, a lean, weather-roughened face, a generous head of sandy hair cut neat and short, and a broad mouth set in a pleasant expression. Appearing totally at ease, well in command of himself, he surveyed her with a relaxed, easy gaze from a pair of friendly blue eyes. He nodded at the introductions, then asked, "What do we know so far?"

"The victim's a young woman," Kate responded. "Seventeen, eighteen. My guess is she's been dead for a good couple of days."

"Taken your medical boards, have you?" the M.E. growled at her. He turned to Franklin. "You watch out for this one. She'll tell you how to run your department, you let her. Well, I gotta go, got a date with a corpse. Report back in before you clock out for the night, Len." He bobbed his head toward Kate and stomped off.

From a distance, Sam frowned as he eyed the M.E. climbing in his car, hesitated a moment, then came over to Kate. "Where's he headed?"

"He has a heavy date." She made the introductions between the two men.

Sam studied Franklin a moment. "The Midwest? Whereabouts?"

"Wisconsin." The blond man smiled slightly. "Eden, Wisconsin. Village population, six hundred and twenty-three, give or take a birth or two."

"What's your background?" Sam asked.

"Pathologist, and all the accompanying medical training. When I decided to move into forensic pathology, I picked up the advanced course work I needed. I've also taken a couple of sessions at Quantico in evidentiary preservation and techniques at the scene of the crime."

Kate was impressed. Not everyone got into the FBI schooling sessions. It wasn't for your run-of-the-mill cop. In fact, if truth be known, she was a bit envious. She'd love to have that kind of chance to increase her skills and training.

Sam studied him a minute longer, weighing the man in judgment. Finally, he nodded. "Okay. Welcome aboard, Franklin."

With Franklin on a conditional acceptance as part of the team now, Kate led the way into the woods. The crime scene photographer came with them. When they reached the clearing, Kate watched the new M.E. with a critical eye. A careless medical examiner could do untold harm.

But Len Franklin took his time. He stayed glued to the trail, gazing slowly around, studying first the body, then the scene as a whole. Next he squatted down and skimmed a glance over the fern bed, looking for broken stems or other signs of trampling and crushing. Then he straightened up and did a long-distance, head-to-toe visual evaluation of the body. Finally, he nodded. "You're right," he said to Kate. "A couple of days, I'd say." He stood silent a moment, studying the scene in general. "You'll want to keep the scene as intact as possible," he said thoughtfully. "I think we'll do this bit by bit in tandem with the lab crew. Pictures from here, then we'll let them clear a path to the body for us. If there are any footprints, they'll have a chance to cast them before we go tiptoeing through the tulips. Once they've cleared an approach, we can go in then for close-up shots and a hands-on examination of the body." He looked at Kate. "Make sense?"

She nodded. It was a good approach. Any footprints embedded in the damp earth beneath the fronds would be preserved and uncontaminated by official personnel. "Sounds fine," she said. "Why don't you go ahead and start?"

"Gotcha," he said with unconcealed satisfaction. He turned to the photographer. "You're up next, my friend. Go to it."

She stayed awhile, merely watching. Franklin was as careful as he'd said he'd be. But still, he was an unknown. Either she or Sam would have to stay and supervise. Which was a waste of manpower, given all the things that had to be done. She pondered it a minute, then skirted the photographer and the M.E. and moved to where Sam was making his own notes on the crime scene. "We need to divvy up the work," she said quietly.

He nodded, and they drew off to one side, well out of earshot of the other two.

Without gesturing, she indicated Franklin behind her. "One of us needs to stay here and supervise. It's his first time on his own. And the other should start organizing teams for a door-to-door canvass of the area around here to see if anyone knows the victim. Or what they might've seen, if anything. And the rider and the park ranger need to be interviewed."

Sam glanced at his watch. "Okay, but I'm out of here at five. I've got a five-thirty appointment I can't miss."

That was so unlike Sam that it brought her to a dead halt for a moment. In two years of working with him, she'd never known him to quit at a certain time just because his shift was over. It had to be this happy reconciliation he was undertaking. She frowned slightly. "Can't you reschedule it?"

"No," he answered shortly. "Not this one." His look warned her not to ask any more questions. "And I probably won't be back again tonight. Sorry, Katie, but you'll have to handle this on your own until tomorrow morning."

"All right, Sam," she said quietly. "That gives us half an hour, a little better. You baby-sit Franklin while I at least talk a little with the rider and the park ranger. Come get me when you have to leave, and I'll come back here and take over."

He nodded, and with another glance of his watch, walked back to Len Franklin's side. He stood next to Franklin while the photographer roamed the trail, taking shots from various angles. Sam didn't look at her again.

Kate turned away from the small group and retraced her steps along the trail. The woods were tall and dark around her, their inner black deepening as the sun dropped lower into the western sky. A few birds sang their evening song, and the faint hum of the freeway beyond the evergreens across the street from the park had thickened into a dull roar as commuter traffic increased. But nothing could be seen through the trees. This section of trail and the clearing were as remote from civilization as a mountaintop in Mexico. A killer could take his time here without any fear whatsoever of discovery. Not a pleasant thought.

Well north of the parking lot a large clearing had been carved out of the woods, containing a riding ring, a small grandstand, concession buildings, a park maintenance shed, and picnic tables set in a grove of trees. Two women were sitting at one of the tables, each lost in her own thoughts, with Styrofoam coffee cups in front of them and a tall thermos bottle standing off to one side. Both women, Kate noted, were pale, but composed.

As Kate moved clear of the woods, the younger of the two picked up on the motion instantly and stared at her, eyes alert and wary. Cop's eyes, Kate thought. The woman didn't relax until Kate introduced herself as a Homicide detective, then she held out a hand. "I'm Barb Denton, the park ranger."

She was a small, well put-together woman with long dark hair threaded into a single French braid that wound around the back of her head into a tidy knot. She wore a khaki shirt with a Washington State insignia on the sleeve, deep green uniform slacks, and rubberized work boots. Next to her hands lay a pair of thick work gloves. Large, clear, wide-spaced eyes calmly observed Kate as she indicated the older woman seated across the table. "This is Miss Lucy Gray," she said, "one of our regular riders here."

Lucy Gray was a tall woman, late sixties, early seventies, whip-thin and straight-backed, with hazel eyes that peered brightly out of a network of age wrinkles. She was dressed in jeans, riding boots and a white shirt with the sleeves rolled up on strong, muscled forearms freckled with the liver spots of age. There was the stern, weathered look of sturdy pioneer stock about her, and she simply nodded once at the introduction, saying nothing, merely watching.

Barb indicated the thermos. "There's still a bit of coffee left. Would you like some?"

Kate accepted it gratefully, settling across from them, notebook out and ready. As she took the first sip of coffee, she glanced around the perimeter of trees encircling the clearing, feeling the sense of peace and quiet that filled it as the late afternoon sun slanted in over the spired tips of ancient firs. "Nice park," she said easily. Then she focused her attention on Lucy Gray. "Nice horse tethered out there," she said to her.

"That's Maisie," Lucy said. "She and I've been together eight, going on nine years now, ever since I retired. Used to be a teacher."

"Tell me how you found the girl."

Lucy outlined her routine. "Maisie and I ride here every day, from three to four, like clockwork. No sooner, no later. Spent too many years with a classroom buzzer to miss it more'n a minute or two." She described how she worked her horse in the riding arena the first part of every ride, then they'd take to one trail or another for the rest of the time. "Got twenty miles of trail twining through these woods, and we know most every inch of them, Maisie and I, right, Barb? But the majority of them are north of the parking lot, so that's where we ride mostly. But today I said, Maisie, old girl, you and I are getting in a rut, so I decided to ride through that one small section of trail on the southwest quadrant.

Besides, we kind of give Barb a hand here with keeping an eye on the trails—"

"We?" Kate interjected.

"The Lake Washington Saddle Club. It's a riding club. Almost everyone who rides here belongs to it. We're the ones that have helped clear the trails, and we've raised all the money to build the ring and the grandstands and the judges' booth. So we keep an eye out for what's going on. That's why I decided to check out the southwest quadrant, and that's how I stumbled on that poor girl lying in there, dead and gone as my teaching career."

Kate was making notes as she talked. "What did you do next?"

"I took a long-enough look to make sure there wasn't any breathing some life back into her, then I turned Maisie and we raced hellbent for leather for help. Barb was doing some trail work on the northern edge of the park, and when I found her, we both went back to the girl, just to make sure there was nothing to be done. Then we called you folks."

"Was she a member of the club?"

The two exchanged quizzical glances, then shook their heads.

"I've never seen her before," Barb said.

"Nope, nor I." Lucy Gray was positive.

"Are horseback riders the only ones who use the park?"

Barb shook her head. "No. We've got businessmen who come here to get away from it all, with their laptops and pagers." Her eyes twinkled a moment at the irony of that. "We have the lovers who walk around all starry-eyed, holding hands, completely lost in each other. And now and then, we have a student or two from Northwest College, sitting in the sun, reading their Bibles."

Kate made her notes. Riders, Bible students, businessmen, lovers. Where did the dead girl fit in? Bible student? The drab outfit she was wearing would fit with that. "Bible students," she said to Barb. "Any particular time of day?"

"Mid-morning through early afternoon."

"And the businessmen?"

"Midday," Barb answered promptly. "Right around noon."

"Saddle Club members?" Kate gestured toward Lucy. "Do they all have set times for riding like she does?"

"Pretty much," Barb answered. "Especially weekdays. They usually have to plan around work and school schedules. Early morning's a favorite. So is the dinner hour. Particularly for the kids. Then stay-at-home moms and retired folks like Lucy usually ride anywhere from after breakfast through mid-afternoon."

"You mentioned lovers. Daytime, nighttime?"

"Both."

"The gate's not locked at night, then?"

"No. We're on the honor system here. First one in the morning opens it, last rider at night swings the gates closed." She explained that while the stated hours on the park signs were from six-thirty A.M. to dusk, that was a mere formality. The main gate was never padlocked, only latched closed. Generally, the park was open to anyone at any time who cared to use it.

Wonderful, Kate thought. "Are you the only ranger here?"

"Yes. This is my permanent assignment. But I usually start my day at headquarters over at Lake Sammamish State Park, doing paperwork. I don't usually get here until about ten or so. Then I spend the rest of the day cleaning trails, removing dead trees, chopping up and removing fallen trunks, clearing underbrush—in general, maintaining the trails and managing the park. If there's major work to be done, new trails to be cut, building repairs, fences to be put up, picnic benches to be built—whatever—I'll call a work party from the Saddle Club and supervise everyone. I'm in complete and total control here."

Kate studied her. "So your day is spent mostly in the woods."

Barb look troubled. "Yes. The park's one square mile, and there's lots of maintenance involved."

"That means if you were working in the northwest quadrant, and something was going on in the southeast corner, you wouldn't necessarily hear it."

The troubled look deepened and Barb sighed. "No, I wouldn't hear it."

"Are you armed?"

Barb smiled slightly as she shook her head. "None of the state park rangers are. Though there's talk in the legislature about changing that."

"How do you feel about that?"

"Mixed, I guess," Barb answered slowly. "With all the violence around these days . . . " She let a shrug finish the thought. But then her slender face turned somber. "But there's no use being armed unless you're prepared to kill someone, is there?" she added softly.

Kate had a single notch on her own gun. Her one and only shooting. She agreed completely with the ranger's assessment. No sense in being armed if you're not prepared to kill someone.

She studied the ranger for a moment. The woman had a calm, grave look about her that spoke volumes of her emotional control. *Centered* was the word that came to mind. This was not a lady to run off half-cocked on some wayward whim and regret it later. "What do you do if there's trouble?" she asked.

"We have all sorts of government agencies we can call on. Local police. King County Sheriff's Department. State troopers. They're all on call to the rangers. In my case here, I'd call you guys first, then county cops if I had to. As for trouble, ninety-nine percent of it can be smoothed over with a little chat. Besides, we don't seem to draw those kinds of people. Except for the picnic tables, there isn't much here to keep the general public amused unless they're horse-crazy. And my riders are all responsible folks who take a great deal of pride in maintaining the park and keeping it up." Her gaze drifted away a moment. "At least, so far. With all the new houses going up, the new people moving in . . . " She shrugged and looked at Kate. "It's a dying way of life." She was obviously not happy about it.

"Unfortunately," Kate agreed. "Given a typical day, when is the park most likely to be deserted?"

Barb thought a minute. "Deserted, meaning completely devoid of people? Or deserted, meaning the parking area and points south? We have twenty miles of riding trail in a square mile of woods. You could have half a dozen riders out, and chances are good they wouldn't see each other."

"Except for the trailers in the parking lot," Kate said. "Then they'd know some others were around, wouldn't they?"

"Yes, some of them trailer their horses in. But there are still some farms left close enough to walk in. And we do have a couple of horse trails that lead directly to the neighborhoods. Not everyone uses the main gate."

Kate thought it over. How had the dead girl gotten here? And was the clearing within hearing distance of the parking lot? Would the killer take a chance on anyone overhearing him or her at work? She amended the question. "The parking lot, when would the parking lot be most likely to be empty?"

"I'd say late afternoon, supper hour. Say from four to six. Lucy's about the last of the day's riders, and the after-work folks have to make it home and change clothes first. Most of the after-school kids ride in from one of the outer trails, so they wouldn't be near the parking lot. So I'd say from four to six."

Kate was silent a moment. "Has there been anyone else you can think of hanging around the last few days?"

"You mean a stranger?" Barb searched her memory, but finally gave a shake of the head. "That's pretty much it. This park's out of the way. Unless you happen to drive past and see the sign, it's not something you'd stumble over."

Lucy was starting to get restless and finally she interrupted. "Maisie's gonna be wondering what became of me," she said in her blunt way. "It's coming up on her suppertime."

"Just a couple more questions," Kate said. "Did either of you see a purse, or any schoolbooks lying around?"

Barb shook her head.

"Nope," Lucy said. "But she attended Woodhaven Academy, if that's any help."

Instantly, Kate's eyes narrowed. "You said you didn't know her."

Lucy's eyes took on a mischievous glint. "Now don't go getting your knickers in a twist. No, I didn't know her. But I recognized the uniform. Woodhaven's a private Christian school and they all wear the same drab gray jumpers and white blouses. I know because my neighbor sends her kids there. Even the boys wear drab . . . gray trousers, white shirt, black vests."

"Do you know where I'd find this Woodhaven Academy?"

"In the phone book, I expect," was the tart answer.

Kate had to smother a smile at that.

Sam appeared at the edge of the woods and nodded her way. It was time for him to leave. Kate nodded back, closed her notebook and rose. She walked down the access road with the two women toward the parking lot. As they walked, the ranger pointed out various trees—madrona, hemlock, big-leafed maple, alder, cottonwood—and named many of the shrubs they passed, like the huckleberry bushes and the red elderberry shrubs. There were a couple of kinds of ferns, sword ferns as well as lady ferns, and bracken spread throughout. The pride in the ranger's voice, the sense of ownership that she exuded over her park, was plainly evident. If something had been going on here the least bit out of the way, Kate was sure it would've been noted.

At the edge of the parking lot, Kate extracted a promise from the ranger for a list of names and addresses of members of the Saddle Club, then walked Sam's way. He was in an obvious hurry. He didn't ask her about the case, or what the women had said. He simply said that the new M.E. was cautious, careful to a fault, and probably among the most professional Sam had seen. Then he apologized for deserting her and said he'd catch up with her in the morning. He never quite looked her in the eye.

She watched him drive away for a long moment before she turned away and headed down the southern trail to the death site.

She was rounding the third bend and just about clear of the trees encircling the clearing and the dead girl when she came to a standstill and let out a fierce breath that whistled between pinched lips. Goddard. He must've arrived while Sam was fetching her from the riding ring. Sam hadn't mentioned him, and he certainly would've warned her if he'd known.

From a distance, Goddard looked like a beautifully sculpted Greek god, tall, blond, tanned and trim. The sheer physical perfection of the man was breathtaking. It was only on a second look that you noticed that he walked with a bit of a swagger. And it was only up close that you noticed that the blinding smile he habitually put on was tainted by a subtle twist of cruelty. And it was only after the smile was switched off that you noticed the icy coldness behind the pale blue eyes. He'd been her first partner when she'd joined the Homicide division and he'd turned out to be the Partner from Hell.

And Kate knew exactly why he was here, at this park, at this time. Ever since the lieutenant's vacancy in Homicide had been funded, he'd collected murder cases like a sharpshooter collected medals, grabbing every high-profile case that came along, knowing the top brass would be watching and judging him. Photogenic as hell, he played the media like a pro, coming across as a cop's cop. The brass loved it. He made them look good. Now he was here, talking to the new M.E. and surveying the scene, acting as if he owned the case.

Still standing in the deep shadow of the path, she stood and thought a minute, then slowly, so as not to attract his notice, she backed up the trail the way she'd come until a bend in the path hid her from his view. Then she turned around and walked briskly back to the parking area.

She went directly to George and borrowed his squad car and radio. When the communications operator came on, she had the call patched through to the Captain. He was curt and abrupt, as if she'd disturbed him in the middle of a critical meeting, but he listened to her all the way through as she described the dead girl and what was known. She made no mention of Goddard.

When she was through, he told her to stick with the case, which was part of what she'd wanted to hear, but not all of it. "I will, Captain," she said, "but I need some authority here to get some things moving. I need to be appointed DIC."

"Where's Sam?" the Captain barked.

She had no idea what Sam might be telling the Captain about his personal situation, and she wasn't going to allow herself to go on record with any explanations that might contradict whatever he was saying. "I caught the call," she said firmly.

"Christ." There was a moment of silence, then he grumbled, "Yeah, go ahead, MacLean, you can take it. But only until I can talk to Sam." He hung up before she could respond to the implied gibe.

But she'd gotten what she wanted. Acting Detective-In-Charge. That would cool Goddard down for a while. Climbing out of the car, she paused to survey the official personnel roaming the area. She was hunting for one man, and it took only a minute or two to find him.

Standing well back among the trees, watching the action from the deep shadow as he always did, was Goddard's partner, Fry. His eyes, hooded and shadowed, roamed past her with an indifference that was as fake as Goddard's smile. He'd been watching her, she knew, and sneak that he was, he'd report her sojourn into the patrol car back to Goddard. Fine, she thought, as she headed for the southern trail again. Let them put two and two together. There wasn't much either of them could do about it at the moment.

When she emerged from the trees at the clearing, Goddard had taken control of the scene. He was pointing this way, then that, handing out orders to Franklin, the lab techies and the photographer as if they hadn't a whole brain between them. Brought up short by the arrogance he displayed, she couldn't help but think, If the brass could only see him now . . .

He caught sight of her and made an imperious gesture for her to approach. "Well, now, here's old Earth Mother herself," he said with false heartiness for Franklin's benefit. His stare, though, was filled with pure disdain. "Long as you're here, MacLean, you might as well make yourself useful. The neighborhoods around here have to be canvassed. I want you to go door to door, looking for witnesses."

She gave a slight smile. "You're a mind-reader, Goddard, that's just what I was going to have you do. Find out who saw what, when, going back over the last—" Goddard's eyes started to narrow. Ignoring him, she turned to Franklin. "What do you think, two days, three?"

Franklin stared out at the body for a long moment, running his eyes up and down the length of the dead girl, making some judgments. "Go back three. It won't be that long, I'm sure, but to be safe . . . "

Kate nodded. "Cover the last three days. Anything odd, unusual, strangers hanging around . . . anything," she told Goddard, his face frozen by then. "I figure you and Fry have—" She glanced down at her watch. "—a good two, three hours before you start running into people's bedtimes. Oh, yes, I should probably tell you, the Captain's put me in charge."

Then she let him stew. He was trapped, and he knew it. The DIC operated with the full authority and powers of the Captain's office. When the Captain ordered, the rank and file hopped to it. Same with the DIC's orders.

The open, friendly look on Franklin's face had faded as he caught the tension strung out between them like a taut power line.

Goddard started to glare, but checked himself suddenly. Instead, he gave her a contemptuous smile that was usually a harbinger of some cruelty to come, and said, "Sure, MacLean." Then turning to Franklin, he shrugged, exchanging one of those male looks that said, Women, what're you gonna do?

The M.E., accepting the sudden camaraderie at face value, relaxed at what he perceived as the easing of the tension, grinned and shrugged back, Damned if I know. He suddenly sank in Kate's estimation.

But she ignored the exchange and said to Goddard, "Fry's in the parking area, waiting." That he wasn't waiting for Goddard, that he didn't even know of the assignment yet, was something she didn't bother to add. Goddard simply nodded and walked off.

The technicians from the crime scene unit had made progress. They'd already cleared a path to the body for the M.E.'s photographer, who was out there taking close-up pictures of the body. But a false darkness was quickly closing in on the park, the early evening light of the outside world chopped off in here by the thick walls of trees. One of the crime scene crew working the clearing looked up at the sky in frustration, then hustled down the trail and returned a few minutes later with some technicians stringing a snaking trail of thick cables. They began setting up sodium arc work lamps around the perimeter that brought a glaring false daylight to the scene.

Len Franklin watched silently awhile, then turned to Kate. "We're about ready to examine the body. Joe's taking the last of the in situ pictures now."

Kate indicated the crews combing side brush for any evidence. "They found anything yet?"

"Some crushed ferns. That's about it."

"No purse? Schoolbooks? Anything to identify her?"

"Not so far. When I roll her over, I'll look for nametags on the clothes. Her dress has the look of a school uniform."

"My information says it is."

He looked at her curiously, but let it go.

The photographer finished with close-ups of the body, then waved to the M.E. "You're up."

"All right, let's see what we've got." He hesitated, studying Kate a moment, then said to her, "If you're not squeamish, I could use a note-taker."

She nodded. "Let's go."

He picked up a folded tarp and led the way out. She followed right behind him, stepping where he stepped, careful not to walk outside of the narrow path that had been cleared, and equally careful not to disturb the lab men still probing the fern bed for evidence. Now with the night chill moving in, the place smelled damp and dank, full of death and decay, like a place primeval, eons removed from the suburban life that teemed less than a mile away.

Franklin began his examination with the extremities. He lifted fingers, tested joints, swung a foot back and forth on its ankle. "No remaining signs of rigor mortis." His hands palpated the abdomen through the clothes. "Abdominal gases building up. Still some pliability left. No pregnancy that I can detect." He examined the throat and upper chest area above the jumper line. "No visible wounds to the chest or throat. Victim is cold to the touch. Skin feels waxy." He raised both hands and examined her fingernails. "Nails look clean. Doesn't appear to be any scrapings under them." Nevertheless, he paused to carefully bag both hands, then continued his examination. "No sign of assault, no sign of rape."

He rose then and said to one of the lab crew, "Okay, I'm going to roll her over." He pointed to an area on the far side of the body, away from the trail. "That spot been gone over and cleared?"

At the lab man's nod, Franklin unfolded the tarp and laid it next to the body, then squatted down, lifted the girl's left shoulder and rolled her away from him. The photographer hovered nearby for more shots.

The dead limbs flopped from one side to another like a rag doll's. The head followed last.

Kate saw the wound as soon as the back of the head cleared the last fern. At the lower back of the skull, the fullness of the hair was pasted to the scalp in a mess of blood, flesh, bone, and some dark bits that could've been wood chips. Below the collar, though, the hair fanned out in clean loose curls once again. The wound was like a barrette, drawing the long hair tight into the scalp at that one point. A barrette of death, Kate thought.

Looking up at her, Franklin nodded. "That's it," he said quietly. He reached out to roll her on her back again.

"Hold it a sec," Kate said.

The girl wore bobby sox and plain brown oxfords and Kate

squatted down to examine the back of them. The shoes were beautifully shined, clean and still firm in the rounded backs. There were no rough spots anywhere to indicate the girl had been hoisted up by her armpits and dragged into the clearing, already dead. Of course, she could've been carried in. As slender as she was, it wouldn't have taken all that much strength to hoist her up and tote her around like an armful of logs.

Or . . . the girl could've walked into the clearing of her own accord. Which would imply a certain measure of trust in the person who accompanied her there.

Kate checked for a label or brand name on both blouse and jumper. Nothing. The clothes were hand sewn. Thoughtfully, she stood and nodded at Franklin, watching as he gently rolled her back over.

"We'll bag her head and take her in," he said. "But unless there's something hidden by her clothes, there's your cause of death."

They picked their way back across the clearing to the trail. "When can you autopsy her?" Kate asked.

"Tomorrow some time. I've got a couple ahead of her, but I'll keep at it till she's done."

"Any thoughts as to the weapon used?"

"Yep, but I'm not going to commit until I know for sure." He stared back at the girl. "A pretty thing. I wonder what she did to deserve it."

That was the question, wasn't it, Kate thought.

She stayed until the body had been taken away, then she put George in charge of a full-scale search of the park for a purse or schoolbooks. Things about as organized as they could be at the moment, she drove out of the park, working her way through the mass of official cars jamming the park entrance and roadside.

Once past the logjam, the two-lane road from the park was empty, and as she drove through the corridor of night-blacked trees lining both sides of the road, a chill swept over her. In spite of the trappings of progress and growth on every side, this one section of land was remote and isolated. The hope of someone having seen or heard something shrank to a kernel. Unless they'd happened to be in the park at the moment of the murder. And of course parks, remote and wooded like this one was, gave rise to the haunt of a serial killer, Seattle's legacy from Ted Bundy and the still-uncaught Green River killer.

She set that appalling thought aside and made a mental review of the notes she'd taken. Description of the victim. Sketch of the crime scene. Notes on the interviews with the ranger and the rider. Notes she'd taken for the M.E. Miscellaneous notes on the park itself, and the people who used it. Including the Northwest College students who wandered across the freeway for an hour or two of respite. A Bible college and a private Christian school. Too good a connection to pass up.

The nearest public phone was at a gas station on Rose Hill. She checked the Yellow Pages under *Schools* and found a listing for Woodhaven Academy. It advertised a "Christ-centered" education from preschool through twelfth grade. Then she looked under *Churches* and found a Woodhaven Church listed for the same address. A check of the plat map she carried in her car showed it wasn't far, only a couple of miles northeast of where she was now.

She glanced at her watch. A dead girl. No ID. And it was suppertime already. Not good. Chances were both school and church would be closed for the dinner hour. Not good, either. But she decided to risk a useless trip. If luck was with her, someone would be there. If not, she'd at least have a chance to scope out the territory without interference or influence.

Chapter Three

Woodhaven Christian Church and Academy was set in the middle of a forest, carved out of one of the few undeveloped areas left between Kirkland and Redmond. A vast clearing extended from one dead-end road on the south to another at the north, with large parking lots off to the side servicing each end. Several low cedar buildings were scattered around, with a simple wooden church set apart from the others, dominating them. The evergreen forest formed a dramatic backdrop for the stage setting of the compound.

The northern parking lot, directly behind the church, was empty of cars. Kate pulled into a slot near the rear of the church, turned off the engine, and climbed out into a world filled with the fresh, nose-tingling scent of fragrant pines. She followed a maze of interconnecting pathways to the main road and stood quiet, surveying the whole.

The church was definitely the showpiece of the place. Set off by itself on the northern third of the compound, it was built of simple cedar, with deep overhangs and a heavy timbered roof which spired high into the sky. Slender stained-glass windows on either side of a pair of thick wooden doors rose from ground level to follow the steep roofline upward toward heaven. A rugged cross made of hefty, rough-hewn timbers hung between the colored shards of glass above the heavy front doors. A long wing of offices and meeting rooms extended out from the side of the church toward the center of the campus.

She walked up the main walkway to the front of the church. Next to the double doors, a simple hand-carved wooden sign announced Woodhaven Christian Church. Beneath, in script, was etched the name *Thomas Barnes*, followed by the single word, *Pastor*.

The doors into the church were made of slabs of planks held in place by crossbeams and thick black hinges. The handles were wrought iron topped by heavy push latches with an old-fashioned keyhole above. The latch pushed down, but the door was held fast by a deadbolt. She followed the walkway around to the office wing and tried the doors there. The church was locked up tight. The days of leaving churches open for the stray soul who sought spiritual comfort were long past.

As the early evening shadows deepened into a false dusk created by the thick woods to the west, she wandered a series of interconnecting pathways, identifying buildings, noting exits and entrances. Whoever had laid out the complex had brought some intelligence to the job. It was well thought-out, organized loosely into three self-contained sections, with maintenance sheds to the south, classroom buildings to the west, and church to the north. Broad sidewalks from the two parking areas guided the casual visitor to the front entrance of every building. But there was also a myriad of smaller rear and side entrances into all of the buildings, with their own series of narrower interconnecting walkways.

The lower grades were housed in a pair of buildings set side by side at the rear of the main rectangle of lawn. Behind them was an elementary-school playground, part cement and part tanbark, with heavy-timbered climbing equipment scattered around. Tall hedges of slender arborvitae lined the three outer sides of the play area, screening it from the rest of the campus.

The two-story high school was set at right angles to the elementary school, separated from it by the thick screening of trees.

A broad walkway wound from the church's parking lot to the school's main entrance, and like the other buildings, there were smaller, less imposing entrances at both ends.

She noted in particular that the furthest end of the high school butted up fairly close to the woods behind the campus. But a quick scan of the trees and undergrowth showed no paths or trails; it seemed a solid wall of tangled underbrush and interlaced tree limbs. Without a trail or path through the woods, Kate wondered, could one young girl have slipped away from the compound during school to meet her death a few miles down the road?

Absolutely. Out the far end of the high-school building, move along the woods which few of the windows overlooked, skirt the southern parking area, and off she'd go down the main road, no one the wiser.

If indeed, she'd been killed during the school day.

Absorbed now in her examination, she walked around once more to the very front of the campus and surveyed it from the main road. At first glance, the entire compound, with its low, rustic buildings scattered among stately firs and spruce, seemed extravagant and lush. But a close analysis showed that the buildings were at least ten years old, the church even older, twenty at least. There was a vast amount of acreage here, but this wasn't expensive land. There was no waterfront, no views to drive the cost up. And it would've been bought back in the days when the Kirkland-Redmond area was mostly rural lands and some old farmer had probably been very pleased to get a section of useless tangled woods off his hands. She could see how it had come into being, starting with a simple church in a clearing in the woods, and adding wings and buildings one by one until it had evolved into the vast complex it was today. The only sign of self-indulgence was the pair of stained-glass windows on the church.

She made her way back to her car. Pausing a moment with her hand on the door latch, she looked back at the campus impassively brooding the last of the day away in the forest. It was remote and isolated, she noted again. Removed, really, from the outside world.

She retraced her route back to Kirkland and headed for Northwest College. It was a good-sized campus, with brick buildings and shaded lawns spread over a graceful rise of hillside adjacent to the new Seahawks training ground. Pathways connected the buildings to a simple chapel with a trio of crosses hung on a stone wall flanked by windows. A peaceful quiet rested lightly over the grounds.

Groups of students were lounging on the lawn, catching the dying sun's final rays. As Kate slowed at the college driveway, a red Miata convertible, top down, roared up behind her and started tailgating her. She made a quick left into the campus drive, allowing the convertible to swoop on past, its gears grinding in anger. She parked as the rear of the Miata vanished over the next rise of road. One of your lost souls, Lord? Then her attention turned to the clusters of students scattered around.

She moseyed from group to group, selecting those that seemed to be the closest in age to the dead girl. The kids were friendly and approachable, and when she identified herself as a policewoman, they seemed eager to help. She couldn't detect any flickers of uneasiness shadowing the apparent openness. They answered her questions with regretful shakes of the head. No, they'd never heard of a Woodhaven Academy, and no, no one they knew spent any time at the state park. Why would they? one of the fellows asked. A sweeping gesture indicated the peaceful, spacious campus, with the night-darkening waters of Lake Washington shimmering in the near distance. Why indeed? she wondered.

However, her queries about Woodhaven did made a connection with the third group. A tall, skinny youth, not fully filled out into adulthood yet, thought over her questions, then nodded slightly. "The name's familiar. Seems to me I've heard of the school."

The girl sprawled next to him bobbed her head in agreement. "Wasn't that Norm's school, Jeff? Norm Overholtz? Didn't he come from Woodhaven?"

"Yeah, I think he did," Jeff said. He thought some more. "In fact, I'm sure he did."

"Would you know where he is?" Kate asked, suddenly hopeful. "I'd like to talk to him a minute if he's around."

"I think I saw him heading for his room after dinner hall," Jeff said. Then curiosity struck at last and he eyed Kate a little closer. "Why do you want to talk to him?"

Kate smiled reassuringly. "I'm just looking for some information about the school, is all."

There were another few seconds of thought, then finally Jeff accepted her explanation. "Hang on a minute, I'll roust him out for you." He bounded up from the grass and raced away.

The group, suddenly shy, smiled at Kate, then looked at each other, at a loss as to what to do or say next. The girl who'd made the suggestion about Norm stared at Kate for a long minute, then finally rose and held her hand out. "My name's Peggy. Peggy Lansing. The guy who went to get Norm is Jeff, Jeff Anderson. If there's anything we can do to help . . . ?"

Even in the fading evening light, Kate could see the flush of embarrassment climb her face, but the eyes were bright and eager, open and friendly. Kate smiled at her. "Thanks. I'll remember that."

Biting her lip, the girl flushed further and nodded. She hesitated, then she said to Kate in a soft voice, "I've often thought of going into police work." She was turning a bright crimson now, as if ashamed at her own boldness. "I'd like to help children if I could."

Kate surveyed her with a sudden measure of skepticism, but the girl seemed perfectly sincere. "Why don't you?"

The girl shook her head sadly. "I couldn't. My parents would never allow it. They'd never approve."

Several of the girls in the group nodded agreement.

Kate was confounded. In this day and age, kids still did what their parents felt best for them? My God, she thought, with some amusement, what's this world coming to?

Jeff Anderson bounded back into the group. "Yep," he said, between panting for breaths, "I found Norm and he did attend Woodhaven. He's on his way now. I told him you were looking for information on the school and he's gathering up some stuff for you. His school annual and some names and phone numbers, stuff like that." Then he added confidentially, "He's a frosh here, so he's still toting some of that junk around."

Kate's amusement deepened. "And what year are you?"

"Second. Sophomore."

Ah, she thought, the older-and-wiser man-about-campus. She glanced around the group, their faces open and friendly, and felt a sudden pang of nostalgia for her own youth. Not that she was that far removed from these kids, age-wise. Maybe a decade. Give or take a year. Yet compared to them experience-wise, she was ready for the old folks' home.

A movement off to her left caught her eye. A short, thickset boy was trundling out of one of the brick dorms, a picture-book-sized volume under his arm. He was plump enough so that his hips pumped like an elephant's as he crossed the lawn toward her. He had a round, fleshy face, with heavy, thick glasses that were slowly sliding down his nose, and as he neared, she could see the rough scarring of a major case of acne pitting the pumpkinlike cheeks. God had not been kind to this boy when the looks were handed out, she thought.

He stopped a few feet from her, peered at her in a nearsighted way, then looked around the group in a puzzled manner before his eyes returned to her. "I'm Norm Overholtz. You the police Jeff told me about?"

"Yes, I'm Kate MacLean, Eastside Police Department."

He pushed his glasses up on his nose and looked around the group once more, as if he needed to identify each and every person there, then finally looked back at Kate, his face still hesitant.

"Is something wrong?" she asked.

"Well . . . " For a moment, he fell silent, then he took a deep breath, shoved his glasses bravely back up his nose, and said in a low voice, "But you're not a man, you're a woman . . . "

At that comment, Kate expected the girls in the group to hoot and holler, to verbally tear the guy to tatters. But they stayed quiet and watched her carefully, a couple of them nodding agreement with Norm's implied protest. The girl who wanted to be a juvenile cop looked on, watching, taking it all in.

Kate thought of and discarded several acid responses. Instead, she gave an easy grin and merely said, "How observant of you."

The group laughed then, and relaxed a little.

Norm blushed, but he lost some of his disapproval and managed a sheepish grin. It gave him a suddenly engaging look. "Dumb comment, hunh."

He wasn't being difficult, Kate decided, just socially awkward. "Believe me, I've heard worse," she said lightly. She changed the subject. "Jeff says you attended Woodhaven Academy?"

Norm nodded with some pride. "From kindergarten to graduation, all thirteen years."

"Who's the principal?"

"Pastor Ellsworth. He's not actually a principal. He's the Pastor of Education. It's an education ministry, you see."

"Would you happen to have his first name, or a phone number?"

"First name is Charles." He tapped the book under his arm. "This is last year's yearbook. It's all in here. But I don't have a phone number. What I do have is the phone number for the youth pastor at church. He'd have Pastor Ellsworth's number."

"And Pastor Thomas Barnes?" she asked.

He seemed surprised she knew the senior pastor's name. "I have his number, too."

Kate took out her notebook and wrote as he dictated the information from a piece of scrap paper he'd stuck inside the front cover of the book. Then she held out a hand. "May I take a look through that a minute?"

"I guess." He didn't sound too sure but he handed it over anyway.

The book was softcover and spiral-bound, not the hardcover of most annuals, and it looked suspiciously homemade. The front few pages, obviously run off on a copy machine, were given over to a description of the school and its purposes, complete with pictures of staff and administration. Then the first of the class pictures started.

She didn't want company while she paged though it. She looked up and around and gestured to a nearby globe-shaped post lamp where an automatic sensor had turned the light on against the failing sun. "I'm going to take this over there where I can see it better for a minute, if that's okay with you."

Norman turned hesitant again, his fleshy face carved into a cascade of frowns. "Sure, I guess." He still didn't sound too sure about all of this and he looked around the group again, seeking support.

"I'll bring it right back," she said in a firm tone that allowed no room for argument and walked away, forestalling any offer to accompany her.

The artificial lamp was still battling the failing daylight for supremacy and just a faint cone of light reached the sidewalk area. Kate found a spot beneath the cone, holding the book well out of her own shadow, and quickly scanned through the student photos.

The book covered the entire school, from kindergarten through seniors. The high school pictures were individual shots, but the early grades were group pictures—a class with a teacher standing tall over them. As the classes aged, the height disparity between adult and youngsters decreased until by the middle grades, the teacher was standing off to one side of the group. From kindergarten through eighth grade, there were two group pictures per class, with fifteen to twenty students per group. Rough math indicated an elementary-school population of at least three hundred. Toss in another two hundred or more for the senior high school individual portraits and there'd be a total school population of from four to five hundred students.

All the girls, from kindergarten through seniors, were dressed in the same gray wool jumpers, with white blouses buttoned to the neck and black ribbons with tiny bows tied at the collar. The boys wore gray wool trousers, with white shirts and black vests. The clothes, for some reason, looked homemade, though she couldn't exactly pinpoint why she thought that. The fullness of the girls' jumpers, maybe. Or possibly the looseness of the boys' trousers, which were pleated and much fuller than even the baggy grunge today's kids were wearing. But whether store-bought or handmade, Lucy Gray had been right—all the girls wore the same type of outfit the dead girl had worn, clear down to the black ribbon tied in a bow at the neck.

She turned the pages until she reached the high-school section. Individual pictures started at ninth grade, small photos for the first three classes, larger ones for the graduating seniors. She found Norm's picture, thick glasses, acne and all. He looked a trifle dismayed, as if he wasn't sure what exactly the camera was seeing, but knew already the photo wouldn't be anything to be proud of. In years to come, she guessed, he would grow to hate that picture.

She turned back to the junior class. Only they didn't call it junior. Each grade, even in high school, was given its numerical year. There were three pages of eleventh-graders, alphabetically arranged. She started with the *A*'s and mechanically scanned the columns. The picture of the dead girl was near the bottom of the third page.

Taft. Sarah Taft. Sixteen, possibly seventeen, at the time the photo was shot. A beautiful girl, with high cheek bones, a slender face with a gently rounded chin, and thick brown hair pulled back from a low forehead and held by a clasp of some kind. Her lips were curved into a warm, gentle, easy smile, the kind of smile that said Here, let me help you. The brown of her eyes was a deep, placid brown—the color of Sam's eyes, she thought, kind of a rich walnut shade—deeply set, with thick lashes curling slightly upward out to the brow, and with a serene, almost grave look about them in spite of the smile she wore. That look reminded her of someone, and it took a moment for her to remember the ranger. Both of them—woman and girl—exuded that same sense of quiet strength and unshakable calm. Kate's first, instinctive reaction was, What a loss. She'd been so lovely, so young, so innocent-looking . . .

So dead.

Why?

Kate made a few notes in her pad. She would've liked to have scanned the activity pictures, to try and glimpse the girl in action. But Norm was hovering protectively around, halfway between his peers and his book, as if he wasn't quite able to trust her enough to rejoin the others, yet didn't quite distrust her enough to stand right at her elbow. She gave that a moment's thought. It was late spring now . . . May. He had almost a full year of college under his belt. His attachment to the yearbook had hung on a little long, hadn't it?

She thought back to her own first year of college. Yeah, she'd brought the old high-school annual along. Sure she had. She wouldn't have dreamt of leaving home without it. Within two days, though, she'd hidden it in her dorm room at the bottom of her sweater drawer, safely buried beneath layers of cable-knit until she could smuggle it home the first chance she had.

Yet that didn't seem to be the case with Norm. Why? Because he hadn't had to leave town to attend college? Because college and high school campuses were only a couple of miles apart? Or were there other emotional ties binding his loyalty so firmly in place? Like a tie to a lovely young woman with soft brown eyes and a warm, gentle smile?

That thought was worth pursuing, and Kate turned to the inside covers, reading the typical end-of-school yearbook signings.

Most of them were the diplomatic generic "To my buddy, Norm," that one wrote to the class geek. But there was one, in a corner of its own, outlined with a neatly drawn box, that was different. "To a very special friend," someone had written in a well-rounded, feminine script. "All my love . . . always. Sarah."

Sarah Taft?

Thoughtfully, Kate closed the book. The last of the group had risen and were milling about, getting ready to disperse for the night. The air had chilled with the fading daylight, driving them inside. But a reluctance to leave the scene of what was clearly to them an unexpected—and welcome—interruption in their routine was apparent in their aimless milling. They quieted at her approach.

She'd have liked to have quizzed Norm a little on the school, the Taft girl, and his feelings about both, but that was for another day and another time. She didn't want to start any jungle drums beating until the parents and the proper church and school officials had been notified. And even the subtlest of questions might set off some premature alarms.

She handed the book back to Norm with her thanks and nodded more thanks to the others for their help. The girl who wanted to become a juvenile cop watched her with a mixture of awe and admiration. Kate gave her a special parting smile of encouragement, then made her way to the car.

Before leaving the parking lot, she noted her mileage, then retraced her route north to the freeway overpass, crossed over and made the turn south to Bridle Trails State Park. Two miles exactly, from college to park. A long walk just to sit and read your Bible.

A killing walk?

She drove slowly past the park. By now, an assortment of TV vans and press cars were pulled off onto the gravel shoulder of the roadway. The media had arrived. For a minute she considered using them to make a public appeal for anyone who'd seen anything unusual in the vicinity of the park. But she didn't have a lot of specifics yet. No specific time of death. No specific method for transporting the girl here. No specific information to seek. No, she decided, not yet. The case would be best served by a downplay of the drama. Anonymous in her old Honda Civic, she passed the tangle of media cars without stopping.

While in the state park area, though, she toured surrounding neighborhoods and cul-de-sacs, looking for some sign of Goddard and Fry at work. She saw neither a departmental car nor either of their personal ones parked anywhere on the streets. Fine. She'd expected nothing less. They'd done this to her before, on the Fletcher case, and she had signed affidavits attesting to this tucked away in a bank safety-deposit box. Maybe it was time to dig them out and use them to derail Goddard's pitch for lieutenant. As she drove off into the dying day, she decided she'd have to give that some thought. It had an unsavory kind of appeal.

Chapter Four

She stopped at the Totem Lake Denny's for a quick dinner, ordered a cheeseburger and French fries, then used the phones next to the rest rooms while she waited for her food. It took three tries to get through the busy signal and when she finally had Thomas Barnes on the line, she didn't mention the dead girl. She simply told him she was from the police and said that it was urgent she meet with him. After some hesitancy, he agreed to come down to his office at the church.

By the time she'd returned to the church grounds, full night had fallen and the church was softly washed by strategically placed floodlights hidden among the foundation shrubbery. Dozens of cars half-filled the parking lot. As she emerged from her car, a rich blend of voices from within the church filled the night with song. She stopped and listened a moment, caught up in the musky rhythm of a lively gospel song accompanied by the deep richness of a full pipe organ. As she entered the rear of the office wing, the music strengthened, the beat strong, swirling around her like an air current, catching the rhythm of her blood. She had to resist an impulse to clap along with the tempo. She stood and listened another long moment, until a swell of song was chopped off in midflow. There was a second of silence followed by a sudden burst of laughter. Someone had blown it, she thought, smiling slightly. Then she turned and followed the pastor's directions to his study and gave a soft knock. A rich baritone voice bade her enter.

His office was a spacious book-lined study, softly lit, that radiated quiet and comfort. A couch and a couple of wing chairs were grouped around a low coffee table at one end. At the other end, his desk sat facing outward from in front of a bank of bookshelves, with a couple of comfortable side chairs for guests. Thick carpeting in a deep rich red deadened outside noises, and the room had a hushed, intimate aura that was soothing and comforting, like a rampart against tragedy. He was sitting behind his desk as she entered, and he quickly rose, rounded the corner and came toward her.

Pastor Thomas Barnes was a plump man in his fifties, medium height, maybe five nine, five ten, whose weight through the years had definitely shifted downward. His chin was blurred at the edges and beneath the opened jacket of the black suit he wore, an excess layer of flesh around the waist pushed against his trouser belt, blousing out the white shirt and black vest. The excess weight wasn't unattractive, though. He simply looked well fed and comfortable.

He shook her hand in a warm clasp, then held it tightly for a moment, his other hand covering hers in a comforting sort of way. His voice as he greeted her was a well-modulated baritone, thick with inflection and vibrancy and empathy. There was a velvet feeling, almost sensual, to his voice as he invited her to sit down, gesturing to the chairs in front of his desk. He took his own place in a high-backed upholstered chair behind it, sat forward, hands folded on top of each other. Kindly blue eyes fixed on hers. "How may I help you?"

Charismatic. That's the only word that came to Kate's mind. He was charismatic. In the same way a good politician was charismatic. She could see him standing in the pulpit in flowing black robes, the rich baritone mesmerizing the congregation as he delivered his sermon, those clear blue eyes moving here and there, stopping now and then to focus on first one, then another of his parishioners. All by himself he would chase away sin.

Before she could answer his question, the choir started up again, with the same joyous song of celebration they'd been singing when she'd arrived. But the music was muted now by the closed door, like angels singing softly from the heavens far away, preserving the sense of hush within the book-lined walls of the pastor's study.

Pastor Barnes had noted her cocking her head to listen a moment and smiled. "They wanted to soundproof my study," he said, his blue eyes filled with that special warmth he projected. "And there's been a time or two through the years when it probably should've been. But I said no. And it's moments like this that make it worthwhile." Then his face turned serious and he said quietly, "You said it was urgent, Miss MacLean. I hope none of my parishioners are in any serious trouble with the police."

Reluctantly, Kate brought herself back to the real world and the ugly news she was bringing that intruded into such comforting surroundings. It was too easy to lose hold of reality in here, she thought.

She didn't respond directly to his statement. Instead, she said, "I'm checking into the whereabouts of one of your students at the school here."

"One of ours?" He looked a bit surprised. "Which one?"

"Would you have a yearbook handy? Last year's?"

Puzzled, but nodding a yes, he glanced over at a row of oversized paperbacks filling a bottom shelf of one of the bookcases on the opposite wall, then pushed his chair back, rose and crossed the room in long strides. He pulled a book free and straightened up with an easy grace. "Here we are." His face alive with curiosity, he handed it to her before resuming his seat. Again, he sat forward, hands folded on the desktop, patiently waiting for the unfolding of the purpose of her visit. In the distance, the choir finished the joyous song and began on a slower, more somber hymn.

To test her own mental image of the dead girl, instead of turning directly to the class pictures, she leafed through the pages of the candid activity shots at the back of the book, taken over the course of the year during various school activities. She spotted the dead girl in several of them. Choir, swing choir, quilting club. One in particular caught Kate's eyes. The girl was climbing a stepladder, a roll of streamer ribbon in her hand, helping to decorate a plain long room for some event. A broad smile creased her cheeks and her face glowed with happiness in a typical carefree-youth type of pose. The caption identified her as Sarah Taft.

Confident of the match now, Kate turned to the individual photos of each eleventh-grader, found the girl's picture and turned the yearbook to face the pastor. "Do you know this girl?"

He nodded. "Of course. Sarah Taft. Eleventh grade then, twelfth grade now. A wonderful girl, very bright. One of our best students." He eyed her. "Why do you ask?"

"Would you know where she is now?"

The beginnings of a frown nibbled at his eyebrows. He leaned back in his chair, his chin firming up. "What's this about, anyway?"

Kate held up a palm. "In a moment, Pastor Barnes. Would you happen to know where she is now?"

"She's on retreat. Or should be." His benign blue eyes turned shrewd. "I'm beginning to think that maybe she's not."

Kate ignored that. "What kind of a retreat is it?"

"The church has a campground over on the Olympic Peninsula. It's the custom of the school to send the twelfth-graders there for a week shortly before graduation. We call it their Week In Christ. The boys went last week. The girls are there this week."

"And they left when?"

"Monday. They usually leave about noon on the church bus."

"And it's mandatory they all go?"

He hesitated. "Basically, yes," he said finally. "However, there are always those one or two who simply cannot go. Because of family commitments, for instance. They may not be able to be spared from home. We have one young girl whose grandmother is dying. She's needed at home to help out. Or the student himself may be ill. One of our boys is battling cancer and is in full radiation treatment. He couldn't go last week. But there has to be compelling reason for a student *not* to attend the retreat." His kindly face creased into a fond smile. "Besides, few students would scrape up an excuse not to go. The retreat is restricted to twelfth-graders. By the time our high-schoolers spend four years looking forward to their turn, when it finally gets here, they can hardly wait for the bus to pull out."

"Do they come to school that day in camping clothes, then?"

His face turned suddenly stern. "Absolutely not. They wear their usual school clothes. They change when they get up there." He leaned forward in his chair, intent that there should be no misunderstanding of what he was going to say. "We've discovered, Miss MacLean, that different clothes lead to different behaviors. That's true for adults as well as children, but it's especially true for children. The campgrounds are where high spirits can break free and a lot of energy can safely be released. But on the school grounds here, our students are expected to act with modesty and decorum at all times. From the earliest grades on. And camping-type clothing on campus far too easily lends itself to unruly behavior." He didn't quite point to her own jeans and denim jacket, but his disapproval was clear. The pale blue eyes were fixed hard on her now, intensifying the depth and color of them, and a frown cut deep into the flesh of his forehead. "Do you have reason to believe that somehow Sarah Taft did *not* go on retreat?"

Again she answered the question with a question. "Is there a phone at the camp?"

His eyes narrowed, then with abrupt motions, he pulled his phone closer to him. He punched in a number, then leaned well back in his chair as he held the receiver to his ear, his eyes never leaving hers. When he spoke into the mouthpiece, his voice was a soft murmur. He asked only a brief question or two, spending a lengthy time merely listening. Try as she could, Kate couldn't make out what he'd asked.

The choir voices raised to a triumphant conclusion, the organ swelled in a final étude and held the last note until it faded away into memory. A couple of minutes later, movement could be heard as people clattered down the stairs, laughing and talking as they poured along the hallway to the rear of the church. From the parking lot came a final flurry of hails and goodbyes, then engines roared to life and one by one disappeared into the night. A deep silence descended over the church.

A soft knock sounded at the door. Without waiting for a response, a man entered, stepped clear enough of the door to close it behind him, then leaned back against the wood, quietly waiting for the pastor to finish his call. He was a couple of years younger than Kate, twenty-eight or so, she guessed, tall and lean, dressed the same as the pastor in a dark suit with white shirt and subdued tie. His gaze on Kate was calm and quiet, only slightly questioning, and he gave a small nod, his thin face creased with a polite half-smile. Then the tight, clear eyes moved to the pastor finishing his call, and he patiently waited.

When the pastor finally hung up, his face was troubled and his motions slow in replacing the handset in its cradle. "It seems," he said to Kate in a reluctant voice, "that Sarah became quite ill here at school Monday morning. It appeared to be stomach flu and the counselors couldn't take the chance of exposing the rest of the senior girls to any kind of a bug going around. So one of the counselors took her home at noon."

Monday noon, Kate thought. The girl was still alive Monday at noon. "Would that be proper procedure?"

"Under the circumstances, yes." He tilted his jaw at a firm angle, a strong jawbone suddenly appearing beneath the drawn-up flesh. Under the soft, pudgy exterior, Kate decided, was a man of purpose. He turned now to the man still waiting in his quiet, easy stance. "Matt, this is Detective Kate MacLean from the East-side Police Force. Miss MacLean, this is Pastor Matthew Jacobson, one of my associates. Everyone calls him Pastor Matt. He's been helping me with some of our family counseling, and I asked him to sit in on our meeting once choir rehearsal was done. He's our choir director, too."

Remaining where he was, Matt acknowledged the introduction with a quiet smile and a nod.

"One of your associates?" Kate asked. "How many are there?"

"Five of us altogether," Pastor Barnes answered. He turned serious eyes on Kate. "Now I must insist on knowing why you're here."

But he already knew. Kate could tell. He already knew something tragic had happened to Sarah Taft, and was already girding himself for the news. Nevertheless, she spoke as gently as she could. "This afternoon a young girl was found dead in the woods at Bridle Trails State Park. I'm sorry to have to tell you this, Pastor Barnes, but I'm pretty certain it was Sarah Taft."

Pastor Barnes stared at her for a long, frozen moment. "That can't be," he protested. "Not our Sarah. We don't allow any of our students to wander free. Ever. Especially to a state park like that."

Her voice was a soft but firm murmur. "I'm sorry."

There was another long silence as he read the truth in her eyes. "How?"

"She was killed."

The pain grew in his eyes. "Murdered?"

She nodded.

His body sagged then. "Glory be to God," he whispered. He steepled his fingers, much as her Captain had a habit of doing, closed his eyes and bent his head low over his hands as he immersed himself in prayer.

Kate had to resist the urge to shift in her chair in response to the sudden discomfort she felt. She wasn't particularly religious. She wasn't particularly antireligious, either. She'd been brought up Episcopalian, but had wandered away from those simple childhood beliefs during her college and postcollege years. As a cop, it was hard to believe in any God, and so she seldom thought about religion, or higher beings, or any of the myths that formed the basis of any theocracy. When she did think about it, however, she knew that if she looked deep enough within herself, that somewhere inside she still believed in a God of some kind. But that was as far as religion took her these days. To her cop mentality, faith was a five-letter word in the dictionary. As was trust. Still, now and then, in times of difficulty, she did find herself praying. Or more accurately, bargaining with God, and to her, it was a terribly personal moment, something one did in private, in total solitude. Thus now in front of Pastor Barnes, she had to fight back her own pschyic discomfort. She glanced over at Pastor Matt.

He'd gone completely still, his face paling with the news as if the blood was being drained out of his body. His eyes had found a spot on the floor some feet ahead of him, and he stared sightlessly at it as a winterlike bleakness settled over his features, his breathing so shallow the rise and fall of his chest was barely discernible. Kate couldn't tell if he was praying, or looking straight into the depths of Hell.

Pastor Barnes finally heaved a deep sigh, ending his prayer, and raised up to face her once more, his eyelashes darkened with moisture. "Even a pastor has trouble remembering that God has a holy plan for each of us," he said softly. "and that His will and His ways are not meant to be always clear to us." He gave Kate a sad look. "You're sure it was our Sarah?"

Pastor Matt raised his head up, waiting for her answer.

"As far as I can tell, the victim matches Sarah's photos, so yes, I'm almost positive it's her. But that's partly why I'm here. We need to get in touch with her family and have them confirm her identity."

At that, Pastor Barnes stiffened in protest. "Couldn't I do that? Surely I could spare the family that indignity, at least." He rose, his motions surprisingly quick and brusque for such a large man. "Matt, you come with us. If it is Sarah, I'll need help telling her parents." Then he turned stern eyes on Kate. "I certainly hope you're wrong about this."

For a moment, Matt Jacobson looked hopeful. But a quick glance at Kate as she shook her head and murmured, "I don't think so," sent the hope crashing once again.

The King County morgue was located in downtown Seattle, which was inconvenient as hell for the Eastside, so the EPD had contracted with a local hospital for the use of their pathology department. The white subterranean hallway leading to the hospital's morgue was one long tunnel glaring with a glacial brilliance beneath a ceiling of artificial light. No shadows, not even subtle shadings, were tolerated in the harsh light. Stainless-steel gurneys lined one wall of the hallway, their emptiness pristine and unspoiled, a blanket waiting like a shroud folded neatly at the foot. There was nothing discreet about the place. You knew instantly that this was a way station for the dead. Kate led the two pastors down the hallway, their footsteps echoing eerily on the hard white floor, a human noise desecrating an inhuman place.

The lanky figure of Len Franklin bobbed out of a doorway at the end of the hall. Kate had called him from the church, so she was expected, and now, for just a moment, his eyes lingered on Kate's, crinkling with a welcoming warmth at the corners, then his gaze moved on to the men with her and his face grew thoughtful.

Kate did the introductions, her voice unconsciously low as if not to disturb the dead who lay behind the closed doors near them. As the men shook hands, she noticed that both pastors seemed a lot more comfortable in this harsh, barren place than she felt. It occurred to her that these men were accustomed to dealing with death, and for a fleeting second, she glimpsed the many facets of their pastoral life far beyond the obvious one of Sunday-morning preachers gently haranguing and badgering their flock into observing all of God's laws. Then Len Franklin was speaking to her and the vision vanished.

"We've got your young lady ready to view," he said to Kate. He gestured to a closed door set in a long section of wall all its own. "There's really not a proper viewing room here. Most deaths occur upstairs on the wards and the deceased are already known, so establishing a place for identifying bodies was never a priority. But I'll wheel her out here for you, and you can take a look-see."

Kate knew he was sparing them from the sight of the other bodies the hospital had collected that day. In spite of her years as a cop, Kate had never gotten over the initial clutch of the gut at the sight of death, and she simply nodded a bleak, appreciative agreement, and watched him disappear.

She would've liked to have been the cool, street-hardened cop that death couldn't ruffle, but she wasn't. That was the problem. Or rather the core of many problems. She *wasn't* street tough, and somehow couldn't seem to get there, and fellow cops like Goddard and Fry knew it. Earth Mother, they called her, not always behind her back. Good old Mother MacLean. Certainly no compliment. She girded herself for the appearance of the sheet-covered body.

On silent swivels, the door across from them swung open and clicked into a holding slot, revealing another sterile white passageway beyond. Franklin guided the gurney out into the hallway, pushed it lengthwise next to a wall, then carefully closed the door to the inner sanctum before approaching the coarse white hospital sheet with the obscene lumps beneath it. With gentle care, he lowered the top of the blanket down to the neck, exposing only the girl's face.

In spite of the harsh lights glaring off floor and walls, the girl still looked beautiful. Franklin had fanned the dark hair out over the pillow to hide any evidence of the wound, and it softly cradled her head like a silky brown veil. The eyes were closed and the long dark eyelashes lay gently against the finely sculpted cheekbones. She was the lovely sleeping princess from childhood fairy tales quietly lying upon her pristine bier, waiting for the prince to come along and kiss her back to life. It was only the cementlike grayness of her face that spoiled it.

Kate stood across the gurney from both pastors, keeping watch on them.

Pastor Matt, who had recovered some of his color on the ride over here, once again, sharply and suddenly, paled to a dead white, the lean planes of his face sinking in as a deep, unbidden grief stripped away all the supporting muscle structure. One forefinger reached out hesitantly, as if to trace the outline of Sarah's face, then the hand clenched and fell uselessly to his side.

Next to him, Pastor Barnes drew in a sharp breath. "Yes," he said in his low, rich baritone, "that's our Sarah. That's Sarah Taft." His voice throbbed with sorrow, and his eyes moistened once again with uncontrollable emotion.

That was what Kate needed. She nodded to Franklin, who covered the head as gently as he'd uncovered it and wheeled the gurney away.

While they waited for Franklin to return, Pastor Barnes stared into the distance, his face creased with sorrow. "We'll have to tell the family," he said in a deep, quiet tone to Matt. "This is going to be a terrible shock to them. Terrible."

The cop in Kate came alive then. "I'll have to accompany you." A slow frown crossed the pastor's face, but before he could verbalize his protest, she added, "This is a murder case, not a natural death. I'll have to ask them a few questions."

He stared at her, wordless, for a long moment, then gathered his thoughts together and finally nodded at the inevitable. "I do hope you'll keep it brief."

She didn't respond to that. Instead, she said to both of them, "Would you wait for me down the hall, please? I need to talk to Dr. Franklin a moment before we leave. Then I'll have you lead me to the Taft home."

At that, without a word, both pastors turned and headed back toward the elevator. Eyes narrowed, she leaned against the wall, arms crossed, and watched them go.

It was her first good look at Pastor Barnes from a distance. The excess padding of flesh on his frame gave the impression of solidity and stability. He still had all of his hair, sandy-colored gradually going gray, and it was cut full at the back, stopping just above the collar. His motions were slow and easy, as if he were comfortable within his own body, but without the swagger and vanity that characterized someone like Goddard. Once again she had an awareness of sensuality just from the way his solid body moved, and she tried to square that with the image of what, in her mind, a minister should be. Which was stern, uncompromising, judgmental. Sensuality not only didn't top the list, it didn't even make the cut.

Pastor Matt, on the other hand, tall, dark and lean, was made mysterious to some extent by his remoteness and self-containment. They were an odd pair, these two pastors, she thought. One, plump, emotional and easily read, the other slim, quiet and remote, with an elegant, almost poetlike sensitivity.

The door to the holding area opened and Len Franklin emerged. Kate uncrossed her arms. "The autopsy?"

"Scheduled for tomorrow afternoon. Want to sit in on it?"

She grimaced and shook her head. "Not unless I have to."

"You don't," he assured her. "The cause of death appears to be clear-cut. I don't anticipate any surprises." He glanced at his watch. "I'm going to be working late tonight. Another couple of hours, at least. How about a midnight snack when I'm through?"

"I'm not sure I'll be done by then," Kate demurred.

His eyes crinkled with amusement. "Strange hours you cops keep."

"Not like pathologists, right? Who get to bed early and stay there?" She straightened, wanting only to get off the personal. "About the snack, thanks, but I don't think so. I'll be going until all hours of the night on this."

He made no effort to hide his disappointment. "Maybe some other time."

"Maybe," she said noncommittally. "By the way, Sarah was seen alive at noon on Monday. That should narrow down the time frame a little."

"You mean *your* time frame. You need to have the time of death narrowed down as much as possible, don't you, to help you pin down the suspects?"

She nodded, then was silent a moment. "You know, if you keep looking at things from a cop's point of view, you're going to be a crackerjack of a forensic pathologist."

He grinned. "Is that an encouragement to stick with it?"

"Absolutely. Bad path reports make life pure hell for us." Then she shook her head with sudden impatience. "Oh, what the hell," she said with some exasperation, "somehow the system works regardless, I guess. I need to quit being an idealist."

"Being an idealist isn't all bad."

"It is when you're a cop." With a simple nod of farewell, she turned away and started the long walk down the glacial tunnel where both pastors were waiting for her. Her mind had already moved from Franklin back onto the case. Five pastors, she mused, as her footsteps echoed around her. Just for one church. Would the other three be as intriguing as these first two were?

Chapter Five

The Taft house was in an old neighborhood where the lots were huge and the houses small. It was a simple rectangle, bedrooms across the rear, and a living room and eat-in kitchen in the front. A single-car garage next to the kitchen filled in the front corner of the rectangle. The street was empty of cars and the house was dark, as was the rest of the neighborhood at that time of night. Kate stood on the small cement stoop next to Matt Jacobson as Pastor Barnes rang the doorbell, waited, then rang it again. After a moment, a glow sprang to life behind the fiberglass drapes pulled across a picture window facing the front, then the porch light snapped on.

Daniel Taft, blinking sleep from his eyes, peered out into the night, gray hair spiking like a thorned crown, flannel robe tied at the waist. At first, he smiled at the two pastors, an automatic smile of welcome. But then, as he caught sight of Kate standing quietly to one side, he misread the situation entirely and his face filled with a rush of compassion. With some small measure of astonishment, she realized that Sarah's father thought Kate was the one in trouble and that the pastors were turning to him for help.

"I'm sorry to bother you at this time of night, Daniel," Pastor Barnes said. "This is Kate MacLean, of the Eastside Police. We need to talk to you and Martha. May we come in?"

The smile faltered slightly at the word *police* but still nothing alarming seemed to occur to him. "Of course." He swung the door fully open and stepped back to let them pass.

Daniel Taft was a man in his late forties, gray haired, medium height, with an age-thickened body. He had the same deep brown eyes and strongly arched eyebrows as his daughter. As they entered, he ran a hand over his head to pat some of the gray horns into place and gestured toward the living room. "Have a seat, Thomas, while I wake up Martha. I won't be a minute." He crossed to a rear hallway and disappeared.

Matt and Kate settled in wing chairs placed on either side of the picture window while Pastor Barnes took the couch across from them, settling gingerly on the edge of the seat, ready to rise when Daniel returned. An ancient wooden rocker sat next to the couch, with a colorful multisquared afghan tossed over its high back. A basket of yarn was on the floor next to it, a pair of knitting needles protruding from a tube of charcoal gray wool. There was no television set, Kate noted, only an old console radio tucked into the rear corner of the room. An inexpensive reproduction of *The Last Supper* hung above the couch. A large family Bible lay open on top of a low bookcase next to a stack of Christian magazines.

Across the short span of living room was a door to a back hallway leading to the bedrooms, and soft murmurs came from one of the rooms in the rear of the house. Used to locating and identifying sounds, Kate estimated it was from the opposite corner, behind the kitchen. Parents' bedroom, she decided. The murmurs grew louder for a second, though she couldn't quite make out the words, then came the measured swish-swish of slippers on carpet. A woman stopped in the hallway door to survey the three of them.

Martha Taft was on the fading side of forty, broad-faced, with little pillows of plumpness collecting on either side of her chin. Long dark hair, threaded with gray, was pulled back and plaited into a single braid hanging down her back. For an instant she seemed to shrink back from the people sitting in her living room, seeking the protection of her husband's solid body behind her.

Then she drew herself together and walked slowly into the room, a quick, worried glance flicking from Kate to each of the pastors, then back to Kate again. Her eyes were apprehensive, as if her mother's intuition had already divined from which direction trouble was coming, and she clutched her flannel robe closed at the throat as she stared at Kate.

Pastor Barnes had risen as she'd entered the room, and now he went to meet her, clasping her hand in his. "Let's sit down, Martha," he said quietly. He guided her as one would an invalid to the rocker.

Daniel followed her in and settled deep into the end of the couch nearest her chair. He had picked up his wife's apprehension now. His eyes were watchful and wary, and his hand hovered protectively near Martha's as it gripped the arms of her rocker.

The pastor sat on the edge of a couch cushion at the far end, facing the two parents. "Martha, Daniel," he said softly, "we're bringing you some terrible news. The very worst kind. About Sarah." He gave them a heartbeat or two to absorb that much, then continued on. "Her body was found this afternoon in Bridle Trails State Park." Another heartbeat of silence. "Martha, Daniel, I'm so very sorry, but she's dead."

Daniel went into instant shock. He stared at his pastor. "She can't be," he whispered, "she's at retreat." His eyes beseeched the pastor to take back what he'd said, to make it not true.

But Pastor Barnes merely shook his head.

Daniel searched the faces of the other two, seeking refutation from each. But again, the somberness that Matt and Kate showed offered no escape from the news that sat harsh and naked like an unwanted stranger amongst them.

Still disbelieving, he said, "But how? How did it happen? *What* happened?"

Kate spoke up then. "She was killed," she said in a quiet voice. "Killed by a blow to the back of her head."

His struggle continued on for a second longer, then ended in a sudden collapse into grief. "Oh, my God," he whispered.

Martha had sat perfectly still throughout this, her eyes fixed on her pastor as her husband fought to grasp the ungraspable. As Daniel breathed out the three words in a voice laced with horror, her gaze swiveled to some unseeable vision in the center of the room and she began to rock. Slowly. A shallow rock, her arms crossed and clutching the opposite upper arm as if she were gripped in an everlasting chill from the grave.

Instinctively, Kate rose and slipped the afghan from behind the woman, pulling it free from the back of the rocker and folding it gently around the woman's shoulders. She couldn't begin to imagine a mother's grief. To nurture a babe from the womb to the brink of young adulthood, then to have her snatched away, brutally, without warning. She wrapped the woman warmly, patted her hand, then headed for the kitchen. Her New England mother always said there was no problem too big that a nice cup of tea couldn't handle. Of course, her mother had never worked Homicide. Still . . .

After a moment, Pastor Matt followed her and got busy on the phone hanging on the dinette wall, rousing some church families to come help. The detritus of death, Kate thought, openly listening as she put water on to boil. After about the third call, he said to Kate, "We'd better get some coffee brewing, too. Would you mind?"

While he picked up the phone again, Kate started searching cupboards for a group-sized coffee urn. There was none she could find lurking in the depths anywhere and she went looking in the adjoining garage. It was as neat and tidy as the house, with tools hung on a back wall of Peg-Board over a workbench, and shelves all along one side wall that held enough jars of canned fruits and vegetables to feed the homeless for a year. The third wall held a gun rack. A couple of hunting guns were propped on its wooden arms, an old shotgun that gleamed with care, and an even older Winchester thirty-ought rifle showing the same care. Beneath them was a chest-style freezer filled, Kate assumed, with the bounty of the hunt. The coffee urn was in a niche below the canning shelves, in its own box, protected from dust. She slid it free and carried it back into the kitchen.

Matt was dialing another number. "I'm going to be late." He wore a wedding ring and Kate assumed he was talking to his wife. "No, I can't give you an exact time. I'm over at the Tafts, there's been a death—" His explanation halted midsentence. He held the receiver and stared at it, then slowly hung it up. He lost himself in a view of the black night pressing against the window pane.

Kate kept herself busy gathering tea things, as if she hadn't heard a thing out of the way. But her mind was busy trying to fathom the meaning of the aborted call. Obviously, Pastor Matt's wife hadn't cared to listen to the whys and wherefores of his proclaimed lateness home. Why not? Because he'd been late so often, it was just one more late night in a life filled with late nights? Because they'd had some argument that morning, some disagreement that had left behind a rankled and short-tempered wife who wasn't anywhere near ready to be reasonable yet? There'd been no sympathy expressed for the family, no offer of help; instead, she'd simply hung up on him. Curious behavior for a pastor's wife.

In the other room, Pastor Barnes was explaining what he knew about Sarah's death. She'd gotten sick at school on Monday and instead of going on the retreat, she'd been brought home by the counselor at noon. He told them of Kate's visit earlier that evening, and her identification of the body in the woods from the school annual.

"You're sure it's Sarah?" Daniel asked at that point.

Without mentioning his own visit to the morgue, Pastor Barnes said, "Yes, it's Sarah." Then he began reading some verses from the Bible. One he'd chosen was the Twenty-third Psalm and Kate listened as he intoned in his rich baritone, ". . . Yea, though I walk through the valley of the shadow of death . . ."

The shadow of death, Kate thought as she rummaged through the cupboards once again, looking for a serving tray, caught by the aptness of the old, familiar line. Drifting overhead like a thundercloud, heavy, ominous, stealthy, never knowing where it would solidify and strike next. A fire shard that would leave a charred smear of the living behind.

Matt was standing in the doorway now, slouched against the doorjamb, listening to the readings. Kate watched him a minute, noting the look of weariness. The initial shock seemed to have exhausted him, yet he and the other pastors were the ones who'd have to give unstinting support and counsel. But who supported the pastors while they gave so heavily of themselves? How did the well of giving refill itself? She thought again of the strange, aborted phone call.

When she'd judged enough time had gone by for the parents to move from shock into some semblance of numbness, she loaded up the tray she'd finally found and brought the tea into the living room.

A younger daughter had appeared, about nine or ten, skinny as a licorice stick, with a pair of sleep-mussed braids hanging over her shoulders. She'd obviously woken up, come out to see what was going on, and heard enough to realize what had happened. She now sat huddled beneath the comforting arm of her dad, staring at all the grownups with eyes huge and round and scared.

As Kate passed around the cups of tea, she smiled over at the girl. "Would you like some hot chocolate?"

The child's eyes widened further at being addressed and she shrunk against her father even more and gave a wordless shake of the head, no.

Martha was still staring at the invisible center of the room. She seemed to have no idea of what was coming next, the questions, the probings. Grief forms its own vortex that swirls around the soul and sucks a person inward, Kate thought, and that's where Martha Taft had gone. She didn't notice the teacup Kate placed on a table next to her.

But Daniel was watching her with some dread, his arm tight around his youngest daughter, his hand patting the sleeve of her robe in an absent rhythm of comfort.

Kate placed the last teacup next to Matt, back sitting in the wing chair again. Then she took a seat at the far end of the sofa, on the edge where she could see both parents. "I have to ask some questions now," she said quietly.

Pastor Barnes had pulled one of the wing chairs to within touching reach of both parents. At Kate's quiet statement, he rose and placed the chair next to Martha Taft's rocker. His message to Kate was plain. He was ally to the family and, on their behalf, he would suffer Kate's questions only to a point. Daniel's hand flew out in a protective gesture and came to rest on Martha's arm.

Kate took them through the easy questions first and elicited routine information about the family and their daily routine. Daniel did all the talking while his wife stared into midair and his daughter peered out with those large, mournful eyes.

He was a hardware clerk in Redmond, he explained. Martha was a housewife. Lizzie was in fifth grade. Sarah, twelfth. Rising time for the whole family was five-thirty, breakfast at six, with Daniel leaving at six-thirty for the traffic-clogged commute over Rose Hill. The store closed at five, but he usually didn't get home until after five-thirty because of traffic. Dinner hour was at six sharp, every night, and the whole family was expected to be at the table then, washed up and ready for evening prayers.

Once a week after dinner on Tuesdays, the family went to church to attend age-related Bible Study groups. Otherwise they were home in the evenings. Martha did needlework while Daniel read, sometimes to himself, sometimes from the Bible, sometimes an article in a Christian magazine that caught his fancy. The children did their homework until they were finished, then there was a short prayer time for the family, with bedtime for Lizzie right afterwards. Most nights, Sarah would stay up later to work on her sewing projects, which was fine as long as she was in bed no later than ten, when the parents retired for the night. Friday nights were potlucks and social hour down at the church, Saturdays were usually work parties at the church and school, with families pitching in on cleaning, maintenance and ground work, and Sundays were filled with Bible classes and church services, followed by a large Sunday dinner. Then a quiet evening before the work-week began all over again. The picture Daniel Taft built was of an old-fashioned family, doing simple, old-fashioned things, living a simple, old-fashioned life.

Kate listened patiently to all of this detail, making no effort to hurry him, sorting out times and schedules for herself as they arose.

The mundane questions and detailed answers had lulled the group into some semblance of calm, almost like a casual getting-acquainted visit between neighbors. Pastor Matt sat motionless, listening quietly. Daniel had relaxed a little, his hand not hovering over Martha's quite so protectively. But it was only a temporary calm. Kate had circled the tough questions that would rouse the shock-numbed emotions once again. And Pastor Barnes, she noted, was maintaining his rigid vigil.

She began homing in on the subject of Sarah by including Lizzie in her questions at first. What time did the girls leave for school, what time did they get home, what were their likes and dislikes, what activities were they involved in?

Again Daniel did the answering, as familiar and comfortable with his family's individual routines as his own. The girls left for school at precisely 7:25 every morning, driven by their mother. Twice a week, on Mondays and Thursdays, the girls were involved with after-school activities. Sarah, in high-school choir and quilting club. Lizzie, in beginning sewing classes and the school band. The other three days they came home directly after school to help their mother with household chores and the cooking. These extracurricular activities were coordinated with Martha's church work, so that when the girls were at home, so was their mother, and when the mother was doing church work, the girls were busy at school at supervised activities. And regardless of the time their school day ended, Martha was there to pick them up.

Pastor Barnes interrupted at this point. The coordination of students' and parents' schedules, he explained, was one of the basic commitments demanded by the church and school. The children of the congregation were under strict supervision by a responsible adult at all times, from rising until bedtime. That was why, he added, neither Sarah nor any of the young people of the church were allowed driver's licenses or any of the accouterments so liberally handed out by parents these days that gave freedom to children too young to handle it.

Listening, Kate made note after note. Then she added a last one in strong script: *Kids are tightly governed and controlled!* Now the questions toughened. She looked up at the parents. "When was the last time you saw Sarah?"

And there it was, the younger daughter eliminated from the queries now, Sarah alone in the spotlight, and the realization she'd never come home again, hitting. And hitting hard.

Lizzie shrunk further back into her father's arms. Martha's eyes began spilling tears in a cascade down her cheeks. Daniel had to blink hard and rapidly to keep himself under control. "Monday morning," he said hoarsely. "At breakfast." His voice suddenly choked on him. Shaking his head at Kate, asking for a moment, he cleared his throat twice before repeating, "At breakfast, God help us."

Kate turned to Martha then. "Did you see her at noon when the counselor brought her home?"

Martha's eyes were filled with a heavy sorrow. "Monday afternoons I sit with Mr. Dixon." Her voice was a husk of a whisper.

"One of our older parishioners who's quite sick," Pastor Barnes explained. "He needs round-the-clock care, and our churchwomen take different shifts."

"What time's your shift?" Kate asked her gently.

"Noon to five."

"What time did you leave here?"

"Eleven-thirty."

A half hour before Sarah had been driven home, Kate noted. For what sounded like the first time in her life, the girl had come home to an empty house. What had she done? Called a friend? No, Kate thought, the girls would've been on the bus, on their way to retreat. The boys would've been in class. Unless one had skipped school? Would she have gone out to meet a boyfriend? Not if she were sick. She wouldn't have gone out at all.

But she had. Somehow she'd ended up at Bridle Trails to meet her death. Voluntarily? Involuntarily? Still feeling sick? Feeling better by then?

While everyone in the room sat hushed, waiting for her next questions, Kate made hurried notes, writing down all the questions as fast as they occurred to her. Then she led the next series of questions onto the subject of Sarah's friends.

Sarah had friends everywhere, it seemed. She was popular with the teachers, popular with her peers, and adored by everyone from babies to old folks. In soft tones halted now and then to push back the terrible emotions that welled up like ocean waves, Daniel told Kate about his eldest daughter. Warm, giving, kind, quiet, respectful, thoughtful, considerate and helpful. She loved everyone and everyone loved her. They were just naturally drawn to the tremendous warmth and compassion and empathy she had for everyone.

As he extolled her virtues, her character, her even temperament, Lizzie poked her head out from under his arm and nodded agreement.

Again, Kate made notes as Daniel described his daughter. "What about close friends?" she asked the group. "Girlfriends, boyfriends? Any disagreements, arguments, feuds of any kind going on?"

"Boyfriends are not allowed." Pastor Barnes's back had gone rigid at the term. "Boy-girl relationships are strictly forbidden until all schooling is completed and our young people are out in the work world, capable of supporting a family. We don't allow *anything* that would encourage early marriages or foolish behavior. They simply are not old enough to handle that kind of pressure."

Foolish behavior meaning sex? Kate made a note to check into the real situation there. "Girlfriends?" she said mildly.

Sarah liked everyone, she was stiffly informed by the now irritated pastor. She didn't like any one person above any others. And no, disagreements were not allowed either. Those few that did crop up were promptly settled to everyone's satisfaction.

Kate made a note to check into that, too.

She kept her skepticism of this idealistic view of teenage behavior to herself, though, and asked the question that would be at the core of her investigation. "Do *any* of you know of *anyone* who would have a reason for wanting to hurt Sarah, for wanting her dead?"

Pastor Barnes looked shocked that Kate had even asked such a thing. "It was obviously some stranger who did this," he asserted. "Some sick, misguided soul just looking to do harm to someone."

She refused to debate him. He could be right. Instead, she watched the others. Daniel's look of suffering had increased tenfold at her question, and incapable of speech, he merely shook his head. Fresh tears flowed down Martha's cheeks and her chair speeded up its rocking. Matt slumped back in the wing chair and ran a hand over his face as if he were fighting off a terrible urge to cry.

It was Lizzie who answered the question directly. Peering out from the safety of her father's embrace, she said loudly, "Nope. Everyone loved Sarah. They *always* smiled when she was around. She just made you feel like smiling."

Then, her little speech done, she blushed bright red, shrunk back under her father's arm again, buried her head against his chest and began to cry.

Kate needed to search Sarah's room, and Martha Taft slowly pulled herself together, rising from the rocker as if weighted down with a double dose of gravity, hugging the afghan tight around her stocky figure as she led the way into the hallway. Sarah's room was directly to the right, tucked in behind the living room. The door had been closed and Martha hesitated before turning the knob, as if a specter would jump out at her given the slightest opening.

Kate indicated the closed door. "Was this shut when you came home Monday night?"

Martha gave a dull nod. "We always close off the bedrooms. Saves heat."

"Did you go in her room at all while she's been gone?"

Martha merely shook her head. Then, drawing in a deep breath to steady herself, she gave the knob one firm twist and pushed the door back.

It was a room done up for a typical teenager. Pale blue walls, crisp homemade white curtains at the single window. The walls were lined with a miscellaneous collection of bookcases and wooden chests, all painted a fresh white, with delicate floral transfers stenciled here and there. In a corner stood a large old worktable used as a sewing table, and next to it a desk, painted white, with a pale lavender trim around the edge. A beautiful handmade quilt with patches of blues and greens and lavenders on a pristine white background covered an old twin-sized wooden bedstead. Another quilt in bright reds and blues and greens, partially completed, lay upon the sewing table. They were each an exquisite piece of work, the quilting stitches tiny, evenly spaced and ruler straight. A bright rag rug in the same colors as the quilt patches lay in front of an old porch rocker painted a fresh sunny yellow. The whole room was fresh and light and airy.

Martha still stood frozen in the doorway, her gaze drifting from place to place around the room, like someone taking inventory, toting up the items there. The schoolwork that wouldn't be done now. The quilting project that wouldn't get finished. The clothes that wouldn't be worn again. The bed that would stay neatly made up, the covers never to be tossed back into thick clumps as the sleeper rose to face a new day. Martha examined each item there, the vast sorrow in her eyes mixing now with wistfulness and pain that deepened until in defense they fused into a dull-eyed stare that saw none of it.

Kate turned away and began a discreet but thorough search of the room. She explored the dresser drawers, ran her hands along the bottom of each one, looking for anything out of the ordinary. She checked beneath the mattress, below the clothes in the drawers, along the closet shelves. She searched the floor of the closet, looked under the bed, and examined the bookcase.

What she was hoping for was a diary. In a perfect world, there'd be one. Names, dates, and times. In a perfect world. That was the maximum hope. Minimum was a scrap of paper with something meaningful written on it. All she needed was a little something, anything, to steer her in some direction or another.

She did find a backpack filled with camping clothes on the floor of the closet, a purse currently in use on the back of the dresser top, and a pile of schoolbooks and notebooks on the center of the worktable. That answered the question about Sarah's missing things at the park, Kate thought. Obviously, Sarah had come into her room after being brought home by the counselor Monday noon. Had she lain down? The bed quilt showed no imprint, no wrinkle to suggest that she had. Impossible to say.

She turned to Martha. "On Monday night, when you got home, were there any signs that Sarah had been here? Any signs at all?"

Martha looked at her with dull eyes. "Like what?"

She wasn't making connections yet, Kate thought. Numbness had dulled her mind and she wasn't connecting a murder investigation and its resulting questions with the death of her daughter. "Oh, the door open when it should've been closed," Kate said. "Scraps of food in the kitchen. Lunch dishes in the sink. Mail brought in. Anything that was out of place at all."

"No, nothing," Martha said in that same dull monotone. "Besides, Sarah had packed a lunch to eat on the bus up to camp."

Kate picked up on that. So, they were missing a lunch sack. "What did she pack?"

"Cheese, I think. A cheese sandwich. An apple."

"What about the garbage? Was the lunch thrown away? Had it been eaten, and the wrappings tossed out?"

Martha shrugged, obviously not considering it worth bothering about. "I don't know, the garbage got picked up yesterday."

"And you'd emptied all the wastebaskets?" Kate asked with some dismay.

Another shrug and a dull stare. "I always do."

"This one, too?" Kate pointed to the empty wastebasket sitting next to Sarah's worktable.

"No. Sarah did that Monday morning before she left for school."

Inwardly, Kate sighed. Sometimes she wished only cops were allowed to people the world. The simplest thing could complicate a cop's life so. Tossing out the garbage for pickup, for instance. A common, ordinary, everyday event, yet who knew how much missed evidence in how many unsolved cases was due to such a simple thing as the tossing away of the garbage of a daily life. She let it go as a lost cause and concentrated again on the things Sarah had brought home Monday noon.

The purse contained only a wallet, a small hairbrush and comb, a half-eaten roll of Tums, and an assortment of pens and pencils that had fallen to the bottom. The wallet held six dollars in bills, a five and a one, a handful of change in the coin purse, and a simple identification card commonly supplied by wallet manufacturers, filled out in neat printing with Sarah's name and address. There were no pictures of friends or family in the cellophane windows, nor any other form of identification. And no loose scraps of paper in either of them. Purse and wallet were as neat and tidy as the room.

She explored the backpack next. Just typical camping clothes. Navy blue shorts and slacks, white short-sleeved shirts, a bathing suit and a terry cloth cover-up made from old bath towels. Underwear and socks, flannel pajamas, also homemade, and a light windbreaker, all neatly folded and packed. A pair of old tennis shoes, some thongs for swimming, and a pair of handmade slipper-socks. Plus a bottle of shampoo and a toothbrush and toothpaste. No curling iron, no blow-dryer, and neither purse nor backpack had yielded cosmetics of any kind, not even lipstick. Neither did the dresser top, nor any of the drawers.

Sarah's school papers and notebooks came last. But all Kate found was regular schoolwork, notes on future assignments, and papers already graded and handed back. Sarah was a straight-A student. Her writing was neat and well rounded, easily read, and her work was thorough, all assignments completed and correct. This was one well-organized young woman, she thought. Absolutely nothing was there that shouldn't have been. And there was no date calendar. Homework assignment book, yes. Date book, no. It was impossible to tell if she'd made arrangements to meet anyone at the state park.

The only signs of a personal Sarah in the schoolwork were a few doodles marching around the margins of some class notes. Mountains, lakes, valleys and rivers had been lightly sketched in the broad flat spaces, top and bottom. Stately fir trees climbed the side margins. The girl had had a natural gift for art. The lines were sure and true, with only a slight erasure here and there to allow a small correction. The scenes were vivid and meticulously detailed, down to the pine cones on many of the firs. But there were no names or initials doodled anywhere.

By now, the first of the family's friends had arrived and the little house began to reverberate with talk, tears and confusion. A couple of women came to the bedroom doorway, encompassing Martha in their arms, making soft, soothing murmurs, their own eyes filling with tears. With the first hug, Martha maintained the same stalwart stoicism she'd managed to hold onto from the beginning. But with the second woman's hug, she laid her head on the soft shoulder and the sobs finally broke loose. "Oh, Emma, she's gone," she kept whispering over and over. "Sarah's gone now."

The intensity of the emotions was getting to Kate. She glanced at her watch. After midnight. She felt a sense of urgency to be done with her work and be gone, to get out of the family's way for the night at least, so they could get their emotional feet under them and the grieving process could begin. She gave one last look around the bedroom before leaving. There was nothing anywhere that gave a clue as to why a sheltered young woman like Sarah would be wandering around a state park.

Deep in thought, Kate slipped into the living room. She took her leave of the Tafts, merely nodding at the openly curious glances aimed her way by the church folk milling about, and was by the front door when Pastor Barnes stopped her. His eyes bored into hers. "It has to be a stranger," he stressed, "it has to be."

For a moment she was caught up by the strong, piercing gaze pinning her like a butterfly to velvet. Then she broke free of the stare. So that was to be the official party line. "We'll see," she said calmly. "We'll have to see."

Then the pastor, with the skill born of one who shepherds his flock through the church door every Sunday morning to keep the postservice greeting line moving steadily, escorted Kate into the night chill. Behind her, the blank-faced door was firmly shut, closing the family back into their tight world, with the outsider right where she belonged . . . on the outside.

There were several cars parked in front of the Taft house now, including the two pastors' cars. Her own was across the street. As she stepped off the curb, by training and habit she glanced up and down the block, automatically checking the neighborhood for anything out of whack.

The only thing she spotted was a car in front of a house several doors down the street. It was definitely parked apart from the others. A streetlamp shining behind it outlined the head of a figure sitting still behind the wheel. The person inside was making no effort to climb out.

Kate reached up and casually unbuttoned the front of her denim jacket, placing her automatic within easy grabbing reach, then began moving down the sidewalk toward the parked car. Through the windshield, she could make out a woman in the driver's seat, a small pale figure bundled up in a heavy coat, with light-colored hair pulled back in a wispy ponytail.

The woman caught sight of Kate. With quick, jerky motions born of fear, her hand lunged for the ignition key. The engine roared to life and the car leaped away from the curb.

Kate jumped sideways to safety. She was too far from her car to even make an effort at a chase. She swiveled instead, rapidly noting the details. Two-door brown Ford Escort, '85, '86, no nicks or dents. A car a narc would love. She memorized the license number at a glance, kept an eye on the Escort until it had raced around a corner and disappeared, then slowly walked back to her Honda. The times she could use a radio, she thought.

She found the incident strange. Unsettling. Although the car had been parked several houses down from the Taft home, and there could've been any number of reasons for the woman being there. Except she'd been left with the distinct impression that the woman had been watching the Taft house.

Why did she have that impression?

She started the Honda, then let it idle as she replayed her memory tapes. The woman's head hadn't turned, that's why. The whole time, from when Kate first spotted it from down the block to that final nearing, the woman's head had been focused on something straight ahead. She'd seemed to be watching and waiting. And the Taft home had been directly in her line of vision.

A second reason occurred to her. There was the lack of the sound of a car door closing. If the woman had just left a home in the area, the door would've made some noise as it closed shut behind her. Or if she'd dropped someone off at their place, same thing. The street was too quiet at this time of night not to hear even the slight click of a car door closing.

No, the woman had been sitting and watching and waiting.

For what?

Or . . . for whom?

Thoughtfully, Kate shifted out of neutral and pulled away from the curb.

Chapter Six

Her adrenaline running too high for much sleep, Kate was up and on her way before dawn. Not yet absorbed in the process that would take on a life of its own, she wanted everything done at once—she wanted witnesses found, suspects questioned, contradictions discovered, motives examined, alibis checked—and, of course, the killer identified. And she wanted it all done now.

At headquarters, she parked in the side lot off the main road, well back among the firs surrounding the perimeter of the grounds, and headed inside, her mind busy organizing the next steps to be taken. The bullpen was daylight bright and nighttime empty. It was one vast open area broken up into detective divisions by a curving maze of four-drawer filing cabinets. As she swerved first one way and then another around Robbery, Arson and Vice, she passed a lone detective here and there laboring over paperwork. Most of them didn't bother looking up as she passed. The one or two who did raise up at the sound of her footsteps gave her a faint, tired-eyed nod and sank right back into their own murk. The Captain's office was dark, the door closed.

She wound around the last curve into Homicide, slung her blazer on top of the filing cabinet nearest her desk and adjusted her shoulder harness for more comfort. She'd be spending a good portion of the day at the church and school, and mindful of the roomful of women she'd seen at the Taft's the night before, all wearing dark-colored dresses, she'd selected a dark navy blue skirt, a prim white blouse and a dark blazer as the uniform of the day. She wanted to blend in as much as possible, looking less like a cop and more like she belonged there.

Without pausing at her desk, she continued following the maze to Narcotics to check out any drug connection to the church and school. A possibility not unheard of in this day and age. Besides, Narcotics had the only coffeepot on the floor.

Brillo was seated at his desk, in deep conversation with another guy she didn't know, speaking in near-whispers. He glanced at her with open irritation as she rounded the last filing cabinet and came into view, annoyed as hell at the interruption.

The man with him was young, early twenties, thin and bony, with a good three days' worth of grisly black stubble bristling from his jaw, and long, greasy black hair that drooped down over the collar of a grimy biker's vest. He wore a belligerent look on his face, his eyes were narrowed with suspicion and distrust, and he had enough dirt beneath his fingernails to start a wheat farm. A beast straight from the sewers of hell. It was impossible to tell if he was narc or slime. Either way, she had a feeling the guy wouldn't smell pretty.

She leaned back against a filing cabinet well out of aroma range and signaled Brillo over. Resigned to being interrupted now, Brillo motioned to the guy to stay where he was, rose and came over to her. Hands on hips, he loomed over her and grumbled, "What?" Brillo was six two, black, broad-chested and fearsome. When he loomed, he loomed.

His mood didn't faze her. Brillo got short like that when something heavy was coming down. "I caught a new case last night," she said. "A young girl found dead in the woods. You guys have anything on Woodhaven Christian Church? She went to their school."

Brillo stared. "You gotta be shuckin' me, right?"

Kate shook her head. "Nope, I'm serious. I'm going to eliminate two possibilities right away, and the first one is a drug connection."

Brillo was already shaking his head. "Doesn't ring a bell."

"Could you check into it for me? It'd help."

"I guess." His displeasure was obvious.

She glanced pointedly at the strange guy. "Nice looking specimen. One of ours?"

"You know I'm not gonna answer that," Brillo snapped.

He hadn't said no. Grinning, she helped herself to a cup of coffee and walked away.

After sending out queries to various police agencies in the Puget Sound area about any similar homicides they might have on the books, she tried to settle down to paperwork, but the various reports on the crime scene, the body, the pastors and the family seemed to take forever to do. The words just wouldn't come easily, and the written picture she drew seemed to be, at best, murky and confusing. She tried to figure out a way to fix it, to make the interview with the family seem more coherent, couldn't, and tore up the first draft and started over.

She kept her impressions out of the reports, but as she wrote, she was again struck by the strictly controlled and supervised environment the triumvirate of church, school and families imposed on their young. At least the Taft young. There didn't seem to be an inch of give anywhere in their upbringing that would account for Sarah being on the loose in Bridle Trails State Park. Or any state park, for that matter. Her conclusion was brief and to the point: This girl shouldn't be dead. But she was. So how had she gotten there? And why had she gone?

She finished up the paperwork and copied Sam and the Captain on everything. She knew ahead of time the Captain wasn't going to like this. He was going to be one unhappy gorilla when he read exactly how few hard facts had surfaced. All they really had was the dead girl's identity, the last known time she'd been seen alive, the fact that she wasn't at her family's supper table that night, and the bit of background Kate had been given on church and school. No motive had surfaced at all.

Without a motive, Kate couldn't focus the investigation on any one aspect of the case yet. She had her cop instinct that told her to concentrate on school and home. Still, she couldn't ignore the other possibilities as outlined by the ranger. There were the Bible students from the college who frequented the park. A strong connection there. There were the members of the Saddle Club. A weaker connection, but still one that had to be explored. And there were the ranger's "stray" businessmen. That one definitely concerned her. A young girl falling prey to a stranger with ungovernable impulses might be the stuff of thrillers, yet it happened too frequently in the real world to chalk it up as sheer fiction.

She began to outline the areas that needed investigating and the resulting manpower needs. The first thing she'd do would be to dump Goddard and Fry. Trade them in on a more reliable second team, who could finish canvassing the park neighborhoods for her. And since there was bound to be an overlap between park neighbors and park riders, they could work the Saddle Club membership for some kind of a link to Sarah. She and Sam would divvy up the rest—the Taft home, neighborhood, church and school. They'd also explore the Bible college connection. And maybe Barb Denton would be able to identify some of her "stray" businessmen.

She looked the list over. A dozen places and a few hundred people to question. Would the Captain assign a third team to the case? Yeah, sure, Katie. Right after a Republican Congress increases welfare benefits.

She shoved the manpower list into her briefing folder and was about ready to go get some breakfast when, as if conjured up by her depressed imagination, the Captain in real life lumbered past her desk. Without slowing a step, he pointed one finger toward his darkened office. "Inside."

And he hadn't even seen the reports yet, she thought with a

sigh. She scrambled after him, heart thudding with apprehension. Hatch had that effect on her.

He took his time settling in. He was a huge man, tall and massive, with a belly shaped like the Kingdome. His skin was mottled and coarse-pored, his eyes were the near-black of a mud pond, thick, glutinous, unreadable, and his mouth had a natural downcurve at the corners.

Without asking her to sit, he moved his ponderous bulk around his desk, lowered it into a wide-armed swivel chair, grabbed the pile of overnight reports stacked in the center of the desk and shoved them out of his way. Including hers on top. He saw her name on the cover sheet. Ignoring it, he leaned way back in his chair and steepled his fingers across the gargantuan bulge of his stomach. "Okay, tell me." The dark eyes were ice-coated muck reflecting the glare of the overhead fluorescents, unwavering and hard-fixed on her.

She helped herself to the edge of a side chair and kept her summary brief and to the point. It took less than a couple of minutes to convey over eight hours' worth of work.

Even she was dismayed by the small amount of progress. And he was frankly appalled. "That's it?" He stared at her with disbelief. "No motive, no suspects, no nothing?"

She nodded, swallowing hard.

"Boyfriend?"

"None."

"Family problems?"

"None."

"Wild crowd?"

She shook her head. "They're all good Christian folks."

"So far," he said cynically.

"So far."

"Well, *someone* had it in for the girl."

She sat that one out.

He studied her with his hard gaze, making summary judgments. He looked exhausted. His eyes were sunken into circles of blackness, the lids red-rimmed and drooping. He had heavy jowls that sagged now around rigid muscle cords running up the throat. He was not one to ever act harried or hassled. That wasn't his style. When he was pressured, he simply acted weary. The heavier the pressure, the deeper the weariness. She couldn't remember the last time she'd seen him smile. Or even if she ever had.

Finally, he spoke up. "Okay, MacLean, I'll keep you in charge for now. But chase down a motive, will you? And you'd better check with surrounding P.D.'s, make sure there's not a whacko on the loose again."

At least he hadn't proclaimed it a nice ladylike case, safe for her to handle. Maybe that meant she was finally being accepted as just another cop. Wouldn't *that* be a refreshing change. She withdrew the sheet of paper with the team assignments listed.

Before she could proffer it, he spoke again. His look was gentle now, his voice mild. "By the way," he said, "guess maybe I forgot to mention it, but I assigned Goddard and Fry to your team. Keep 'em busy and outta sight, will you?" He raised a stubby forefinger to forestall the protest he saw forming and continued on. "Guess I also forgot to mention Sam. You're to keep him inside awhile. He can do the desk work for you."

Speechless, she stared at him. There went her manpower list. She could read absolutely nothing from his expression or his eyes.

He jerked upright in his chair, yanked the stack of reports to center desk and slid the bottom one out to read, dismissing her.

She finally found her voice. "But—"

Without looking up, he pointed toward his office door. "Out."

Dazed, she backed out of his office. No Sam. And she was stuck with the Wonder Twins. Which basically left all the work for herself. The whole church setup, their hierarchy and members. The school, teachers and classmates. Sarah's friends. The Taft neighbors. The Saddle Club. The Bible students. The ranger's "stray" businessmen with their laptop computers and electronic pagers.

And at the same time, she'd sure as hell have to monitor Goddard and Fry. Without Sam.

God help her, what the hell was the Captain thinking of?

She grabbed her jacket from the top of the filing cabinet and headed to Papa's Diner for a fix of food.

Sam didn't show up for breakfast again, as he hadn't for the past couple of weeks, and Mama Stopolous, lined face creased with warm sympathy and her dark expressive eyes showing concern, hovered over her with the coffeepot in hand as if Kate had been orphaned and coffee would make up for everything lost. Kate ordered one of Papa's enormous Greek omelets and borrowed the diner's copy of the *Eastside Journal.*

She was halfway through her food when she reached page four. As she folded the page back, a publicity still of Goddard peered out at her under the head, Girl's Body Found in State Park. In the article, Goddard sounded smooth and in command. It was the usual no-hard-facts-yet police pablum assuring the public that all was under control. He managed to sound as if he were in charge of the case. *Her* case. Exasperated, she folded up the paper and set it beside her plate.

Now the Captain's order to keep Goddard "out of sight" made sense. As did his orders to keep Sam at his desk. It was this damned lieutenancy business. The top brass favored Goddard; the Captain wanted Sam. A classic struggle for power, as she saw it, the brass wanting to exercise their political muscle, the Captain fighting for the autonomy needed to do his job.

Sam, though, had ripped the Captain's game plan to shreds by asking for a transfer to the Duty desk. She could just picture the Captain's reaction to that. Well, by God, if Sam wanted desk work, he'd see to it Sam *got* desk work. Plenty of it. Give him the work without the transfer. See how Sam liked the taste of it, the feel of it, being chained to his chair, all day, every day. In the meantime, bury Goddard, keep him out of sight, and especially out of the newspapers, and hope that old saw worked with the brass—out of sight, out of mind.

But would the Captain be that devious?

Kate snorted at her own question and tossed a bill on the table to cover her tab and tip.

She was back at her desk before six-thirty to tackle the last few details for the briefing she'd be holding. Fortunately, it would be short and to the point, then she'd be out of there.

The Wonder Twins arrived together shortly after she did, slicked up in three-piece suits like the top brass wore. Fry veered off toward his desk with only a cursory nod in her direction, but Goddard made a point of hiking his hip on the outer corner of her desk and presenting her with a sheaf of pages stapled together. He bowed. "Your report."

Wordlessly she took the sheaf and riffled through them. Names, addresses and phone numbers of the people canvassed the night before and the results of the interviews. There must've been four dozen homes listed there. All in the space of a couple of hours? She sincerely doubted it. Yet . . . the phone numbers were there. It would be so easy to check up on the two of them. Surely, they wouldn't be stupid enough to try and pull one of their stunts, then hand her the weapon to investigate it. Would they?

She set her doubts aside for the moment and scanned the lists for any nugget of information. But no one that lived around the state park had seen or heard anything out of the way. Not a car, not a person. A big dud. And Goddard looked pleased.

She looked up at him. He was wearing the same superior, sardonic smile of the previous evening. What the hell was he up to anyway? "Thanks," she said mildly, then dropped back to her work, dismissing him.

He bowed once again, then swung off the desk and moved to where Fry waited. Goddard made some comment that brought a sly grin to his partner's face before the two of them settled down to desk work. Kate would've given a month's salary to know what Goddard had said.

Sam came in just in time to catch her on the way to the briefing room. "Anything I should know ahead of time?"

If you wanted to ask that, she wanted to snap, why didn't you show up for breakfast? She simply shook her head. "We've identified the dead girl, and I've interviewed the family. I'll cover all that in the briefing. The best we've got is that she was seen alive on Monday around noon. And she wasn't at supper with her folks. The family thought she was on a school retreat, the school thought she was with the family. The autopsy's scheduled today for one o'clock, and I'm hoping that'll give us a narrower time frame to work in. But so far, hard facts are few and far between, and there isn't a sniff of a motive. That's pretty much it."

"Not a lot to go on," Sam said.

"Tell me about it."

Their glances locked for a moment. His eyes looked bloodshot and haggard, too tired to show emotion of any kind, caged with tiny lines splaying from the corners. His mouth was set in deep trenches. She turned her back on him and led the way into the briefing room.

As if the tension between herself and Sam, and herself and the Wonder Twins wasn't enough, at the very last minute the Captain came in to sit in on the briefing. He piled his intimidating mountain of flesh onto one of the folding chairs she'd grouped around, leaned back, crossed his arms over his massive stomach and watched her every move with hooded eyes.

She bit back an exasperated sigh and kept the meeting brief. She went over the dead girl's identity, age and family situation, and the heavy church involvement by the family. She added in the same time parameters she'd outlined to Sam, and summed it up by saying they were looking for anyone who'd seen her alive after lunchtime on Monday.

Normally at a briefing, once the DIC had finished with the verbal summary, the team would brainstorm together, tossing around theories about the homicide, seeking some direction that made sense, especially when there wasn't a suspect in sight and the motive was unknown. But these four men sat there, stone-faced, arms folded across their chests, eyes ranging from disinterested to sad to cold. They made her feel like some prissy old schoolmarm lecturing on and on and on.

She quickly handed out their assignments. Goddard and Fry were to continue on with the canvassing in the Bridle Trails area, and follow up any leads that might develop there. Goddard looked bored. Fry said and did nothing, simply watching from the shadows as he always did—even when there weren't any shadows to watch from, she thought. As there weren't in the brightly lit briefing room. She wondered how he did it.

When it came to Sam's assignment, she obeyed the Captain's orders. She stuck him at his desk to follow up on her queries to the surrounding police agencies.

He started to protest, but her look warned him off. "I'd also like a plate run through DMV," she said, handing over the license number of the Ford Escort she'd written down the night before. Taking the note without responding, he gave her the sad look of a mistreated basset hound.

Throughout the briefing, the Captain said nothing. He took no notes, made no comments, and changed expressions not at all. And when the meeting was over, he simply rose and walked out. The whole session had lasted less than ten minutes, and she had no idea what he thought or felt about it, or her. Sometimes he must have the feeling he was running a kindergarten filled with obnoxious little brats. She brought the whole charade to an end.

It was a relief to get out of there. She could concentrate on the hunt now. And compared to confronting that group in there, tracking down a brutal killer qualified as recreational activity. She sat for a moment behind the wheel of her car before starting it up, doing nothing but taking deep breaths to calm the tensions that had climbed during the morning session.

It was only seven A.M., and the day, as far as she was concerned, was on a steep, downhill slant.

Chapter Seven

By the time Kate drove into the church parking lot, the sun had already topped the Cascades and the tarmac behind the church was striped with the long black fingers of shadows from the taller trees at the edge of the complex. A clear blue sky stretched from treetop to treetop with not even a puff of cumulus to hold out hope for a sprinkle or two. Another hot, dry day ahead. She pulled her nondescript Honda well out of the way of any arriving traffic and sat and watched for a while.

Several aged school buses pulled into the lot and curved around to the curb. It had been a while since she'd watched any school buses unload. In her memory kids burst through the bus doors in shouting, screaming packs like puppies bursting out of their puppy pens in exuberant freedom. These kids, though, filed off in an orderly manner, grouped in twos and threes, and walked calmly up the school sidewalk, talking quietly among themselves. The low pulse of the bus engines made more noise than they did.

Girls walked with girls, all dressed in the same rough-wool gray jumpers and white blouses that Sarah Taft had worn, and boys walked with boys, wearing loose trousers made of the same rough gray wool, long white shirts and black wool vests. No jeans, no tight pants, no cutoffs, no T-shirts, torn or untorn, no casual clothes allowed. From the littlest kindergartner to the oldest high-schooler, they all wore the same uniform.

Many parents drove their kids to school. Cars swung into the lot and pulled around to the sidewalk, slipping in behind the buses, disgorging anywhere from one to a carful of kids, then pulling back out into the drive-around and disappearing into the street. She kept a close watch out for a brown Ford Escort, but didn't see one.

At the double front doors to the high school, one boy from each approaching group would hold the door open for the nearest bunch of girls. It was done without smirks and giggling, just courteous smiles and simple nods of thanks. Obviously an accepted procedure. Kate watched in amazement. These were not kids, she thought, they were clones of kids.

Promptly at eight, the campus went abruptly silent. The double doors closed behind the last student and the last of the parents and school buses rumbled away. The complex slumbered peacefully now in the early morning sun.

She gave it another minute or two, then headed for the door. The interior of the building was lifeless when Kate entered, the only sound drifting down the hallway the peck-peck-peck of a typewriter. She followed the sound to the school office halfway down the entry corridor and peered around the door. The school secretary was working at a typewriter set in the middle of an untidy pile of sheets and scraps of paper. Kate wanted to look the school over before announcing her presence. She slipped past the open doorway without attracting her notice and began exploring.

The first floor of the high-school building contained the academic classrooms, English, social studies and math, with a small library containing study tables sprawled across one end of a rear wing. Upstairs were the secretarial and homemaking labs for the girls, and science labs for the boys. In the basement was a quasi gymnasium, with basketball hoops, volleyball nets and locker rooms using up half the space, a compact kitchen and lunchroom filling the rest. The school was small, but complete, Kate thought, a scaled-down version of any modern-day high school.

She stayed well back from the classroom doors, peering in from the side of the windows out of the line of sight of the teachers. Class sizes were small, with no more than twenty students in each of the academic classrooms, and half that many in the second-story labs. Except for the labs, there were no informal seating groups. All desks were arranged in rows, in formal classroom style. The classes she saw through the windows were quiet, well controlled, the students either intent on taking lecture notes or working quietly on assignments at their desks. A few of the classrooms contained only boys, scattered amidst a dozen empty seats, and Kate assumed they were seniors and the girls were missing because of their retreat.

The windows drew her eye. In all the classrooms, long panes of glass ran across the tops of the outside walls, large enough to flood the room with daylight without being low enough to tempt the daydreamer. Not even the teachers were tall enough to glance out the windows and see anything more than sky. There was absolutely no chance of anyone having seen anything occurring on the grounds during class time on Monday.

She headed back to the school office.

The secretary looked a bit glum staring down at the sheet of paper in the typewriter until she saw Kate, then her face creased into a warm smile of welcome as she shoved her chair back from the disorganized desk to come to her side of the counter.

Pastor Ellsworth was tied up in a staff meeting, Kate was told when she presented her ID. The woman's hand fluttered to her breast. "It's about poor Sarah Taft, isn't it." The eyes teared up. "I heard about it this morning in the coffee room. It's shocking. Absolutely shocking. That poor, poor thing."

She was a middle-aged woman, bespectacled and plain, as dumpy as a lump of pastry dough, but with plump cheeks and kindly features. Wisps of gray hair escaped a bun at the back of her head, and she looked almost as unruly as her desk. She'd be a cookie-jar grandma, Kate thought, or a donut grandma, the one who'd ply the grandkids with treats.

"And those poor parents," she continued on. "What they must be going through."

Before Kate could respond, the phone on the desk rang. The woman's hand fluttered again to her breast as she glanced between her desk and Kate, unsure which needed immediate attention first, cop or phone. She'd been hired more for her warmth and friendliness, Kate deduced, than her efficiency.

The phone won.

The woman kept her voice as low as possible to keep the conversation confidential, but Kate eavesdropped shamelessly. It was obviously a parent who'd heard the news about the murder. "Yes," the secretary said, "it's true. We have the police here now. Dreadful, isn't it, a young girl like Sarah? . . . Oh, no, she wasn't taken from the school here, no, she was taken from her home by some stranger . . ." Her voice was soothing, always soothing.

Calming the fear. Kate stared unseeingly at a series of framed class pictures arranged on one wall, each class bigger than the next. Tragedies happen to other folks, front-page events read with an impersonal horror. Now it had come to their school and suddenly it wasn't impersonal anymore. They knew this girl. Their children walked where Sarah had walked, sat where Sarah had sat . . . and that realization led to the next leap in logic—would they die where Sarah had died?

The school clock ticked softly on.

The phone call ended and the woman turned back to attend to Kate. "That was one of our parents. They're so concerned."

"I can imagine," Kate said quietly. "So they know the Tafts?"

"Oh, my, yes. Everyone knows everyone else. That's what our church is all about, you see. We're all like aunts and cousins and grandparents to each other. It's part of what makes our school—our whole community here—work so well."

"Have the students been told about Sarah yet?"

"That's probably what the staff meeting's about. When and how to tell them. Sarah was very popular, you know. It's going to be just plain awful when the news really gets out."

"Do her teachers know?"

The woman nodded. "It's all we talked about in the coffee room."

Kate loved it when she found people who liked to talk. It was like panning for gold dust and finding a solid nugget. She leaned informally on the counter, giving the woman a smile of encouragement. "What's Sarah's family like?"

"Wonderful. Wonderful people. Martha and Daniel devote hours to the church. They're always doing this and that. And Martha's so faithful, she brings the girls to school every single morning, and picks them up every afternoon." She shook her head in sorrow. "To be so careful like that, and then to have something like this happen . . ."

"Is this typical of the parents, picking up and dropping off their kids?" Kate asked.

"More or less. We have a few buses, so some of the students ride those. But I'd say a good half of our student body are brought here by their mothers. Or a car pool."

Kate fell silent a minute. She had a couple of ideas bouncing around and decided to try them out. "I'm just a little confused," she said quietly. "Maybe you can help. According to what I've learned, Sarah got sick at school on Monday morning, had to miss going on the retreat and was taken home at noon, right?" Another nod. "Now supposing it was one of those quickie bugs, that come, make you sick as a dog, then suddenly you feel better. Wouldn't Sarah have tried to figure out some way of getting up to her retreat after all?"

The secretary's face wrinkled in heavy thought. "It would go against everything they're taught," she said hesitantly. She thought about it another minute, then shook her head firmly. "No, I'm sure she wouldn't. She wouldn't have a way up there, first of all. And secondly, our students are drilled from kindergarten on to never, but never leave the house without a parent. We're very strict with our children here. They're not allowed to go anywhere without a parent or another adult. No, once she was home, there's no way she'd leave the house. Sarah simply wasn't the disobedient type."

"Supposing she felt better and decided to come back to school then?"

The woman was already shaking her head. "The same thing would apply. She wouldn't leave the house without her parents' permission."

"How can you be so sure?" Kate asked quietly.

"Because that's how we bring our children up." It was a quiet statement of truth. The way she saw it.

Kate fell silent a moment, studying the woman. She truly believed what she was saying. Yet Kate had proof—the dead-body kind of proof—that Sarah *had* disobeyed parental, school and church edict and *had* left the house without their permission. If she wasn't a disobedient young woman, then who had the power over her to convince her to go against her entire upbringing and head off to a state park like that?

But badgering the secretary about it wasn't going to get her anywhere. "Do you have any idea how long Pastor Ellsworth will be tied up in his meeting?" Kate asked.

"No. It could be five minutes, or all morning. We're all so distressed by this that the schedules have gone by the wayside."

"Then I'll talk to some of her teachers while I'm waiting. Do you have a list of her classes, and the locations of the classrooms?"

"Oh, you'd need Pastor Ellsworth's approval for that." The fluttering began again and a fearful look came into her eyes. "No, I couldn't allow you to do that. That wouldn't be proper at all. Not without his approval."

What kind of a man was this Pastor Ellsworth anyway, to inspire such nervousness? Kate gave an easy smile. "Then why don't I check with you a little later on."

The relief on the woman's face was sad to see.

* * *

Kate left the school building and wandered over to the church office wing. Pastor Barnes wasn't there, she was told by a church secretary, he was helping Sarah's family select a coffin. No, Pastor Matt wasn't there either. But Pastor Garrett was somewhere on the premises. Kate settled for him.

Bob Garrett was the Youth Pastor of the church. She tracked him down over at the elementary school, a large, plain rectangular building almost dead center of the campus. He was working in a staff room at a rear corner of the building, in conference with one of the teachers. Sarah Taft had taught a Sunday School class for the younger children, and the two adults were poring over a series of short Bible verses, assigning them to some of her students to be read aloud at her services. At Kate's entrance, the teacher excused herself and hurried away, and Pastor Bob invited her to sit at the worktable.

He was in his early twenties, with sandy hair, a face full of freckles, and a lithe body brimming with energy. Though he was dressed in the same dark suit the other pastors wore, he looked barely voting age. He greeted her with a somber face at odds with the squirrel-like brightness of his eyes. "We're going to miss Sarah terribly. We all loved her. I was absolutely destroyed when I heard about it." Pastor Bob's eyes on her were frank and open. "It has to be a kidnapping. There's no other explanation for it. One of those random things, pick up a strange girl and do away with her."

"Have you seen any strangers hanging around the church or school?" Kate asked.

"No, but that doesn't mean anything, does it? Look, I've thought of nothing else since I heard. She was taken home at noon, sick, according to what I hear. Someone—anyone—could've grabbed her then, right?"

"It's certainly a possibility," Kate responded with caution.

He shook his head. "Not a possibility, it *has* to be. It's the only thing that makes sense. I don't know of a single person in the whole church community who didn't worship the ground she walked on."

"Did you see her at all on Monday?"

He shook his head. "We were in budget sessions all day. Fighting about the number of hymnals we need." An irrepressible grin broke out. "They didn't tell me in Bible college I'd need an MBA from Harvard to run a Sunday School program."

"What about Bridle Trails State Park? Do you ever take the children there for an outing?"

"Nope," he answered promptly. "We've got the camp retreat over on the Peninsula. It's extremely popular with our church families and seems to answer most of our needs."

"Then you'd have no explanation for why Sarah was in the park?"

"None." His clear blue eyes fixed solemnly on hers. "I wish I could tell you more. I really do. I want to help catch the devil who did this."

She quizzed him some more, but he gave her nothing more than what he'd already said. Over and over he repeated the litany, it had to be a stranger.

She checked back at the high school, but Pastor Ellsworth was still in his meeting. She wandered back to the church. Neither Pastor Barnes nor Pastor Matt had arrived yet, but Pastor Lang had come in, the secretary informed her. Could he help?

Mentally, Kate shrugged. Her morning was spinning past with no headway at all. Why not?

Ansel Lang was the finance minister for the church. He was pushing fifty, small, slight, bald, with wire-rimmed glasses. He seemed nervous, tense and rushed when she was ushered into his office. His office was bare, austere, with a tall cart holding computer and printer rolled off to one side of his chair. The old wooden desk was covered with a fanfold of printouts, heavily redlined. He stood behind his desk and gave several pointed glances down at the spreadsheets, letting her know she was interrupting his work. He remained standing, not inviting her to sit.

Immediately he started protesting her presence on the grounds, giving her what was quickly becoming the standard litany. The church couldn't possibly be involved in Sarah Taft's murder, he said in a testy tone of voice. Absolutely not. There was no earthly reason anyone would want Sarah Taft dead. She'd been a wonderful girl from a wonderful family, who were prompt with their tithes and tuition. No, Miss MacLean, no one in the church community would want to hurt her or her family in any way. You'll have to look elsewhere, sorry. Then he strode around his desk and ushered her back out, closing the door on her.

Thoughtfully, she stared at the blank-faced wood a moment. It was clear now the church was circling its wagons around the stranger-killer theory. But Ansel Lang had been blunt, testy and rude. Not the greatest way to deal with the police. Was he afraid of something?

Kate turned away and paused to take stock. So far, she'd spent a couple of hours on the grounds here and had come up with nothing new. She felt a need to move on. Yet she still had one more pastor to meet, Charles Ellsworth. And she really needed to talk to Sarah's teachers. Since she was here anyway . . .

She retraced her steps out the rear door of the church and headed back to the high school. Third time's a charm, she encouraged herself.

She had a twenty-minute wait on a hard chair before a tall man dressed in a dark suit strode into the office with the unmistakable air of ownership. His glance around the office was the same that Kate gave her house when she entered every night, an automatic checking to see that things were as they should be.

He glanced at Kate, then approached the secretary at the counter and murmured something in an undertone. The woman nervously whispered something to him, then nodded her head Kate's way. The man turned and stared at her a moment, running his gaze down the length of her in judgment. Then he strode her way, hand outstretched, and introduced himself.

Pastor Charles Ellsworth was a handsome man in his forties with the bony good looks of a New England ascetic. He had sandy hair going gray, pale skin and features, a tall, gaunt body and strong blue eyes that would pierce and shrivel the soul of the devout if found wanting. With brisk motions he ushered Kate into his office behind the counter, eyeing his secretary's desk with disdain as they passed. Her desk was still a discordant symphony of chaos, and her hands scrabbled ineffectually with the top layer of the mess, trying to straighten piles that were hopelessly tangled. Then they were through the outer office and into the pastor's sanctuary.

His office, in keeping with the tone of the overall complex, was simply but comfortably furnished. There was a walnut desk and matching credenza, with a high-backed, cloth-covered desk chair. Within easy reach on top of the credenza was a single stack of file folders, squared off and aligned with military precision. His desktop was neat to the point of austere. A small wooden box held sheets of memo paper next to the phone in one corner, a calculator sat on the other, and a stack of computer printouts covered with numbers was set precisely in the center. Above a bank of filing cabinets hung an oil painting of the school and grounds, done at an angle that set the long, low building against a background of rich, hunter-green firs. Though he wore a wedding ring, there were no personal pictures or mementos of any kind. Not on the desk, not on the credenza, and not on the bookshelves set beneath a broad span of side windows.

The windows overlooked the center of the campus, with the same stand of woods at the rear that had been used as a backdrop in the painting. Next to the last window and bookcase, there was an outside door that gave him his own private entrance. Convenient, Kate thought, though he'd have to skirt the bulk of the rear wing of the school to get from office to parking lot. But why did he need one?

He settled into his chair behind the desk and motioned her to take one of the straight wooden side chairs placed dead center facing him. He quickly picked up the printouts and set them behind him on the credenza. "Sorry, budget time." He turned back and eyed her. "Well, this murder has certainly put us in a dreadful mess. Sarah was one of our best students, an outstanding young lady."

Kate ignored his complaint. "Describe outstanding for me."

His gaze wandered the far wall for a moment. "Straight-A student. Sunday School teacher. Active in choir and one of the sewing clubs. Quilting, I believe. Outgoing, pleasant, kind. Steady, reliable. Even-tempered. Loved children. Especially her younger sister." The strong gaze found Kate's. "Really, she was an exemplary young woman. Wish I had a school full of them."

That confirmed everything Kate had been told to date. "Who were her close friends, some of the people she was closest to?"

A frown began, slight, nibbling at the edges of the high forehead. "Why are you asking?"

"I need to find out as much about Sarah as I can. Names of her friends, list of her classes, her usual daily schedule, periods of free time, who she ate lunch with . . . Basically, I need to be pointed in the direction of those who knew her best."

"Surely you don't think anyone within the church or the school had anything to do with harming her?" he asked sharply.

She ducked a direct answer. "In a homicide investigation, we have to start broad."

He waved that away with an impatient gesture. "There's no one within our community who'd do something like this to her."

"I still have to know these things," Kate said quietly.

His eyes were turning fierce now. "Sarah was well liked and respected by everyone. There is no one here who would hurt her."

"I'm not saying there is. But she might've done or said something that would give us a clue as to who did kill her."

That drew a deeper frown and a strong, piercing stare. "I would've heard about it if she had."

"Maybe. If the person she said it to realized it had enough importance to report it to you. Sometimes, though, someone can have a critical piece of information and not know it."

His strong blue eyes pierced her. "There's a flaw in that argument, Miss MacLean. You're assuming that Sarah was killed by someone she knew, that she felt some sense of danger and that she made a comment to someone about it. And that's simply not the case."

"But what if she'd seen someone lurking about?" Kate said mildly. "Someone stalking her the last few days? There is a chance she might've mentioned it to someone. An offhand comment of some kind or another. Or possibly someone from the school saw something, a strange car parked near the campus, or someone watching the school from the woods . . ."

"Then I'd have heard about it."

She stopped trying to use reason with him. It was getting her nowhere. "I still need to talk to these people," she said mildly.

"Absolutely not."

They were back where they started.

The clock ticked softly on the wall as she gave the situation some thought. Her choices were two. Pull rank on him, or work around him. Pulling rank would mean bringing the Captain in on it, or worse, some of the higher brass. Which would probably get her the information she wanted. But this man would not take kindly to being coerced into anything. And when the brass had pulled their rank and disappeared back into their fortress, she'd be the one out in the cold left to deal with a hostile man on an ongoing basis.

Yet, she wasn't sure exactly how she was going to get around him. She didn't know enough yet about the church, the school and the power structure to be able to figure out a path through the maze. Still, her instinct was to not pull rank yet, and have a bit of faith that she'd find a way to get what she needed. Maybe Matthew Jacobson could help. Of all the pastors, he seemed the most approachable.

She dug one of her business cards out of her purse, rose and handed it to him. "In case you *do* hear of something . . ."

As he escorted her out of his office, his face expressed complete certainty that he wouldn't.

She was walking slowly, deep in thought, on her way back to the parking lot when she came to an abrupt halt. Pastor Matt had emerged from the rear of the church office wing, one arm around the shoulders of an obviously distraught Norm Overholtz. Kate backed up a step into the shadow of a screening shrub and watched.

As they moved slowly down the sidewalk toward the parking lot, Pastor Matt's head was bent low, talking earnestly into Norm's ear. At one point, the boy stopped and looked up at the pastor, protesting something that had been said. From where she stood, Kate had a clear view of Norm. His face was blotched with red patches—from tears, Kate judged—and his chin was visibly trembling as he struggled for emotional control.

With utmost patience, Pastor Matt listened to him through, his head cocked to one side, then reached out and patted his forearm in an understanding gesture. He began speaking once more. What he said seemed to calm the boy. The pastor said something further, then gently guided him to the parking lot.

Norm reached the bike rack that was tucked into its own niche in the parking lot and pulled an old, dull green three-speed free. None of the bikes were locked, Kate noted with a professional eye. She shook her head at the innocence of the school in this day and age of casual thievery.

Norm swung a leg over the seat and straddled the bike, one foot supporting him. He listened, nodding again now, to the last few words from the pastor. There was a final pat on the arm, then the boy was up and off.

Pastor Matt stood quiet a moment, watching him pedal out of sight. Then head down and shoulders slumped, he slowly retraced his steps back up the sidewalk to the church offices.

Kate thought of stopping Matt for help with Pastor Ellsworth, but decided against it. She wanted her request to be more than just a casual Oh-by-the-way. She waited until he was safely out of sight inside the building, then stepped out from behind the shrubbery and continued on slowly to her car.

Norm Overholtz.

Mourning Sarah?

Chapter Eight

She checked in with Sam from a pay phone at a nearby gas station. So far, he wasn't having any luck with the neighboring P.D.'s, he said. No homicides similar to Sarah Taft's had shown up. Then he gave her her messages. One was a phone call from Barb Denton, the park ranger, who'd wait at headquarters for Kate to call back. The second was from Len Franklin. Kate took that one down with hope. Maybe he'd moved Sarah's autopsy up and had some hard information for her. The third message was an order from the Captain. He wanted her calling in to him directly at regular intervals.

Smothering a sigh, Kate said, "Is he in now?"

"Yeah, but he's on the other line."

"Perfect. This is my check-in call, then. Sorry he couldn't take it. Which takes care of that." She looked down at her notes. "Last item on my list. License plate. Did you have a chance to run the number I gave you through DMV?"

"Nope. Their computer's down."

"The wonders of the electronic age. Any sign of Goddard and Fry?"

"None."

This time the sigh got away from her. "All right, Sam. I'm headed over to the Taft neighborhood now. Maybe somebody saw her leave the house that afternoon. Lord, I hope so, I need help here. This thing is going nowhere fast."

"Let's meet for lunch. Las Comidas at noon. Maybe something'll break by then. Oops, the Captain's light just blinked out, he's off the phone now."

"Las Comidas at noon. Bye, Sam." She hung up fast, then stared off into the distance, absently eyeing the cars roaring by. She'd gone to a station up on Rose Hill, and even though it was mid-morning the street was clogged with traffic. At first she was irritated, as she always was at the constant busyness that encompassed the Eastside nowadays, but then her attention moved inward and the roar simply became a background rumble for her thoughts.

It was a toss-up, which call to make first. She wanted to hear Len Franklin tell her he'd finished the autopsy ahead of schedule, but she was afraid that Barb Denton would get tired of waiting for her call and head out to the park before Kate could reach her. It could be she'd discovered something important. She tossed a mental coin and it landed heads up, Barb Denton. She plugged another quarter into the phone and dialed.

But Barb didn't have any fresh information. She'd called simply to warn Kate that Lucy Gray was playing detective and was quizzing the members of the Lake Washington Saddle Club. "My concern," Barb said in her calm, quiet way, "is that she'll ask the wrong questions of the wrong person and find herself in a dangerous situation."

Kate mulled it over. If the church's official stance proved out, and it was a stranger who'd killed Sarah, then Lucy Gray could very well be headed for trouble. "Okay, let me have her address. I'll try and get to her today. In the meantime, sit on her, will you, Barb? Just get her to cool it until I can talk to her." Barb wasn't encouraging, but she'd try.

Kate plugged another quarter in and called the church. Pastor Matt could see her at one-thirty. She agreed, then made her last call.

She caught Franklin between autopsies, and to her extreme disappointment he wasn't calling with news about Sarah, he was calling to invite her to lunch. She listened, fighting to control the sudden impatience she felt. She didn't have time for boy-girl games. Not with this kind of a case on her hands. And she wasn't too sure she wanted to get cozy with Franklin anyway, even if she did have the time. Or the energy. Or the desire. "I've already made arrangements for lunch," she said, "I'm sorry." Then a sudden suspicion took hold, and she asked, "Did you happen to mention it to Sam when you called?"

"Sure," Franklin said, in his cheerful voice. "He wanted to know if I was calling about the autopsy results and I said no, I was calling to grab you up as a lunch partner."

She apologized again, though why she should apologize at all wasn't quite clear to her, then stared back out at the traffic after she'd hung up. Just what kind of a game was Sam playing anyway? Why should he care whether someone else wanted to take her to lunch or not? He was being taken care of these days, wasn't he?

She climbed into her Honda and edged toward the street, waiting for a break in traffic to take off. So Sam had aced Franklin out. Deep down in that feline part of her soul a tiny little grin began.

She retraced her route to the church, made a U-turn, then headed for the Taft house, taking note of the mileage as she drove. One-point-one miles from school to home. Easily walkable. Easily bikeable. And about that far again to the state park. She was finding the juxtaposition of the various locations interesting. Though she was damned if she knew how it applied to the case. Yet.

The crowd of cars in front of the Taft home of the night before had thinned to a single sedan that Kate didn't recognize. It didn't belong to either Pastor Barnes or the person who'd nearly sideswiped her last night. She passed on by, parked at the far corner of the block, and began knocking on doors.

The neighborhood was in transition, much like her own. People who'd originally bought there four or five decades ago were moving on into old age now and their homes were being sold for the usual reasons—retirement, health, nursing homes or death. So it was a mixture of ages and people who answered Kate's knock on the door as she trudged up and down the block.

About half the houses had someone home. Sarah had been identified by name on the morning newscasts. Some of the old-timers were able to make the connection between the dead girl and the family down the street, and were eager to answer questions. She helped a couple of mid-morning gardeners pull some weeds, and downed several cups of coffee and an assortment of muffins, sweet rolls and cookies in kitchens that differed only in their wallpaper and the pattern of the curtains hung at identical dinette windows. But no one had noticed any strangers in the neighborhood. There'd been no one seen lurking about, no prowlers, no one who didn't belong.

And no visitors to the Taft family. According to the neighbors, the family lived quietly and kept to themselves. Churchgoers, you know. Nice people, though, polite and well-mannered whenever paths did cross. And there was never any screaming or fighting coming from their direction.

Only one elderly woman had seen Sarah being brought home at noon on Monday. She lived across the street from the family, and had been weeding her front flower bed when a car had stopped in front of the Taft house and Sarah and an older woman had gotten out. Yes, Sarah had been loaded down with backpack, school books and a purse. The other woman had gone in the house with her, stayed a few minutes, then left. Then about an hour and a half later, around one-thirty or so, the old woman had been eating lunch in front of her dinette window and had seen Sarah at the side door of the garage, crumpling up a brown paper bag and tossing it in the garbage can. The girl had gone back in and closed the door. The old woman had seen nothing more.

At the news of the crumpled paper bag, Kate felt a slight stab of hope. Lunch sack? Had she begun to feel better and eaten her lunch after all? Would the autopsy show any residue in the stomach contents? If so, maybe they could set a time of death. She kept mental fingers crossed and pursued her line of questioning, but the old woman had told all she knew. Shortly afterwards, she said, she'd washed up her dishes, then gone in the living room to watch her afternoon soaps and talk shows. With the drapes drawn to cut down the glare on the television screen, she'd seen nothing else the rest of the day. She brought the kettle over from the stove. "Another cup of tea?" With her white hair crimped tight to a pink scalp, the light blue eyes gone watery with age, the liver spots covering the plump hands, the porcelain-fragile skin, she reminded Kate of her grandmother.

Kate smiled slightly. She had a dozen houses left to canvass, a church to investigate, a school to penetrate, a killer to catch. But it all seemed far removed from this quiet, well-ordered kitchen with its old-fashioned, ticking wall clock. And there was no denying the appeal in those watery blue eyes, nor the loneliness that was starkly there. Mother MacLean, she sighed to herself as she pushed the cup toward the old woman. Wouldn't Goddard love to see this. And the Captain. "Sure."

Later, finally escaping, Kate paused on the sidewalk in front of the old woman's house. There was an unobscured view across the street of the Taft's side yard. Next to the side door leading into their garage stood an old metal garbage can, streaks of long-dried rain-grime running down the corrugated sides. The old woman would've had that same clear view from her kitchen window. So Sarah Taft had been alive at one-thirty. Yet she hadn't been there at dinnertime. One-thirty to five-thirty. Four hours. They were beginning to narrow down the time frame. With renewed hope, Kate moved on to the next house.

No one else had seen anything, though. The new America. TV and drawn drapes. It seemed as if the old-time neighborhood friendliness was in serious decline. Television was a plague on the land, Kate thought, isolating and segregating people, acting as sole companion to too many people suffering from the loneliness that its existence created in the first place. Oprah and Phil filled the void that used to be filled with neighbors, friends and family. It was sad. All these lonely people . . . just plain sad.

By lunchtime, she'd finished the block. Those neighbors that weren't at home were working, she'd been told. And yes, they'd have been working Monday, too. But at least Sarah's arrival home at noon on Monday was confirmed. There was a possibility she'd eaten her lunch. And she'd been seen alive at one-thirty.

Behind the wheel of her car, she shook her head. Slim, Kate, pretty slim pickings. And no sniff of a motive. The Captain wasn't going to like that.

Las Comidas was a little Mexican restaurant in one of the dozens of strip shopping malls that lined Redmond Way, sandwiched in between a dry cleaners and a Mail Boxes Etc. Little more than a storefront with Formica tables, it had none of the Mexican ambience of an El Torito or a Chi-Chi's. But it served a chili that cauterized the throat.

Kate got there ahead of Sam and snagged a high-backed wooden booth for the both of them. Neither one of them liked to sit at tables out in the open. Being cops, they liked having the security of solid wood at their backs, with no way for anyone to sneak up behind them. Shades of the Godfather, she thought, as she slid into the booth and opened the early afternoon edition of the Seattle *P-I.*

She was munching salsa and tortilla chips and had just started on the front page when Sam arrived. His face was long, his dewlaps droopier than ever, and his eyes were as sad as she'd ever seen them. She wanted to reach over and lift the corners of his mouth into some semblance of a grin, to bring some life back into his features. "Rough morning?" she asked.

He grunted as a disinterested waitress slouched their way. He ordered the tostada special with a bowl of chili on the side, and an Ixtapa. She'd need her throat later on, so Kate went for the quesadilla and iced tea. Beer for her halfway through a workday was not the brightest idea.

When the waitress left, Kate held up the front page of the *P-I* for him to see. "Sarah got the front page, above the fold."

"That's a tough way to make the big time."

She turned to an inside page for the continuation of the story, read two paragraphs, then exhaled an exasperated breath. She lowered the page to glare over the top of the page at Sam. "Guess who they quoted as official authority?"

"Don't tell me."

"Right. Listen to this, Sam." She read him a quote Goddard had made to the press about how the Homicide department would hold nothing back in their zeal to find the killer. "Damn him anyway. You ever hear from him at all this morning?"

"Nope, all's quiet on that battlefront."

Kate sighed slightly. "They say that no news is good news. Whoever said it didn't know Goddard. He's like the plague getting ready for a fresh outbreak."

Sam didn't say anything. He became absorbed in scooping salsa on a chip, avoiding her eyes.

She folded the paper back up and tossed it aside. Casually, she dipped a chip into salsa and, holding it up to her lips, said, "You know, Sam, if the brass had their way, he'd be appointed lieutenant already." She popped the chip in and munched, waiting for his response.

Mouth tightening, he stared down at the salsa bowl as if the bits of tomatoes and hot peppers swimming in their juices were a work of art, fascinating to behold. Ravines deep enough to hike in were carved in the lean planes of his cheeks. He looked tired, glum and every one of his forty-plus years. When he realized she was still waiting for a response, he looked up at her, not quite meeting her eyes, and shrugged. "What can I say?"

She said quietly, "You can say you'll fight for the job."

He took a long sip of his brew, then moved his brooding from the salsa to the beer foam.

She let the restaurant noises fill the silence between them, sugaring her tea and stirring it as if getting the tea sweetened just right were her sole assignment in the world.

Finally, he rubbed a hand down the length of his face, pulling the long planes of his cheeks even longer, a habit of his when his world didn't go exactly right. "Forget it, Kate," he said curtly.

She ate another chip.

The food proved a blessing. Sam's tostada was about the size of a Thanksgiving turkey, a mound of meat and cheese heaped on a platter-sized tortilla. The bowl of chili was large enough to wash dishes in. His dark eyes warmed with pleasure as he dumped hot salsa over the top of each and dug in. Then suddenly he noticed her watching him and his fork paused in midair, on its way down to pick up its first load. "Something the matter?"

"Of course not. I was just thinking of Christmas."

He stared at her. "Christmas."

"Yeah. I was wondering what size belt you'd need by then." She gave him a blinding smile of innocence. "You think a fifty-six would do it?"

The slightest grin crept in at the corner of his mouth and the fork scooped up a shovelful of food. "You're just jealous."

"Jealous of what? Causing a self-inflicted stomachache?"

He swallowed the first mouthful and followed it with a gulp of beer. "It's all in the training. Besides, it's comfort food, to soothe the soul." The grin faded and he began to grumble. "Guess what exciting and intellectually stimulating project our wondrous Captain has me working on today? Rotation calendars. For you, for me, for Homicide, Vice—for every damned detective under him. While you're out working the case, I'm figuring out who needs their wedding anniversary off, or their kids' birthdays off. Or worse, whose mother-in-law's coming to visit, and for God's sakes, be sure and schedule them that day. In fact, assign them to a double shift, no, make that triple while you're at it." He grumbled on and on until he'd worn it out, then he sighed heavily and looked up at her from beneath the strong brows. "You get the idea maybe I'm a mite perturbed with the Captain?"

"Perish the thought."

His grin came back. There was nothing nicer than Sam's grin. His skin was swarthy, his teeth white, a beautiful contrast of color. And when he grinned, truly grinned from the inside out, the brown eyes warmed up and the long, lean face furrowed into folds a basset hound would envy. If he did transfer to the Duty desk, she thought sadly, she was going to miss him. A lot.

As he relaxed more and more, he began questioning her on her morning, and she was finally able to unload all her concerns. Between bites of taco, she described her canvass of the Taft neighborhood and the various interviews she'd had on the church grounds. She did a general synopsis of where they stood in the case—basically nowhere—then told him in detail about the meeting with the Education Pastor.

"Pastor Ellsworth's attitude sort of sums it all up, Sam," she said. "He said if Sarah had any kind of a problem at the school, he'd have heard about it. There seems to be no reason anyone can give why Sarah Taft was in the state park, and not even the sniff of a reason why anyone would want her dead. I've never run into a victim held in such high esteem before. Usually, somebody somewhere doesn't like them, but not Sarah. She was universally loved by everyone. All any of them can say is that it has to be a stranger. One of the sick whackos roaming the world."

"Do you feel like you're getting the runaround from them, maybe a cover-up of some kind?"

She probed back into her impressions of the morning. "No, I can't honestly say I do. I think they're sincere. They really believe it. But what it's done is to shut down my access to them. Since they won't treat the idea seriously that anyone they know can be involved, they won't make information I need available to me. For instance, Sam, I was turned down outright by Ellsworth when I tried to get hold of a class list. It's a small thing . . . I can get hold of a yearbook somehow, and get the names that way. But that's what I mean. He's so damned convinced it was a stranger that he's absolutely blocking my access."

"What do you think?"

She shoved the last two quarters of the quesadilla away and concentrated on her iced tea. "I'm getting concerned that maybe they're right," she said slowly. "Maybe we do have a random killing on our hands. As ludicrous as it seems, it really could be that some sicko came walking up her front walk that afternoon, and he just happened to find her there alone and made off with her for his own nauseating reasons."

He considered it through the last few bites of food. He scraped up every last morsel of food from his platter, soaked up the last of the chili juices with the last of the flour tortillas, then waved his hand at the waitress for a cup of coffee and sat back with a contented sigh. He didn't undo his belt a notch, but he patted his stomach as if he'd like to.

He mulled over what she'd said, then slowly shook his head. "You're talking serial killer. If that's what we've got on our hands, it's the first one of the series. I've talked to every P.D. around. There are no similar M.O.'s in any of the homicides they're working."

"How about older women found in the woods?" Kate asked. "Or younger ones, for that matter. Or girls with their heads bashed in but not found in the woods?"

"Nope."

"Males, then, not females."

Sam shook his head. She was reaching, and he knew it.

"What about missing girls that haven't been found yet?"

"There are some of those," he admitted. "But I talked to the folks handling those cases this morning, and there's usually some kind of a troubled background there. Drugs, bad home life, divorce, bad grades, boyfriend trouble, a rap sheet of some kind . . . whatever. In every case, there's a reason why the kid could've taken off."

She gave him a quizzical look. "In every case? There's not even one that might come close to this?"

Sam looked thoughtful a minute, replaying tapes in his mind. "Well," he said slowly, "I guess we can't eliminate every single disappearance. That wouldn't be reasonable. Some girl might be having problems at home or in school and still fall victim to a random killing. It's just that there are no strong pointers that way."

"Okay, let's leave it for a minute. The murder weapon. Any leads there at all?"

"Nothing. The search drew a big zip. They even got the Explorer Scouts involved. Nothing."

"The license number," she said with some desperation. She needed something. Anything. "How about that license number I gave you? Did you have a chance to run the plates yet?"

He nodded. "It's registered to a Matthew and Patricia Jacobson."

She stared disbelievingly at him for a moment. Pastor Matt's car. Then that had to have been his wife watching the Taft house last night. But why would a pastor's wife sit on a dark street late at night like that, simply watching, instead of going in to help the bereaved family? And exactly how did this little juggernaut fit into the case?

But maybe she hadn't been watching the house. Maybe she'd simply been trying to remember something, something she forgot to bring for the family, for instance, then suddenly did remember and took off in a roaring hurry to go get it. If that were the case, then so much for her mysterious sideswiper. But that scenario didn't play right to her. It seemed a stretch—off-base somehow. Well then, was this little side trip worth pursuing? Or was it one of those odd twists that crosses a case every now and then that lead absolutely nowhere.

"Any help there?" Sam asked.

"If there is, I can't see it." She fell silent, but as she tried to tease the small bits and pieces into some kind of a meaningful picture in her mind, she grew more and more discouraged. She toyed with the pieces for several more moments before giving it up and finally looked up at Sam. "Maybe the autopsy will come up with something."

"Why are you so intent on the autopsy results?"

"I want it simpler, Sam. I want to find out that maybe it was a baseball bat instead of a tree branch, and we'll find it lying around the school locker room, complete with fingerprints and bloodstains. I want to be told she died at two-sixteen, or four fifty-three in the afternoon, so the time of death is sliced down to the minute and I can go hunting down whoever isn't firmly alibied. Lord, what a mess," she said, glumly. "As it stands now, we're nineteen hours into the case and we've got nothing. Absolutely zilch. Not even a reason she was killed." She looked up at him. "Is the Captain going to parole you to cover Sarah's autopsy this afternoon?"

"Nope." He picked up the check and began figuring out her share. "Looks like you'll have to do it."

Her eyes widened. "I can't. I'm meeting with Pastor Matt then. Sure you can't get away?"

"I'm sure. In fact, I've gotta head back now. The Cap gave me exactly one hour for lunch." His voice was matter-of-fact, but the bleak look was back again.

"Okay, then, maybe you can help me out. Supposedly the Wonder Twins did some canvassing last night around the Bridle Trails area. Their reports are in the case folder on my desk. Complete with phone numbers. How about doing some double-checking for me on that whole thing?"

For an instant, Sam's eyes warmed with humor. "Are you saying you don't trust our Fabulous Duo?"

She started to give him a light answer in response, but the whole case was digging at her, and the thought that Goddard and Fry might be taking shortcuts put her nerves on edge. If she and Sam were missing a piece of information simply because Goddard and Fry hadn't done their job . . . "I just have a hard time believing Goddard had time to cover forty-eight houses or more at the same time he was giving interviews to the media. All in a couple of hours? It doesn't add up."

"Okay," Sam said, making a note. "I'll handle it. Where will you be this afternoon?"

"Lucy Gray's, then back to the church. When I'm through there, I'll head on in."

"You're going to wimp out on that autopsy, eh?"

"You bet. I've seen my share. One."

"And the Dreadful Duo? If they happen to wander in, what would you like them to do for you?"

"What in hell can we do with them? I don't trust them to do any serious inquiries for me."

A wicked look came into Sam's eyes and a lazy smile began to cross his face. "You know, Katie, I had seven confessions this morning over the phone."

"With names and addresses?"

"Complete with . . ."

A blissful feeling began deep inside of her and spread like the warmth of wine throughout her being. Goddard interviewing the crazies. Perfect. "What fun," she murmured to Sam.

And they grinned at each other like a pair of Cheshire cats, proud of themselves.

In her car, she dug out Lucy Gray's address and studied the plat map. She had time for a quick visit before her appointment with Matt Jacobson. She'd see about getting this self-appointed helper of hers chilled out a little.

Lucy Gray's place was near the 405 on Slater Avenue, a road of fields, firs and old farms between Kirkland and Totem Lake that the developers hadn't hit yet. Lucy had a nice-sized piece of land, a couple of acres at least, with a small barn in the rear, a tiny house next to it, and a front yard that was all green pasture. Maisie was grazing in the field near the rail fence running along the roadside, her flanks gleaming a rich chestnut beneath the midday sun. Kate pulled into the long graveled drive and slowed to admire the horse a moment, then continued up to the small house at the rear of the property, her tires kicking up sand and rock behind her.

There was a large turnaround area to one side of the house, with a horse trailer backed in next to the barn, and the pickup truck parked next to it, ready to move out, hitch up and take off. A strong sun glinted off the windshield and hood of the pickup and the metal top of the horse trailer. Kate pulled well off to the side, out of the way of both, and climbed out. Instantly, the rich smells of a farm hit her. The scents from a sun-warmed field, the sweet smell of hay, the pungent aroma of manure combined into one deep, earthy aroma. Some bees were buzzing around a stand of wildflowers behind the house, droning their way through the heat of the day. It was a serene, pastoral setting with the grazing horse, green pasture, white fences and deep blue sky. Calendar perfect. And completely spoiled by the roar of traffic from the freeway just beyond a row of fir trees across the road. A crime the D.A. couldn't prosecute, Kate thought.

The back door to the little house shot open, and Lucy Gray stood in the doorway, peering out. She was dressed in jeans, work boots and a plaid shirt with the sleeves rolled up. In her hands was a shotgun held in firing position, pumped and cocked, barrel aimed at the center of Kate's chest.

Kate stood stock-still, hands spread wide in a nonthreatening gesture. "It's the police, Lucy," she yelled. "I'm Kate MacLean. I talked to you yesterday at the park. Remember? I came to visit with you a minute or two."

Lucy's eyes narrowed against the glare of the sun. She peered once again, then recognition came and she upended the shotgun. "Ever thought of calling first?" she snapped. "I could've filled your backside with buckshot, you know." She held the door wide open as Kate climbed the rickety back porch.

Still keeping a wary eye on the shotgun barrel, Kate moved slowly toward her. "Do you always greet visitors with a gun?" she asked. It was a Model 98 Winchester pump, a good seventy to seventy-five years old. And oiled like new.

"Only since yesterday," the old woman said. "Can't ever be too old to change your ways to keep up with the times. And these times are violent."

She uncocked the hammer and leaned the gun against a corner of the back entryway, then led the way into the house.

The kitchen was a tiny room that wasn't much more than a shed tacked on behind the house. A sink on legs, an ancient black iron gas range with an old enamel coffeepot burbling gently on a rear burner, a round-shouldered refrigerator at least thirty years old and a small round table with two chairs by a back window crowded the room. But the room's walls were painted the palest of buttermilk yellows. It was sunny and cheerful, and the aroma of fresh-brewed coffee filled the room. As Kate looked around in admiration, she made an instant decision to paint her old dark and dingy laundry room the same buttermilk yellow that so brightened this room.

Lucy motioned her to sit, then pointed to her own place where a small plate held a half-eaten sandwich next to a partially empty glass of milk. "Caught me in the middle of my lunch, you did. Can I fix you something?"

Kate shook her head. "Thanks, but I've just had lunch. I can only stay a minute."

"Oh, long enough for a cup of coffee, surely." She took a thick heavy cup down from a cupboard and poured out a cup of coffee for her anyway. "Nice to have you drop by, though, no matter how long you can stay. Cream or sugar?"

Kate took the chair pointed to. "Neither, thanks." She watched the old woman move, spine straight, motions brisk and lithe. The jeans outlined a slim body and tiny waist, giving her a fragile look that was deceptive, for her forearms were wiry and well muscled, like oak limbs in their prime.

Lucy set the cup in front of Kate, then took her own seat. "If you'll excuse me . . ." She picked up her sandwich half and began munching.

Kate gave thought to how best to approach this. She decided to lead into it sideways. "Did Barb Denton happen to call you?"

Nodding, the old woman chewed twice more and swallowed. "Sure did," she said, once her mouth was empty. "Gave me some nonsense about keeping my nose out of your work."

"Did she happen to mention that you could get yourself into a bit of a bad situation if you weren't careful?"

Lucy snorted. "Now who's gonna tangle with an old broad like me? First of all, I'm stronger than most men twice my size. Comes from the work around the place. And second, who would want to?"

"The killer," Kate said quietly.

Her response was designed to dramatize the dangers inherent in what Lucy was doing, but it didn't faze the woman one bit. She simply snorted again. "Well, now, all I'm doing is asking a few questions of the Saddle Club. It's your job to catch him, right? So how's that catching going anyway?"

"Now hold on a minute—"

"Oh, pshaw, girl. Clear to me you could use the help. So how's it going?"

It was the old schoolteacher look, pointed, stern, demanding a response. "Now listen, Miss Gray," Kate said in stern tones of her own, "I appreciate what you're trying to do, but you have got to stay out of this. We can't have civilians going around playing detective. It's too dangerous."

Lucy had taken all of this in while munching the rest of her sandwich. Without saying anything, she drank the rest of her milk, picked up a paper napkin and wiped the milk mustache off her upper lip, then crumpled the napkin and tossed it on the plate. She rose, carried the plate over to the sink, poured herself some coffee, and brought it back to the table. She sat with elbows on the table, cup held at her lips, and took a deep breath of the coffee aroma. "Nothing like the smell of good fresh-brewed coffee in my book." That said, she took a long sip.

Kate knew she'd made no impact at all with this woman. Stubborn old broad, she thought with some exasperation. She leaned across the table and said in blunt, no-nonsense tones, "Stay out of it, Lucy. That's an order."

The old woman's eyes met hers over the coffee cup, and Kate could see the amusement in their depths. No way, they said. "Of course," Lucy murmured out loud. "I wouldn't want to add to your worries." And she began to drink her coffee.

Chapter Nine

Matt Jacobson was running late. When he finally did appear at the church secretary's desk, he was in shirt sleeves and reading glasses, looking more like a harassed grad student than an associate pastor of anywhere. "I'm sorry, I didn't mean to leave you waiting like this." He escorted her down the hall to his office. "We had to tell the kids about Sarah this morning, and they're taking it pretty hard. And the parents are just as upset. Paranoia's setting in real fast."

His office was plain, with a utilitarian desk much like hers at headquarters, only wood instead of metal. There were a couple of file cabinets and a bookcase, with stacks of papers and file folders piled everywhere. A fan of computer printouts she recognized now as budget spreadsheets were spread out across his desk. A mug being used as a pencil holder stated *A Pastor a day keeps the Devil away.*

Matt folded up the budget sheets and tossed them aside. "I don't know about you, but I could use a shot of coffee. Join me?" At her nod, he said, "Be back in a minute," and disappeared.

He was gone a long time, and she took the opportunity to wander around the room. A collection of engraved crosses was arranged in a display around an old family Bible on top of one of the bookcases. Groups of framed photographs and snapshots were everywhere. Some were Sunday School classes, the children standing at stiff attention for the camera in their Sunday best. Others were candid shots taken at various church activities, all of them with the collegiate-looking Matthew Jacobson involved. A few had been taken outdoors, the glossy sheen of blue water showing in the background. The setting didn't match what she'd seen of the campus. Taken up at the church campgrounds? she wondered.

Several had Sarah Taft in amongst the group. Kate looked at the lovely young woman with the calm gaze and the warm smile, and was struck anew by the loss.

She turned away from the pull that the dead girl exerted over her and paused by a low bookcase running beneath the window. Set in a prominent spot was one large eight-by-ten portrait of a young woman in her mid-twenties. She was a pale, thin woman, with fine, light-colored hair pulled back and clipped at her neck. She was pretty in a delicate way, but worry wrinkles were already setting in at the cleft of the brow above her nose. Though she was smiling, it was an anxious, tense smile, as if she weren't sure she was doing the right thing posing in front of the camera. There was enough resemblance to Kate's flash-image of the woman in the Ford Escort to link them together. Patricia Jacobson, Matt's wife.

Matt poked his head in the door, holding two Styrofoam cups of coffee. "Let's move down the hall and get away from the phone."

He led her to a large, pleasant sitting room at the end of the corridor. Several comfortable-looking club chairs formed a semicircle around a low coffee table, facing a sofa against one side wall. The walls were painted a soothing rosy-beige and a large sliding glass door overlooked a small walled garden area. The monochrome color scheme and the garden greenery framed by the glass created a soothing atmosphere, with nothing controversial to upset the psyche. "Is this where you do your counseling?"

"Yep." He grinned. "I'm afraid if the women caught sight of

my office, they'd be more inclined to tidy it up than to listen to some counsel and advice."

At his gesture, she took a club chair. It was soft and deep, cupping her body like a feather bed, much like her couch at home. She resisted an impulse to kick off her shoes and tuck her feet up under her, as she took the proffered coffee.

He'd taken a swivel tub chair opposite her and held out a small basket from a nearby table providing sugar packets, dry creamer and an assortment of stirring sticks. She shook her head in refusal and he poured generous helpings of both into his cup.

He was staring down as he stirred the lump of powdered creamer into the coffee, and for a moment, his face was unguarded. Sadness edged the clear hazel eyes, an emotional weariness that she recognized, not so different from Sam's. For in retrospect, that's how Sam struck her, as a man who was exhausted at the moment by the push-pull tensions of his emotions. It was an odd linkage in her mind, relating these men to each other, for Matt was so much younger than Sam that one would assume they'd be at different stages of life. Especially given their differing professions.

Finally he looked up at her. "Sorry I was so long. Another call came in from one of our churchwomen, and it took a few moments to calm her down. I do hope I'm doing the right thing by assuring them the church isn't involved?" He directed a questioning glance her way.

Kate let the question slide. "Is anyone offering any theories as to who or why?" she asked.

He shook his head, still intent on sugaring his coffee. "No, they're asking us for answers. Us meaning the pastors. And, of course, we're asking you for the answers." His coffee finally fixed, he slumped back in his chair, his eyes fixed on her through the wire-rimmed glasses. "Do you have anything at all yet?"

She gave her answer careful thought. The usual police assurances, or the truth? She wanted his help. Empty reassurances wouldn't do. "Nothing," she admitted finally.

He accepted that news glumly. Now it was his turn to study her. "Do you have a family, Miss MacLean?"

"Parents and a brother. All in Connecticut."

"Is that where you were raised?"

She nodded. "A good Episcopalian upbringing. Very traditional."

"Yet your line of work can hardly be termed that."

"True." She grinned. "And it raised all kinds of havoc with my psyche. Not to mention my mother, who's horrified by what I do. She wanted me to become a lawyer."

He tilted his head quizzically, and she had a near compulsion to pour out all the inner conflicts her soul harbored. It was the warmth on his face, the encouragement clear in the light eyes, the quiet of the room. . . . She wondered if it was soundproofed. It amused her how easily he'd slipped into the counselor role. She took back the initiative. "Do you counsel many families?" she asked.

"My share," he admitted.

"Sarah's family?"

He hesitated. "Normally, that'd be confidential. But in their case, I can say no, I didn't. The Tafts live a very Christ-centered life and they practice their beliefs to the fullest. They never seemed to have any problems they couldn't solve themselves . . . with God's help, of course."

Kate phrased her next question carefully. "What are some of the problems you do deal with?"

Matt saw through that in an instant. "None that would make the headlines," he said in an amused tone of voice.

"No rape, no incest, no pedophiles?" she asked lightly.

He shook his head. "Nothing so dramatic."

"Do you do one-on-one as well as family counseling?"

"Sure, whatever's needed."

"What about Sarah? Did she bring any of her concerns to you for help?"

"Usually the teens go to Pastor Bob with their concerns."

She noted the indirect way he answered the question. "When did you see her last?"

"In church. On Sunday."

"And how did she seem?"

His gaze wandered back to the window. "As usual." Then his focus sharpened and he brought himself back to the present. "How do you start something like this, an investigation of murder?"

"You ask a lot of questions of a lot of people," she said quietly, "then you start comparing the answers you're given."

"For what?"

"Areas of agreement. Contradictions."

"Contradictions like how?"

He seemed serious in his inquiry. As if he really wanted to know. As if it were more than simple idle questions to make polite small talk.

"People who say they were someplace else at the time of the killing, but weren't. People who say they don't know the victim, but do. People who say they have no reason to harm the victim, but do. Why? Have you run into some contradictions about Sarah's death?"

"Just the fact of her death itself," he said in an even tone. His features took on a more businesslike cast. "Now what can I do to help you?"

Matt turned out to be every cop's dream. He was quiet, reflective, a true listener, listening to the story of her aborted interview with Pastor Ellsworth without interruption. When she was through, he reflected on it a little, and said, "Why do you need the class lists, what is it you're after exactly?"

"I need to talk to her classmates, to talk with her friends, to the teachers she felt closest to. I want to check the absentee list for the day. Was someone else absent that day? What about in the afternoon, when she was home alone? Had someone else come to school in the morning, but missed afternoon classes? I want to know how she was feeling. Aside from being sick that day, had she been depressed lately? Was she having problems with someone, with anyone, an argument or a fight, perhaps? Had there been unexpected mood swings that would indicate a problem somewhere? I want to know why she was in Bridle Trails State Park. Was it a favorite haunt of hers? Did she go there often? Occasionally? Never? Who else was familiar with the park? Had she been followed, had she seen anyone lurking around? Had *anyone* seen anyone lurking around? These are just some of the questions we need to get answered."

He raised an eyebrow. "That's quite a list. What was Pastor Ellsworth's response when you made the request of him this morning?"

"He simply said he'd have heard about it if she'd had problems of any kind."

For a moment, his gaze wandered again to the garden behind her and he idly swiveled the chair back and forth, lost in thought. The silence lasted awhile, then he seemed to reach some decision. The swiveling came to an abrupt halt and he rose. "I'll be back in a minute." He crossed the room in long strides and was gone.

Within a couple of minutes, he returned, carrying a file folder. "In here," he explained, holding it out to her, "is a complete church roster, names and addresses. The children are listed under their parents' names, with ages given. I've also called over to the school office for a copy of Monday's absentee list. It'll be here in a minute or two."

Kate smiled her relief. "And Sarah's class schedule?"

He gave a half-smile. "Let's wait until the bulk of the donations come in before we scrounge up the last few pennies. There are a dozen ways of finding that out if we have to. But the people you really need to see are still up at retreat. Nancy Wells is our English teacher. She's also counselor for all the girls. And Denise Hickman was probably Sarah's closest friend. She's up there, too. We have cut the retreat short and called everyone home early, but they won't be coming in until mid-afternoon."

She took the folder with thanks and started glancing through the thick sheaf of papers clipped together. Pages and pages of names, hundreds of them.

Before she was finished going through the list, a light tap sounded at the door and Matt opened it just enough to slip his hand through the crack and draw back a single sheet of paper. He murmured his thanks, then closed it again. Whoever had been there had no chance to see into the room, Kate noticed. Or to see her.

He brought the sheet to her. "The absentee list from Monday."

She took it and scanned the length. Possibly a dozen names all told. Plus a separate grouping of girls under the heading Senior Retreat.

She looked up at him then. She was appreciative of his help and frankness, but he must've read the speculation in her eyes, for he said, "You're wondering why I'm doing this when Pastor Ellsworth wouldn't, right?"

She nodded.

"I don't believe in playing ostrich," he said flatly. "I want Sarah's killer found. I'll do anything to help. But I have to honestly say I don't think any of this stuff's going to help you at all."

He leaned forward, then, eyes intent on hers, face earnest. "Let me tell you what you're up against. From babyhood on, our children are *never* left unsupervised. They are either at church, at school, or home. Even our teenagers. Especially our teenagers. They never go to malls by themselves. They are not left alone to wander the streets—or even their own neighborhoods. They are not allowed to go anywhere without an adult. This doesn't mean we hover over them every single minute of the day. In their spare time, they play together, they work together on projects, or spend time reading or doing individual things that interest them. But there's always an adult close by.

"Let me give you a typical schedule for a twelfth-grader," he continued. "Dot, Joe and Suzy, let's say, are dropped off by either their parents or their car pool each morning. They're in classes until noon. Lunch is assigned seating with a faculty member at every four tables. More classes, then it's either home, or after-school activities and then home. In either case, again they're transported by parents or church bus. They have dinner and homework. Once a week they're required to come to an evening Bible study. Again, though, it's with their parents. The whole family has Bible study classes. Other than that, once home, they stay there.

"Weekends are much the same, minus school. Friday nights are church socials for the families. Saturdays, they either do chores at home, or attend work parties at the church, or both. Saturday nights, the church puts on various activities for the youth. Sundays are church, Sunday School, prayer groups, Sunday dinner, and family time, a time for rest, relaxation, a time to prepare for the upcoming week. This schedule covers the youngest kindergartner through the graduating senior. Then, by the time they're adults, habits of responsible behavior and discipline are ingrained, and as young adults, they can be trusted to do what's right. So when Pastor Ellsworth says it's impossible for any of our students to have done this to Sarah, he means just that—it's logistically impossible. Their schedule doesn't allow it. Sarah being alone that one afternoon was simply one of those flukes that could never happen again. Believe me."

Kate had an image of cattle being shuttled from chute to chute to chute, with no chance of escaping the stockyard. Her instincts for independence and freedom were too strong; they stood up and rebelled inside. "What if the mothers work?"

He grinned at that. "You're not going to like the answer at all. You see, we don't encourage our mothers to work outside the home. We're not very modern that way. Our whole focus—spiritually, emotionally, psychologically—is on the family, the well-being of the family, and particularly the proper raising of a child. And the mother's role in the home is critical to the success of the child-raising. We do have instances where the women have to work—the husband is sick or injured, and can't work. Or he dies. And we've had a desertion or two. In that case, there's no recourse but for the woman to go to work. But we do everything in our power to see to it her children are cared for while she is at work. But as for having careers . . . motherhood and wifehood are their careers. Anything else outside the home is for single women—or childless women."

"In other words, you'd never have a female cop in your Mothers' groups."

He smiled slightly. "I told you you wouldn't like the answer."

Kate nodded agreement. "What about simple things, like dating, going to the movies, going out for burgers or a pizza, stuff like that?"

He shook his head. "Dating's not allowed. It too often leads to early marriages. Marriage requires maturity, flexibility, a deep love, and a full commitment by both to make it work. That requires an emotional stability that most high-schoolers simply don't have yet. So dating's outlawed until they're adults. The activities offered on Saturday nights substitute for dating. Game nights, movie nights, pizza nights, sing-alongs, even debates. There's more than enough things for our high-schoolers to do. And by insisting they participate only in group activities, eliminating the pressure of dating on them, boys and girls get to know each other as they really are. The chances of successful marriages increase considerably. And successful marriages create successful families. Our real business here is training our children to please God."

Kate left that one for now. "Then what about logistical things, like grocery shopping, running errands, even just buying a new pair of shoes?"

"We've founded a buying co-op group. Everything from food to clothes to furniture and birthday presents are bought through it. There's no need to go to the malls for anything. As for running errands, the kids don't get driver's licenses until they're out of high school. And most times, they don't get them until they're out working and self-supporting."

"Books, records, TVs?"

He shrugged. "We have our own Christian bookstore nearby. It carries everything from fiction to music tapes. And television sets are absolutely forbidden in the home. Advertising is a dreadful influence on the young. If kids don't know what's out there, they can't want to have it. As for the programming content, well, anything goes, it seems like. There just are no limits on indecency these days, and we're extremely careful what our young folks are exposed to."

Original thinkers need not apply, Kate translated. "So what you're saying is that all of the children in the school, from kindergartners to graduating seniors, are kept away from the real world."

He smiled slightly, not taking offense at that. "If you mean protected from gangs, drugs, promiscuity, knifings, drive-by shootings, random violence, metal detectors on the school doorways, why yes, then, our children are protected. But if you mean protected from responsible adulthood, commitment to others, a strong sense of community and their place in it, and experiencing the true joy of devoting their life to Christ, the answer is no, they're not."

"And you never have families that bend the rules a bit?"

"No." He paused then, frowning. "Not to my knowledge, at least."

"And the kids don't rebel at these restrictions."

"They're brought up with them, so they accept them as the norm. Like spaghetti for dinner. It's an accepted part of their life."

Kate quirked an eyebrow as she thought back to her own teenaged years. There'd been a flexing of a strong, independent spirit combined with the intellectual questioning of everything she'd been told and had accepted as Gospel as a child. Maybe these kids accepted their restrictions; maybe not.

He pointed a finger at her coffee cup. "Are you through?"

She nodded.

"Then why don't I show you around a bit. Maybe it'll help you understand it better." He led her outside through the rear door of the office wing, around to the front of the complex. "We'll start at the beginning."

They walked to the edge of the road and turned to face the complex. The church was beautiful in its simplicity. The rich hues of the cedar stain absorbed the strong rays of the afternoon sun, the colors of the stained-glass windows in front shone pure and vibrant, and a sense of comfort emanated from the serene symmetry of the eaves and roofline rising up to the strong blue sky. It seemed to say that the rest of your world may be chaotic and askew, but within my doors, you'll find only peace and a sense of order to things.

Intrigued, she stood silent, a dozen questions tumbling through her mind. The whole complex was a magnificent, well-groomed layout, with walkways, lawns and evergreen gardens gracefully contoured and interlaced throughout the grounds. When had they bought the land, how much had they paid? What did it cost to run a church/school such as this? Was it funded solely from tithes and tuitions, or were there some wealthy donors hovering in the background, helping as needed? When had the other pastors been added? Who governed the whole? Who held the power, and how did the grapevine loop work? Who were the insiders and who were the ones on the outs? Who decided the what and when of things? Where were the checks and balances? The old five *W*'s, she thought. Who, what, why, when, where. And the one *H*—how? How had it come into being?

Matt's eyes never left the church. It was as if he couldn't get enough of it. His gaze continually went over the front, like a lover memorizing the face of his beloved, examining the thick castle doors, exploring the stained-glass window piece by piece, following the roofline up to its peak, then dropping to the large wooden cross hung just above the door.

Finally he spoke. "This was built with donated materials," he said softly, "and the labor of a couple of dozen dedicated souls. I think it ended up only costing the congregation something like twelve thousand dollars all told. Hard to believe, isn't it?"

"When was it built?"

"Twenty-two years ago. Pastor Barnes had founded his church a couple of years before that, and his message was so inspired, his vision so clear, that his congregation quickly grew and they built the church two years later. And everything else grew from that."

He led the way to the heavy double oak doors then. They were unlocked and he pulled one open and they moved from the warmth of the sun into the cool dimness of the interior. The theme of simplicity had been carried through from the exterior. A plain wooden cross hung on a whitewashed wall behind the altar. A simple carpet runner in a deep, rich royal red ran down the center aisle and spread outward over the three broad steps up to the altar platform. The pews were plain benches, painted white, their backs topped with a half-round of oak stained a light honey color. The choir loft ran the full length of one side wall, while the organ itself was at congregation level on the opposite side of the altar, which provided the organist with a clear view of both pastor and choir. And over all of it, rays of soft blues and rose and gold bathed the interior as the strong sunshine outside played kaleidoscopic games with the stained-glass windows. It was breathtakingly beautiful in its simplicity. She hesitated to use the word, but holiness was the one that came to mind.

An old woman bundled in a cloth coat and scarf in spite of the heat of the day outside sat motionless in the third row. Her head was tilted up to face the cross, and her lips were moving in soundless prayer. If she'd heard or noticed them, she gave no sign. They watched her for a moment, then Matt shook his head in sadness. They quietly backed out of the church. The heavy door swung closed behind them.

"She lost her husband a few weeks ago," Matt explained. "She's having a rough time of it. We've asked her to come in and spend some time in prayer each day. She wasn't getting out of the house at all. Wasn't even getting dressed most days. Now, one of the churchwomen picks her up each day and brings her here, and another's always waiting for her when she's through, and she'll take her down to the meeting room just to have a cup of coffee and a visit with the other ladies down there. She seems better since she's getting out a little. She doesn't feel quite so abandoned and alone, I think."

He led her through a side door into the rear of the church, explaining rooms as they went along. "What is now the choir-robe room in the church was Pastor's first office. And down here in the basement used to be the Sunday School classrooms, a community room and a small kitchen. Then, as the congregation continued to increase in numbers, Pastor moved his office down here. The good churchwomen stood it awhile, but eventually they squawked at having their kitchen and meeting rooms taken over by filing cabinets and put their foot down. The office wing was built and the ladies reclaimed their basement."

They walked down the back stairs, and when they hit the community room in the basement of the church, a dozen women were gathered in clusters around tables of quilting patches, faces somber, talking in low murmurs about the tragedy of Sarah's death. Their faces brightened a little when they saw the pastor.

As for his part, Matt set aside his own sorrow and his hazel eyes creased with warmth as he spread hugs and a few reassuring words all around. Kate stood apart, watching. Intent as he was on his comforting, he didn't seem aware of the strength of the impact he was having on his parishioners. As he spoke with each group, their expressions softened and the terrible sorrow that was there eased into sad smiles.

Kate began to see some of the demands made upon him. His job certainly entailed a lot more than red-lining budget spreadsheets or directing a church choir. He was an important element in these women's church lives, and it required of him a nonstop, non-ending supply of warmth, empathy and compassion. She wondered again how the well of caring within him refilled itself. Or did he chance running dry?

They left the basement and strolled the grounds. Matt pointed out some of the other buildings, the day-care established so young mothers could join in the daytime activities at the church, the maintenance buildings and workshops that handled most of the complex's upkeep, and of course, the schools.

As Kate walked by his side, seeing what he saw, listening to him tell the stories of how each unit of the complex had come into being, it was clear to her that purely and simply, Matthew Jacobson was in love with his church. It was clear in the way his gaze lingered on the buildings, the way his face flooded with warmth when he saw a member of the community, the way his voice resonated with pride when he talked about the church's evolution.

Silently, Kate walked beside him, double-stepping now and then to keep up with his enthusiastic long-legged style, listening and watching as he waved open, expansive arms, first one way then the other, to point out this and explain that. He was so clearly a man of God, and he reveled in it. It made her feel a bit envious. Had he truly found something of value that she had somehow missed in her Episcopalian upbringing?

"Shortly after they built the church office wing, the school started holding its first classes in the basement," Matt said at one point, his face breaking into that young, appealing grin. "Those poor ladies. After reclaiming their basement from Pastor's filing cabinets, they lost it again to a bunch of school desks. But shortly afterward, the grade-school building was built. And then, about five years ago, the high-school building came into being."

"And the next stage of growth for the church?" Kate asked.

Matt gave a faint smile. "Ah, next to 'Have you saved a soul today?' that's the big question. Pastor's a man attuned to the needs of his congregation, and the thing he notices now is that we're an aging population. Many of the original parishioners are grandparents of the kids in high school. A few are even great-grandparents. Health problems are becoming a factor in their lives. Many have lost their spouses and are left on their own to cope. Like poor Mrs. Norris in there. Some need intermittent care, some need daily care and some need someone there at all times, day and night. We've organized the church membership to put in regular shifts of time, helping wherever there's a need. But these people are scattered all over the county and the setup's far from ideal. So what we're planning for the next stage is to take an area of land well away from the noises of the school grounds and build a senior-citizen complex with homes designed for independent living, along with a full-care facility for those who need it."

Kate put this into context with the overall complex, starting with the day-care center they'd just left. "It sounds like a cradle-to-grave philosophy."

"That's what a community is, isn't it?" Matt said, quietly. "In biblical times, the world was a series of small villages and hamlets, in which you were born, you lived, and you died. People stayed put. Accordingly, they had a sense of deep roots, of ancestors walking the hillsides they walked, and they knew their progeny would walk the same paths. They were able to pass on time-tested values and morals from one generation to the next. This is what we've attempted to establish here. To reconstitute that sense of community."

She stood silent beside him, fitting the pieces together into an overall picture and time frame. Her thoughts moved from building to building, from pastor to pastor, examining the evolution of it all. How it fit into a homicide investigation wasn't clear yet, but she was fascinated by the setup.

The general tour of the complex was complete. He said quietly, "Because of Sarah's death, you're seeing us at our lowest ebb. It's a horrible, wrenching loss for us. So let me show you what our church is all about through eyes too young to be affected by what's going on." He guided her back to the southern end of the grounds.

The day-care center was divided into three large playrooms, segregated by age, plus some crib nurseries and a kitchen and small dining area. Two of the playrooms had been dimmed for naptime, and sleeping children were scattered around, lying on mats and covered with light blankets. As Matt and Kate paused in the doorways, a couple of mothers looked up with warm smiles from corner chairs where they sat reading quietly and held fingers to their lips for silence. Matt nodded, returned their smiles with a warm one of his own, and ushered Kate on.

The last room in the building, separated by the kitchen/nursery area from the others, held a group of children too old for naps anymore. Some were sprawled on their stomachs on the floor, drawing on large sheets of paper. Others were scattered around at low tables, weaving colored strips of paper into mats, chattering and giggling as they worked. Their busy happiness was unadulterated by the grief surrounding them. It was a sun-filled oasis in the midst of a sorrow-filled desert, and Kate saw what he meant when he'd commented on the low ebb of the congregation at large. Matt paused, enjoying watching them for just a moment, his face warm with pleasure.

A slender woman in her late twenties came forward to greet them. "Hello, Matt. We've just finished our quiet time," she explained, "and when we're through with art, we'll be going out to play." She pointed toward a well-equipped play yard that ran behind the building.

"Terry Wright's one of our mothers here," Matt said to Kate, introducing the two women. "We run the day-care with volunteer help. There are several sessions a week, and each mother works during one of them. The rest of the time she's free to join the other mothers at the church for group work, or club meetings, to work on joint projects, or just for some good old-fashioned socializing."

Terry, a pretty woman with sparkling eyes, gave a mischievous grin. "That's my favorite, the socializing. I do love my gossip. This day-care center is a lifesaver for us. Otherwise, we'd go nuts, stuck at home alone all day." Then the grin faded and the same somberness came over her that Kate had seen in the other churchwomen. "I've heard about Sarah, Matt. I just can't believe it." She turned to Kate then. "Sarah was the best volunteer we had. She'd spend hours here every Saturday. She'd help with the babies and play games with the older ones. She was simply enchanted by the children."

"Why Saturdays?" Kate asked.

"Whatever needs doing for the church, we do," Matt explained. "Repairs, painting, building, planting, ground maintenance. Whatever. Every family donates a couple of Saturdays a month to helping the church out. Child care's provided, of course, and Sarah was one of those who helped us with that."

"Had she missed a Saturday lately?" Kate asked Terry.

"No, not a one," Terry said sadly, shaking her head. "Her family's one of the stalwarts who're here every week, so Sarah was, too."

"Did she seem troubled by anything? Worried, concerned, depressed in any way?"

Another shake of the head. "No, on the contrary, she was looking forward to graduation."

"What were her plans?"

"College. She was going into teaching. Either elementary or preschool, I don't think she'd decided which."

"And there was no indication she'd changed those plans?"

"None."

"What about other areas of her life? Friendships, romances, parents, teachers—any problems there?"

"Nothing she spoke about," Terry answered slowly. "There were no romances, they're not allowed at that age. As for the rest, she got along with everyone. I've never known Sarah to have an argument of any kind. Ever. She just wasn't that kind of person."

"What about outside of school?" Kate asked. "What were some of her outside interests?"

"Quilting was one, I know. She talked a lot about that. Her latest project was a quilt for her sister's bed. She showed me the pattern. It was beautiful, all bright reds and blues and greens . . . kind of a garden spray." Terry frowned in concentration. "She liked to read. And she loved to sing. She loved music in general, actually. She lent me a few of her gospel tapes. And she had quite a good collection of classical music. Mostly piano concertos. Then there was swing choir . . ." She looked up at Matt. "She was in swing, wasn't she?"

He nodded.

"What's swing choir?" Kate asked.

"Our music's not the stuffy, slow, ponderous hymns," he said, grinning slightly. "That would be more the Episcopalian way. We have joyful, upbeat songs of celebration. That's what our church is, a celebration of the Lord. You add in a touch of syncopation, and you've got some rousing, toe-tapping, hand-clapping, finger-snapping tunes. That's our swing choir. And it's made up of a select few of the high-schoolers. It's an honor choir, if you will. Anyone can join—and indeed is welcome—in junior choir. But swing choir's by invitation only."

"And Sarah was in it?"

"Yes. She had a wonderful sense of rhythm, and a pure, clear voice. Contralto. She could carry a counterpoint melody on her own, in key. A requisite for swing."

Kate absorbed that, then turned back to Terry White. "What about horses?" she asked. "Did Sarah ever do any riding?"

Terry shook her head. "Not that she mentioned. Although I know she was as crazy about animals as she was about kids. But no, I don't think she went through the horsey stage."

That confirmed what Barb Denton had said, that she hadn't seen Sarah at the park before, and didn't think she'd had any contact with the Saddle Club. "Did she mention anything unusual going on in her neighborhood," Kate asked, "like maybe someone watching her from a distance, across the street, from the woods? Someone following her? Anything like that at all?"

Terry sighed at the implications. "I've thought of nothing else since I've heard. In my mind, I've gone over and over all the conversations we've had lately, trying to find some clue she might've given that something was wrong, but I can't think of a thing. Sarah was—well, just Sarah, you know what I mean? She was solemn and wise, and warm and funny, and caring and joyful—

her heart went out to anyone with a problem. She'd just scoop you in and warm you with her love." Terry's eyes were filling with tears now and her voice cracked. "That's why it's so hard," she whispered. "She was such a good person—it's such a loss. Such an awful loss."

Kate stared off into thin air. At the phrase, "anyone with a problem," her thoughts had instantly jumped to Norm Overholtz. He struck her as a person with a myriad of personal problems. Had Sarah's heart gone out to him, too?

She had a chance to ask Matt about Norm as he walked her through the strong afternoon sunshine to her car.

"Oh, Norm." He eyed her as if trying to deduce what she did and didn't know. "I'd guess you'd have to say Norm had a crush on Sarah. That was very obvious to everyone. Everyone except Sarah, that is. She didn't seem to notice, and treated Norm as just a friend. Drove him crazy. But since the kids aren't allowed to have boyfriend-girlfriend relationships, there wasn't anything he could do. He's over at Northwest Bible College now. Hopefully, being over there will help, and at some point, he'll move on with his life."

She frowned. "That's a strange way to put it, move on with his life. Hasn't he done that already, just by virtue of going to college?"

He was cautious in his answer. "In some ways, yes. But regrettably, he finds excuse after excuse to hang around the school here. In his defense, though, there are some valid reasons for it. His family all are church members, of course, and he still lives at home, so he partakes in more activities here than another college student would. But we have a special Young Adult service on Sunday mornings, yet he skips that and comes for the early service that Sarah attends. And you'll see him staying for the main service whenever swing choir's scheduled. I don't think he's missed a performance all year. He's a good kid, Norm is. But he simply hasn't broken the ties that bind yet."

Kate thought about it. "I stopped by the college last night. He had his yearbook there. That's how we identified Sarah."

Matt gave a sad shake of the head. "That's Norm." He sighed. "He can't quite let go."

"Then his feelings for Sarah must be pretty strong."

He was silent at that.

"Did you see him on Monday?" she asked. "Was he on campus here at all that day?"

"I can't honestly say. We're into budget developments—our fiscal year runs from October one through September thirtieth. And before we can present a unified budget to the board of deacons, each pastor has to come up with figures for his own department, then defend them to the other pastors. That's what we were doing Monday. And the day tends to run long. It's a rigorous testing of a man's faith, I can tell you."

She grinned in sympathy at the distaste obvious in his expression. "Pastor Bob told me he hadn't realized you needed an MBA from Harvard to run a Sunday School program."

"Surprising, isn't it? But in this day and age, churches are a far cry from the old-time evangelistic dog-and-pony road show passing a hat through the crowd. It actually is a business. Which is why we have both Pastor Lang and a board of deacons. What escapes one is caught by the other. Pastor Lang is fond of quoting the old saw that if you watch the pennies, the dollars take care of themselves." His unexpected touch of humor surfaced again. "Of course, inflation has jacked that up a bit."

"What kind of an annual budget does it take to run an outfit like this?"

He smiled. "What a subtle way of asking what we spend a year."

She smiled and let it go. "What did you do after the budget session ended?" she asked casually.

"After the budget session, I hunkered down in my office to prepare for a couple of counseling sessions scheduled for that evening. I didn't see anyone else until I left for supper. Just in case I'm on your suspect list, too."

She didn't respond to that. Everyone was on her suspect list for now. "Did you eat out, or at home?"

"Home. My wife is well aware of my schedule, and prepares the meals accordingly."

His tone now was formal, and she noted the use of "my wife" rather than Patricia, or Patty, or Patsy, or whatever he called her. The warmth that had been there whenever Sarah's name had been mentioned was noticeably missing. She said casually, "Any children at home?"

"No."

The answer was curt and abrupt. The subject was definitely off-limits. For now, Kate thought. Just for now. She decided not to mention seeing his wife watching the Taft house the night before.

They'd reached her car by then. As she opened the driver's door, she smiled over at him. "Well, the tour's been fascinating. And unexpectedly pleasant. I expected to have Bible verses spouted my way all day long."

"I certainly can if you'd like. How about Philippians Three, Verse Two—'Beware of dogs, beware of evil workers, beware of the concision.' "

"Concision?"

"The too-concise."

She smiled. "Yes, it's apt. Especially for a cop. We tend to like talkers."

For the first time, he laughed. It was a warm sound, resonant and openhearted. "Yes, I bet you do. Which is probably a warning to me to shut up now."

She grinned. "You did just fine. You talk, I'll listen anytime." She held out her hand. "Thank you for the time you've taken with me, Pastor Jacobson. You've got quite a setup here. Kind of a real-life Garden of Eden. A perfect world with perfect parents and perfect children."

The amused tone came back. "Oh, we're not perfect. We just strive to be."

She gave a neutral smile and climbed in her car. Behind the smile, though, her mind was running down a list of questions, wondering what exactly *were* the imperfections that existed in this fairy-tale world. And was murder one of them?

Chapter Ten

There were two problems with driving on the Eastside any time of day—traffic and weather. When it was rainy and cold, everyone outside hurried to get in. When it was sunny and warm, everyone inside hurried to get out. Regardless of which it was, traffic was always a mess. And now, in the middle of a warm, sunny afternoon, Mount Rainier was sitting like some benign Buddha in the southern sky, drawing people out of their shells like a bunch of goofy turtles, and streets had produced their typical gridlock.

And the commute hour hadn't even started yet, Kate fumed, stalled at an intersection for yet one more turn of the same red light. The mental images of the wide-open spaces of Wyoming and Montana spread across the landscape of her mind. Surely crime visited the Wild West now and then. Surely they had a need for cops on occasion. If only for a cattle rustling or two. Why she continued to live in what had become a traffic hellhole was beyond her. Then finally, the snarl sorted itself out and she broke free and roared away.

The parking lot at headquarters was less than half full. Detectives and other assorted species had found excuses to be out and about in the warmth. She took the handiest slot and made her way through the security checkpoints, then wove through the filing-cabinet maze to Homicide. Sam's desk was empty and the Captain's office was dark. There were no signs of Goddard and Fry. Of course.

She bent over her desk for messages, and frowned when there were none. Sam had left no note about his whereabouts, the Wonder Twins were still on the loose somewhere, God only knew where or doing what, and there'd been no word from the pathologist. Even Brillo hadn't gotten back to her on any drug connection. Though with what she'd learned about school and church today, she doubted there'd be one. She slung her purse over the back of her chair, plopped down into it and punched out Franklin's number on the phone.

He wasn't at his desk, and she left a message and hung up, trying not to feel frustrated. This is when time played its tricks. On the one hand, she had a dreadful sense of time passing much too swiftly for the progress being made. On the other hand, the clock crawled when it came to spitting out the information she needed. She wanted a time of death. Narrow it down. Pare down the possibilities. Figure out where to go next.

On impulse, she scrawled notes to Sam and the Captain, dumped them on the appropriate desks, then, her conscience clear if not quite pure, she grabbed up her notebooks and the folder of information Pastor Matt had given her, and headed back out. The autopsy report was next. Sam could wait; the Captain could wait; Goddard could go to hell.

It was the same glaring white hall of the night before, though it was broad daylight out, and it was the same echoing noises and the same acrid odors wafting about that stung the nose and made the stomach clutch. Kate cooled her heels for a good half hour in the two-chair waiting room of the pathology department before the lanky figure of Len Franklin came loping down the hall like a loose-limbed dog, a manila envelope in one hand. "Good," he said, "you waited. I had to check a few things out and was afraid you'd leave."

"You have the autopsy report, I hope?" At his nod she exhaled a heavy sigh of relief. "Find anything special?"

He looked around the cramped room with distaste. "Let's go get a cup of coffee." Without waiting for her approval, he started out of the room with his quick, long stride.

Kate jumped out of the chair. "Hey, wait up."

He paused for her to catch up, then with a light hand on her arm, propelled her through a maze of corridors to a hospital cafeteria. The good smells of food replaced the grisly smells left behind and her stomach settled back down and purred. They got their coffees, then found an empty table in a rear corner far enough from the nearest group of diners to provide them with some privacy.

He took a chair across from her, handed her the manila envelope, then busied himself sugaring his coffee.

She undid the clasp and slipped a black-and-white glossy paper free. The photo was a close-up of Sarah's face, taken in the morgue. As it had been when the pastor had ID'd the body, her hair was fanned out over the white-sheeted gurney, pillowing the head. A look of calm repose transfigured the face. Sarah Taft looked peacefully deep in slumber.

Len pointed to the picture. "I thought you might need that."

"I do. I'll have it duped and spread around the department when I get back. Maybe it fits another case someone else is working."

Len nodded, then extracted some folded sheets of handwritten notes from his lab coat pocket. "The formal report'll come in a few days. But this is what we've got so far. In clear, simple terms, she was killed with one broad swipe to the back of the head."

Kate took out her notebook and pen. "Any more details about the weapon used?"

"A tree limb of some kind. A dead branch, not too heavy, with some of the bark left on. I've sent the bits and pieces buried in the skull and hair on to the state lab for analysis. Marked urgent. With luck, the lab will be able to identify the tree it came from.

Then you'll know if the killer picked it up at the spot, or had it with him, carried in from someplace else."

"Him?" she repeated softly.

"There was a lot of strength in that blow. It wasn't a typical feminine tap on the head."

There were different implications in that statement that ran through Kate's mind, starting with the idea that only a man could deal a strong blow and ending with the stereotype of women as the weaker sex. She let it pass. "How big a limb?"

"Halfway between the thickness of a walking stick and a baseball bat."

"Swung like a bat?"

"Yes."

"If the branch was big enough, how much strength would it actually take to swing it and kill someone?"

"Well, given a piece long enough and thick enough, not all that much, I guess," he admitted. "The clearing formed a good batting circle, there was plenty of room there. Even the littlest guy on the team could've gotten a good swing going and knocked the ball out of the park."

"The ball in this case being her head."

"Unfortunately."

She nodded. "What about signs of force? Was there anything that would suggest she'd been taken to the park against her will?"

"Nothing. There were no surface abrasions at all. No raw spots on the skin, no rope burns, no scratches, no ligature marks. And most telling of all, no scrapings from her fingernails. There's no sign she fought at all."

"Was she doped?"

"Toxicology will have to tell us that. But there were no puncture marks for an injection of any kind. Generally, Sarah had been a well-nourished female, eighteen years of age, five six, one hundred and fourteen pounds, small-boned, good muscle tone."

"What about time of death?"

"Definitely on Monday. From the condition of the body, I'm

saying she died anywhere between fifty and sixty hours before autopsy. That definitely places it on Monday, say between breakfast and suppertime. I'm going to get the official hour-by-hour temperatures from the weather service. Once I have those, I'll be able to figure out the rate of cooling and narrow the time down for you. But it was approximately two and a half to three hours after she'd eaten last."

"I think I know when that was." Kate shifted in her chair. "Let's reconstruct this a minute. She was sick Monday morning, throwing up. That would've emptied her stomach. Then she was seen later that day, about one-thirty, throwing away what could've been a lunch sack. The vomiting would've emptied out breakfast, so what you're saying would confirm that she really did eat the lunch."

He nodded. "If she was seen tossing away her lunch sack at one-thirty in the afternoon, then the only sequence that fits the facts we have right now is that she went home, had some lunch, and was killed between four and four-thirty."

That was a big piece of news. With the time of death known now, whereabouts and alibis could be examined, and the field quickly narrowed down. Well, maybe not quickly, she amended. There were still a few hundred families to be eliminated. If she just had a motive, she might be able to winnow those down real fast. Unless she was dealing with a kidnap victim and a random killer. There'd be a worldful of suspects in that case. Not a cheerful thought.

Len was watching her with a grin, as if he was divining what she was thinking. "And," he said, "we have one more little piece of information to fit into that computerlike brain of yours. Your little gal didn't have stomach flu. She was pregnant."

Kate sat back and stared at him.

"Eight weeks. Far enough along for morning sickness to set in. Not far enough along to show. That wasn't stomach flu she had, just plain old morning sickness. That's why by noon, she'd have felt well enough to eat."

Kate drifted off into her own thoughts. With any other girl, she'd already have been suspicious of a case of morning "flu." With Sarah, she'd accepted the surface explanation. Why?

The atmosphere, she decided. The atmosphere and the environment. The first was heavily marbled with piety. It permeated everything—conversations, attitudes, responses. The whole general approach to life that the church fostered around itself. That alone, though, wasn't enough. The Bible was rife with passion and illicit couplings.

It was the environment that argued against it. Sarah Taft wasn't some street kid turned loose without a care to wend her way through life by hook or crook. She existed in a heavily controlled environment, her hours and days and weeks highly structured. In part, Kate thought, to prevent just this sort of thing from happening. The girl hadn't been allowed to date. She hadn't been allowed to have a boyfriend. Though how you prevented a lovesick teenager from making cow eyes at some good-looking guy escaped her. Still, it was a long way from daydreaming to actually having sex.

Pregnant? No way.

And yet she was.

"Boy," Kate said quietly, "is this ever going to cause an uproar among the saints that be."

Franklin nodded. "I got the distinct impression from Pastor Barnes last night that his flock was just that—*his* flock. My reading of the man says he won't take kindly to any straying lambs."

"That's my feeling, too." She sighed and pushed back her half-empty mug. "I suspect the good church people are going to raise holy Cain about this."

Len grinned. "So to speak."

"So to speak," she echoed.

The street in front of the Taft home was jammed with cars. What she had come to recognize as the Taft family cars—an old Chevy sedan and an even older GMC pickup—were parked in the driveway. The rest crowded the curbs up and down the block. Kate cruised along the row and found a slot half a block away and walked back. She had a focus for the case now and had decided to start her quest with Sarah's parents.

The woman who answered the Taft door had a round, kindly face, gray hair pulled back into a simple bun, and was dressed in an old-fashioned, Sunday go-to-meeting dress. She'd opened the door with an instinctive smile of welcome that changed to a look of polite query when she realized it was a stranger.

Kate introduced herself. "I need to speak with Mr. and Mrs. Taft."

Instantly, the chin dimpled with distress. "I'm Emma Barnes, Pastor Barnes's wife. I'm sorry, Detective MacLean, the family can't be disturbed. We're in the middle of prayer group right now."

The front door opened directly into the living room. Taller than the pastor's wife, Kate looked past the plump shoulder blocking the doorway. Folding chairs common to any community meeting room had been moved in to fill the gap between sofa, rocker and wing chairs, and a group of church folks sat in a circle, heads bowed, holding hands and praying.

Martha Taft still sat in her rocker, as she had the night before, though she wore a somber church dress now instead of the old flannel robe, and instead of her hair hanging in a braid down her back, it was pulled back into the same tight bun Mrs. Barnes wore. Which seemed to be standard for the churchwomen above a certain age, Kate noted. Her head was bent low, her mouth moving soundlessly along with the Bible verse being read by the prayer group leader. Her hands clutched a well-worn Bible with a white-knuckled grip. The younger daughter, Lizzie, was nowhere in sight. Neither was Pastor Barnes.

There were only two men in the group, and one of them was Daniel Taft, staring at her. He disengaged his hands from the ring and crossed quietly to the door. His face was haggard and drawn, and his eyes were red-rimmed from lack of sleep or tears or both.

He stopped just behind the pastor's wife. "Any news?" he asked in a soft, hoarse voice.

"Not of the sort you mean," Kate answered quietly. "But I do need to talk to you and your wife a moment. Privately."

Mrs. Barnes's face took on a look of distress. "Oh, surely, not now . . ."

"It's all right, Emma," Daniel said in a gentle voice. "Get Martha for me, would you? We'll use the kitchen."

Her plump cheeks firmed into doughy lumps of disapproval, but Emma Barnes merely nodded, then moved off to the circle.

Daniel escorted Kate through the corner of the living room into the kitchen. A couple of curious heads unbent themselves to follow her progress, but most of the others in the group kept their prayer positions firmly in place, their heads bowed.

Food had been pouring in and the kitchen table was covered with casseroles, salads, desserts, plates of cold meat and cheeses and a wide variety of homemade breads and sweet rolls. On a counter, the group-sized coffee urn chirped away. A teakettle simmered on the stove.

Daniel cleared a spot at the end of the table that held the paper plates and silverware, and motioned to Kate to take a chair. He sat opposite her, staring at her as he waited for his wife.

When Martha finally came in, Kate scrutinized her closely. Though she sank down onto a kitchen chair with shoulders slumped in sorrow, the glazed look of last night was gone. There was some awareness now in her eyes.

Emma Barnes had followed her in, patting her arm as she guided her to her chair, all the while making soothing, comforting murmurs. A born nurturer, Kate thought. But when it looked like Emma was about to help herself to a chair and join them, Kate looked at Daniel and murmured, "This would be best in private."

He nodded. He moved to where Emma was pulling out an empty chair. "Thank you, Emma." With paternalistic gentleness, he took her by the elbow and led her to the doorway. "It's time to join the others now."

"Oh, are you sure? I'd be happy to sit with you awhile."

"No, that's all right, Emma. I can handle it, thank you. Tell the others we'll join them in a few moments." He waited until she'd left the room, then pulled a pocket door out from the kitchen doorjamb and slid it home, closing the three of them off from the others. With the droning of the prayer reader cut down to a murmur, a thick silence engulfed the kitchen table.

The parents were sitting on the same side of the table, silent, both watching her like two well-behaved children in a schoolroom with hands folded on their desk, waiting for the teacher to begin.

Kate had spent the drive over trying to figure out the best way to break the news to the parents. The reaction to an unwed pregnancy would be intense. Impulsively, she reached out and covered Martha's hand. "Are you all right?" she asked softly.

She gave Kate a dull stare. "The Lord is with us," she said in a hoarse whisper. Her voice was thick and guttural, as if she were talking through a throatful of phlegm. Her eyes were weary, her face bereft, and she looked too tired to cope with one single thing more. Her gaze dropped to the table and she stared unseeingly at the pile of food there.

Kate patted the woman's hand, then dug her notebook out of her shoulder bag. Like it or not, she had to begin. "I need the names of Sarah's friends," she said, softly. "Those she felt the closest to."

Daniel was already shaking his head. "Our church doesn't operate like that. We all love one another equally. And life is centered on the home and the family. We have no friends who are closer than any others."

Oh, dear, Kate thought. Somehow she had to breach this wall of illusion and there was going to be no easy way to do it. He sincerely believed what he was saying, though it went against known human nature and all its frailties. There are always people we like better than others. Always. Unless she had badly misspent her life. The tantalizing aroma of the brewing coffee tickled her nostrils. She could do with a cup. "I have quite a few things to go over with you. Would you like some coffee before we begin?"

Flushing, Martha sprang to life, jumped up from her chair and moved to the kitchen counter. "I'm sorry, I should've offered . . . I don't know where my mind is . . ." Her voice wandered off into vagueness, her gaze stalled in midair, and her hands stilled, one cup held before the coffeepot spout, the handle still not pushed down.

Daniel caught sight of his wife's paralysis and went to help her. "Go sit down," he said gently. "I'll bring it."

Dumbly, Martha nodded, trudged across the linoleum and sank back into her chair, weary and defeated once more.

Daniel carried the cups back to the table and handed Kate hers. You're stalling, she accused herself. Damned right, she answered right back. She took a sip of coffee, then stretched her legs out a bit, trying to appear at ease. "Did Sarah talk about her future much?" she asked Daniel, when he'd settled back at his own place. "I know she was planning to go to college and teach later, but did those plans change at all?"

"Sarah wasn't—" He sought the word he wanted. "—wasn't flighty like that. She was a quiet, level-headed girl, who knew what she wanted. She knew from when she was little that she wanted to be a teacher, and she never changed her mind."

"You said last night she was involved in some after-school activities."

Daniel nodded. "Choir. And the quilting club. She used to sit right where you're sitting, Miss MacLean, working on those little squares they use. And she was teaching Elizabeth how to quilt, too. She was awfully good with a needle and thread, our Sarah was." The memory brought a huskiness to his voice. He grabbed his cup, took a massive swig of coffee, then rubbed his eyes furiously, with thumb and forefinger digging in hard.

Kate gave him a moment. "When she chattered on about her

day, both school and clubs, what names surfaced? Who did she talk about the most?"

"Sarah was a quiet girl," Daniel said. "She didn't chatter."

"So there was no one in particular she mentioned?"

"No."

"I notice you have church socials on Friday nights. Who did she spend time with there?"

"Everyone," Daniel said. "She'd visit with everyone from the elderly all the way down to the toddlers."

"Boys as well as girls?"

Daniel went rigid. "Absolutely not," he snapped. "The girls are always kept separate from the boys."

She kept her face bland and said easily, "When I was growing up, at our church socials, some of the boys used to come up and pay their respects to my parents. That wasn't so long ago. Young people can't have changed that much." Though she knew they had. Her days of innocent girlhood seemed like they were from some century long past. Then it was romance and illusion and fairy-tale dreams. Now it was drugs and condoms and cold-hearted decisions to become "sexually active."

Her comments eased Daniel's back a bit. "Well . . ." The admission was grudging. But that was as far as he went.

Kate took a new tack. "I was at the school this morning. I was struck by how polite and well behaved the students were."

Martha's gaze lifted from her cup. "You were at the school this morning? Why?"

Kate couldn't believe the question. *Why?* "This is a murder investigation, Mrs. Taft."

The woman's eyes were glazing over again and Kate reached over and grasped both her hands to keep her from mentally drifting away. "Mrs. Taft," she said with some urgency, "your daughter didn't just die, she was *murdered.*"

It was as if she were explaining that the earth was round to a person convinced she'd fall off the edge of the horizon. Martha merely stared at her, uncomprehending.

Kate gentled her voice down a notch. "Mrs. Taft, I have to find out who did this to Sarah, who killed her. It's my job, you see. And in order to find out, I have to ask a lot of questions of a lot of people. The people who knew Sarah best. So of course I visited the school."

Martha jerked her hands free. "It was God's will. Pastor Barnes told us. It was God's will."

"That may be," Kate said softly, "but He had some help, and it's my job to find out who."

She was losing Martha to the glaze again. She turned to Daniel and said in an urgent tone, "The reason I'm asking about Sarah's friends is that the autopsy report's in, and—"

"Autopsy!" Daniel's bark was sudden, deep and gruff. Fierce eyes fixed on hers with a disbelieving stare. "We gave no permission for an autopsy!"

Kate wasn't going to be sidetracked by that response. "It's routine in the case of a violent death," was all she said, then she moved on. "The report, Mr. Taft, showed that Sarah did have one close friend, at least. A boyfriend of some kind."

The fierceness turned to ice. "That's impossible."

"Far from being impossible," she said softly, "it's most definite. She was pregnant, Mr. Taft. Sarah was eight weeks pregnant when she died."

Martha's jaw sagged and a look of slow horror crept into her eyes. But it was Daniel's reaction that mesmerized Kate. If she'd struck him, he couldn't have been more shocked. He stared at her in total disbelief. Then the fury began gathering in his eyes.

"That's blasphemous!" he exploded. "An abomination to ever *think* such a thing! It's impossible!"

Kate said simply, "I'm sorry," and fell silent.

Her silence was as rage-provoking as her statement had been. Daniel stared at her with fire laced with loathing and slammed a fist on the table. "I *said* that's *impossible!*"

Well in command of her emotions, Kate looked him square in the eye. "It's fact," she said calmly.

"The reports were mixed up!"

"No, sir, they weren't."

"It was some other girl!"

"No, sir, it wasn't."

"How can you be so sure?!"

"I talked to the pathologist personally."

At that, he sat back, crossed his arms, his rage receding into ice. "I refuse to accept this."

Kate nodded. "I can understand that."

"It's impossible. We watched her every minute."

"I'm sure you did."

"There's no way something like that could've happened."

Kate said nothing, she merely looked at him with sympathy.

The ringing of the doorbell, heard clearly beyond the pocket door, distracted Daniel for a brief second. Breathless, caught on the verge of some verbal abyss, the three sat frozen, waiting for whatever was going on in the other room to resolve itself. After a few seconds, a light tap sounded and the door slid halfway open. Pastor Barnes and Pastor Matt filed in. The Lord's troops were gathering, Kate thought. Courtesy of Emma Barnes? All in all, though, not bad timing. Thank you, God.

Daniel pushed his chair back, preparing to rise.

Sensitive to the intent, Pastor Barnes crossed the distance quickly and placed a comforting hand on his shoulder, pressing the half-risen man back into place. "Sit, Daniel. I simply stopped by to see how you're doing." He aimed a half-smile at Martha before turning to Kate. "Well, Miss MacLean, you do make the rounds, don't you."

"I manage to," she said calmly. She noticed Matt was the one who'd carefully slid the door closed behind them. He stood quietly with his back against the painted wood, watching them. Assessing them, she thought.

Pastor Barnes took measure of the tension, then flashed a warm smile at Martha. "How about some of that coffee, Martha?" he said in his deep, easy baritone. "It's been a long day."

Automatically, Martha started to rise.

"No!" Daniel shot out. "Sit down, Martha!"

Martha looked at him, confused. "Pastor said I have to get the coffee," she said tonelessly, as if a robot under orders that couldn't be abridged.

"I said, *no!*"

Martha collapsed like an imploding building.

His fury on the rise again, Daniel pointed one long arm at Kate and said to Pastor Barnes, "This—this *woman* here, has blasphemed our Sarah. She's saying wild, wicked, abominable things about our little girl."

Pastor Barnes gripped the back of the wooden chair and leaned heavily on his hands, elbows locked. "And that blasphemy was?"

Matt's eyes, dark and ungiving, were fixed on Kate.

Kate locked Pastor Barnes's stare with a steady one of her own. "Sarah Taft was eight weeks pregnant."

The words dropped like concrete blocks into the silence. Then Martha let out a soft keen, a tuneless wisp of a wail that cried of a soul in pain beyond bearing. Daniel quickly put an arm around her and pulled her close, protective in his actions while he was directing a ferocious scowl at everyone else. Matt simply kept on staring at Kate.

Pastor Barnes's knuckles went white. "That can't be. We've never had a teenaged pregnancy in our school."

"I told her!" Daniel thundered. "I *told* her she was *wrong!*" His hand slapped the table again, startling Martha. "I *told* her the records were mixed up! I *told* her that!"

Matt's eyes had never left Kate's. His face had gone as white as Pastor Barnes's knuckles, and he looked like he'd been struck. "Were they?" he asked in a quiet voice.

Kate shook her head. "No."

He held her gaze a long moment, then straightened a bit, drew in a long breath and exhaled slowly. His glance now darted from mother to father to mother again. He chose Martha as the one most in need of comforting and went to stand behind her, hands on her shoulders. "It's all right, Martha," he murmured, "it's all right."

Pastor Barnes recovered some of his composure. The paleness eased and some of the rigidity left his body. "This is impossible," he said again. But he wasn't fighting it anymore. His eyes began to narrow with thought. Kate recognized that look. Damage control. They all sat silent, waiting.

Finally he gave a heavy sigh. "All right," he intoned. "Several things come to mind. Firstly, I see no need for this bit of news to go beyond the four—" He glanced at Kate and corrected himself. "—the five of us. There was no sign of expectant motherhood that would lead anyone to wonder. And the child is dead in the womb now, and thus will be buried with its mother. Secondly—"

Kate couldn't let it pass. "I can't guarantee that kind of silence. We have a murder investigation going on here."

Pastor Barnes frowned. "What would that have to do with Sarah's unfortunate condition?"

"Don't you find it odd that a school that claims to have a zero pregnancy rate and a zero murder rate would end up with a girl who just happens to be pregnant and murdered?"

"The father may not have known about the child," Pastor Barnes countered.

"Possibly not," Kate said, allowing her skepticism to show fully in her voice. "But that's in doubt, isn't it? The girl had to have someone to turn to for help. Who better than the baby's father?" She turned to eye Matt speculatively. "Unless to you, as a pastoral counselor?"

He shook his head.

"Or you?" She turned back to Pastor Barnes.

He shook his head sorrowfully.

"You two?" she asked the parents. But she knew that answer already. The mother under the husband's thumb, and the husband given to outbursts of biblical rage. Where would be the comfort for a young woman in Sarah's situation? Kate didn't need the two negative shakes of the head to guess the answer to that one.

"A teacher then," Kate pushed on.

The two pastors exchanged glances before giving dubious negatives.

"A girl friend . . ."

More dubious negatives.

Kate shrugged. "Well, then, the father's the only one left."

Matt shook his head. "Sarah was quite capable of keeping her own counsel," he said firmly. "She wasn't given to going on about herself. She was a listener, not a talker."

This man fascinated her. He denied counseling Sarah, or her family, yet seemed to know her well enough to be able to characterize her in such a definite way. There'd been no qualifying words in his statement. No seemed-to-be's, no she-appeared-to-be this or that, but rather a flat-out statement leaving no doubt that this was the way she was . . . a girl who kept her own counsel.

Sounds of the prayer group breaking up filtered through the pocket door. The soft shuffling of feet on the carpet, the murmur of several conversations, the general commotion made by one large group of people breaking up into smaller groups came to Kate, partly through vibrations on the floorboards, partly through the drone filtering through the door. Their time of quiet was about through.

Pastor Barnes sensed it, too. He leaned toward Kate, his face intent, his voice urgent. "There really is no need to pursue this. The last thing this family needs is scandal. And if you pursue this, that's exactly what they'll have—scandal. And all they've got left of Sarah now is her good name."

Who are you really protecting? Kate wondered. Sarah and her family? Or the school and your church?

The last of Daniel's defenses suddenly crumbled. He continued with a defiant stare at Kate for a moment longer, then his head dropped down and he buried his face in his hands. "Oh, the shame of it . . ."

On his right, the soft keening began again.

Chapter Eleven

Kate left the Tafts and headed back to the school, struck once again by the proximity of home and school. It was clear Woodhaven drew the majority of its students from the immediate towns surrounding the campus rather than from Seattle and its suburbs across the lake.

The bus home from the retreat should've been in by now, but there was no sign of it when she pulled into the north parking lot. She checked with the secretary in the high school. The bus had already come and gone, she was told. All after-school activities had been canceled and everyone had gone home. No, Pastor Ellsworth wasn't there either. At this pronouncement, the secretary let out a small sigh of relief, glancing inadvertently at the desk still heaped with the untidy piles of papers and work. However, Nancy Wells, the girls' counselor, was still on campus.

The counseling room was at the back of the building on the second floor. Kate's knuckles were poised to knock on the solid door panel when she heard a male voice raised in a sudden, sharp tone. There was a low throaty murmur in response. Try as she could, Kate couldn't make out the words. She waited for silence, then tapped lightly.

Heavy footsteps thumped and Pastor Ansel Lang swung the door open, his face pinched and tense. It took him a minute to place her. He stared at her tight-lipped a moment, then recovered himself. He swung the door wide, inviting her in, and turned to a woman seated in a deep, soft chair. "This is Detective MacLean, the homicide investigator."

Nancy Wells was a small, plump woman in her late thirties, a comfortable looking woman with a halo of bouncy brown curls encircling a round face, still dressed in camping clothes of navy slacks and white blouse. At first, she'd flashed a friendly smile Kate's way, but it died away when Pastor Lang introduced her and her eyes clouded over with sorrow. "Oh, dear." She sighed. "So that's who you are."

Kate nodded. "I need to talk to you about Sarah."

Pastor Lang still had hold of the doorknob. "I was just on my way out," he said to Kate. Then he aimed an unreadable glance—almost a warning glance, Kate thought—at Nancy. "Catch up with you later," he said to her, and marched out of the room, back tense and rigid.

Nancy watched him go with a thoughtful stare before she turned her gaze back to Kate. She indicated another chair twin to her own. "Come, have a seat and we'll talk. Would you like some coffee?" She made a motion toward a coffee machine surrounded by mugs set up on a small table against a side wall.

"That would be nice, thanks." Kate watched her as the woman moved about, getting the coffee. She seemed relaxed, composed, in easy charge. Which was at odds with the tension that Lang had shown. Obviously, Kate had interrupted a discussion of some importance and she was wary now, all her senses at full power.

Nancy handed Kate her cup, took her seat and looked at Kate, the same sorrow in her eyes. "I can't tell you what a tragedy this is. Sarah was so special. She simply was."

"She sounds like she was the ideal student," Kate said.

"In almost every way. I wish I had a whole class of Sarahs." She bit her lip. "I shouldn't say that. All our kids are good kids. Not a bad apple in the bunch. But still, they're kids, and immature, and they have their spots of trouble now and then. Sarah wasn't like that. She never had been. She had a good head on her shoulders. I swear she was born with all the wisdom of an old woman in her soul."

"Had she seemed troubled these past few weeks?"

"Not particularly. But then Sarah kept her troubles to herself. She was never one to go prattling around about things that were bothering her. She'd just grow extra quiet. And since she was quiet to begin with, it wasn't always noticeable." Nancy gave her a knowing look. "I suppose you're trying to find out if anyone knew she was pregnant."

Kate's eyes narrowed. "How did you find out?"

"I got off the phone with Pastor Barnes a bit ago. He started quizzing me about any boyfriends that Sarah might have had. Since I was the one who took her home sick Monday morning, I added two and two and came up with four. When I made the connection, he confirmed it. He had to. It was either that, or lie, and I don't think Pastor Barnes could lie to save his soul. He'd spend an eternity in Hell before he'd do that."

"Did you suspect on Monday what the problem was?"

"For an instant, I kind of wondered," Nancy admitted. "It kind of plays in the back of your mind with girls that age. And she'd been looking a bit green around the gills for a week or so. But then I thought, Oh, no, not Sarah, and I simply chalked it up to good old-fashioned stomach flu."

"So who'd be your candidate as the dad-to-be?"

Nancy brought her mug up for a sip. "I really couldn't say."

She was a lousy liar.

"Aren't you concerned about where your own soul will be spending eternity?" Kate asked lightly.

Nancy gave a wry grin. "God forgives all sorts of sins we weak mortals fall prey to." She set the cup down. "Look, Miss MacLean, I could make a guess. Probably even a couple of them. But I know both these boys—I should, I taught each of them for the full four years of high school. Over that length of time, you get to know your kids pretty well. And while these two may have had a crush on Sarah, and may even have had a licentious thought or three about her, their commitment to the church and their religion is about as strong as I've ever seen. One's already studying for the ministry. The other one's not sure exactly what his path through life will be following graduation, but whatever he does, his work will also be dedicated to God. Neither one of them could possibly have done something so vile and evil as was done to Sarah. So knowing both these young men, I think God will forgive me for protecting their good names."

There was enough information there to make a guess that one of the two was Norm Overholtz. But who would the other one be? Obviously, a senior, not yet graduated. Kate let it pass for the moment. "What kind of procedures has the school set up to deal with the teenaged, unwed mother?"

"None. Our pregnancy rate is zero."

That's what Pastor Barnes had said. Kate hadn't argued with him at the time, but she hadn't believed him either. Now she let her skepticism show. "Zero?"

"Zero. The students are strictly governed, their days highly structured, their home lives and free time thoroughly supervised. And it works."

"Except for this one case."

"Evidently," Nancy said sadly.

"Well, then, what resources would a girl in Sarah's predicament have? Who would she go to? Where could she turn for help?"

Nancy lost patience at that. "We're not without compassion, Miss MacLean. Any one of us in the school or church would've helped her."

"All right. Let's say she'd turned to you. What would you have advised her to do?"

"Go to her parents, have them arrange for her to stay with relatives out of the area, arrange to give the baby up for adoption, then come back and get on with the rest of her life."

"Wouldn't that have seemed a little strange?" Kate asked. "A girl suddenly disappears for six or seven months and then just as suddenly reappears? Wouldn't that have raised all kinds of red flags in people's minds?"

"Not at all. Sarah was near enough to graduation to complete the school year with no problem, and a goodly number of our kids go on and do missionary work after graduation. Some during the summer, others a bit later. Some even take a year or a semester off from Bible College. It's a wonderful experience for our young people. We're always sending groups out. Under chaperone, of course."

Kate bit back a sudden impatience as she mulled the situation over. She just couldn't believe that these teens were so special, so removed from all the temptations facing their peers out in the world at large, that they didn't have romantic relationships just like everyone else did. And that sometimes—often, actually, in this day and age—those relationships went too far. Was it herself that was the problem? Had she become so cynical that she could no longer believe in an innocent span of teenhood?

"What about abortion? Wouldn't that be considered?"

Nancy quirked an eyebrow. "I wouldn't go asking that question around here," she said coolly. "Abortion's murder, plain and simple. It's an abominable practice and our church in no way condones it."

Kate looked at her mildly. Abominable seemed to be a favorite word among the congregation. Used often in sermons? she wondered. "Okay," she said agreeably, trying to forestall any kind of an argument. "When you took Sarah home on Monday, what did you tell her mother?"

"Martha wasn't there."

"But I thought students were never to be left alone," Kate said mildly. "Even in their own home."

Nancy raised an eyebrow. "You *have* done your homework, haven't you." Then she shook her head sadly. "That's what makes this such a tragedy. It's the first time Sarah *ever* was left alone. It turns out that Mondays are Martha's days to care for Ellis Dixon.

He's terribly sick and requires full-time care now. But I didn't know that. I thought she was just out on errands. Since we're not supposed to leave any of the kids alone ever, I hung around a few minutes, hoping she'd get back, but then I had to leave for retreat. Sarah had gone in to lie down, and I fixed her a cup of tea and made her promise to stay put until her mom got back. I waited until she'd drifted off to sleep, then I had to go."

"Did you tell anyone that Sarah was alone?"

"Yes. I mentioned it to the school secretary when I got back here. She promised to track Martha down and let her know about Sarah."

"Did she?"

"I don't know. I can tell you, though, I've gone through the 'what-if's ever since I learned what happened."

"When did you learn about Sarah's death?"

"When Pastor Barnes called the campgrounds early this morning."

"And when did you decide to come home?"

"Immediately. Pastor thought it was best if we canceled the rest of the week. We both agreed the girls would be too upset to benefit any from the program. We also felt they needed their families around them at a time like this."

"What's the purpose of the retreat?"

"It's a coming together of a group of schoolgirls who are about to graduate into womanhood. A rite of passage, if you will. It validates all the years that have been, all that they are, and helps readjust their focus to the upcoming world of adulthood."

It sounded like a quote right out of a brochure. "That doesn't tell me very much," Kate said. "That's a nice policy statement, a mission statement, but it doesn't tell me anything specific."

Nancy frowned. "Do you want a day-by-day breakdown of our activities?"

"That would be helpful. Anything to help me understand."

Nancy's frown deepened. For a moment, it appeared she was going to argue with Kate's request. Finally, all she said was,

"Why? This won't bring Sarah back, it won't undo what's been done."

"Maybe it won't," Kate replied. She looked curiously at the woman. "Why are you reluctant to tell me about the retreat?"

"It's not that. I just think you're going far afield."

Kate grinned suddenly. "I've got a Captain who'd probably agree with you. But humor me, anyway, Miss Wells."

Nancy cocked an eyebrow at her in skepticism. "All right. You're a stranger to our ways, and you're trying to grasp it. Okay, specifics. Day one. Arrival. Naturally, the girls are excited, so there's a settling-in process. Which is why we choose to leave the school at noon, rather than first thing in the morning. That puts us there late in the afternoon, and there's much to be done to get organized. It's a calming process, as work generally is. After dinner, we have evening services around a campfire, and then we reminisce. We look back over all the school years and share our memories with one another. The girls don't know it, but it's a form of saying goodbye. Goodbye to childhood, goodbye to childish things.

"The next few days," she continued, "are devoted to looking ahead. Pastor Barnes comes up on day two, and leads it off. He talks in pastoral terms about what life means as an adult. Taking responsibility for yourself, what an adult's commitment to God entails. He talks about stewardship, and the idea that each of us is a steward for his or her own life. He spends the whole day with us, talking with the girls as a group, then talking with each one individually. He's there to help answer any questions and deal with any doubts of faith."

"That would have been yesterday?" Kate asked.

"Yes. He was there for the day."

"All right. And then?"

"After he leaves, and for the rest of the week, the retreat leaders take his words and translate them into what it means in everyday living. We discuss what will be expected of them as wives and mothers. We explain some of the temptations they'll be facing as they move beyond the protection of the church and family. We tell them about the materialism that'll surround them, the superficial values they'll be exposed to. And then we teach them how to maintain their own value system in the face of all the temptations out there, and we show them how to use the Bible as a resource in times of confusion. In short, Miss MacLean, we start preparing these girls for living adult life in a godly manner."

Her glance probed Kate's to see how much understanding was there. "Our church is a very practical church. We know the attractions that are out there, that can seduce the naive, the unwary, and the idealistic, and we use every weapon in God's arsenal to combat that. We don't believe in merely preaching all this high-sounding spiritualism, then setting our members free to sink or swim for the week between the Sunday sermons. We not only preach the Gospel, we teach them how to live it. It's a process that will continue throughout their lives. That's what the retreat is all about."

"Do you have any wayward ones, any who fall off the wagon, fall by the wayside?" Kate asked.

"Of course. Every day. We all have problems we face, just like in biblical times." The pert grin appeared again. "If we were perfect, Miss MacLean, we'd be sitting at God's right hand instead of enduring our time on earth. In other words, we're human. The Lord does have a way of humbling us all."

"When you received the call from Pastor Barnes this morning, what did you do?"

"We were preparing breakfast, so I met with the other leaders and we decided to go ahead and feed the girls, then tell them as a group."

"What was the reaction?"

"Shock, tears, disbelief, grief. The whole spectrum. Mostly disbelief, I'd say. Shock and disbelief. As it sunk in, though, the grief grew stronger and stronger."

"Did any of the girls seem more upset than the others?"

"They were all upset. Sarah was loved by everyone."

"I realize that, but were there one or two who seemed to take it harder than the others?"

"Denise Hickman. She and Sarah were very close."

"Anyone else?"

"Not that I can think of."

"And of the boys back at school, who would be the most affected by Sarah's death?"

Nancy Wells just shook her head and grinned. "Nice try, Miss MacLean, but as I told you, I'm not going to get into a guessing game as to who might be the father of Sarah's baby. Besides, pregnancy or no pregnancy, you're going to have to look elsewhere for your killer. There is absolutely no one among our congregation who would've done such a thing."

"Not even a panicked father-to-be?"

Nancy Wells's eyes were cool on hers. "Not even."

At Kate's request, Nancy walked her down to the main office to check on whether the secretary had ever passed along the counselor's message to Martha Taft on Monday. The secretary looked confused a moment, then memory set in and she slapped her own cheeks with horror, her gaze drifting over to the piled-up desk. Then she started pawing through the stacks, a wave of excuses pouring out. Pastor Ellsworth had come in just as she'd finished taking the message. He'd needed a report she'd been typing for him right away. There'd been a rush of students through for one reason or another. One of the teachers had needed some work sheets copied immediately. As she poured out the story of her Monday afternoon, her hands scrabbled among the messy piles until, with some triumph, she pulled free a small tatter of scratch paper and held it up. Then the triumph collapsed as the reality of what it meant set in, and she dropped into her chair and wept.

Kate left the counselor comforting the hapless woman. They'd never know whether or not Sarah would still be alive if that simple call had been made. For the want of a nail . . . Kate sighed.

The woman would have that on her conscience for the rest of her life.

Denise Hickman's family lived in Kate's neighborhood, across the street and down a few houses from her own corner Cape Cod. The Hickman home was an old two-story Craftsman house built in the twenties, one room wide, three deep, with an old-fashioned veranda crossing the narrow front. The sidewalk looked scrubbed, the porch was swept clean, and the parlor window on the front gleamed with window polish. Kate rang the old-fashioned bell-turn and waited.

A lace curtain over the upper window of the front door was pushed aside, and a middle-aged face, worn and drawn, peered through the pane, scanning the visitor with an anxious glance. Seeing no one other than Kate, she pulled back the door to the length of its security chain, and whispered, "Yes?"

"Mrs. Hickman?" Kate gave her name and showed her ID. "May I come in a moment, please?"

The security chain stayed taut as slow suspicion overtook the timorous fear that had been evident in the plain broad face. "What about?"

"Sarah Taft."

The woman said nothing. She considered Kate for a long moment of silence, then, her face set into deep worry lines, she swung the door closed enough to release the security chain and stepped back to allow Kate just enough room to enter. She quickly shut the door and slipped the chain back on.

Kate watched her going through the rigmarole of locking the world out, taking her measure. She was an older woman, wearing a dark, shapeless cotton dress pulled on loosely over a stout body. The graying hair was pulled back into a severe bun, and like the other churchwomen, she wore no makeup, which made her small, pale eyes appear washed out and flat-looking. She couldn't have been much more than in her early forties, but the way she dressed and wore her hair, she looked ten years older than that. Did she just not care? Kate wondered. Or had life whipped her into a defeat so strong that any attempt to fight it would be futile? Whichever, the woman was a walking cauldron of fear and timidity.

Kate examined the chain on the door. It was a flimsy piece of work, the kind found in cheap discount stores, not strong enough to keep a weak kitten out.

Mrs. Hickman saw Kate eyeing the chain and said timidly, "With everything going on . . ."

"I understand." Instinctively, Kate felt a need to reassure her. "Murder is a frightening thing. It scares everyone. You know, I've got a much sturdier chain than that somewhere in my garage. I'll bring it by when I've got the chance. You'd feel much safer with that."

The offer didn't impress the woman one bit. She neither refused it nor accepted it. She simply ignored it. "What is it you want?"

"I need to speak to Denise for a minute or two."

"That's not possible." The whisper was accompanied by a firm shake of the head. "The poor girl's gone to bed, she's so upset."

"This is important, Mrs. Hickman."

"No." The whisper was still soft, but the small flat eyes had turned stubborn, almost hard.

Kate's empathy vanished. This woman was one of those who appeared weak, but were totally unbudgeable underneath. The meek submissiveness was a sham, a form of control and domination all its own. "Then we'll have to call a police doctor in to verify that Denise is too upset to talk," Kate said easily, not bothering to argue with her. "This is a homicide investigation, after all."

Kate had neatly trapped her. Either produce the girl, or she'd produce a doctor who'd produce the girl.

The woman's eyes slithered left, then right, seeking a way out, but if there was one, she couldn't find it. Finally, she turned and marched up the staircase set off to one side of the front door, her stocky body rigid with resentment and disapproval.

The sound of muffled voices drifted down the stairwell, then heavy footsteps pounded across the ceiling overhead. A teenaged girl descended the stairs, two steps ahead of her mother, reluctance in every move. The sober, pale face of a little boy about seven peered down at Kate from the gloom of the upstairs hall above.

Kate smiled up at him.

His mother stopped mid-stair at the smile, turned and looked upward, then snapped her fingers at the boy and pointed past him to a doorway beyond. With a face filled with sudden guilt, he vanished back into the shadows.

Kate noted the mother's control without saying anything, then turned her attention to the girl.

Denise Hickman had the same stocky body as her mother, was about the same height, with a thick waist, the same broad, plain face, and nondescript brown hair pulled severely back from her face and clipped behind. But her eyes, though red from crying, were gorgeous—a deep-set greenish blue, with thick long lashes that curled up beneath thick, well-shaped brows. Given a shorter haircut with a slight body wave to soften the harsh planes of her cheeks, and about twenty pounds less body weight, she'd be a stunner.

Kate smiled encouragingly at her as she reached the bottom of the stairs, and held out her hand to shake. "Hello, Denise. I'm Detective MacLean." Kate deliberately used her title to establish authority and to leave no doubt who was in charge here.

The girl's eyes darted toward her mother a couple of steps behind her, as if seeking permission to speak.

"Mind your manners," the mother hissed.

Instantly, Denise dropped her gaze to the floor. "Pleased to meet you," she mumbled.

Kate gestured through an archway into an old-fashioned parlor. "May we sit in there?"

Denise darted another quick look at her mother again. Her mother sighed, but nodded, yes. Then Denise nodded yes, too.

This wasn't going to work, Kate thought, as she followed the other two into the parlor. The girl was thoroughly dominated by her mother. She needed to get the mother out of there. The interview would be pointless, otherwise. But how?

Kate settled onto the hard-cushioned settee indicated by Mrs. Hickman, her mind racing with ideas. A cop had a few choices when it came to defusing tense situations. She could try and placate the mother. But the stubborn set of the old lady's jaw told her that would get her nowhere. The woman was not about to be charmed. She could try out-bullying the mother. But then she risked upsetting the girl and losing the interview anyway. Or she could phrase her questions so they appeared to be innocuous, yet would still garner her the information she wanted. All she needed was a name. One name. That's all she needed to have in hand when she walked out of there.

Kate smiled at Denise. "I'm going to have to ask a few questions about Sarah," she said gently. "I know it'll be upsetting to you, but let's see if we can tough it out together, okay?"

Denise looked at her mother before nodding agreement.

"When did you last see Sarah?"

"Monday."

"When on Monday?"

"Monday morning. We have first class together."

"Did you see her again that day?"

Denise nodded. "Between second and third periods."

"How was she feeling?"

"Sick."

"Describe 'sick' for me."

"Sick to her stomach. I think she threw up a couple of times. She had stomach flu."

"Did she tell you that's what she had, or was that a guess on your part?"

"No, that's what she said she had. She had a touch of it at

church on Sunday, but on Monday it was a lot worse. She was going to have to stay home from retreat."

"Did you try to talk her out of staying home?"

Denise looked at her mother again. "A little," she said in a small voice. Her mother frowned at that.

Kate didn't want to give the mother another chance to beat the girl down further and changed directions. "What were Sarah's plans for after graduation?"

"She was going to go to Northwest Bible College, and study teaching."

"Had her plans changed recently?"

Denise's curiosity was up now, and she forgot her mother for a minute. She gave Kate a puzzled look. "No. Why? Should they have?"

Kate didn't answer the question. "Did you talk a lot on the phone with Sarah?"

Denise looked down at the floor. "No. The phone is for God's work, and God's work only. It's not for fooling around."

That had to be a direct quote from the mother, Kate thought. And the girl was lying through her teeth. "Well, what about problems? Did Sarah ever talk to you about her problems?"

"No, she didn't really seem to have any." She looked sideways at her mother and a bit of defiance came into her eyes. "Besides, her parents supported the idea of her going to Bible College."

While the *her* of "her parents" wasn't exactly emphasized, there was enough verbal underlining there to let Kate know that Denise's folks didn't like the idea of college. Mrs. Hickman's jaw took on a tighter cast.

"Did Sarah seem—distracted at all the last few weeks? Preoccupied a little? Possibly not quite as with it as she used to be?"

"No." Then Denise thought about it. "Well, maybe a little daydreamy. She'd doodle now and then in her notebooks."

"Doodle what? Anything specific?"

"Trees, a lake, and mountains. She was always sketching mountains."

"Did you ask her about it at all?"

"The mountains?"

"No, the daydreams."

"Well, I'd ask her what she'd been thinking about. And she'd just say she was thinking about graduation, and after graduation, and that kind of stuff."

"Did she give any sign or hint at all that her own plans about college might change?"

Denise grew puzzled, forgetting her mother again. "Why do you keep asking that? Is there something that makes you think she *wasn't* going to college?"

"Oh, I was just kind of wondering about boyfriends, and love and marriage and all that."

Mrs. Hickman's back went rigid at that.

Instantly, Denise cowed back down again. A spot on the rug midway across the room held a particular fascination for her. "We don't think about stuff like that at our age," she whispered. "We're too young."

Mrs. Hickman gave Kate a glance of the strangest mixture of disapproval at the question and triumph at the answer, as if to say, See? None of this will do you any good.

Dealing with the mother was like circling a powder keg. The older woman sat on the edge of her chair like some squat toad, her glance flicking back and forth between detective and daughter, ready to strike with venomous tongue if the questioning got the least bit out of line.

Kate mustered her patience and asked Denise other routine questions about school, trying to get the girl to relax. But with the mother perched right there, it was nearly impossible. And if she even neared the subject of boys, the old woman would go rigid and Denise would hang her head again.

Finally, Kate tried a new tack. When she'd carried the question-and-answer session as far as she could, she sat back as if the interview was over and smiled at mother and daughter. "Thanks, Denise. Now that wasn't so tough, was it?"

Denise glanced again at her mother, then shook her head.

Kate could see the girl start to relax. The old woman was as suspicious as ever.

She adjusted her position deeper into the settee, apparently ready to linger for a bit of small talk. "I'm pretty impressed with what I've seen of your school," she said in an easy conversational tone. "It seems so nice and friendly. And it's small enough so everyone knows everyone else, right?"

Denise shrugged. "Pretty much."

"I bet a lot of the girls in your class are planning on becoming teachers."

Denise nodded. "Some."

"And the guys? Will some of them go into teaching, too?"

"Yeah, I guess."

"What about the ministry? Being a religious school like it is, are any of the guys planning on becoming pastors themselves?"

"A couple."

"Oh, really, who?"

Mrs. Hickman had started scowling again. She knew something was going on, but wasn't quite sure what. Kate could practically see her going over the sequence of questions in her mind, looking for the dangerous one. So far, though, she didn't see the harm in the last few. That didn't mean she liked it, though. Come on, Denise, Kate urged, give me my answer.

The phone rang.

The girl had been giving Kate's question some thought, but the phone ringing stopped the process. Denise glanced at her mother and sat back, waiting.

Mrs. Hickman was torn between a lifelong upbringing in which one answered the phone when it rang, regardless of the inconvenience, and the need to monitor every word her daughter said. When the phone wouldn't let up, she finally yelled, "Billy! Get that!"

But that was a worry, too, Kate could see. Mrs. Hickman's glance darted from doorway to daughter, not sure now which kid needed her attention the most. Her plight resolved itself when loud footsteps thumped down the stairs and Billy showed up at the parlor door. "Mom. It's Pastor. He says he *has* to talk to you." Then, having delivered that pronouncement, he aimed a shy smile at Kate and thumped back up the stairs.

Mrs. Hickman pointed a stern finger at Denise. "Don't you say anything till I get back." She swooped out through the doorway and headed toward the back of the house.

Kitchen phone, Kate thought. She had a bad feeling about the call. It was Pastor Barnes, she was sure. He was the only one of the five to be referred to as simply Pastor. The other four always had names attached.

Sensing the session would come to an abrupt end at any moment, Kate said in a low voice, "Denise, you were going to tell me the name of the two boys who're going into the ministry."

Denise's green-blue eyes widened with shock. "Mama says I'm not supposed to say anything."

"Oh, I won't mention it," Kate said casually. "I just need to know who was planning to go into the ministry, is all. Someone who liked Sarah. Someone who liked her a lot."

For a quick second, Kate thought she had her. The girl had thought about it and had begun to nod, as if there weren't any harm in telling her.

But then the hardwood floors began to vibrate with the heavy footsteps of Mrs. Hickman coming back down the hall.

"Denise!" Kate whispered urgently. "The name!"

But Denise had felt the vibrations, too. Her head fell forward and her gaze found the spot in mid-rug again as Mrs. Hickman barged through the doorway, suspicious eyes flicking from detective to daughter.

"Pastor says we shouldn't be talking to you, Miss MacLean," the woman said, not bothering to hide a look of triumph in her eyes. "You'll have to leave now. Denise, go on up to your room. Right this minute."

Denise ran for the stairs.

The interview was over.

Kate stood for a long moment on the Hickman porch, staring off into the dying day. She needed that one name. If only she could work on Denise just a little more . . .

It was her car parked the wrong way that gave her the idea. It was facing her own house, and the thought of Mrs. Hickman's chain came to her. She turned around and eyed the front door. Old. Solid wood. Mind made up, she bypassed her car and walked the short distance to her house. Kate was never in her neighborhood during a weekday afternoon, and the isolation of the area surprised her. There were faint traffic noises from Main Street a few blocks east and the mosquitolike whines of boats running up and down the lake a couple of blocks west. Other than that, the street dozed, still and silent, in the late afternoon sun, drowsy from the day's leftover warmth. It was an eerie feeling, for anything could be going on in those houses, and no one would know.

She cut through the backyard to the freestanding garage at the inside back corner of the lot. There was plenty of daylight left. She dug her keys out of her shoulder bag, unlocked the side door, then raised the main door to let the lowering rays of the sun drive the inside shadows away. A series of old wooden shelves built high on the studs of all the walls held rows of open cartons and stacks of piled, sealed boxes.

She went on a discovery tour of the cartons, shoving aside odd finds like half a doorknob and a set of rusty old keys that fit Lord only knew what. She finally found the chain in a back corner box, a good thick one that would offer some real protection to the timidly domineering woman down the street. Chain in hand, she dug out her cordless drill and screwdriver, the single woman's best friend in the hardware department, and started to go after a can of wood putty. Then another idea occurred to her, and she left the putty on the shelf.

Mrs. Hickman's eyes glittered with ice when she peered through the chained door once more and saw who it was. "Pastor said we don't have to talk to you."

"Of course you don't," Kate answered cheerfully. She held the chain up to view. "I'm doing this as a neighbor."

The conflict of fears within the woman was quite clear. She was afraid of Kate, afraid of the cops, afraid of what Kate would do to her family and, in particular, afraid of what Kate would do to her daughter. And there was probably some fear of God, her pastor and her church mixed up in it, too, Kate thought. But there also was a real honest-to-God fear of the outside world. As much as Mrs. Hickman tried to control herself, she couldn't help the quick flick of the eyes between the two chains—the light one, easily popped, and the thick, sturdy one that Kate was holding out. The difference was notable. Like the difference between a piece of string and a hanging rope. The conflict was easy for Kate to read. Did she bar the door against the cop, as her pastor had ordered, or did she bar the door against an outside world so frightening that, at all costs, it had to be held at bay?

Kate took advantage of the ambivalence. "I really am here just to help you, Mrs. Hickman," she said gently. "That's what my job is, to help when I can."

Suspicion took the foreground once more. "You live nearby? Where?"

Kate pointed out her house. "Across the street. The Cape Cod on the corner." She displayed the chain one more time. "Really, I just want to help."

Mrs. Hickman peered down the street at the house, then had to think about it all, and the ambivalence continued on. Then, reluctance in every move, she closed the door to, slid the chain free and opened it back up again. Just wide enough for one person to slip through, Kate noted. But she said nothing. Inside, Kate closed the door and went right to work, ignoring Denise and

Billy, both watching this development with interest. She placed her tools on the floor, then examined the lock and selected a bit to remove the screws.

The kids watched her from a safe distance, Billy hovering in the hall behind her, Denise sitting on the bottom step of the stairs. Mrs. Hickman stood in the archway to the living room, arms folded across her broad chest, eyes as glacial and suspicious as ever. As curiosity got the better of Billy and he inched gradually closer to see better, Kate smiled at him. "Want to take a turn?" she asked, holding up the cordless screwdriver and pointing to the next screw to be loosened.

His shyness faded away and he nodded eagerly.

Kate stepped aside. "Well, come on, then, I'll show you how this magic little tool works."

She showed him the slot in the top of the screw, then guided his hand so that the bit slipped in tight. "Push against it a little, Billy, so it doesn't slip, then push down the rocker switch on the screwdriver, like this." She placed her thumb over his and pressed lightly. The driver burred loudly and the screw jerked once before the bit slipped off the head. "That's fine, Billy. A little more pressure then." She let his hand work alone this time.

It took time for him to coordinate the motions, his forehead screwed up in concentration, but he finally was able to get the screw out. He held it out to her with a look of triumph. "Can I do the next one?" he asked.

Kate grinned. "You bet. Then we'll give Denise a turn."

Mrs. Hickman twitched at that, but settled back onto her heels and said nothing.

Kate let Billy finish the next one, then turned to Denise. "Okay, young lady, your turn." She guided Denise's hand as she had Billy's, then let her struggle with tool and screwhead until the first one was out. As with Billy, the second came out faster and easier. "Not hard at all, is it?" Kate smiled at her.

The girl shook her head shyly.

They took turns after that, first Billy, then Denise, until all the screws were out and the chain and plates were off. Kate set the tool and the old chain down, then started taking the new chain out of its packaging. She freed the screws and brought one up to the door frame. Since the whole mechanism of the new one was sturdier and thicker than the old, the screws were larger and there'd be no problem using the same screw holes again. There'd be ample wood to catch and hold them securely.

But she was counting on Mrs. Hickman not to know that. With a look of casual innocence, she turned to her and said, "We'll need to do some filling in of the holes here. Would you have some wood putty in the basement?"

The woman looked confused. "I don't know . . ."

Kate moderated her voice carefully, seeking that one note of casual authority that would make the woman respond without making her get her back up. "Check for me, please, while I sort out the rest of this stuff."

The old conflict was back, fear of the cop if her kids were left unattended, and fear of the world if the door was left unchained. She stared at Kate a long moment, then her glance flicked first to Billy, then Denise. Billy looked eager to go, but he wouldn't know what to look for. And Denise simply hung back, shaking her head. She wouldn't know, either.

Not daring to push any harder, Kate left Mrs. Hickman to work it out for herself and squatted down to sort out plates and chain, taking her time, studying every link as if it were the most critical link in the world, dawdling over it, stretching out the silence like the Captain did when he was staring at her and not liking what he was seeing. She didn't look at the woman again.

Finally, Mrs. Hickman turned from the archway and marched with her heavy tread to the back of the house. The sound of thick heels thudded across the linoleum, a door squeaked open and there were more thuds on steps disappearing below.

Kate eased up her position, and glanced at Denise. The girl was avoiding her eyes. She turned to Billy. "I'm awfully thirsty. Could you get me a drink of water?"

Billy considered her a best friend now and said, "Sure." He scooted back down the hallway toward the kitchen. The kitchen faucet sounded with a loud whoosh of water.

Kate concentrated then on Denise. "Well, Denise, I need you to help me," she said softly. "I still need that name."

The girl looked down at her shoes, thought a minute, then glanced shyly up. "Am I getting anyone in trouble?"

Kate gave a soft, sad smile. "I wish I could answer that. I can tell you this, though, you'll be helping Sarah. In the long run, that's what you'll be doing. You don't want to cover up for a killer, do you?"

The girl looked shocked. "Oh, no, never!"

"Good. Then tell me the name."

There was another long glance down at her shoes, another long moment of thought, then just as the kitchen faucet shut off with a clank of pipes, Denise looked at Kate and whispered, "Peter. Peter Dickerson."

Kate exhaled a mental sigh of relief. "Thank you," she whispered back. Then she moved to where Billy was walking gingerly down the hall, trying not to spill an overfull glass of water. "I'll help you there." She took the glass from him and drank deeply. "Thank you, Billy," she said, bestowing a broad grin upon him, and returned to her project spread in pieces all over the floor.

She was still concentrated on gathering them up when Mrs. Hickman returned, a small, stained can in her hands. There were suspicious looks all around, but Billy was sitting cross-legged on the floor, intent on watching Kate, and Denise was sitting silent on the bottom stairs again.

The icicle glare directed her way didn't faze Kate in the least. She filled the screw holes with the putty, and using the door-frame plate as a template, quickly made new ones slightly above the old. Within minutes, the new chain was installed.

Kate gave it a strong pull, checked to make sure everything worked all right, then gathered up her tools. "This is going to work just fine," she said to Mrs. Hickman. "We'll both be feeling better about this now."

For an instant, there was an almost-thaw as Mrs. Hickman relaxed a little and nodded slightly. But then she remembered who Kate was, and how she was supposed to act. The spine went rigid and the disapproval thermometer dropped to arctic depths again.

Kate ignored the reaction, smiled at all three as she said her goodbyes, stashed her tools in the trunk of her car, then casually drove away from the house as if she didn't have another thing in the world to do. But once around the corner and out of sight, she put on a burst of speed and raced away.

Bingo.

Chapter Twelve

A mile north of Kirkland, a shallow depression in the hills east of Juanita Beach held a cluster of modest homes built on a half-dozen streets that wound up and down the hillsides. The houses were a random mix of boxy ranches and small split-levels designed as first homes for young couples just starting out. Thirty years ago they'd sold for maybe twenty-five thousand dollars, max. Now they went for close to a couple of hundred grand. Progress, Kate thought. The Dickersons lived at the back of one of the cul-de-sacs, a small hillside ranch house with a walk-out basement below.

A young man, seventeen or eighteen, opened the door at Kate's ring. He was tall and slender, not quite past the awkward stage of middle adolescence, with a forelock of sandy-colored hair falling on his forehead, and a thin face with good lean planes from cheekbone to jawline. The blue eyes were frank, without suspicion, as he surveyed her. "Yes?" he said.

When Kate showed him her ID, his eyebrows skyrocketed and his mouth formed a perfect O. "Are you Peter Dickerson?"

He nodded.

"I'm here to visit with you a little about Sarah Taft."

At that, he sagged against the door frame and swallowed hard a couple of times, struggling against a sudden welling of tears. "I'm not sure I can," he croaked. "Not yet."

"I understand. Why don't we go inside a minute and we can talk about it."

Wordlessly, he nodded, stepped back to allow her in and led her down the entry hall into a living room at the rear of the house. To the right, bookcases flanked a fireplace centered on the far wall, with a single sofa and a couple of comfortable chairs arranged in front. To the left, a large archway opened into a dining room holding an old trestle table polished to a satin smoothness. Both rooms had broad banks of windows overlooking a tree-tangled ravine out back, letting in the few rays of late afternoon sun that could pierce the treeline. There were no neighbors behind the house, Kate noted, and the fir trees growing along the sides of the house sheltered it from any prying eyes on either side. Then she turned her attention back to the boy.

He was still struggling against the emotion welling up. He indicated a chair for her, then collapsed into the one opposite her. His face torn up with grief, he covered his eyes with one hand.

She watched him a long moment. "Is your family home?"

Unable to speak yet, he shook his head.

"Then can I get you something? A coke, a glass of water?"

"No," he croaked out in a whisper. "There isn't anything that'll help." Then his shoulders heaved. With a muttered "Be right back," he lunged from the chair and stumbled down a hallway next to the dining room.

From the depths of the house, she could hear the sounds of water running and a nose being furiously blown. It sounded like a Canadian goose honking its way north, and she smiled slightly. The water shut off with a wracking of pipes, and when he appeared, his eyes were swollen and red-rimmed, his face pale and drawn. He tossed his body into the chair and leaned his head against the back. "Sorry," he mumbled.

"Don't worry about it." She hesitated. She was in a dilemma.

Questioning a kid who'd become a suspect without parents or another adult around was risky. "How old are you, Peter?"

"Eighteen."

Okay. Legally, Kate was safe. Morally and ethically, though . . .

And why was the kid alone? Were the church's strict controls beginning to show a few cracks, first with Sarah, now Peter? "Where are your folks, Peter?"

"Dad's an engineer at Boeing. He's not home yet. And Mom's helping out up at the campgrounds for the girls' retreat."

Kate relaxed a little then. The bus was back, the mother would be here soon. "Tell me about you and Sarah," she said gently.

His gaze drifted into the distance. "I loved her," he said simply. "She was warm and wonderful and gentle and kind, and I loved her with my whole heart." He was silent a minute. Then his face took on the forlorn cast of an old man, wearied by life. "Pastor Matt says death's hardest on those left behind. He said that death is the glory and the resurrection of the person who died, but it's a satanical hell for those left behind."

"When did you talk to Pastor Matt?"

"This morning, when I heard the news. I called him at home before breakfast."

"How did you hear about it?"

"One of the church ladies was organizing food for Sarah's family and called for Mom, so I took the message. That's how I found out."

"What did you do when you heard? What did you say?"

Flushing, he squirmed a bit in his chair. "I was so stupid. I can't believe how stupid I was. I listened to her all the way through, then I said, 'Thank you, I'll give Mom the message.' Can you believe that? This lady calls to tell Mom Sarah's—" He faltered. "—And all I can say is 'Thank you, I'll give her the message.' "

"What did you do then?"

"I got Brenda and Douglas ready for school."

"Who are . . . ?"

"My little brother and sister. Brenda's ten, Douglas is seven. Dad had already left for work, so I made their lunches and got them ready for their bus. Then after they were gone, I called Pastor Matt. See, it didn't hit at first. I just couldn't believe it. I was just numb. So I kept on doing what I was already doing when the phone rang—I finished making the little guys' lunches and made sure they had their homework, and stuff like that. But all the time I kept thinking, 'Dead? Sarah dead? She can't be!' I just couldn't get used to it. But when I called Pastor Matt, he said, yes, it was true, and then he asked me how I was, and I guess I wasn't so okay, and I'd already missed my bus by then, so he came over and talked to me awhile, then he took me to school. He said school's the best place for me. It'd keep my mind from going nuts."

He fell silent a moment, then gave a weary shake of the head. "But I still can't believe it. Today, all day, I watched for her in the hall, like I always do, then I'd remember, she's dead. Or lunch. We're not allowed to sit with the girls at lunch, but I'd always sit someplace where I could see her, and when she wasn't there, I thought, 'Right, the girls are on retreat this week.' Then I remembered, Sarah wasn't on retreat, she was *dead.* And every time I'd forget, and then remember, I'd go blank, absolutely blank inside. Sometimes I didn't even know where I was, or what time it was, or what I was supposed to be doing. And at first, none of the other kids knew—I mean, the word hadn't gotten around yet—and one of the guys made some kind of a joke about something, and we all laughed, and then I thought, 'Why am I laughing, Sarah's *dead*!' But I'd forgotten it again, you see." He turned a grief-stricken face to Kate, his eyes as bleak as a November day, and he whispered, "Why? Why would someone do this to her?"

"That's why I'm here," she said in a quiet tone. "So I can start finding out some of the answers. When was the last time you saw Sarah?"

"Monday morning, at school," he answered promptly. "I saw her before first class, then between second and third periods."

"How did she look?"

He started to answer, Fine, then stopped. He said, somewhat surprised, "Sick, actually. She looked like she didn't feel good. She was real pale, like maybe she was coming down with flu."

"Did she say anything to you?"

"Just 'Hi' each time we passed. We only have a couple of minutes between classes and it doesn't do to be late."

"What happens if you're late?"

He wrinkled his nose. "It becomes a big deal with Pastor Ellsworth. He can't stand tardiness. Says it's a sign of a sloppy soul."

"Who was she with when you saw her?"

"No one. She was in a hurry, rushing down the hall both times."

"Rushing to where?"

He shrugged. "Class, I guess."

"Were the girls' rest rooms in that direction?"

He thought a minute, then nodded. "I think so."

"So she might've been rushing to the bathroom?"

"Oh, to be sick, you mean? Yes, I guess that's a possibility."

"What about Sunday. Did you spend any time with her that day?"

"A little. We both taught Sunday School classes in the church basement. We talked a little in the hallway while the kids came in. Then afterwards, I lent her a Bible lesson on Daniel and the lion that she'd asked me about."

"And how did she seem then?"

"You mean was she sick?" He frowned. "No. Pale, maybe. And a little tired, maybe, like maybe she hadn't slept well. No, she seemed okay."

"Was she quiet, talkative? Friendly, withdrawn?"

"Sarah was always quiet. She wasn't one of those giggly, shrill kind of girls. And she was always friendly. So, no, she didn't seem much different."

"What did you two talk about?"

"Bible lessons, mostly. Her class was second-graders and she was thinking of having her kids draw the lion's den."

"Anything on a personal level?"

"Nothing, really. Pastor Ellsworth was hanging around. He supervises all the Sunday School classes, and he doesn't like a lot of visiting going on between the teachers."

Pastor Ellsworth was a real killjoy, Kate thought. "What about after Sunday School?"

"The junior choir was singing for services that day, so I walked upstairs behind her and Denise. But I didn't actually talk to them."

"Could you hear what they were talking about?"

He suddenly turned cautious. "A little," he admitted grudgingly.

She eyed him. "Don't wimp out on me now, Peter. What were they talking about?"

He stared down at his hands a moment, then said reluctantly, "Denise and her mother had had an argument. According to what I heard, her mom felt she was spending too much time on the telephone, and Denise didn't agree."

That confirmed Kate's suspicion that Denise hadn't been exactly honest about her use of the phone. "That doesn't sound so terrible."

"It would've been if one of the pastors had heard them. We're not supposed to argue with our parents. Ever."

"What did Sarah say to Denise about the argument?"

"Nothing, really. She mostly just listened, and sympathized. Sarah was a good listener. She always cared about others, about what they were thinking and feeling. So she just listened. Made sympathetic noises."

"Did they talk about anything else?"

"No. We reached the top of the stairs then, and they separated. Denise isn't in choir, so she went to sit with her folks in church and Sarah and I went on up to the loft."

"Did she say anything to you then?"

"No, she was quiet all the way up."

"And then what?"

"Nothing. We took our seats and waited for church service to begin."

"And after church?"

"Well, I kind of hung around until Pastor Ellsworth started glaring at me, then I said 'Bye' to Sarah, and went and joined my folks."

There was something wrong here, Kate thought. What he was describing didn't sound anything like two kids madly in love, trying to steal private moments together. It sounded more like a case of distant worship on one side and friendliness on the other. "Peter, you said you were in love with Sarah. How did she feel about you?"

He blushed. "I don't know, I never asked."

"Yeah, but usually people can tell without asking."

He went from pink to red and then a flaming scarlet. "I think she liked me. A little, at least." His voice was soft, almost wistful.

"You keep talking about Pastor Ellsworth watching the two of you. Where did you two go to get away from him, to have some private time together?"

"We didn't. We're not allowed to be alone together. Not at our age."

"But I'm sure," Kate said gently, "as creative as kids can be, that some couples manage to steal away for a few minutes every now and then."

He shook his head. "Maybe. I never tried."

"What about simply taking walks together? A picnic, maybe. A day at the beach. Or slipping away from one of the church socials for a few minutes?"

He leaned forward. "Miss—am I supposed to call you 'Miss,' or 'Officer,' or what?"

" 'Miss MacLean' will do. Or 'Katie,' if you'd rather."

"Miss MacLean, see, the way it works is we're not supposed to be left alone, ever. My mom goes every year to help out on the girls' retreat, and up until this year, we've always been parked at someone else's house until Dad can pick us up after work."

"What made your mother do it differently this year then?" Kate asked.

"She didn't. She made all the arrangements for us to stay with another church family. But there's been a flu going around, and the folks we were supposed to go to came down with it, and couldn't keep us. Dad parked the little guys with other families, but he agreed I was old enough to be on my own, since it's only a couple of hours a day from after school until he gets home."

The lad exercising the first rights of manhood, Kate thought. But what a week he chose to do it. "That means that on Monday afternoon, after school, you were here alone?"

He hadn't made the connection of Monday afternoon with the time of Sarah's death yet, and he nodded with pride. "Yes. And I had dinner ready for the family when Dad came in with the little guys."

Maybe the meal would provide an alibi. "What did you fix?" she asked casually.

"Hot dogs," was the proud answer.

Kate sighed.

She poked and probed and pried, but Peter was adamant in his statements that he'd never spent any time alone with Sarah Taft. She took him through the last couple of months at school again and again, and the picture he drew was one of a boy very much in love with a girl who may or may not have felt the same way about him. With the tight trinity of the home-school-church social structure, he saw nothing unusual in his arm's-distance love. They were in no hurry.

"But, Peter, we know she was seeing someone. We *know* that. If it wasn't you, who would it have been?"

He was drained by then from the emotional ups and downs . . . forgetting one minute that Sarah was dead, then having it crash in on him with fresh shock. Worn out from the jolt after jolt his system was taking, he simply shook his head mutely.

There was no one.

She was on the verge of leaving when the vibrations of the garage door opening rumbled through the walls. Peter quickened at the sound, and glanced at the mantel clock. Quarter to five. Frowning, he said, "That's too early for Dad."

A few seconds later, a female voice rang out from beyond the kitchen. "Hi, I'm home! Anyone here?"

Peter's eyebrows rose. "That's Mom. What's she doing here?" Then he yelled out, "Me, Mom, I'm here." With an alert look, he scanned the room, made a minor adjustment in a stack of Christian magazines, then sat back with the look of a satisfied householder. It was such a mixture of the little kid wanting Mom's approval and the man of the house putting order into his world that Kate bit back a smile. Neat kid, Peter Dickerson.

Peter's mom was slender and petite, with hair the same sandy color as her son's, brushed back and clasped with a plain barrette at the back. She was around forty, with an athletic grace and bony good looks that would age well. She was dressed in a pair of loose navy blue slacks and a white short-sleeved blouse, and carried a small suitcase with her.

She paused at the archway into the living room when she saw Kate, and her glance flicked back and forth between her son and the strange woman. "What's going on here?" she asked in a neutral tone.

Kate rose and introduced herself.

She paled. "Police?" Then a sharp intelligence came into her eyes and her face filled with sympathy as she peered at her son. "It's about Sarah, isn't it?" She set the suitcase down and sat on the end of the couch nearest his chair, reaching out and clasping one of his hands in both of hers. "Oh, Peter, I'm so sorry."

Suddenly, he was on the verge of tears again. She patted his hand in understanding, then turned to Kate. "This is why we decided to bring the girls home early from retreat," she said softly. "Everyone's devastated by what's happened." She patted her son's hand again. "Peter was very fond of her."

"Yes," Kate responded, "he's shared some of that with me."

She looked at Kate with curiosity. "I'm Alice Dickerson. If there's anything we can do to help. . . ." Then she caught sight of her son struggling for control and said in a calm, matter-of-fact voice, "Peter, I could do with a cup of tea. And I'm sure Miss MacLean could use one, too. How about playing butler and fixing us some. My old knees would really appreciate it." She smiled slightly at Kate. "Arthritis. Old age is roaring straight down the road, I'm afraid."

Alice had kept her tone light and the pleasant smile in place, but her eyes were concerned as her gaze followed her son out of the room. She sat deeper into the couch and sighed. "This is going to tear his heart out. From the time they were in grammar school together, he's had eyes for no one except her. And the Tafts . . . I thought about how I'd feel if I lost any of my children, and I honestly don't know if I could handle it and stay sane." Her clear blue eyes were filled with distress as she studied Kate. "We were talking on the bus on the way home. We all pretty much think it has to be a stranger of some kind. Someone sick who takes girls they don't know and does this to them."

"This doesn't have the earmarks of a serial killer," Kate responded. "There aren't any other cases around similar to Sarah's. We've checked."

"Couldn't she be the first?"

"It's possible, I suppose," Kate said cautiously. "From what we've been able to determine so far, though, it's almost a certainty that Sarah was killed by someone she knew. And the only people she really knew were members of the church. I wouldn't spend much time on the stranger theory, if I were you. It might be comforting, but it's not realistic."

"That's frightening," Alice said in a grim tone. "Terribly frightening. To think someone from our church family felt enough hate and anger in their soul to do this horrible thing to an innocent young girl." Kate sat silent, waiting for more, but Alice turned briskly practical again. "All right, Miss MacLean, what can we do to help on this serpent hunt of yours?"

"Names," Kate said promptly. "Names of those Sarah felt closest to."

Alice's response was just as prompt. "Denise Hickman. The girls were as thick as thieves. And Denise has been in nonstop tears since the news arrived at camp this morning. She's absolutely destroyed by this. They were the very best of friends."

Kate said, casually, "Pastor Ellsworth scoffed at the idea of anyone having best friends . . ."

Alice grinned. "Pastor Ellsworth lives on a higher plane than us mortals."

Kate nodded acknowledgment. "Anyone else? Another male friend, perhaps? Besides Peter."

Alice shook her head. "No, Sarah didn't have any close male friends. Not at this stage of her life."

"She had Peter," Kate pointed out.

Alice smiled. "Not really. He was love-struck at a distance."

"Then let me rephrase the question," Kate said thoughtfully. "Aside from him, who else had their eye on Sarah?"

Alice thought a minute. "Norm Overholtz. He's been eyeing her for years. But he's over at Northwest Bible College now, and his mom said just last Sunday she thought he'd finally met someone he really likes." She glanced in the direction of the kitchen. "I think I'd better check on my son. He must be growing those tea leaves. Excuse me a moment, please."

While she was gone, Kate mulled over that small bit of information about Norman. Could this be another version of *An American Tragedy*? Get one girl pregnant, then fall in love with another?

Alice's words, serpent hunt, came to mind. A good term for it. A serpent hunt in the Garden of Eden.

And was Norm destined to be her serpent?

Chapter Thirteen

One did not drive on the 405 during commute hour. First of all, there were five lanes of traffic that suddenly narrowed down to three. Second, lanes six and seven of bumper-to-bumper traffic incoming across the 520 bridge from Seattle tried to merge into those same three lanes. Then toss in all the road construction on the interchange that caused the whole mess to begin with, and in the time it took to drive the four miles of freeway from Kirkland to Bellevue, you could read an Anne Rice novel from cover to cover.

Kate took a variety of back roads to headquarters, seeking that one elusive road that would be relatively traffic-free. Of course she didn't find it. It no longer existed. Everyone with the slightest bit of sanity was avoiding the freeway too, and it was one gridlocked intersection after another. The sad thing was, she thought, as she angled for advantage, her little Civic beat out again and again by the BMWs and the Jags and the Jeep Cherokees, was that by the time the road-widening was complete in a year or two, another ten million cars would've moved into the area and they'd have to do it all over again.

Kate would've gone to see Norm right away instead of driving in that mayhem, but there was a good chance that the Northwest Bible students would be at dinner hour. She did not want to interrupt Norman then. He was plump; he liked his food. She wanted him sated and mellow, not edgy and irritable with hunger. Besides, her little notes spread in the afternoon around headquarters would mollify the Captain only so far. He'd be expecting her to check in.

She finally reached headquarters just ahead of quitting time and had to drive around for three or four minutes before she found a slot way at the rear of the parking lot. Relieved finally to be shed of the car, she grabbed her notes and the school information Matt had given her, strode the length of the lot, pushed into the public foyer and came to a dead stop.

Goddard and Fry. They were coming through the security doors from the direction of the bullpen, still in their three-piece suits, headed toward the public elevators to one side of the lobby. Their elevator arrived and the two men allowed the people riding down to unload, then both stepped into the empty cage, Fry hunching back into the corner behind Goddard. Only then did Goddard acknowledge he'd seen her standing there, watching. Eyes fastened on hers, he bowed his head once, punched a button and the doors slid closed on a sudden, smug smile.

Kate waited to see on which floor the elevator was going to stop, but Goddard had outsmarted her. It stopped on every one. She turned away and headed for the doors to the bullpen.

Sam was at his desk, head bent low as he cleared away the day's debris, getting ready to head home. The noise of her arrival—the click of her low heels, the thud of her purse catching a corner of her desk as she slung it on the back of her chair, the squeal of its one squeaky wheel—broke through his concentration and he looked up and gave her a grim nod. She had hoped for a smile. Some sign he was glad to see her. But she got nothing. One thing about Sam, she thought glumly, when he was unhappy, he didn't bother hiding it.

The Captain spotted her as soon as Sam did. He was standing several desks away from her, conferring with a couple of his men. He was out of his suit jacket, shirt sleeves rolled up over meaty forearms, stomach pushing gaps open between the buttons straining to hold his white shirt together. When he saw her arrive at her desk, he broke off the conference with a last word and a stern pointed finger, then lumbered her way, his tie flapping against his shoulder like a wind-whipped flag. "My office," he snapped without breaking stride. "Now."

Frozen a moment, she stared after him, then glanced at Sam for help.

He shook his head. "I don't know what's up, Katie," he said in a quiet undertone. "All I can tell you is Goddard and Fry just left him."

"Damn."

The Captain had paused at his doorway and was glowering her way.

Reluctantly, she picked up her notebook and walked slowly toward him. God, there were times she hated working for this man. Maybe she'd have a heart attack and drop dead right here and now.

Hatch lumbered around his desk, pointed his finger first at the door, then at the visitor's chair next to it. "Close it and sit." He sank into his chair, yanked his tie clear of the desktop and smoothed it down over the mound of his stomach, then leaned over a scratch pad filled with heavy black scrawls and studied it, ignoring her.

Kate tried to maintain some measure of equilibrium as she sat in the thick silence he was deliberately letting build. The good news was that he hadn't closed the blinds on the window overlooking the bullpen. He never fired anyone without lowering the blinds.

Finally, without raising his head a notch, simply by lifting the black caterpillar brows just high enough to clear a line of vision to her, Hatch looked up at her. His eyes were pure mud. "Goddard was in. Says he's gotten reports from the Bridle Trails neighbors of some strange men hanging around the park. Says the neighbors have been worried about it for some time now. Says he's gathered enough specifics to track some of the pukes down. Thinks we're dealing with a whacko here. He wants me to put him in charge of it." Speech given, he fell silent, hard gaze glued to Kate, waiting for her reaction.

Strange men? That didn't square with what the park ranger had told her. Unless the neighbors meant the occasional businessman with his laptop computer and portable phone. But she set that aside for the moment and concentrated on what Goddard was after. "In charge of what, the whole case?"

Hatch looked at her as if she were stupid. "Of course in charge of the whole damned case."

"Really," she murmured. "How considerate of him. Wanting to save me all that work."

For a moment, they stared at each other, each one as impassive as the other. Then Hatch snorted at the quiet sarcasm in her voice.

Tableau broken by the snort, Kate went on. "Unfortunately for Goddard's theory, Sam's already checked out the whacko angle. None of the neighboring P.D.'s have anything similar on their books. There are no missing girls fitting the profile, no signs of a whacko on the loose. If there is one, no one knows it yet."

"Hmmph." He let it pass. But he wasn't done yet. His voice deceptively mild, he said, "I also heard from those church folks today."

He held up four fingers and ticked them off individually.

"One, a preacher who says you're harassing his school."

Pastor Ellsworth, she thought.

"Two. A preacher who says you're harassing him."

Pastor Lang.

"Three. A preacher who says you're making wild accusations about the goings-on of the teens in his church."

Pastor Barnes. Kate bit back a sigh.

"And a mother who claims you're badgering her daughter."

Mrs. Hickman.

Now he leaned way back in his swivel chair, chin resting on

steepled fingers. "You been harassing the school, you been harassing the preachers, you been making wild accusations, and you been badgering good church folks in their homes. You got something working I don't know about?"

She waited to make sure he was done, then she gave an elaborately casual shrug. "There's the preliminary from the autopsy. Sarah Taft was pregnant."

In this day and age, that was no big deal. Hatch scowled, unimpressed. "So?"

"The church forbids premarital sex and the school claims a zero pregnancy rate as a result of their strict controls."

"So you see it as a motive," he said, studying her.

"You bet."

"The boyfriend?"

"Pretty much has to be, don't you think?"

"Which dumps the whacko theory overboard."

"Seems to."

"Any leads?"

She held up a pair of neighboring fingers. "Two."

"Hmmph." His fingers stayed pointed beneath his chin as he pondered it. And her. His eyes narrowed into black pinpoints. Taking her measure as he always did.

She resisted the impulse to squirm like a little kid caught at the cookie jar and sat waiting for his next move, meeting his gaze with a calm, level one of her own. But she could feel the hot seat she sat on growing hotter.

Finally he jerked upright in his chair. "That's it, then. You stay in charge of the case. But you keep those damned preachers outta my hair. You know how fucking hard it is to talk decent to them?" Then he leaned an elbow on his desk and stabbed a stubby forefinger in her direction, his eyes fierce. "And you take control of Goddard. You bring that guy to heel and you keep him heeled, you got that? And for Christ's sakes, keep him away from the goddamned media!" That said, he gave her one final glare, then bent his head over the mess of paperwork on his desk, dismissing her.

He let her get to the door before he added, "And stick to the boyfriend theory, will you? It's a nice simple little murder case. Don't complicate it."

She escaped before he could issue any other orders.

Sam was keeping watch for her. "You okay?"

"Minor skirmish." She smiled to take the worry out of his eyes. "Nothing major. Hey, let's go—" She broke off suddenly and finished lamely, "back to work."

But they both knew she'd been about to suggest going out for Mexican. And Sam couldn't do that. He had to go home to his wife.

She grabbed her purse from the back of the chair and got the hell out of there.

She spent the evening racking up useless mileage on her car.

First stop, Northwest College. It was the same group of kids doing the same thing, catching the last of the sun's rays. They were as open and friendly as the previous night, but this time they were unable to help. Norm Overholtz hadn't been seen at school all day. Sharp kids, they linked her query about Norm to the Taft case.

"How did you hear about it?" Kate asked.

Jeff Anderson, her helpful rouster-outer of Norm from the night before, fielded the answer for the group. "We read about it in the newspaper."

One of the girls hanging back had a quiet, thoughtful look on her face. Now she said to Kate, "Norm isn't a suspect, is he?"

There was something almost protective in the way her question was said that caught Kate's attention. Did she have something going with Norm?

"I just need to talk to him," Kate said lightly.

They didn't buy it. She could see their faces close down one by one. Kate swore at herself. She'd closed down a conduit and the case had few enough of them as it was.

Her next stop was the Overholtz house, a small brown rambler, typical of the modest dwellings of the church members. Norman's father answered the door. He had the same striking gray eyes as his son, and they fixed on her with a mixture of worry and distrust. Norm was not home, he said in answer to her queries. He was sitting with the Taft family and wasn't expected home until late. He stood at the door, watching her return to her car.

She swung by the Taft house on the off-chance that she could corner Norm there, but the house had so many cars crowded around it that she knew it would be senseless to try and talk with him there. She drove slowly on past.

She was pretty much at a standstill now. The one thing she hadn't done was check the absentees for Monday. The only male on the list was a senior in Sarah's class, Dennis Cooper. His address was listed clear out in Fall City and coasting past the Taft house, she debated whether to make the twenty-plus mile drive out there or not. Sooner or later, though, he'd have to be interviewed. She gave a tired sigh. It might as well be sooner.

It took longer to get to Fall City than it should've. For some reason, even with the evening well underway, traffic was horrendous. As one traffic jam after another brought her to a stop and she fended off the rudenesses of the Jags and BMWs—and the Cherokees, don't forget the Jeep Cherokees—she climbed back up on her mental soapbox again, grumbling the whole way. Just before reaching Fall City, she finally broke free.

The Coopers were home. All of them. Mother, father, and three sons. All in bathrobes, all recuperating from flu. Which they'd had since the weekend. Dennis had been in bed all day Monday. He had four other family members who could testify to that. And yes, the mother said apologetically, Peter Dickerson had been scheduled to stay with them while his mother was up at the girls' retreat, but they'd had to cancel that because of the bug.

Kate accepted the news philosophically. Sometimes it just went like that. At least she'd confirmed part of Peter's story. She thanked them for their help and trudged back to her car.

Full darkness had fallen by the time Kate made the drive back to Kirkland. Weariness began to settle into her spine and back. It was well after eight-thirty, and she'd been going since six o'clock that morning. Almost fifteen hours, working alone. She'd pushed herself far harder than if Sam had been around, and she'd carried it about as far as she could for one day. Now, in her mind, she could see a rack of balls racing around on the smooth green felt of a pool table. Like Maya Angelou playing solitaire while composing her poems, pool kept the front, worrying part of the mind occupied while the rear, free-wheeling portion of the brain was left independent to mull and ponder.

She crossed the 405, still clogged with creep-crawl traffic even at this time of night, and topped the hill above downtown Kirkland. At the first light she turned off Central onto Kirkland Way, and as she rounded the last curve at the bottom of the hill she passed Kirkland Hardware and noticed its lights still on. She glanced at her watch. A few minutes to nine. Still time.

She swerved into the parking lot, raced into the store and had them mix up two gallons of buttermilk yellow paint for her. Then she headed for the tavern. If she couldn't solve a simple murder, she could at least get the damned laundry room painted.

There was an open parking space in front of George's and she grabbed it. She stopped in the restaurant to have a cheeseburger and fries sent next door, then wandered into Smokie Jo's. Only one of the pool tables was busy. The sound of the clicking balls was like prayer bells to a novitiate, and Kate paused in the doorway to watch a minute. The two guys playing were pretty good. She plunked her quarter down on the table to rotate in.

Pearl was bartending, and she grinned a welcome at Kate and waved at a vacant stool midway down the bar. Pearl was above fifty; how far above, no one really knew. The tight reddish brown curls hugging her scalp came compliments of the nearest beauty shop. But her body was slim and youthful, and her face, high-cheeked with pointed chin, was as unlined as a girl's. The only thing that gave her age away at all was the bit of a turkey neck that dropped down beneath her chin.

Kate took the stool Pearl indicated, her back to the wall, then sat quietly a moment while she waited for her glass of rosé, letting the tavern atmosphere wash over her. It was dim and relatively quiet for a Thursday night. A couple of after-work regulars were talking quietly together at the horseshoe-shaped bar jutting from the rear wall. A dressed-for-success group had commandeered one of the high tables angling out from one wall and had formed an inclusive group beneath the neon beer signs on the wall above them. The jukebox was playing the no-longer-new Prince song, "I'm on Fire."

Pearl brought her wine and Kate stared down into the deep pink depths a moment. This was when she missed Sam the most. In the quiet of the evening when they'd sit and rehash the day. She could feel depression gathering around the edges, weighing in on her.

Pearl finished delivering a beer across the bar, poured herself a fresh cup of coffee, and sank onto her stool inside the bar across from Kate with a sigh of relief. She took a sip of the coffee, then leaned on the counter. "We missed you last night. You working a new case?"

Kate nodded, watching the progress of the pool game.

"So where's Sam these days?"

"Don't ask."

Pearl gave her a quick look. "Uh-oh, trouble in paradise, right?"

"Hey, Tess Truehart, you're up!"

Kate nodded at the pool player and slid off the stool. She racked the balls, then chose her cue while the guy broke. Chalking up, she watched the balls scatter. A stripe went in, which gave her solids. He missed his second shot, the cue ball rolled harmlessly into the center, and it was her turn.

She eyed the placement of her balls, working out a strategy. With icy coldness, she sank the first, gave herself a good leave, and proceeded to run the table. Every one of those round, shiny balls had Sam's face on it, and she sent them all flying to their doom.

"Whoa," the guy said, "you're wicked tonight." He turned to his buddy. "You take her on."

They'd played three games when Kate's dinner order from George's arrived. Feeling better, she relinquished the table back to them, then settled over her cheeseburger basket across from Pearl and scooped up a fry. "How about some ketchup?"

Pearl slid off the stool and brought her a packet kept for the microwave sandwiches the tavern served. "Don't ever let anyone accuse you of eating healthy," she grumbled. She slid back on her stool, and let Kate get a bite or two down before leaning toward her again. "So tell me, what's with Sam?"

Kate continued to chew until the bite was gone, then smiled. "Have I told you about my new paint for the laundry room? It's called buttermilk yellow. Kind of a cream with the palest hint of sunshine in it. It's just what that laundry room of mine needs, something light and cheerful and sunny. I saw it today on a lady's kitchen wall."

"He got married," Pearl guessed.

"I think I'll paint it this weekend. Want to help?"

Pearl snorted. "No, I don't want to help. I want to talk about your love life. Or lack of one. What'd you do to him anyway? He's positively nuts about you and what, you let him get away from you?"

Kate swallowed another bite of cheeseburger. "You're relentless, you know that, Pearl? You've only got one thing on your mind."

"That's because my mind can only handle one thing at a time."

"Yeah, but does it always have to be the same thing?"

Pearl gave her a stern look. "He did get married."

Kate felt the glumness spread inside again. "You're close." She told her about Sam's reconciliation with Janet. She described how Sam had been acting the couple of weeks before he'd broken the news to her, and repeated what he'd said on the wharf by Ivar's.

Pearl took it all in, listening without interruption. When Kate was through, she simply said, "Why?"

"Like I said, he feels this obligation to try again—"

"No, no, you misunderstand. I *know* why he's doing it. Let's face it, Sam's lovable, but he's an emotional klutz. No, Katie, why's *she* doing it? I mean now, after all this time?"

Kate set down her wineglass and stared at her. "Well, Sam said she'd been in counseling, that she's realized she'd caused some of their problems. He said she wanted to try—"

Pearl was still shaking her head. "But why didn't she just take all this wonderful insight and move on to the next guy? Why Sam?"

Kate shifted her gaze to stare into space, thought about it a minute, then shifted back to stare at Pearl again. "Damned if I know . . ."

They were about to dissect the situation when Pearl spotted a new customer coming through the door and hopped off the stool to meet him at the head of the bar. That was the start of the evening rush, and Pearl didn't have time for further talk.

Kate played a couple more games of pool, then called it a night. The minute she was out of the tavern, her mind returned to Pearl's question, Why? Why *had* Janet wanted to reconcile?

She was still puzzling over it when she pulled into her garage and walked around the house to her front porch. She picked up her mail, unlocked her door and entered the little front hall, then flicked a casual glance around, much as Pastor Ellsworth had done in the school office that morning—the householder arriving home, assuring himself that his world was in order.

Except hers wasn't.

Someone had been in her house.

* * *

Brillo came at her call, bringing a print man with him. "Low-key," she'd warned him. "I don't want the neighbors knowing." He and his man slid into her house like a couple of shadows passing through the night.

They fingerprinted her for comparisons, then Brillo took her over the story while his tech-man dusted the front door for prints. She was still pretty shaky from the scare of it, but managed to give a lucid account of her homecoming.

The first thing she'd noticed was the phone out of place, and she'd frozen in the front hallway. It belonged on the lamp table by the couch, not on the coffee table. The second thing out of order were the magazines on the coffee table; they'd been shoved to one side by the phone. At that point, she'd set the mail and her purse down and drawn her gun, listening hard. But all she heard was silence. The place had *felt* empty.

Cautiously, room by room, she'd gone through the whole house. And it actually had been empty. She then checked to see if anything was missing—TV, stereo, jewelry, her piggy bank, her portable strongbox—but everything was there. Yes, she'd checked all doors and windows, and no, there were no telltale signs of anyone forcing entry. Whoever had done it had known how to break in without leaving traces.

And since there were no obvious signs of a break-in she hadn't bothered reporting it to patrol, and since she couldn't call Sam, and knew better than to call the Captain, she'd called Brillo.

He listened to her, his black eyes playing over her face, making their judgments. As he measured the situation, the lack of immediate danger in it caused him to relax somewhat. "Okay, let's take it room by room. Tell me what's been touched and what hasn't been."

The amount of things out of order was quite small. One dresser drawer in her bedroom, another in her bedside table, the bookcase in the living room, and her desk in the den. Letters, bills, bank statements and various books looked like they'd been pawed over.

"How can you tell?" Brillo asked, watching her at the desk.

She pointed to a basket of mail. "My VISA bill was on top, to remind me to pay it. It's buried in the stack now."

He nodded. "Anything else?"

She turned around and scanned the room, shaking her head.

Deep in thought, Brillo led the way back to the living room. He dropped into a soft chair set at right angles to the sofa. "You still working that church case?"

She nodded.

The first humor broke through the worry and his teeth flashed white against the dark skin. "You gonna attribute this to divine retribution?"

She only half-laughed, not quite through with the scare yet.

"Who's your backup on the case?"

"No one, really."

He was appalled. "You mean you're working it *alone?*"

She felt compelled to defend the Captain. "It's a manpower shortage."

"Bull*shit!*" Brillo gave her his best world-weary look. "Listen, Mother MacLean, you *gotta* quit taking things at face value like Little Mary Sunshine. You just gotta. You're gonna get your tits in a wringer if you don't. Where the hell's Sam in all of this, anyways?"

"Chained to his desk by Hatch."

"What's going on?"

She was too tired and too upset to fight him. She told him about Janet, the reconciliation, Sam's request for a transfer to the Duty desk, and the Captain's retaliation.

Brillo fell quiet and leaned way back and stared into space for a while. She could sense the mental tape running. She sat on the couch and waited.

Finally, he started speaking, his eyes still locked on the distance. "Okay, Mother MacLean, here's what I think's coming down. Some puke with some B and E smarts broke in here without leaving a trace. He doesn't seem to have taken anything, but he messes around enough so's you know he's been here. That smacks of scare tactics. The unwritten threat. The warning."

His gaze drifted lazily down to meet hers. "But you're working a case involving a bunch of saintly types. Something isn't adding up here. What you gotta figure out, Katie, is what that warning means. And who'd want to deliver one." He began shaking his head. "You better watch yourself, Mother MacLean," he said slowly. "You're hanging out there all alone, and you're letting yourself get tied to a limb while someone below's sharpening the old family saw."

It was well after one when the two men finished up. They left her with some final words of reassurance, and she knew Brillo waited outside on the porch until he'd heard her click the lock home. The door had no chain, and the irony of her situation didn't escape her. Here she'd made the investment of time to see to it that Mrs. Hickman was safe behind the sturdy chain Kate had given her, while she herself was vulnerable to anyone with a key. She shivered at the thought as she went around the house, checking the back door and the windows yet one more time to make sure they were safely locked.

Sleep would be impossible, she knew. With hands that weren't quite as steady as she'd like them to be, she lit a fire, pulled an afghan free from its storage trunk in the den and huddled beneath it on the couch, making herself as small and invulnerable as possible, trying only to watch the flames, trying not to think.

But that was as impossible as sleep. Who would've done this? Was it as Brillo had suggested, connected to the case somehow? Could the church folks have figured out where she lived? And if they had, what were they after, why would they bother? And could they break in without a trace, were they that sophisticated in B&E techniques?

But the same mind that thought up the questions supplied the answers. She had a clear memory of Mrs. Hickman peering through her door down the street to the corner where Kate had pointed out her house. A simple matter for her to pick up the phone and call someone to share that little goodie of information. And breaking in as clean as this? Any locksmith could do it. They were bound to have one in their congregation. Or know someone who knew one. As for the why . . . well, scare tactics had been used to intimidate man since the beginnings of time. She huddled further beneath the afghan and stared at the flickering flames. She'd have to fight it. But how?

A firm tread sounded on the steps of her porch, then an even firmer tread crossed the wooden planks to the door.

Kate jerked upright, heart thumping, ears tuned like a wild dog's to the noises outside.

A hard knock sounded. "Katie?" a deep baritone voice called out. "It's Sam. Let me in."

She flew to the door. She fumbled some with the lock, pulled the door open, then stood and simply stared at him with relief. He'd pulled on the same clothes he'd worn that day at work, brown slacks and his old tweedy sports jacket, and his hair was mussed as if he'd just climbed out of bed and hadn't taken the time to comb it. A slight bulge beneath the left armpit said he was wearing his holster.

Her knees were threatening to give way and she sagged against the door frame. "Guess Brillo called you, hunh?" Her voice shook slightly.

"I guess he did." He gave her the professional once-over, cop to victim, measuring the injuries. When it was clear to him she was okay, he gave a single nod of the head, then lazily stretched out one arm, planted his hand on the door frame, leaned against it and said, "You gonna make me stay out here all night?"

She managed a slight smile. "What would the neighbors think if I ask you in?"

"What would the neighbors think if you don't?"

"True. Either way, I'm lost, I guess. Three men in one night, my reputation's made." She swung the door wide for him.

They'd both been keeping up the casual tone, but the minute

he was inside the hallway and the door was closed behind him, he held out his arms to her and she fell into them, burying her head on his shoulder, feeling the good strength of his arms tighten around her. "Oh, Sam," she whispered into his chest. "It was scary. Really scary."

He held her for long moments, stroking her hair down to her shoulders, smoothing it back from her face, planting soft kisses on her forehead, murmuring soft reassurances until some of her tension eased. Then he released her and led her over to the couch. He settled her into the corner where the afghan was heaped, drew it over her lap, and disappeared into the kitchen. She huddled under the afghan again, but this time not curled into a tensed ball as she had been, content to listen to his movements in the other room. The kitchen faucet came on and she heard the ping of a rush of water hitting a glass bottom and recognized the sounds of the coffeepot being filled, the slight *thwap* as the filter basket was shoved in, and the clunk of the glass pot hitting the burner.

When the coffee was ready, he brought out two steaming mugs, placed one on the table next to her, then took the same low, soft chair Brillo had used. His eyes on her, he took a tentative sip of his coffee, then leaned back in the chair and stretched his long legs out in front of him. The only lamp on in the room was a low one on the round table next to her, and it cast a soft golden light over the right side of his face, while his profile was lit by the fire off to his left. "Okay, tell me about it." His eyes were in deep shadow and their dark brown depths were unreadable.

She'd taken a sip from her own mug. Now she held it in one hand and curled the other around the body of it, shivering slightly from the sudden heat that warmed her palm. Then she began to speak. She told him the way she'd told it to the others earlier, calm and factual, without dramatics, beginning with her homecoming all the way through the visit with Brillo.

"Did he come up with any theory?" he asked, when she was all through.

"He thinks it may be related to the case."

"You agree?"

"It could be."

"You think they'd go to all the trouble to find out where you live?"

She told him then about her visit to the Hickmans and the story of the door chain.

He listened with interest, his eyes still taking her measure, judging her emotional equilibrium. Which was still shaky, and made shakier by reliving it again for him. He asked a few more questions, similar to the ones Brillo had, then he said. "Now tell me again."

He took her through it another three times, until the shakiness in her voice was replaced first by weariness, then by irritation. The next time he said to tell him again, she finally snapped at him, "The story isn't going to change, Morrison, no matter how many times you make me tell it."

"Good. That's the way you need to be. Angry. Mad as hell." He grinned then. "And just to make you madder . . ."

He set down his mug and withdrew a pack of playing cards from his shirt pocket. He slid the cards from the case and riffled them like a Las Vegas dealer. "Gin rummy. You don't stand a chance."

Chapter Fourteen

By five A.M., Kate was dressed for the day and at headquarters to start in on her reports. Sam had stayed until after three. She thought she'd be able to sleep, but the moment he drove away, her eyes popped open and the adrenaline started flowing again. She gave sleep up as a lost cause and headed in to work.

In spite of the support given her by both Sam and Brillo, she felt acutely alone, like someone tossed off the roof of a skyscraper, expected to grow wings and fly to save herself. If she thought about it, she was sure she'd find one discouraged cop inside, but the emotional ice shards left over from the break-in gave an edge to her despair, keeping her outwardly calm, and she pulled form after form from her desk and started in on the paperwork.

By six-thirty she had all the reports done, and leaned back in her chair to analyze the case. She had the motive, and she had the background to put it into context. All she had to do now was to retrace the routes of both Norm and Peter on Monday, looking for the arrow of guilt.

She glanced at her watch. Six forty-five. She had a full day ahead, and a strong sense of urgency to get going, yet it was too early for most everything that needed doing. Except for one item on her agenda that had taken on a sudden significance.

She made a tour of headquarters, starting with the Duty

sergeant. He not only assigned first-response teams, he assigned the unmarked cars, too. But he merely shook his head at her. "Sorry, Katie, they're all checked out."

That was no surprise. Cops were supposed to sit around and admire the palatial architecture that had gone twenty-three percent over budget, shorting the department everywhere else from coffeepots to cars. And normally, simply because of the mileage she was paid, she wouldn't mind using her own car. But working a homicide without any assigned backup at all made her pretty dependent on a radio should the case take an unexpected turn and something nasty start coming down. Especially after the break-in of last night. And it was beginning to irritate her that she could never get a car, while the Dreadful Duo always seemed to have one. "Excuse me, but exactly when does my turn come?"

He gave her the kind of look that he'd give a lowly file clerk demanding a promotion to Chief. "Think of the mileage check you'll be getting at the end of the month, Katie. Plenty enough to retire on, right?"

She trekked downstairs to Equipment to see what they had. Guns they had. Handcuffs. Tape recorders. But portable flashers and radios that would work in her car? Zip. The fact that they never asked the make and model of her car didn't escape her notice. They simply shrugged her predicament off. It was her problem, not theirs. They just worked there. Their attitude stemmed from the old town-and-gown split. Only in this case, it was the Uniforms against the Suits, men against the women, and Equipment came down solidly on the side of the male uniformed officer.

She still had a couple of shots left to try. She swung through Narcotics to grab a coffee. A rare bird or two, looking more like crooks than cops, were bent over typewriters, painfully tapping out reports with stiffened forefingers. She knew better than to ask who they were. She filled a Styrofoam cup with the muddy black liquid, then left a message for Brillo. "Hunt me up. I need some equipment." She was explicit in her message. After last night's scare, she didn't want to have him come charging in on a white horse, ready to tilt at her windmills when there wasn't even a breeze stirring.

She carried her coffee back to her desk, glancing at her watch. Seven o'clock. Finally. She called the state crime lab and asked for Homer. Homer was a cop's dream crime analyst. He had an instinctive sense of what counted and what didn't, and could cut through reams of tests to cull just the right one. Then, wonder of wonders, he'd actually take the time to call the detectives involved and give them a verbal report so they could act on it. He was one of those rare ones who didn't view cops as a nuisance.

"Hi, Katie, how's my girl?"

She automatically grinned when he came on the line. There was nothing cool about Homer. He was young, enthusiastic, impetuous and infectious. To him, cool meant below-zero weather in Rochester, New York.

She was on the verge of asking him about his latest girlfriend, but thought better of it. His romances changed with the seasons. Tall, lanky, with great horn-rimmed glasses that had a habit of sliding down his ski-slope nose, he held a certain appeal to women. All he wanted out of life was a wife and a large brood of merry little Homers, yet he was attracted to strong career women eyeing the corporate vice-president's office, who vanished when his intentions became clear.

She skipped the personal and went straight to the point of her call. "I'm working the Taft case, Homer. Sam told me yesterday the crews searching the woods for a killing tree branch drew a blank."

"Right. Not a thing that even came close, Katie. There are hundreds of acres of jungle at that state park, six hundred and forty of them to be exact, and they fine-combed a good portion of it, but they found zip."

"Would that mean the killer carried it away with him?"

"You can bet on it."

"Like in a trunk of a car?"

"Possibly."

"Then there'd be trace evidence, wouldn't there? Bits of bark, maybe some splinters, leaf debris, things like that?"

"Again, possibly. Can't tell until you've found me a car to examine," he said cheerfully.

But would it be a car? Early driving licenses were forbidden among the church youth. Cars meant freedom, and the church wasn't geared that way. "What about bicycles, Homer?"

"Well, there you might have a problem. A bike basket might or might not hold some trace. Saddlebags would, definitely. Unless the guy's as good at cleaning up as we are, which he won't be. But if I were gonna knock someone over the head with a dead branch, and was riding a bike, I'd hold it with one hand, ride a ways away, and dump it in a trash heap somewhere. You'd get some trace on the clothes, maybe. Chances are, though, you're not going to find much of anything of any use. You gotta remember, Katie, bikes come in for some hard wear. They get tossed on their sides in fields, on lawns, shoved through brush and woods and branches— You're better off hoping the killer used a car and dumped the branch in his trunk. Even then, he can claim he was toting firewood and maybe get away with it."

"But you can compare traces from a car trunk with traces caught in the victim's hair, can't you?"

"Oh, we can probably produce a miracle or two, sure. We do it daily, on command."

"In other words, keep my eyes open and pray," she sighed.

"Those who say prayer and science don't mix have never watched me at the test tubes."

"Okay, Homer, I get the message. There's one other thing I need from you. You've got some loose equipment roaming the shelves in the communications lab over there, don't you?"

He turned cautious. He'd helped her with the climax to the Fletcher case, and that had created an uproar that had lasted for months. Since then, he'd trod the straight and narrow. "Why do you ask?"

She explained her situation with cars and personnel, and gave him her car profile.

He sighed with relief that he was able to give her an honest answer. "Sorry, Katie, can't help you out. I got a few portables roaming around, but nothing that's going to do you any good. Tell you what you should do. You need to go to some kind of a commercial vendor and have them fix you up with the right antenna and equipment. They can outfit you with anything you want."

"What am I looking at, cost-wise?"

"A few hundred bucks, maybe a little more."

She thanked him and hung up. Could she requisition the equipment? She could just see the amusement come creeping into the Captain's eyes. It would be the highlight of his day.

The bullpen was filling up by the time she hung up the phone, and there was the usual noise and bustle of a new day beginning. At Goddard's desk, the Wonder Twins had arrived, dressed again in three-piece suits. They had their heads bent together, Goddard talking and Fry nodding, saying nothing as usual. The Shadow and the Shadowee. She narrowed her eyes slightly as she watched them. What did make those two tick? Ambition, she knew, in Goddard's case. Ruthless ambition. But Fry? Reflected glory? They finished their conversation, and Fry settled down to some desk work while Goddard ambled her way. She gave him the don't-mess-with-me evil eye and he ambled right on by without saying anything.

Next to her, Sam had just reached his desk. He looked like hell. His face was drawn and ashen with tiredness, and he wore the same brown slacks and tweed jacket he'd worn yesterday and again to her house last night, badly rumpled now as if he'd slept in them. To sum it up, Kate thought, he looked old and miserable and disheveled, and in definite need of a sympathetic back rub.

She smiled at him. "Want a cup of coffee?" she asked.

He nodded.

He was settled in his desk chair by the time she got back with the coffee, and he took his cup from her with gratitude. "Thanks." His eyes were warm on hers. "How come you look so fresh and cheerful and I feel so damned whipped."

"It's the good, pure life I lead. And probably the amount of Mexican I skip." She perched on a corner of his desk. "Sam, did you have a chance to start Goddard interviewing the crazies yesterday?"

He shook his head. "He never reported back in. When he did finally show up, it was with Fry, and they both headed straight for the Captain."

"Yeah," she muttered, "well, I know why they wanted to see him. And when they left the Captain they headed upstairs."

He gave her a sharp look. "To see the top brass?"

"Goddard pushed all the up buttons so I wouldn't know which floor he got off on." She gave a wry smile. "Just because he's slime, I keep thinking he's dumb. Bad error on my part."

Sam nodded agreement. "I'll tap my jungle line and see if anything's brewing."

"Thanks, that'd help. And what about the Bridle Trails neighborhood they supposedly canvassed?"

"Just a slight shortcut there. The folks I called back and checked with were interviewed . . . by one plainclothesman and a couple of uniforms."

"Fry and a patrol unit."

Sam smiled. "You got it. Technically, they fulfilled your orders."

Kate mulled that one over. Calling in a patrol unit like that meant Goddard had strings he could pull among the uniformed ranks. Not good news.

The phone on her desk shrilled, and she moved across the aisle separating them to take the call.

"I just knew you were an early riser," a cheerful voice chirped out.

She recognized Lucy Gray's voice instantly. "Good morning,

Lucy. You're not calling to tell me you've solved my crime, I hope."

"Absolutely not," Lucy said with some indignation. "You told me to stop, so I stopped."

Kate didn't bother relaxing. She may be saying she stopped, but that didn't mean she had.

"It's just that I got to feeling neighborly yesterday afternoon and did a little visiting around. You remember me telling you I recognized that poor girl's uniform 'cause my neighbor sent her kids to school there?"

Kate closed her eyes. "Yes," she said with some resignation.

"Well, I was wrong." She said it triumphantly, as if it were a blessing. "She *used* to send her kids to that school. She pulled them out a few months ago. Said girls were disappearing from there."

Kate frowned. "What?"

"Sure enough," Lucy said in satisfied tones. "Said at least a couple a year kind of just got lost. When she asked about it, she was told they'd transferred to other schools. But guess what? They hadn't! She checked. Then she was told they were off doing missionary work. She had no way of checking that, but she didn't believe it either. Since she's got a couple of girls, she just yanked them out and is sending them to public school. Says it's safer, even with metal detectors on the doors."

Kate's mind was racing with possibilities. "I want to talk to this woman."

"Of course, that's why I'm calling. I made an appointment for you to see her at eight. Her kids leave for school at seven-thirty, and that gives her time to make the beds and clean up the kitchen."

Kate buried her head in her hand. Dear Lord. Missing girls, but we gotta make the beds and clean the kitchen. Her mind was leaping every which way like a frog with a hotfoot, and she drew in a deep breath to slow it down. She pulled her pad and pencil in front of her. "Okay, Lucy, I'll see her at eight. What's her name and address?"

"Donna Wilhelm. And her driveway's directly across the road from mine. Can't see the house from the road, though. Too many trees."

"Okay, Lucy, I'll be there. Now listen to me—"

"I know, quit poking around in your case. See you later, Katie." And she was gone.

Kate hung up slowly. Missing girls? She swung her chair around to face Sam. "You're not going to believe this . . ."

He'd watched her from the time her phone had rung, ready to fly if something had broken loose on the case. Now suddenly, he glanced beyond her, then directly at her, sending her an urgent warning message with his eyes.

She swung around. Goddard was there, lounging up against one of the filing cabinets. "What isn't Sam going to believe?"

Kate ignored the question. "Nice of you to check in," she said in a casual tone of voice. "Been missing you lately. What'd you get done yesterday?"

There was only so far Goddard could go in his arrogance. As DIC, she was in charge of the case. Which meant she was in charge of the team. And as long as he was on the team, she was in charge of him. He didn't like her question, and his eyes glittered with malice, yet he didn't dare say anything. Especially with Witness Sam listening in one desk over. "Why, we did exactly what you commanded us to do, we talked to the neighbors around the park."

"Really. And what've you got planned for today?"

"More of the same."

She studied him. "You mean you didn't finish yesterday?"

He shrugged. "Lots of folks not home." His shrug and tone said he didn't give a damn whether she believed him or not.

She considered it a moment. He was close to skirting insubordination in the look in his eye, his tone of voice, the attitude. But he was smart enough to avoid putting it into words. If challenged, he'd simply repeat the same words with a softer tone of voice, a softer look—probably one with some humor and lightness in it—and come off as an easygoing, cooperative team player. And she'd look like the over-sensitive, hyper-reactive feminist looking for slights in every exchange of the day.

She rose abruptly and moved toward Sam's desk, beckoning Goddard to follow her. Fry was standing off in the distance watching them, and she waved him over, too. "Okay, guys," she said when they'd formed a circle around Sam, "this is the way it's going to play. Goddard, we've had some confessions phoned in. You take the list from Sam, and interview every one. Fry, you stay here and type up all your notes and reports from yesterday, so I have a full record of everyone you two interviewed. Be sure you list the folks who weren't home. Sam, you're point man. You man the phones and coordinate any calls from the three of us. If Goddard turns up any leads, you hand out the follow-up work. Oh, and Sam, make notes of the orders I've just given, so that there's no misunderstanding among any of us."

Without waiting for any kind of response, she turned away and grabbed the shoulder bag slung over the back of her chair and smiled at Sam. "See you later, friend."

Goddard had been bullied beyond his tolerance and he stepped in her path to block her way. "And just exactly what will you be doing?" he asked, his eyes narrowed and hard.

"Excuse me," Kate said lightly, "haven't you mixed up the dialogue? The DIC asks the team that, not the other way around." She was rubbing it in, and she knew it. She also knew it was a dangerous thing to do, to provoke him any further. But it felt so damned good. She smiled sweetly and strode off into the filing-cabinet maze toward the front entrance of the building, not bothering to look behind her.

But she could feel the heat from Goddard's glare scorching her back clear down to the shoulder bone.

* * *

Donna Wilhelm lived in a mobile home set back in a stand of woods next to the 405. It was a small trailer, several years old, with the beginnings of some rust dribbles running down the corrugated siding from the metal edging of the roof. The walls were too thin to keep out the freeway noises, and the continual growl of cars and trucks blurred together into one vast roar that sounded like a gale wind rushing through the treetops.

Donna was a thin, nervous, intense woman, given to tossing her head back to flip limp tendrils of mousy brown hair out of her eyes.

Kate turned down an offer for some coffee, withdrew her notebook from her purse and took her over the story of the missing girls.

"It's true," Donna said, defensively, before Kate ever challenged her on it. "My Marcie was in high school and saw it happen with her own eyes."

"Saw what happen?" Kate asked calmly.

"They'd be there one day, and gone the next. Just"—Donna waved an extravagant hand—"*vanished!* Why, Josie Hendrix is a perfect example. There in October, gone in November. A perfectly nice girl, too. That's when I knew. And that's when I yanked my girls out of there, you can believe me."

"That's when you knew what?"

"Why, where they're being sent." She leaned forward, eyes fixed on Kate's, and said in a low whisper, "You know they closed the retreat down for a year, don't you?"

"No," Kate said slowly, puzzled by the sudden shift in topic. The woman offered it as the most personal of confidences shared.

"They did." Donna nodded with satisfaction, then sat back. "They had to. To get everything set up."

Kate was at a total loss now. "Set up for what?"

"The buyers."

"The buyers."

The woman nodded. "You know, for the harems."

"Harems?"

Donna made an impatient gesture, as if Kate was being deliberately dense. "Yes, that's what they're doing with the girls, they're selling them to those foreign sheiks who run all those harems. They pay big money for young girls, those sheiks do," she added, confidentially. "You just do some checking and you'll see. You'll see that every time a girl disappears, sooner or later the church ends up with a big gob of money. You just check it out and you'll see."

Not caring a whit about the shotgun or propriety, Kate drove directly across the road, marched up to Lucy's back door and pushed her way right in. Lucy was sitting calmly at the kitchen table, sipping coffee, and Kate banged her purse down on the table and stood with hands on her hips. *"Harems?!"*

Amused eyes fixed on Kate. "I didn't say she was exactly normal."

Kate exhaled an exasperated breath. "You might've warned me."

"Would you have gone to see her?"

"Probably not."

"Well, then . . ." Lucy took another sip of coffee.

Kate collapsed into a chair. "Look, Lucy, you can't keep doing this. You can't keep stirring things up like this. I've got my hands full, I skipped seeing a potential suspect to talk to this lady, and I've wasted time I don't have."

Lucy nodded. "I understand. Of course. But when you do have a spare minute, you might want to follow up on Josie Hendrix. You see, I made a few calls yesterday afternoon after talking with Donna. Josie Hendrix really is missing. And the church really did close down the retreat for a year. To reestablish the ecological balance, they said."

Kate's eyes narrowed a minute, then she sighed. "Okay, Lucy, I'll check it out. But damn it, stay out of this. You could get hurt!"

* * *

The day's sunshine held a foretaste of summer in its heat. Outside, in Lucy's yard, she lowered the windows of her Honda to let the baking air out. The fresh smell of sun-warmed pine drifted in and she breathed deeply of it for a long moment. Then sighing, she picked up a Woodhaven yearbook, the most recent of the four she'd wrested from Donna Wilhelm, and paged through the pictures of last year's high-school students. Sure enough, in the eleventh-grade class there'd been a Josie Hendrix. That would make her twelfth-grade this year. Kate turned then to the file folder with the church roster Matt had given her. No Josie Hendrix listed. No Hendrix family at all.

Closing both yearbook and file folder, she tapped the steering wheel with one finger and stared off into a distant treetop. Would she be wasting her time to follow up on this?

Then she thought, Harems?

Harems?

She started her car and headed toward Northwest Bible College to do what she'd been planning to do before Lucy's call came in . . . corner Norm Overholtz.

The green of the Bible College's lawns was cool and inviting in the hot morning sun and already, at nine, students were lounging around in casual groups. Kate slowed for the turn into the driveway and parked on the circular drive. Climbing out, she scanned the lounging students for any familiar faces, but none of the evening group she'd been talking to the last two days were there. She climbed the hill and headed for the administration office at the top of the campus.

A secretary, pleasant and friendly, greeted her with a broad smile. Kate showed her ID and asked her help in tracking down Norm Overholtz.

Instantly, the secretary's face turned sad. "Yes, we've all heard about that poor girl found at Bridle Trails," she said, shaking her head. "I can't believe it, not there. Why, that's just across the freeway from us. A lot of our students here take picnic lunches over there. Just imagine, it could've been one of them. It makes you shiver, doesn't it?" She shook her head in dismay, then focused back on Kate's request. "Let me look up Norm's class schedule." She riffled through a book of laminated index cards overlapping in columns. "Ah, here we are. Let's see . . ." She glanced up at a wall clock, then back down at the card. "Yes, he's in a theology class right now. Christian Doctrine. I'll call down for him if you like."

"Yes. Thank you." While she waited, Kate wandered over to a nearby bulletin board filled with notices. A schedule of final exams and a list of commencement activities were posted, as was an invitation to all graduating seniors to a special faculty tea. Smaller hand-printed notices advertised bikes, desks, lamps and used textbooks for sale. Typical end-of-the-school-year college items.

A reminder to turn in library books and a warning that no grades or diplomas would be handed out until all overdue fines were paid brought a nostalgic grin to Kate's face. Religious school or not, some things about college never changed. Her own overdue fines had totaled a couple of hundred dollars after four years of schooling. It'd be triple that today. A lot of money. She hoped Bible students were more disciplined than she had been. Or wealthier.

"Detective MacLean?"

Kate turned back to the counter where the secretary waited.

"I'm sorry, Norm isn't in class. One of the students said he didn't come to school today."

The news didn't surprise her. She simply nodded. "What is his weekly schedule like?"

The secretary swung the card around so Kate could see. Three one-hour classes early on Mondays, Wednesdays and Fridays. Two classes on Tuesday and Thursday mornings—and one three-hour seminar on Tuesday afternoons. Monday afternoons from two o'clock on were a blank.

"Thank you." Kate handed the card back. "I appreciate your trying at least . . ."

"Anything we can do, *anything,* just ask. That poor girl . . . it could've been one of ours, you know. . . ."

She drove straight to Norm Overholtz's house. It was almost nine, and the neighborhood should've been stirring a little, but the street was quiet, people hidden behind curtains drawn against the bright sun. An old Chevy station wagon stood in the Overholtz drive, wet patches apparent in the self-shade it created. The car's metal fenders, dimpled and worn from age, gleamed in the stream of sunlight poring over it. Off to one side, Norm squatted by the front wheel of a green bike parked in a smaller patch of wet cement, polishing the spokes. The rest of the bike gleamed like the car. Kate's heart sank. Washed. Damn it.

She parked well down the street from him. Her rubber-soled walking shoes were soundless on the sidewalk, and Norm didn't notice her until her shadow fell across the drive in front of where he was working. He looked up then, squinting into the sun to see who it was.

She smiled down at him. "Hi."

"Oh. Hi." He went back to his polishing.

He wore a pair of ratty old knockabouts he'd outgrown several pounds ago, a short-sleeved checkered shirt with a button missing at the belly, and a no-name pair of tennis shoes with the big toes pushing up through holes in the canvas tops. Squatting, his body looked plumper than ever, with thighs pushing against the seams of the trousers and the fleshy stomach overlapping the waistband. Beneath the short sleeves of his shirt, fleshy forearms jiggled as he moved the polishing rag back and forth. Though the day promised heat, it was still relatively cool, yet sweat ran in rivulets down the plump cheekful of freckles.

She moved so that her shadow was out of his way, leaning back against the car fender. She eyed the runoff puddling in the gutter, wondering what would be left for the lab to find if it proved necessary. Even the thick balloon tires shone a rich black, obviously washed down with the rest of the bike. Any dirt, twigs and leaves that might've been caught in the wheels were history. Indicating the bike, she said, "Looking good."

He darted a glance upwards, then concentrated back on the rag. "Pastor Matt said to keep busy, it helps."

"Has it?"

"Not much." Suddenly, he bowed his head down and rubbed the spoke with a vengeance.

Kate moved a couple of paces away to the edge of the front lawn to give him a chance to recover his composure and sprawled on a sun-warmed patch of grass near him. "Hard, isn't it?"

He was silent a moment, then raised a face where sweat and tears wove a network of crisscrossed trails. "I feel like my guts are gonna rip open and spill out. I can't think, I can't concentrate—but I can't stand just sitting around, thinking of her, either." Fighting a fresh surge of tears, he bunched up the rag in one fist and gave the spoke another vigorous rub. "The funeral's tomorrow, you know."

"I know."

"That's why I'm doing this."

"Washing your bike?"

He nodded. "She was always so neat and clean about everything. It's a way to pay her a last respect. Going to the funeral in a clean car, riding a clean bike . . . That's what Pastor Matt said, I'd be honoring her in a way." Norm squinted over at her. "You think so, too?"

She could see a defense attorney cornering her on the witness stand. *And isn't it true, Detective MacLean, that you told our defendant here that it was perfectly all right for him to scrub and polish his bike? Therefore, Detective MacLean, how can you now accuse him of trying to get rid of trace evidence?*

Thanks, but no thanks, she thought, ducking an answer. Yet he still waited, his baby face crumpled into one freckled moon of pure misery, waiting for some magic words that would make it all go away. "Whatever works for you," she hedged, wincing inwardly at the bland glibness of the statement. "We each have to find our own way through grief."

He seemed to take it in. "That's pretty much what Pastor Matt said. He said the Bible can help. That God has called her home, and she's happy now, experiencing a serenity far beyond our understanding. He said it's those of us left behind who're suffering, not Sarah."

She waited a moment, then asked, "Did Sarah know how you felt about her?"

His eyes shifted away from her. The silence was so long she wondered if he heard the question.

"She knew," he said finally.

"How did she feel about you?"

"She liked me a little, I guess."

"How do you know she liked you?"

"I didn't say she liked me. I said she liked me a little, maybe."

To defuse his growing agitation, Katie grinned. "I stand corrected."

Surprised, his glance shot back to her. "You believe me?"

"Sure, until events prove differently."

"What events?"

"Oh, like, where were you on Monday afternoon?"

"In class."

"What class?"

"Religious History."

"What time?"

"From one to two."

"And after that?"

"I holed up in my dorm room to work on my term paper."

"Until when?"

"After supper."

"Is that when you usually get home?"

"Depends. Sometimes Mom needs some help, and I'll come home after class. Other times, I need to do some research work or stuff, and I'll stay until after supper. I've got this term paper due in history next week, so Monday I stayed late." He fidgeted with the polishing rag, swiped at an imaginary spot on the spoke, then looked over at her. "I'm not supposed to talk to you, you know."

"You're not? How come?"

"My folks said it's not such a good idea. Pastor Barnes told them that."

"What harm does it do to talk about Sarah?"

He had to think about that one. "None, I guess. As long as you don't think I'm the one who—*did*—this to her."

"Are you worried that's what I'll think?"

He nodded. "I wouldn't hurt her for the world," he whispered.

She chose her phrasing carefully. "I'm sure you'd never deliberately hurt anyone."

And she was sure he wouldn't. He was at that agonizing, confusing age of man-child . . . beyond childhood, not yet fully grown into manhood, still plagued by the round of baby fat that encircled his face and waist. His voice veered from the deep tones that would mark his adulthood to the higher ones of adolescence, yet he was neither/nor. He would grow these next few years, though. He'd grow into his body, he'd grow into his adulthood, but right now, he was all conflicting emotions, child subservience warring with manly needs. No, he'd never deliberately hurt Sarah. He seemed too gentle for that. But on an impulse of the moment? Out of panic, out of rage? Out of jealousy?

She went back to the subject of Monday afternoon. "Term papers," she mused. "How I hated doing them. I never could figure out which was the hardest, choosing the topic, or writing them."

His eyes widened in surprise, as if finally someone really, truly understood. "That's it exactly!" he said, some life coming back into his voice. "I went through four topics before my prof accepted one. Too broad, too broad, he kept saying. I think it took me longer to get the right topic than it did to write the paper."

"Did you ever do one before?"

He nodded. "Last year for Senior English at Woodhaven. But

we were given a list of topics to choose from, so we didn't have to come up with our own, you know? And they made them easy. I did one on the poems of Edward Taylor."

"You like poetry then?"

He nodded shyly. "When it's about how people feel about God. Edward Taylor's poems are rich and lush. Lyrical, kind of. I like those kind."

Stereotypes, Kate thought suddenly. We think the shy, sensitive soul of a poet should dwell in a thin, slender, refined body—an elegant body to fit an elegant soul. In this case, though, the sensitivity was housed in a thick, pudgy stump of a trunk, more coarse-looking than refined. Had Sarah seen past the exterior to the sensitivity hidden within?

"Did Sarah like poetry?"

He nodded again. "I used to copy some poems for her. She really liked that."

It was the first Kate had heard about Sarah liking poetry. And there'd been no poems lying around that Kate had noticed in her room. Sarah, Sarah, she sighed. You're such a mystery. Presenting one face to the world while keeping the inner you safe from prying eyes.

She took a new tack. "Did you know Josie Hendrix?"

He frowned at the sudden change in subject. "Josie? Sure, she was a year behind me in school, in Sarah's class. Why?"

Kate ignored his question. "Do her folks belong to the church?"

"They'd have to, to have her go to Woodhaven."

"Have you seen any of them in church lately?"

He shrugged. "I guess I haven't paid any attention."

"Were she and Sarah friends?"

The grief took over once again. "Sarah was friends with everyone."

Kate nodded. "I've kind of gathered that. I meant, close friends."

He shrugged again. "I don't know, I guess I never noticed."

"Had Sarah mentioned anything about Josie leaving school?"

Another shrug. "I guess she's still there."

The subject of Josie Hendrix obviously did not interest him, and she went back to Sarah. "What else did Sarah like besides poetry?"

He had to think about that. "She liked quiet things, mostly," he said slowly. "She liked to read. That was a favorite. And she loved music. Music meant as much to her as reading. She used to say that reading fed the mind, and music fed the soul, and the love of God glued it all together. That was so beautiful, don't you think?" he asked. "She was so beautiful . . ." His voice cracked. "So beautiful . . ."

"And you loved her very much," Kate said softly.

He nodded, helpless before the grief that had risen and clutched him again.

"And you told her this," she suggested, still in a soft tone.

Another sob-choked nod.

"And when was this?"

"At Christmas. Christmas Eve. It was our candlelight service. She was so beautiful, holding that candle, singing in the choir . . . I couldn't help myself. I whispered it to her after the service."

"And she said . . . what?"

"She was very kind. She took my hand and said I was a dear friend."

"But that wasn't what you wanted to hear."

"No." He stared at Kate, eyes widening in sudden fright. "But I didn't hurt her. I'd never hurt her. You've got to believe me. I'd never hurt her."

She held his gaze through the force of her own. "Was it Peter Dickerson, then?"

He was shocked. "No! He wouldn't do such a thing either!"

She wasn't that sure he was wrong. "Then who, Norman? Who else loved Sarah the way you and Peter did?"

He thought long and deep about it, then shook his head. "There's no one. Besides, Pastor says we're not to tell any names."

"Even to save yourself?" she said softly.

"Pastor says no one from the church did this, and we'd be making lots of trouble for nothing. That would be a terrible sin, he says."

"Norman, that doesn't make sense. We're dealing with a murder here."

There was a stubborn set to his face that told her it would be useless to push it now. She sighed. "All right, then, Norman, let's get back to you. Tell me, who saw you in your dorm Monday afternoon while you were working on your term paper?"

Total misery came over him now. "No one," he uttered in a ragged whisper. "My dorm mate has a late lab on Mondays. No one saw me."

Their eyes held again, his gray ones stricken, her own blue ones filled with sympathy and speculation.

"Okay, Norman," she said, finally, "okay." She gave him one last, long look before getting up from the lawn. "We'll just see how this all washes out, okay?"

Chapter Fifteen

Kate wandered after leaving Norm's. She went to the Tafts to search Sarah's room again. Though it was after ten when she got there, for once the parents were alone. Martha explained why in a weary voice. Sarah's visitation was scheduled for that night at the church, and the churchwomen would be busy with the arrangements. Besides, she said in her soft whisper, they needed some time alone. She seemed terribly tired, as if she were a stone worn down by a continual drip of water. At least the glaze of shock was gone from her expression. But she looked like she'd never smile again.

Daniel was still simmering. He muttered a few words under his breath at seeing Kate on his doorstep again, but after that, he left it to Martha to handle her. When Kate announced she needed to search Sarah's room again, he turned his back on them and marched into the kitchen with the same angry stride she'd used climbing Lucy Gray's back porch, and pulled the pocket door shut behind him.

While Martha stood guard in the doorway to Sarah's room, Kate started examining every single scrap of paper she could find. She was even more thorough than she had been the first time, but she found nothing. No notes, no names, no diary, no initials interlaced in the intricate doodlings climbing the margins of Sarah's schoolwork. Not even a copy of a poem.

She did, however, double-check her memory about the placement of the room in relation to the rest of the house. First bedroom beyond the living room. Once the household was asleep, it would be a simple matter to slip out the bedroom door, cross the front room, and on out the front door. The deep night hours had been open to Sarah any time she chose. Lost in thought, she thanked Martha and left.

She moved on to the school then. Coming in a side door, bypassing the secretary, she roamed the halls, peering in through windowed doors until she unearthed Nancy Wells, teaching a class, and talked to her briefly in the hallway outside the classroom. No, Nancy hadn't seen Josie Hendrix since she'd left the school. The family had moved out of the area, a job transfer, she thought. And yes, it seemed to her that a few years back the retreat had been closed for a season or two. Something about the ecological balance. And no, she still had no boy's name to offer as the father-to-be. Most definitely not, Miss MacLean. Kate kept quiet about Peter Dickerson.

Nancy's classroom was on the second floor, and Kate went back down the stairs and schmoozed with the school secretary a bit. Pastor Ellsworth wasn't around, so the woman was somewhat relaxed, though she was still upset about forgetting to make that phone call to Martha Taft. Kate did what she could to console her. In the process, she learned that the Hendrixes indeed had moved away, to somewhere in Tennessee, the secretary thought. At least that's where the school records had been sent. And no, she had no idea which of the senior boys might've had a crush on Sarah. Most of them, she'd guess. Sarah'd been a popular girl. That statement led the secretary back to her battle with guilt, and Kate consoled her once again. Before leaving, she took the precaution of noting down the Tennessee address. She also wheedled out of her copies of March and April's school and church calendars before moving across the campus to the church.

None of the pastors were in, she was told by the church secretary. Pastor Barnes would be at home working on his sermon, and none of the others had checked in for the morning yet. Kate thanked her and wandered away down the hallway until she was out of sight, then ducked around a back corridor and down the basement steps. As she thought it would be, the meeting room was full of churchwomen busy organizing things for Sarah's visitation to be held there that night. But by now, they knew who she was, and the friendly smiles of the day before dried up like prunes in the hot sun.

After leaving the basement, she wandered into the church and sat a few moments in a side pew, alone. She stared at the simple cross hung behind the altar for long moments before her gaze moved slowly up to the choir loft running along one side. She pictured Sarah standing there, staring down at the congregation, at—whom? Who would Sarah be watching? Norm? Peter? Or was it someone else entirely, possibly someone in the swing choir?

She walked along the road to the southern end of the complex and turned inward to the day-care center. Terry White was on duty again, and she excused herself to come over and lead Kate away from the children. No, Sarah had never mentioned having a friend named Josie. Yes, she had known the retreat had been closed awhile. Had that been for a whole year? she answered vaguely. She guessed she hadn't paid that much attention, it was so long ago. And no, Sarah had never talked about boyfriends or poetry or anything else like that. Just her schoolwork, and the children she helped take care of. That's all.

When Kate left there, she cut back across the main part of the campus, behind the grade school, and paused by the playing field a moment, letting the sun bathe her in its summerlike warmth. It seemed like there was nothing to the Josie Hendrix disappearance. A family job transfer out of state. As for the retreat, that *had* been shut down, but that had happened a long time ago. So much for Donna Wilhelm's harem buyers. Her thoughts went back to the mystery of Sarah.

She was stymied. She needed a source. The church had closed ranks against her, and she needed some kind of a source to feed her the information she wanted. But who? How could she find someone who'd be willing to open up to her? What could she try that she'd overlooked?

As her thoughts began to play along those lines, she started walking back to her car in the northern parking lot. As she emerged from the last walkway onto the graveled parking area, Pastor Matt's car drove in and pulled into one of the vacant slots. She stopped in the shade of an oversized spruce, near the path he would take to the church.

He didn't see her immediately. He climbed out of his car, bent down and pulled a leather file pouch from behind the driver's seat, then slammed the door shut. When he turned her way, his face showed he was clearly upset. His forehead was scrunched down into a worried frown and his lips were pressed into a thin line. He looked like a grad student who'd just failed his orals.

She moved out of the shadows, and squinting against the bright sun slanting down behind her, he pulled up short when he recognized her. She smiled at him. "Good morning. You don't look exactly happy with the world."

With an effort, he erased some of the frown from his face, but not all of it, and he couldn't quite ease his lips into any form of a welcoming smile. "Good morning. Still detecting, I see."

Kate grinned. "My mother calls it snooping. Most unladylike, she says."

The answering smile was brief and halfhearted. It didn't come close to reaching his eyes. "I hope you aren't looking for me, Miss MacLean. I've helped you all I can."

"I'm sure you have," she said mildly. "You do look like you're the new Atlas in the world, though. Is there anything I can do to help?"

The reaction was strong and mixed. It veered from a self-deprecating amusement that he would need help from a cop, to pure, unadulterated anger that he would need help at all. The anger won out, then was quickly suppressed and turned inward into a deep depression. He stared at a tree nearby, his eyes tracing the beams of sunlight filtering down through the upper branches. "Have you ever, ever been at a total loss as to what to do about something?"

Not sure what he was referring to, Kate picked her way cautiously through the verbal land mines she sensed were suddenly there. "Yes. Often, as a matter of fact."

He looked at her with quickened interest. "What did you do then?"

She thought about it. "Most of the time, I guess, I made a decision to make no decision. To let things evolve until it became clear what I should do."

Eyes fastened on hers, he absorbed that. Then slowly, as his thoughts roamed free, his eyes went back to tracing sunbeam paths through the treetops. He was so young, Kate thought suddenly. With his looks and air of maturity, and the strong sense of purpose he'd shown about his life, she'd kept thinking he was so much older than his years. But now he looked young and uncertain and unsure of himself and vulnerable. Something major had happened to him this morning, she thought. Some life-changing event.

Finally he nodded. "Maybe that's best. Let things evolve."

"It usually does," she murmured. He'd had her sympathy, but now she had to be the cop again. "Unless, of course, the problem's related to the murder. Then time is a luxury that can't be allowed."

He nodded. "Let's hope it's not, Kate. Let's just pray it's not."

"Should you be the one making that judgment?"

"I'm the *only* one who can make that judgment. I have a duty to my church."

"I should've thought your duty was to God," she said softly.

The anger simmering just below the surface suddenly gave way to a bleak sorrow. "That's the conflict, isn't it," he said, just as softly.

Without another word, he moved on past.

She stood for a long moment, watching him eat up ground in long, forceful strides. By the time he reached the office wing, his anger was back full-force and he yanked the door open and disappeared inside. She gave a silent whistle and turned once again toward her car. Someone had sure planted a burr under his saddle. Pastor Barnes, perhaps? Or his wife?

The brown Ford Escort popped to mind. She sat in the front seat of her car and paged through the church roster Matt had given her. Sure enough, the last page contained names and addresses of the staff. Including the pastors. She wrote down the address she needed, checked its location on her plat map and set off.

Pastor Matt's house was in an old section of Redmond, two blocks off the main street. It was a small white two-story structure on a large lot surrounded by giant firs. Kate parked in front and went up the walkway to the front porch and knocked. As she waited, she glanced at the gardens. Everything was dead. The only things thriving were some old, overgrown shrubbery that could survive neglect. The rest was all dead stumps, sticks and nubs. Bleak.

The woman who answered the door was anything but bleak. In person, Patricia Jacobson was much prettier—in a fragile way—than the photo in Matt's office had shown. She was in her middle twenties, twenty-six, twenty-seven, perhaps, with a slim build, delicate skin, light blue eyes and pale blond hair that was worn fluffed out around a slender face. She wore a deep rose shirtwaist dress cinched in tight around the thin waist, with a full skirt billowing below and a soft swelling above that clung to the small curves of her breasts. Kate could've sworn there was the slight sheen of pink lipstick on the full lips. Though if there was, it was the first touch of makeup she'd seen on any of the churchwomen.

If Patricia recognized Kate from two nights before, she gave no sign. "Yes?" she said, softly.

"Patricia Jacobson?"

A small smile appeared and her head tilted to one side. "Mrs. *Matthew* Jacobson," she corrected gently.

"I'm Detective Kate MacLean. I'd like to talk to you a moment. May I come in?"

She frowned slightly. "I was just on my way down to the church. Are you the detective investigating Sarah's death?" At Kate's nod, a sad, sweet smile came over her face. "Of course I have time to talk to you," she said in a soft voice, swinging the front door open wide. "Come in please."

She ushered Kate into a living room right out of the pages of *Home* magazine. The walls were a dusty pink with white woodwork, the loose-cushioned sofa and matching love seat were covered in a creamy linen fabric brightened with sprays of large pink cabbage roses, and the delicate Queen Anne side tables were from one of the Drexel-Heritage lines. An Oriental rug woven in the same colors as the floral sprays lay in the center of a sprawl of white wall-to-wall carpet. It was an elegant room, one that Kate would've loved for herself. But not if she were married. She couldn't imagine a man feeling comfortable in such a feminine decor. And she couldn't help noticing that Patricia's dress matched the room.

Patricia saw her eyeing the room with admiration and said, "We're looking for a much nicer house than this. I do try to do my best . . ." She let a sad smile finish the sentence.

At the end of the room, two cream-colored wing chairs flanked a small brick fireplace with built-in bookshelves. As far as Kate could tell from a quick scan of the shelves, they were filled with religious books of all kinds. Not a decorating book in the lot. A hired decorator had either been at work, or the woman had a natural gift for interior design.

Patricia indicated one of the wing chairs for Kate, then took the other for herself. She sat straight in the chair, like Queen Elizabeth posing for an official portrait, and smoothed down the skirt of her dress. Then she smiled again at Kate. "You said it was about Sarah. That poor, poor girl. We're all so distraught over this."

There were two things that hit Kate instantly. The first was the smile. It was sweet, but wholly inappropriate under the circumstances. The kind of smile Kate gave Goddard when she was at her bitchiest best.

The second thing that hit her was the actual statement of feeling distraught. Aside from the inappropriate smile, Kate couldn't help thinking, Really? If Patricia Jacobson was so distraught over Sarah's death, then why had she sat outside the Taft house two nights ago instead of going in to offer her sympathy and comfort?

Kate gave a noncommittal smile. "I wonder what you can tell me about Sarah."

"Why, let me think a moment . . ." Patricia stared off into space, her brow creasing into a thinking frown. "She was such a pleasant girl, you know. So well mannered. The Tafts were very fortunate that way. Not all children are that well behaved. Some of them are quite rowdy actually. They make dreadful messes, and leave fingerprints all over the wall—" She broke off and smiled at Kate. "But I'm sure you know that. It was *Mrs.* MacLean, wasn't it?"

Kate gave her the same noncommittal smile of a moment ago, ignoring the implied question of marriage and motherhood. "Katie will do. You were saying about Sarah?"

"Oh, yes, Sarah. I wasn't that close to her, you understand, though I do try and help everyone as much as I can. But she did seem like a pleasant girl."

"I'd like to find someone who was close to her. Someone she might've confided in. Who would you suggest I talk to?"

"Oh, I wouldn't know that. But you might ask Pastor Bob." She smiled sweetly. "Yes, you might ask him."

"Why Pastor Bob in particular?"

"It's just that I saw Sarah coming out of his office one day last week . . . Of course, that could've been a conference about anything, really." Then she added with a wicked little smile, "Though it did seem to go on a bit long. A good hour or two."

"Really," Kate said in a quiet voice designed to encourage gossip. "You were there the whole time?"

"Of course, I'm often there to see my husband. They cut him up into little pieces, you know." She smoothed down the skirt of her dress again and readjusted the prim position of her knees. "Not literally, of course." She giggled slightly. "Time-wise is what I meant. There's so little of him left when he does get home."

Kate eyed her. The giggle, like the smile had been, had no real humor behind it. And it too was inappropriate. Nervous habit? Like smoothing her dress down again and again?

"You see, we met at Bible College. I wanted to find someone I could truly help in his work. Matthew seemed ideal." She looked down at her lap and fussed a bit more with her skirt. "I don't always go to church on Sundays, you know."

Kate fielded that one cautiously. "You don't?"

"No. Sometimes they don't seem to have the right attitude." Her eyes, pale and luminous now, fastened on Kate. "Religion's a very serious business, you know. It's much too serious for levity. That's why I married a man of God. To be able to devote my whole life to his well-being so that he's free to do God's work."

"I see," Kate said.

"Do you?" The eyes remained fixed on hers. "Not many do, you know. Understand the seriousness of it, I mean."

Kate kept her voice gentle. "Do you think Sarah understood how serious it was?"

Patricia gave a demure smile. "What do children know of anything? Our Lord said, 'Suffer little children.' Even He had no use for them. So you see, I follow the Lord's example and have very little to do with them at all."

A chill raced down Kate's spine. She remembered next to nothing from her childhood Sunday School classes, but even she knew that Patricia had given a distorted meaning to that particular Bible verse.

Patricia's head was bowed as she smoothed her skirt yet again, then she peered shyly up at Kate. "Sarah had a licentious nature, you know."

Again, Kate played it cautiously. "Really?"

Patricia nodded. "Oh, yes, she did. Why, she was after everyone, it seemed. It didn't matter who they belonged to. Or whether they liked her or not. She just—well, *flung* herself at them."

"Men, you mean," Kate said, still cautiously.

"Yes. She was like some nasty bug, crawling all over them. Why, I wouldn't blame any of them if they finally just kind of—shook her off. Know what I mean?"

Kate swallowed against a sudden dry throat. "Would there have been anyone in particular that might've just—shaken her off?"

The sweet smile was back. "Well, as I said, there's always Pastor Bob. He's never married, you know. Why, he doesn't even date. Which makes you kind of wonder, doesn't it. You might also try Norm Overholtz. Or better yet, Peter Dickerson. Sarah never could seem to leave either of them alone. Every time you looked, she was sitting next to one of them, or walking next to one of them. Those poor boys. They were really quite helpless about it." The pale, luminous eyes swung away from Kate to peer at some private vision. Still staring into space, she began nodding. "Yes," she said in a pleased voice. "I'd definitely look at Norm and Peter. And don't forget Pastor Bob."

Kate nodded agreement. "Patricia— Do they call you Patty or Patricia?"

"Mrs. Jacobson, if you please." The woman smiled gently. "Mrs. *Matthew* Jacobson. I *am* the pastor's wife, you know."

"Mrs. Jacobson, then. When exactly did you see Sarah Taft last?"

"I told you," she said, suddenly annoyed. She didn't quite answer the question, Kate noted. "I didn't go to church on Sunday. I also told you I don't pay attention to children."

"Then why were you parked outside the Taft home two nights ago, just sitting there and watching?"

Ice began to form in the blue eyes. She stared straight at Kate and said, "Why, I wasn't anywhere near Sarah's house."

"You were seen," Kate said, mildly. "Parked there outside. Watching."

Patricia locked eyes with her. "You're mistaken." Then she rose with tense, abrupt motions. "You must go now. I'm really quite busy."

Kate rose to face her. "Mrs. Jacobson, if Sarah meant nothing to you, why were you there?"

The thin face was unyielding. Without answering, the woman strode through the foyer archway with tense, jerky motions, the full skirt of the dress swirling around her like a rose mist. She swung the front door open wide. "You must go now. I'm late as it is." Then suddenly, the sweet smile came back and she gave Kate a radiant look. "Thank you so much for coming to call. You must do this again some time."

Giving in to the inevitable, Kate bowed once without saying anything further, walked with even steps through the door and down the walk to her car, climbed in behind the wheel and locked the doors. Without a pause, she shoved her key in the ignition and drove off. Dear God, she thought, what in the world had Pastor Matt married?

She couldn't even think of whom to go to. Sam was out of the question. She didn't want to carry this back to the bullpen until she had her thoughts straight. And he couldn't get away to come to her.

Or could he?

She wheeled onto Redmond Way and hit the nearest phone booth. She got through to him right away, and when he was on the line, she said, "Meet me for lunch, will you, Sam?"

They agreed on Las Comidas in fifteen minutes. Then he gave her a phone message. Pastor Barnes wanted to see her in his office at three.

At that news, her head sank against the plastic cage of the booth and she sighed. The meeting with Pastor Barnes would not be a happy one. He'd have heard of her meanderings around the complex and she had a pretty good idea what the theme of his little lecture would be. "Okay," she said quietly, "I can make it."

In spite of all the stoplights and the heavy noontime traffic on Redmond Way, she beat him to the restaurant and snagged the same booth they'd had yesterday. She'd finished one glass of iced tea and was on the second before he arrived.

He came in looking glum. His eyes were dark and shadowed, his face closed off. They placed their orders, then he sat silent, staring down at the table, toying with his silverware.

She held off talking about the case, her senses fully tuned into him now. Something heavy was going on, something he was reluctant to share. She took another sip of her iced tea and waited.

When his beer arrived, he watched the head die down, bubble by bubble, then started twisting the glass. Finally, he drew in a deep breath and sighed. He raised up to look at her. "Guess I'd better tell you," he said quietly, "a list of promotions came through this morning."

She went suddenly still.

"Goddard got lieutenant, Homicide. Effective July one."

It blew lunch right out of the water.

She left Sam and her food sitting there, drove straight home, headed for her desk drawer and picked up the little red envelope containing the safe-deposit key, cursing her own procrastination the whole way.

She was halfway back out her front hall when she came to a stop and stared down at the little envelope. It was made of a stiff cardboard-weight paper, so it felt firm in her hand. But even so, there was more give to it than there should've been with a metal key inside. She unsnapped the clasp and peered in. No key.

Goddard and Fry. The break-in. The smug smiles in the Up elevator yesterday. The promotion.

She strode out the door and headed straight for the bank.

The lady guarding the safe depository checked her logbook, then looked up at Kate with surprise. The box, she informed her, had been cleaned out and closed yesterday afternoon.

Kate pulled out her badge, pulled rank and raised such a ruckus the manager got involved. She was shown one of the bank's own forms that supposedly she'd signed, authorizing the bearer of the key to empty the box and close out the account on behalf of the box holder. It was common procedure, she was informed, designed to streamline things when a box holder transferred out of the area without cleaning out the box. No, of course they wouldn't remember what the person who had done this looked like. You must understand that a bank as large as this one dealt with thousands of people a day. And yes, the box was definitely empty, its contents gone. All perfectly legal, you understand.

She left the bank with a copy of the form and sent it directly to Homer with a note with her signature on it, then stopped at a pay phone and called a locksmith in Kirkland. She met him at the door to her house and ordered deadbolts and new locks installed everywhere. She also had him check the locks on all the windows and replace any that weren't working. A crook with free and easy access to her house was one thing. Goddard having free and easy access to her house was something else again.

As soon as the locksmith had left with a couple hundred of her hard-earned dollars, she made a big pot of coffee and sat at her snack bar trying to figure out what she was going to do with the rest of her life.

She hadn't brought in the mail, and she didn't really care. Her message machine light blinked once, but she didn't bother listening to the message. She poured another cup of coffee, then on impulse picked up the phone and called her folks.

It was only a little after one, her time, after four in Connecticut, and her mother, in spite of her voice being as cool and proper as ever, betrayed a little anxiety over hearing from her at that time of day. "Kate. Are you all right, dear?" What she meant was, Why are you calling during a workday, dear? But her mother, New England to the core, would never ask such a direct question as that.

Kate sat silent a moment. Well, Mom, Sam's gone back to his wife, my house was broken into, my safety-deposit box was robbed, and a man who hates my guts has just been made my boss. She shut her eyes and nodded. "I'm fine, Mom. It's been a while since I've called, is all. How's everything there?"

Her mother, never one to appreciate problems being thrust upon her doorstep, accepted the reassurance at face value, and chattered on about the rest of the family. Kate's dad was presiding over some complex civil litigation and was poring over books even as they talked, seeking legal precedence for the ruling he was about to hand down. Mark had been chosen for the *Yale Law Review*, and both parents were exceedingly proud. Unspoken, of course, was the underlying meaning, That could've been you, dear. Her mother did say, "We still have that little fund put away for you, Kate, in case you do ever change your mind about law school."

Kate, in a suddenly testy mood, said, "Supposing I wanted a master's in social work?"

Her mother sighed. "Oh, my dear, all those tenement places you'd have to go into . . . besides, dear, you know how we feel about the law."

The strings were still there. My way or the highway. Which is why they lived a continent apart. Just once she'd like to sit down with her dad alone and have a good heart-to-heart, and see exactly how much of this attitude was really the "we" that was constantly flung about so casually, and how much was her mother's alone.

But in spite of the cool, socially correct voice that so aggravated her, as her mother chattered on about the latest doings about town, Kate could picture the tiny village, neat and tidy with its town square and the two church steeples at opposite ends of the narrow, river-valley town, rising above the tops of the shady maples like a pair of slender fingers pointing toward heaven. Everything seemed so orderly there. The seasons came, the seasons went, and life went on unchanged as it had for centuries. By comparison, the west seemed young and raw, everything too new, its traditions too unformed.

Then reality set in, the suffocating routines of living the same life day after day, the social pecking order that never changed from generation to generation, the bloodless discourse that passed for conversation. *Yale Law Review*, she snorted to herself. Sure, Mother, sure.

She ended the conversation with messages of love to her dad and brother, then took the mug of coffee into the living room. It was too hot for either a fire or her afghan, so she simply curled up on the couch and stared at the hearth as if the flames were there anyway, hypnotizing her.

It was after two when she decided to go back to work. She needed to purge her files, clean up her desk, make sure there was nothing incriminating laying around for Goddard to find. She hesitated for a second, unsure, not wanting to face him yet, not wanting to endure his strutting and gloating and cruel power.

Fine. If she didn't want to deal with him right now, then she'd just go back to work on the case. Goddard couldn't do anything with her files for now, not with Sam sitting guard next door to her desk.

She rose and grabbed her purse and headed for her car. She had an appointment with Pastor Barnes at three, anyway. In the meantime, she had to go peel a few potatoes.

Chapter Sixteen

She drove to the church and headed directly for the basement meeting room. Without saying a word, Kate smiled at the women working there, rustled herself up an apron from the pile she'd seen stacked there, and grabbed a paring knife. She ignored the shocked stares of the women and headed for a stockpot filled with cooling boiled potatoes for salad.

Emma Barnes moved her way, her plump cheeks deeply dimpled by a disapproving look. "Can I help you with something?" she asked, in a formidable tone. What she was demanding was an explanation, of course.

Kate simply said, "I saw how much work you had to do."

"That's quite all right, dear, we can manage quite nicely."

"I'm sure you can." Kate smiled warmly at her. "What would you like me to do with the peelings?"

Nonplussed, Emma stared at her. She had two choices. Answer, or create a scene. She rummaged around for a trash can with a liner and plunked it down next to Kate with a disapproving thump. "Here you are, dear." She turned and marched back to her own workstation, where she was frosting a cake.

Without a pause, Kate started in on the first of the potatoes. At first the churchwomen were stiff and silent around her, going about their work with unaccustomed self-consciousness, but as

Kate concentrated on her potato peeling and made no effort to poke and pry, they began to relax and resume some of their normal ways, murmuring quietly in pairs at first, then eventually falling into a more natural kind of chatter.

They were no different from women's groups anywhere, Kate soon realized. There were the gossips and the listeners, the workers and the lazybones. And then there were those few busybodies who preferred to supervise rather than do any work at all. Emma Barnes, Kate noticed, had a smooth way of deflecting those women, drawing them away from their victims and assigning them chores to do off by themselves. One particularly inspired busybody got escorted firmly to the sink in front of a whopping stack of pots and pans. Gradually Kate sorted out the chatter and began picking up little tidbits here and there that built into a picture of the church and its social climate.

It began with a flurry of conversation about how and where the food should be arranged and laid out for the visitation that night. Before anything was really decided or resolved, the talk veered off into memories of other gatherings the meeting room had held, and that led into a discussion of future events. Emma Barnes and the Pastor were coming up on their thirtieth wedding anniversary, and they were planning a renewal of their vows in the church in front of the whole congregation, with a reception to follow in the basement meeting room.

The subject of wedding anniversaries dissolved into a discussion of Pastor Ellsworth's marital status. "He needs to find *someone*," was a firmly voiced opinion. "I don't think he's smiled since Anne died, and that was twelve years ago. He just gets grumpier and grumpier every day."

There was murmured agreement to that, then the talk veered once again to the subject of bachelorhood in general, and Pastor Bob in particular. Evidently the Youth Pastor was adept at sidestepping all efforts at romantic pairings. There was a lot of speculation as to why he hadn't found someone yet. "The problem is, he's just too involved with those kids," was one woman's opinion.

"Why should he marry when he's got all of ours acting like he's their second daddy?"

A woman near her snorted. "That's exactly why he *should* marry. So he could be someone's *first* daddy."

"Well, whoever she is," a third chimed in, "she'd better like children. Lots of them."

"That certainly eliminates someone we know, doesn't it?" the second woman said smartly.

There was laughter and several amens to that.

"What *is* Matt going to do about that woman?" one woman demanded to know.

Emma Barnes spoke up then. "That's enough of that. Patty's his wife, and that's the end of it."

The talk died away for a respectfully guilty length of time. Kate hid a smile, finished dicing one potato, scooped the pieces into a bowl and picked up another one to peel, concentrating on her work.

Another woman, working silently at the counter next to Kate, also had her head bent over her work. While chopping an onion, she started tossing a few glances Kate's way. She was a slender woman in her thirties, with brown hair clipped back at the neck, dressed as the other women were in a high-necked dark print dress. Finally, as Kate seemed to be harmless enough, she looked around to see who was within hearing distance. When she was sure they couldn't be overheard, she said softly, "How's it going? The investigation, I mean. Have you come up with any answers yet?"

Kate nudged her potato stockpot closer. "I keep pecking away at it," she said just as softly.

The woman concentrated on peeling another onion for chopping. After a moment or two, she murmured, "We were talking about this whole thing. We all pretty much think it has to be a stranger of some kind. Someone sick in the head who takes girls they don't know and does terrible things to them."

Kate shook her head. "That would be a convenient solution,

but we've checked. There aren't any other cases around similar to Sarah's."

"Couldn't she be the first?"

"It's possible, I suppose. But from what we've been able to determine so far, it's almost a certainty that Sarah was killed by someone she knew."

The woman shook her head in sadness. "I was afraid you were going to say that." She finished up the one onion and started on the next.

"What's your name?" Kate asked after a minute.

"Evelyn. Evelyn Dietz."

"Did you know Sarah well?"

"To an extent. She was Missy's Sunday School teacher for a couple of years. Missy's my third-grader. And of course I saw Sarah every week at Friday night potluck."

Kate finished one potato and picked up another. The other women were chattering away, no one paying any attention to Kate and her neighbor. Kate decided to take advantage of Evelyn's quiet friendliness and press her luck a little. Watching the strip of potato peel curl away from her knife, she said casually, "I've heard that Peter Dickerson was pretty smitten with Sarah."

Evelyn nodded. "He was gone on her all right. He and Norm Overholtz."

Kate's peeler made rhythmic slices into the peel. She waited a beat or two. "I imagine some of the other guys in school had their eye on her, too."

Evelyn looked doubtful. "If there was anyone else, it was a case of worship from afar. Certainly nothing that was noticed."

Kate fell silent. The response always came down to those two, she thought. Peter Dickerson and Norm Overholtz. Never anyone else. And she didn't like it. Why didn't she? she wondered. Both boys had had a crush on Sarah, big-time. So why did she keep searching for a third romantic partner? Because, she thought, neither Norm nor Peter struck Kate as guilty of anything more than a bad case of lovesickness. Yet there was no denying that each of the boys had been alone when Sarah was killed. Opportunity and motive certainly existed for either boy.

She was still arguing with herself when a pair of high heels sounded on the wooden basement stairs and Patty Jacobson paused for a moment in the doorway as if posing for a *Playboy* shoot.

She'd changed her rose dress for a solid black one, the color more appropriate for this church gathering. But even then it didn't work. All the women there were draped in soft, loose folds of their dark material. Patty's dress, though, while the right color, was the wrong cut. Tight across the chest, outlining the swell of full breasts, it cinched down into a tight belt that spanned a slight waist, then belled out for the hips and tapered back in at the knee, emphasizing her curves. It looked more like a chic cocktail dress than a proper outfit for church.

But it was more than the dress. The church women wore their hair pulled back and confined at the neck in some twist or bun. But Patty's blond hair was fluffed out around her sharply angled cheekbones. Worse, Kate could clearly see the sheen of the pink gloss on her lips and knew for certain she was wearing lipstick. If she saw it, she was positive it wouldn't escape the eye of any churchwoman there.

And last, the total combination of dress, hair, and lipstick all warred with the sweet girlish smile she bestowed around the room. She looked unreal. A walking Barbie doll.

A silence worked its way around the room and next to her, Kate heard a whispered, "Oh, dear," coming from Evelyn.

Then, as smooth as custard pudding, Emma Barnes quickly moved to Patty's side. "Come on in, dear. We can always use another hand." She escorted her to a table where some ladies were sitting making sandwiches and brought a chair up to a clear spot for the younger woman. Bustling from place to place, Emma gathered up a spreading knife and some sandwich wrap and set them in front of Patty. "Any kind will do, dear. Don't worry about a thing." After a sharp, warning glance at the ladies around the table, she moved back to her own workstation and, as if there had been no pause at all, she continued frosting the cake she'd been working on.

The aimless chatter gradually resumed, as it had after Kate had jolted them into silence with her appearance, but she noticed that the ladies at the sandwich table remained quiet. They stared only at the bread before them and concentrated fully on getting the mayonnaise spread just right.

Kate felt a little sorry for Patty, so obviously the outsider. She glanced sideways at Evelyn Dietz and murmured, "That's Pastor Matt's wife. What's the story there anyway?"

Evelyn simply shook her head. "No one knows. They were already married when Matt came here. We simply can't figure her out, and Lord knows, we've tried. She's been a disaster since day one. It's a strange pairing."

"I know they don't have children."

"No, according to the rumor mill, Matt can't have them."

Kate ducked her head down to hide a quick flash of satisfaction. *That* little gem was worth every damned potato she'd peeled. Strike one potential suspect. "What does she do to fill her time then?" she managed to ask in a casual tone.

Evelyn thought about that one. "She drifts. She drifts here and she drifts there. But she never really *does* anything." She bobbed her head toward the sandwich table. "See what I mean?"

And Kate did. Patty's hands drifted over the sandwich bread, then hovered over the tray of stacked meats and cheeses, hovered a moment above the spreading knife, then slowly her hands drifted—still empty—back to her lap. All without touching a single item. She looked down at her lap for a long moment, then pushed her chair back, bestowed her sweet smile on the circle of women at the table and rose. Without saying a word to anyone, she drifted out of the room. Behind her, the women at the sandwich table exchanged knowing glances before each and every one of them bent to their work in front of them. Not a word had been said. None was needed. Their opinion of Pastor Matt's wife was plain.

"Where does she drift to?" Kate asked.

Evelyn shook her head. "Heaven only knows." She looked at Kate. "And I mean that literally. Only Heaven does know."

Kate tucked that away, then glanced at her watch. It was a quarter to three. She finished the last potato, then took off her apron. "I must go."

Evelyn set down her knife and turned fully her way. "Please," she said, in a quiet undertone, "I don't know what theories you're working on, or why you're looking at us, but none of us could have done this. You must believe me. There isn't one member of this church who could've done this to Sarah."

The two of them stared at each other, Evelyn intense, Kate caught by the intensity. "I'd like to believe that," Kate said softly. "I really would."

Evelyn Dietz stared at Kate a moment longer, then, her eyes filling with tears, she turned away and went back to chopping the onions.

The meeting with Pastor Barnes went as she thought it would. He had a litany of complaints, ranging from her intrusion on a grief-stricken family to what he perceived as her total disregard for his church and the feelings and sensitivities of his parishioners. He also came close to accusing her of dereliction of duty by not concentrating on seeking a random killer from the world at large. As he spoke on and on, his face displayed a kindly concern, as a father's might lecturing a beloved but wayward daughter on the evil of her ways. He spared her the flow of biblical quotes she might've expected from a church leader, but he spared her none of the biblical reasonings behind his admonitions. Bemused, she studied him, but all she could detect behind his laments was a grave concern for the well-being of his church and his people.

What she hadn't expected was the presence of the other four

pastors. The meeting was held in the pastor's spacious, book-lined study, and all the men were arranged along the far wall like jurors in a courtroom. Pastor Barnes had put her on a straight chair centered in the room, facing the row of couches where four of the pastors sat. Matt stood apart from them by the window, leaning against the edge of a bookshelf, his body angled so he could see both the group and the view outside.

They were a diverse group of men, Kate thought. Nothing like her preconceived notion of what men of the cloth would be like. Particularly Pastor Bob. The Youth minister had tamed down his natural enthusiasm and vigor, and he sat as sober faced and quiet as the others, his eyes fastened on his senior pastor's face as the sermon went on. But his head continually bobbed in agreement with what was being said. He was the adoring disciple sitting at his master's feet, Kate summed up. And couldn't stop himself from being so.

Pastor Ellsworth, on the other hand, sat back and focused solely on her, a dark, brooding look in his eyes. His repudiation of her was plain. It was there in the way he looked with distaste at the slacks and blazer she wore, at the way her hair swung free when she moved her head, even the way she'd crossed her legs in the casual, relaxed pose she'd assumed for this meeting. To her, he was the archetypical puritanical preacher, stern, uncompromising, unforgiving. A strange leader for a church school professing to be grounded in loving guidance for all.

Pastor Lang was merely there. She suspected it was strictly at the behest of Pastor Barnes and for no other reason. He was late arriving, entering a couple of minutes after she had, and he never quite lost the pinched, worried look he'd worn hustling through the door. He tried to display the appropriate concern, nodding his head in agreement at several points the senior pastor made, but he still gave the impression that he had someplace more important to be, and this meeting was causing him a grievous loss of valuable time. The typical businessman? she wondered. Overbooked and understaffed? And though she never quite caught him at it, she suspected he was sneaking glances at the old-fashioned pendulum clock quietly ticking the seconds away on the wall behind her. Of the five, he showed the most discomfort and uneasiness at this session. And his eyes avoided hers completely.

Pastor Matt spent most of the time staring out at the tree shadows spreading across the lawns. The afternoon sun streamed in through the panes, lighting one side of his face while casting the other in deep shadow. It was an eerie effect, splitting his face in half, creating an image of half-saint, half-devil. Unaware of her scrutiny, he was lost in some private thoughts of his own, his face closed and remote, expressionless. The look reminded her again of Sam. Both men wore that same, closed-off expression that people had when they were having a mighty struggle within their souls. Was this man in as much misery as Sam was these days?

Pastor Barnes had finished his complaints about her, and moved on to a harder-pitched sell now. "You have to look at what we've accomplished here." A new list began. No drug or alcohol problems. No child abuse, no crime, no theft, no guns, no violence. The school hallways were safe, no fights, no lascivious conduct, just good clean wholesome youths going quietly about their business. And educationally, the students consistently rated in the top ten percent of the annual state testing programs. The home life was just as virtuous. No divorces; the family unit intact. Parents lived within their means, no debt beyond their home mortgages, and their families were clothed and well fed. The home life a happy, contented one, based on strong moral values and firm parental control. "We have carved a warm, caring, giving community in the midst of a world gone insane."

He'd leaned toward her as he'd spoken, his eyes intent on hers, the rich baritone voice hypnotic. He smelled of cologne. She became aware again of the great sensuality emanating from the man. He was not just a plump man, well fed, but a man, she judged, of vast and varied appetites, given to excesses in all things.

She fervently wished she had backup here. Sam. Wished he was sitting in on this, his own brooding eyes taking in the scene, absorbing everything, his mind running its quick and sure near-photographic tape for later analysis.

Pastor Barnes finally began to wind down. He gave a heavy sigh. "You see, Miss MacLean, Satan wears many different cloaks. Materialism, greed, lust, lack of faith in God . . . these are what we must strengthen the soul against. And that's why this church was founded. Do you see this now?"

This time his question was more than a rhetorical one and she finally spoke up. "I understand your rationale for founding the church and school," she said in a mild tone. "I'm not here to dispute the merits of either. I'm here strictly to solve a murder. And I fail to see how allowing me access to people who might have information I need is jeopardizing any part of what you've built."

"It implies that the killer is one of our congregation. And that's impossible."

Kate shook her head. "What's impossible is your church's denial that it could be possible."

Pastor Barnes gave an exasperated sigh. "Miss MacLean, you missed my point completely. My point is that if you're never exposed to a certain way of doing things in life, you won't know that it's out there to do. Let me simplify this for you. If you've never seen or heard of heroin, and you don't know it exists, then how would you know to shove a needleful of it in your arm? *That's* the kind of thing I'm talking about. If the concept of murder is unknown to you, how can you then kill?"

"Rage, Pastor Barnes," Kate said softly. "Simple rage. If you wished someone—and her problem—would go away, then it doesn't take a major leap of faith or a whole lot of knowledge of the outside world to come up with a way of making that happen. Death is the great silencer, and heroin needles and sawed-off shotguns aren't its only weapons. As a matter of fact, a most natural means was used on Sarah—a tree limb. How much closer to God's natural world can you get?"

Pastor Barnes looked at her with pity. "And you *still* miss my point, Miss MacLean. Even if the means and the desire are there, because of who we are and the upbringing we've had, no member of my congregation would cross the line between thought and action. Setting aside its grisly outcome, murder is no different than a dozen other sins I could name. Sloth, greed, lust, envy . . . we are all tempted by something at one time or another, by something as simple as coveting a pretty new dress to something as complex as coveting our neighbor's wife. That's why we have church Gospel—to help us resist those temptations. And if you don't succumb to the pretty dress or to the neighbor's wife, how in the *world* do you figure you'd succumb to the impulse to kill?" He shook his head. "That's what makes it impossible, don't you see?"

"You live in a world of high ideals, Pastor Barnes." Kate locked her gaze on his now, all pure intellect. "Tell me, Pastor Barnes, have you never had a deacon, a colleague, or a church member who makes you raise your eyes to the heavens in exasperation when you see them headed your way?"

"Publicly, no. Privately . . ." He shrugged. "Of course, Miss MacLean. We all know people who are difficult, a trial to deal with. But I wouldn't *kill* them to get them out of my hair."

"Raise the stakes," Kate said grimly. "If, in your eyes, they could do you irreparable harm, wouldn't you at least give it some thought?"

"Now we're back where we started. The line between thought and action. There is no situation bad enough that anyone in my church could get into that he couldn't come to any one of us"—his gesture included the other four pastors—"and receive guidance and understanding and counseling."

"And that's *my* point, Pastor Barnes," Kate replied. "Obviously, *someone* didn't feel he could."

"But that *someone* is definitely not from within my church!"

Kate put it crude and blunt. "So you're saying someone *outside the church* came along and got Sarah pregnant, then returned eight weeks later to kill her. Is that what you're saying?"

Charles Ellsworth could stand it no longer. All through Pastor Barnes's speech, sitting with his legs crossed, his agitation had increased, fingers drumming the couch arm, his foot oscillating like a hyperactive pendulum. As Kate had argued with the senior pastor, his face had darkened to thunder and now he could no longer hold back. "You keep insisting they're connected," he snapped. "First of all, the fact of Sarah's supposed pregnancy has *not* been proven to my satisfaction. There is virtually no way she could've gotten pregnant. Our whole school is structured to prevent such a thing from happening. I go to great lengths to make sure that there is no opportunity for any socializing whatsoever between the two sexes."

"The autopsy report's—"

"Hang the autopsy report! A mistake, obviously, by some overzealous bleeding heart out to destroy the very foundations of what we've so carefully built here!"

Kate stared at him, astonished. The other pastors looked startled.

"Charles . . ." Pastor Barnes started to say.

But Pastor Ellsworth was beyond restraint now, buoyed by a deep, fiery rage. "Furthermore, you keep on insisting that this phantom child and Sarah's death are connected. Don't you understand that this girl was left alone and unsupervised for the *first* time in her *life?* Don't you understand that means she was prey for every sick pervert roaming the streets your kind of people let roam that world out there? Yet you waste our time by stalking the innocent while a killer roams free, stirring up dissent and rumors among us, starting trouble everywhere! I've got kids crying in the hallways, I've got classrooms disrupted and schedules out of whack and a senior retreat destroyed, all because of you! You, and your stubborn refusal to listen to what we tell you—"

"*Charles!*" Pastor Barnes's voice boomed the name out.

Kate held up her palm to forestall him. "And don't you see, Pastor Ellsworth," she said in a deadly quiet voice, "how unlikely it would be that a pathological killer would happen to choose the *one* house out of thousands where *one* girl happened to be alone for the *one* time in her life? Think about it. And it isn't just any stranger you're talking about. You're talking about a psychotic stranger, who not only just happens upon her, but happens upon her when he's in a killing mood. No, Pastor Ellsworth, I'm sorry, but that theory's not going to fly."

Then she calmed herself down and leaned forward, hands gripped together in her lap, her face serious and intent. "You know, Pastor Ellsworth, I would love it to be that psychotic stranger. I truly would. I don't like going in and stirring up all manner of suspicion and trouble any more than you like me doing it. I don't like hurting people. But murder does hurt. It hurts a lot more people than simply the victim. When the killer is unmasked there's going to be a profound sense of betrayal on the part of his family and friends. I take no joy in that. I take no joy in inflicting that kind of agony on anyone. You're angry with the wrong person, Pastor Ellsworth. You should be directing that rage of yours toward the guilty party, not toward the police."

Pastor Ellsworth drew in a deep breath, ready to blast her again, when Pastor Barnes leaned over and gripped his arm. *"Charles, that's enough!"*

Under the stern visage of the senior pastor and the unrelenting grip on his arm, Pastor Ellsworth exhaled a long, slow breath and finally regained control of himself. The red gradually faded from his face and the wildness went out of his eyes and he looked around now at the other pastors surrounding him. Pastor Bob smiled encouragingly, as he might at a kindergartner coming out of a tantrum. Pastor Lang was frowning, looking at Ellsworth as if he were a puzzling and unidentifiable specimen under glass. Pastor Matt was fully turned into the room now, leaning back against the bookshelves with his arms crossed, studying the angry man, his face thoughtful.

When Pastor Barnes was sure the man had a grip on himself, he patted his arm then turned his attention back to Kate. "You see, Miss MacLean?" he said quietly. "Emotions are churning like that everywhere. I believe you, Miss MacLean, when you say you don't like hurting people—"

His office phone rang, bringing him to a sudden halt. He frowned at it as if it shouldn't even be in the room. When it rang a second time, however, he gave in to the inevitable, rose and crossed the room to answer it.

He listened a moment, then held the receiver out to Kate. "It's for you."

Kate took the receiver and identified herself. It was Dispatch at Headquarters. She listened, asked a couple of quiet questions, then listened some more. "All right, Phil, I'll be there right away. Ring Sam's desk for me, please. Tell him to go to the Captain and get himself busted loose any way he can, then have him meet me at the state park."

Hand trembling slightly, she returned the phone to the cradle.

She stared a long moment at the wall behind the desk, at a beautiful oil painting of the Crucifixion. Her thoughts tumbled around her brain like balls in a lotto cage, and she stayed put until she had herself well in hand. Then she turned to the others. "I'm sorry, I must go," she said in a low voice. "There's been another killing."

The news sliced through the air like a sword.

The pastors stared at her.

"Who?" Pastor Matt finally asked.

She met his gaze directly, but kept a peripheral eye on all the others. "Peter Dickerson."

Chapter Seventeen

The mid-afternoon rays of a cresting sun found a crack in the thick foliage around the clearing at Bridle Trails State Park and turned the blond hair of Peter Dickerson into a halo of deep gold. He lay near the same spot where Sarah Taft had been found, sprawled face down, arms and legs askew. The underside of his skull was smashed in. Drying blood crusted over the back of his head like a black slash burn across a field of golden hay. Except for a couple of birds chirping and trilling in the treetops around Kate, the woods were still and silent.

There'd been no rain in days now, and the wild grass of the clearing was patched with brown where the sun's rays had reached in to bake it dry. Still on the path, she squatted down and her glance skimmed the heat-dead grass. A lot of the brittle blades were broken at half-mast. He'd met someone there, she theorized, they'd talked or whatever, then Peter had turned to leave and the killer had swung, catching him unawares. There was plenty of room to swing even a long tree branch and still clear the forested perimeter. There was no sign of a tree limb or a dead branch anywhere.

She got out her notebook and began sketching the scene and taking notes on her observations. The whole time she wrote, her mind kept asking, Why? Why, Peter? Why you?

A hail from down the trail interrupted her before she'd finished. Sam came into sight around a bend, followed by the long, easy stride of Len Franklin. They came up to her and for a moment, the three stood side by side on the path, staring at the dead body. Len Franklin squatted down and saw the broken grass, then began picking his way out to the body, following a path where the blades were unharmed. Sam and Kate stayed put, watching him do a cursory of the body.

After a moment, Franklin retraced his steps to their side. "On the surface," he said thoughtfully, "it looks the same as Sarah. Blunt blow to the back of the head. Bits of bark mixed in there, so it was probably a branch, same as with Sarah. But it looks like there was more than one blow this time. A couple, at least. I won't be able to tell until I get in there with a scalpel."

"How long ago?" Kate asked.

Len eyed the body, considering it. "Rigor's just setting in, the small muscles are involved and the neck's stiff, so he's been dead at least four hours. There's no blanching when the skin's pressed in. So that makes it five hours after death. Cornea's milky and cloudy, that happens after six to eight hours. And the skin's cool, but not cold." He swiveled and eyed the sun, then followed its trajectory backward across the sky. "It's just after three now. If that sun hit the clearing full-force midday, keeping the body temperature up, I'm going to guess early morning. If it didn't, I'm going to say mid-morning. When he's on the table, I'll work out definite times from the temperature of the body. It'd also be helpful to know when he ate last. Broadly, though, I'm going to guess between seven and ten A.M. Certainly no earlier or no later. And it's more than likely eight to nine."

Kate stared moodily at the body. "Can you do DNA tests on a dead man?"

"Sure. What've you got in mind? Comparisons to the fetal tissue from Sarah's baby?"

She nodded. "I'd like to prove he definitely was the father."

Sam was shaking his head. "I don't know. Those tests cost an arm and a leg, and the Captain's got a bottom-line mentality these days."

Money, Kate thought. It always came down to money. It affected everything—manpower, equipment, cars, computers, even the damned forensics lab—they lived in a technological age and couldn't afford any of it. "What about blood tests then? Can you type the baby's blood against his?"

"Sure, that's not a problem," Franklin said. "But you have to remember, Katie, that's just an elimination test. If the mother's O-positive, and the daddy's A-positive, for instance, and the baby's B-positive, then we'll know he's not the daddy. He's eliminated. But if Dickerson comes up a match, all we can say is that he *could* be the father. Along with any other male of his blood type."

"Was the baby B-positive?" Kate asked.

"I'd have to check back on that. I honestly don't remember."

"But you did type the baby's blood," Kate pushed.

"Not to worry," Len assured her. "Not only did I type it, I preserved some fetal tissue on the off-chance it'd be needed."

She separated herself from the two men, walking a pace or two to the side, and studied the sprawling body once again. There was a casual violence to this that bothered her. Mentally, she retrieved the image of Sarah lying there, hands folded across her chest, clothes neatly arranged, lying peacefully in her wooded bower. But Peter's body lay crumpled as it had fallen. There'd been no effort at arranging him as had been done with Sarah. Had the killer been interrupted at his work by a rider ambling down the trail?

No. The lengthy time before discovery argued against that. The body was clearly visible from the path, and anyone riding by couldn't help but see it. And it would've been reported immediately.

A noise then? Spooking the killer into *thinking* someone was coming?

Possibly. The faint roar of freeway traffic snaked its way

through the trees. Other than that and a bird squawk or two, the silence of the woods was complete. Even the sounds of a parking lot full of squad cars crunching over gravel didn't penetrate this far.

She moved back to Len with a sudden question. "Would either of the victims have cried out when they were hit?" she asked him.

He shook his head. "Doubtful. They'd go black instantly. Maybe an 'oof' as the breath rushed out of their lungs when they hit the ground. But, no, I wouldn't think so. That kind of a whack on the skull snaps the lights off instantly. Especially a surprise whack."

"A whack," Kate repeated, taken with the phrase. "A whack. Pretty strong person to do that."

"Pretty strong person," Sam put in. "Or pretty strong rage."

Kate gave him a thoughtful look. A filmstrip of all the people she'd interviewed to date ran past her mind's eye. Pastor Barnes and Norman Overholtz were among the strongest who came to mind. And Pastor Ellsworth had certainly displayed his capacity for rage. Did these two kids die because they'd ruined his school's perfect zero pregnancy record?

Len stirred. "Time to get to work. If all your questions are satisfied, for now?" He raised an eyebrow at each of them.

They both nodded. "Thanks, Len," Kate said.

His blue eyes lost some of their professional coolness as he looked at her. "Nice to see you again. But let's make it in more pleasant surroundings next time, like a dinner table."

Deadpan, Sam looked up at the sky. "Oh, my, the vultures certainly are circling."

For a moment, Kate took him literally, and glanced upwards, too. Then his meaning dawned on her and she flushed. She couldn't think of a damned thing to say. She gave him a wry look and started back up the trail to the parking lot.

Pastor Barnes was standing in the parking lot off by himself, looking uncomfortable and out of place among the uniformed cops scattered around the area. They had agreed in his office that he would be the only one at the scene. They'd also agreed that the other pastors would say nothing to anyone about this. Sarah's visitation, scheduled for that evening, was enough of a strain on his parishioners, Pastor Barnes had stated, without adding the drama of a fresh death to it. Kate had concurred. At the moment, silence was to her benefit.

Now, he stood with arms crossed, a slight scowl on his face. Kate stopped just short of the edge of the woods and tried to decipher the man behind the scowl.

Who was this man, really? she wondered. Founder of a church, a visionary, idealist, certainly. Seeking perfection in an imperfect world. Just how did he deal with the human foibles of his flock? Did he take each as it came, guiding the wayward soul, providing enlightenment according to Christian Gospel? Or did he, instead, ignore moral weaknesses, pretending they didn't exist? Or did he sweep them aside as of no importance, a mere hiccup in a mortal's climb to heavenly perfection?

And why the scowl? At events out of his control? Forced to mingle with elements and people beyond his ken? Or simply a busy man with important things to do, forced to cool his heels in a graveled parking lot as the wheels of justice did their slow bump and grind.

Suddenly she was angry with him. Deeply angry. He with his kindly face and visionary soul had blocked her at every twist and turn. If only he'd accepted the fact that a serpent lurked within his professional Eden and had allowed her full access to his church population, then maybe that boy wouldn't be lying dead in the woods back there.

His scanning glance spotted her, and his scowl deepened as he headed her way. She stayed put, waiting and watching. As he walked, the scowl transformed into a frown of concern. "Is it really Peter?"

She made a sudden snap decision and beckoned him to follow her, then she led him along the darkening path to the clearing where Len and his men were working. She lengthened her stride the last few steps so that she was well into the clearing and turned around, facing him, before he cleared the last of the woods. It was time he dealt with reality, not visions, and she wanted a good look at his face as he saw the result of the killer's work.

He stopped dead at the sight of the body crumpled in a heap in the clearing, then backed up a step in involuntary recoil. "No," he whispered in protest. Shock, pain, grief moved across his features in turn, and his body sagged with despair. "This can't go on, you know . . ."

Kate was ready for him. "Then tell your people to cooperate with us," she said simply.

Confusion mixed in with the pain. "I haven't told them not to," he protested.

Kate wasn't going to let that pass. "Pastor Barnes, you and your entire congregation have closed ranks against me."

"These are good people, Miss MacLean."

"Good people often get into strange corners. Sarah Taft *was* pregnant. That baby inside of her *was* a real baby, not some phantom fetus. And chances are better than excellent that we have the father of the child lying here. Now if you had an unmarried mother-to-be killed, and the likely father-to-be killed, what else could the motives behind the murders be except the baby? Yet, I have been stonewalled at every turn. I need you to get up on your pulpit and command your congregation to cooperate. Because—make no mistake about it—I *will* get to the bottom of this. I'll do it with you, or I'll do it without you, but I *will* do it. And no amount of Bible-thumping is going to stop me."

She'd gone a bit further in her speech than she'd intended, but surprisingly, he took it rather well. He simply nodded and said, "I'll see to it."

And he would, she believed.

She led him back to where some of the uniformed patrol guarded the trails. "Stay put," she said to him. "This'll take a while." When he started to protest, she simply raised a palm to stop him. "These things take time." She turned away from him and headed up to the riding arena.

It was the same picnic table, the same thermos of coffee and the same two women sitting in the afternoon sun.

They both watched Kate approach, and without asking, Barb Denton poured some coffee into one of the Styrofoam cups stacked there. "I'm sorry," she said as she handed the cup to Kate. "I should've kept a better watch."

Kate shook her head. "You can't baby-sit every inch of this place. If you had been guarding the clearing, chances are the killer would've simply taken the boy to a different section of the park. Are you both okay?"

When she'd received double nods that yes, they were fine, she focused in on Lucy Gray. "Okay, Lucy, tell me what happened."

Lucy's report was brief and succinct, put in the kind of simple, clear terms the Captain would appreciate. Since Sarah's death, she'd started reading books about murders, and had learned that predictability was a killer's best friend, so she'd taken to riding Maisie at different times of the day now. Today she'd come over about two-thirty, had worked Maisie in the arena for fifteen minutes or so, then had started out for the day's trail ride, heading south to check the clearing, as she did every day now. She'd seen the boy lying there, knew at once he was dead, and she'd done the same thing she'd done when she found Sarah, she'd hightailed it out of there and hunted up Barb Denton. "He wasn't there yesterday," Lucy finished up simply, "and there he was today."

"Were you around here anytime this morning?" Kate asked.

Lucy shook her head. "I was on the phone all morning."

Kate wasn't thrilled to hear that. Especially when the button-bright eyes didn't quite meet hers. "Doing what on the phone?"

"Just visiting around a bit."

Kate bit back a sigh. A vague answer from a very *un*-vague person. *Now* what had she been up to? But she'd have to pursue that later, she decided, and turned to Barb Denton.

"What time did you arrive this morning?"

"My usual," Barb answered calmly. "I left headquarters at ten, and pulled in here fifteen or twenty minutes later."

"Was there anyone here? Any cars? Any bikes?"

"No. The park was empty."

Then Peter was already dead, Kate thought. And the killer well away from the area.

The second murder, though, gave her an advantage. It definitely eliminated any of the Saddle Club members from suspicion. It was all linked to the church now. Which left her free to make use of some civilian help here. "Here's what I want you to do," she said to both of them. "Split the list of Saddle Club members between you and get in touch with everyone. Talk to everyone who was in the park this morning before ten, and see if anyone saw the boy. Or anyone else who might've been here. Write down the time they were here, take down any names they give you, get detailed descriptions of the people they saw, especially strangers, have them describe any cars or bicycles that might've been here, make, model, color and so forth, and write down any license plate numbers they might've noticed."

Barb nodded with a professional calm. Lucy's eyes widened and her straight spine straightened even further.

Kate smiled at them. "And, as my Captain would say, I want it all done yesterday."

She thought Lucy was going to salute.

She walked at a slow pace back toward the parking area. Her mind was clicking now like a computer doing calculations at warp speed. Who was alibied for Monday afternoon around four-thirty?

She stopped walking and ran down a mental checklist. Lucy Gray was here at the park, finding the body. Daniel Taft, at work until five. Martha Taft, sitting with a sick man until six. Nancy Wells, on the bus to the retreat. The school secretary, at work in the school office. And Terry White at the day-care center. She'd check those last two to find when their workdays ended, but for now, they were on the alibied list.

She skipped the churchwomen in the basement for the moment. God help her if she had to start examining their whereabouts and motives.

Now who was left? Norm, working alone in his dorm on his term paper. Patty Jacobson, her whereabouts unknown, probably drifting, but where?

And the pastors.

Their budget session had broken up at three. They all agreed with that. Matt had said he'd spent the next couple of hours preparing for some counseling sessions that night. No alibi there.

And the other four?

Good question. Damned good question.

Then doubt set in. A man of the cloth committing murder? Could that be?

But then she doubted the doubt. She was assigning them virtues because of their professional roles and her own perceptions of what a pastor should be, rather than basing it on the reality of who and what they were as people. She put them back on her mental list and began moving toward the parking area again.

There was a large cluster of vehicles on the scene now. Some squad cars, a couple of tech vans, a Medical Examiner's van, her car, Sam's, the pastor's and the M.E.'s. So far, Goddard and Fry hadn't shown up yet. That was good news, she hoped. Lucy's rig was drawn off to one side as it had been before, with Maisie hitched to the end of the trailer. Kate spared a glance for the horse, again admiring its gleaming flanks. If she lived in Montana or Wyoming, she could have one.

She was turning away from the rig when she caught sight of a bike parked well back in the shadows, its front wheel stuck between two low fir branches to hold the bike upright. She walked to it slowly, eyeing it. A red Huffy, full-sized, three-speed, with a bar running across the center from seat to handlebar. A boy's bike. Without touching anything, or treading on any soft dirt that might've held footprints or scuff marks, she examined it. It wasn't an expensive bike, by any means, and it certainly wasn't new, but it had been well maintained. The fenders looked waxed, the spokes gleamed even in the shade, and the vinyl seat looked like it had had a good scrubbing recently.

She looked over to where Sam and the techies were conferring and raised one arm, catching their eyes, beckoning them over, then pointed to the bike.

"What do you think?" Sam asked Kate. "Could it be Peter's?"

She looked over to where Pastor Barnes stood by himself, still pasty-faced from shock. "I don't know," she murmured. She caught the Pastor's eye and beckoned him over, too.

He made his way to her side, thoroughly chastened now, and waited to see what she wanted.

She pointed toward the bike. "Would that be Peter's?"

He stared at it as if it belonged to some off-beat religious sect. "I don't know, I really don't know which of our young people have bicycles and which don't."

She nodded. That would've been too much to hope for. "We'll be heading for the Dickersons pretty soon now. We'll ask them." Then she tilted her head to one side. "By the way, Peter was killed between seven and ten this morning. What were you doing during those hours?"

Her gaze was as unyielding as the Captain's as she watched a slow horror spread across his face.

Satisfied that he finally understood the true nature of her job, she turned away from him. She'd get the answer to that one later.

Alice Dickerson answered the door when Pastor Barnes rang the bell. She was wearing a simple navy blue dress with dark blue shoes. Headed for Sarah's visitation, Kate thought, standing on the front step next to the Pastor. Sam stood behind her.

She'd shown signs of tension, almost an irritability, when she yanked the door open, as if she'd been expecting someone else and was ready to give whoever it was a piece of her mind. She'd been so focused on her anticipated caller that it took a moment for her to adjust to the reality of who was actually at the door. She stared blankly at them a moment. A stranger who looked like a cop, a lady who was a cop, and her pastor. Then understanding and knowledge came at once. "Peter," she whispered with dread. For a moment, her whole body sagged. Face, trunk, limbs. "Oh, my God, Peter."

Pastor Barnes didn't deny it. "Is Larry home?"

For a second, she stared at him, uncomprehending. Then she shook herself, drew up straight, and with as much dignity as she could manage, she backed away from the door. She nodded and gestured them in.

As she led them into the living room, a hearty male voice called from the rear of the house, "Honey? Was that Peter?"

"Larry?" the pastor called back. "It's Thomas Barnes."

From another part of the house, a young and chirpy voice rang out, "It's Pastor, it's Pastor, Douglas! Let's go see him!"

The floor vibrated with the thumps of running feet and a girl about nine and a boy a couple of years younger ran out from the hallway, the girl leading. Her face turned from cheery welcome to startled shyness as she caught sight of Sam and Kate standing there. She braked to such a sudden stop that her brother smashed into her back. She put out a hand to stop his sideways skid, and he regained his balance, then peered at the strangers over the outflung arm.

Pastor Barnes went to them, bent down and hugged each one. Then he said quietly, "I need to talk to your folks alone for a while. Can you stay in your rooms and play quietly while I do that?"

The little girl's blue eyes rounded at the seriousness of his tone. "Is it about Peter?" she asked. "He's been gone all afternoon, and nobody knows where he is, and he's in big trouble with Mom and Dad." Her eyes turned to her mother for confirmation.

Alice Dickerson stared unseeingly straight ahead, arms rigid at her sides, hands clenched.

Fear crept into the girl's face. "What's wrong with Mommy?" Tears began to well as fright took hold.

"Go along now," Pastor Barnes said gently. "We'll explain it all to you later."

The girl was reluctant, but obedient. She ushered her brother back down the hallway, directing backward glances at all of them until she was out of sight.

Larry Dickerson strode into the room through the dining room archway. "Sorry, Thomas. Blood-sugar problem. Had to get something on my stomach."

He was father to the son, Kate thought. Tall, lean, sandy hair, with a pleasant, open expression. He directed a welcome, if slightly puzzled smile toward the two detectives, then strode across the room, toward Thomas, hand outstretched, ready for the greeting. Then he caught sight of his wife.

As soon as he'd appeared, her eyes had gone to him, silently beseeching him for help. Now he faltered, and the outstretched hand fell back to his side as he paused. He veered to her side instead of going on to the pastor and encircled her shoulders with an arm. "What's going on? What's wrong, Thomas?" Then he seemed to take a mental tally of his family and paled. "Is it Peter? Has something happened to Peter?"

Pastor Barnes gave a simple nod. Then he gestured toward the couch and chairs grouped around. "Let's sit down a minute, please."

Guarded and watchful now, Larry tightened his arm around his wife's shoulder and guided her to the couch.

Pastor Barnes wasted no time. Looking Larry directly in the eyes, he said quietly, "Peter was found late this afternoon in Bridle Trails State Park. The same place where Sarah was found." He was seated closest to the couple, and he reached across empty space and took a hand from each parent in his own and gently squeezed them. "I'm terribly sorry, but he's dead, I'm afraid."

There was a clock somewhere out of sight in the dining room, and the silence magnified the ticks until they merged and blended with Kate's own heartbeat and one became the other, impossible to distinguish.

The thick stillness was broken by a sharp "No!" Alice's voice cracked out like a whipshot. "No!" Her eyes were wild as she looked from detectives to the pastor and back again. "I don't believe it. It can't be! He was at the table for breakfast this morning. He's going to visitation tonight. He's looking forward to the summer. He's going to college next year. This can't be! It just can't happen like that! Here this morning and gone now? It *can't* happen that way!"

Larry Dickerson simply clutched his wife closer, pushing her head down onto his shoulder until her verbal protests subsided. Then he gave a sharp shake of the head, as if to ward off dizziness, and asked hoarsely, "How? What in God's name happened?"

Pastor Barnes slumped back in his chair, his face filled with defeat. "The same as Sarah, Lord help us," he said in a weary voice. He motioned toward Sam and Kate. "They can tell you about it."

Briefly, Kate described what they knew about it. Which was little until the autopsy report came in. When the details had been given, the parents sat silently, struggling with disbelief.

Finally, Alice, still in the tight grasp of her husband, straightened up, separating herself from him. Her eyes were clearing now, the initial wildness of the trapped animal replaced by intelligence as her mind began to function. "I don't understand," she said slowly. "How could this happen? Why wasn't he in school?"

"I don't have an answer for that yet," Kate responded. "You mentioned having breakfast with him this morning. How did he seem? Was he worried, or preoccupied at all? Was there anything he did or said that would indicate he planned any change of routine?"

Alice stared off into space, then gave a weary shake of the head. "Nothing that comes to mind. He ate most of his breakfast. His appetite's been a bit off, because of Sarah, you know. And he hasn't been as cheerful and as outgoing as he usually is. But he's been that way since Thursday. Her death really hit him hard."

Kate took her notebook out and opened to a fresh page. "What exactly did he have for breakfast?"

Slowly, factually, keeping it calm and low-keyed, she elicited the morning's routine. At six forty-five, Peter had had breakfast. A bowl of Cheerios, toast, some orange juice and a glass of milk. Afterwards, he'd gone in to brush his teeth, then had left to catch the school bus at 7:10. Yes, all the children took the same bus. His brother and sister rode the bus with him.

"You're sure he got on the bus this morning?" Kate asked.

Alice's eyes widened at the implications of that. "He left the house with the two younger ones. He acted like he was going to."

"Does he own a bike?"

"Yes."

"What kind?"

Larry fielded that one. "It's an old Huffy. A red one. Three-speed. We got it secondhand from a neighbor and Peter fixed it up."

The same as the one she'd noticed at the state park. Kate dropped the issue of the bike. There was time to identify it later. Right now, she accepted it as the way he'd gotten to the state park. "Did he leave any note or message for you when he left this morning?"

Alice shook her head.

"How about phone calls? Did anyone call him this morning? Did he call anyone?"

Alice shook her head again. "No, he got up, he got dressed, he ate his breakfast, made his bed, and left for school."

"What about last night? Did he get a call last night, did anyone drop by to see him, did he get in touch with anyone?"

"No, we weren't home. We were at the Tafts. All of us." Then Alice remembered Sarah and tears overwhelmed her again momentarily.

Kate eyed her with sympathy. To give her some time to regain control, she directed her next question to Larry. "Exactly who was at the Tafts' with you last night?"

"Hang on, I'd have to think about it." He drew himself together and concentrated a minute. "Lots of people. We were there a couple of hours, and we probably saw half the church come through."

Kate was afraid of that. But there had to be contact somewhere between the killer and Peter. Somehow, Peter had to know to go to the park this morning, and the killer had to know Peter would be there. "Try," she urged. "Try separating out the families."

He did what he could, but it came out a jumble of names as unknown as a page in a phone book. Kate and Sam both took them down as they were spoken to compare lists and cover any omissions either of them would've made. The only ones Kate recognized were the Hickmans, Nancy Wells, Terry White from the day-care center, and Norm Overholtz. And the pastors. All five of whom had managed to stop in sometime during the two-hour period. Everyone else was a newcomer to the case. The pastors had really hurt her by restricting her access to the general congregation.

"Who'd he talk to while he was there?"

Larry looked at his wife, then shrugged. "Everyone, I guess." She nodded agreement.

No help there, Kate thought. "Did he say anything when he got home? Did he mention talking to anyone special, did he mention making a date or an appointment with anyone, or was he surprised to see some one person or another there?"

"No," Alice answered, "he went straight to his room. He's taken this hard and we gave him some privacy. He was too broken up to talk."

"Did he ever offer any theories about Sarah's death? Speculating on the reasons for it, or who might've done it, or anything like that?"

"No," she whispered, shaking her head.

Kate surveyed both parents, taking stock of their emotional condition. They were strong people, struggling to maintain control in the face of horrendous news. The question-and-answer routine had helped in its way, but they were about at the end of their emotional reserves. She set aside her notebook and leaned forward in her chair, forearms resting on her thighs, and tried to ask her next question without implying criticism of any kind. "The school and church is very strict about allowing their children any freedom. Is there any reason, or anything so important, that Peter would disregard his entire upbringing in order to skip school and meet someone at a state park?"

The parents gave it hard thought. Larry finally shook his head, no. Alice considered it longer, then she raised red-rimmed eyes to Kate. "Only Sarah. She's the only one who would have had that kind of influence on him. And she wouldn't have done such a thing. She wouldn't have made him do this." Her eyes were filling again and the first tears topped the lower lash and trickled down her cheek. It was the start of a flood and she gave in to them at last. She laid her head on her husband's shoulder and wept. Her control was at an end.

Kate let her be. "We're going to have to search his room, Mr. Dickerson," she said in an undertone. "We'll need your permission."

He gave a distracted nod, then tightened his arms around his wife, gathering her in even closer and burying his face in her hair.

The pastor had sat quietly through the whole session, obviously not feeling the need to interfere and control and obstruct as he had with Sarah's parents. His own voice was hoarse from choked-back emotions. "They have a rec room downstairs. I'll take them and the children there. Just give us a moment or two."

Kate watched as Pastor Barnes first shepherded the parents down the stairs, then went to the back of the main floor and gathered the two younger children. He led them out, one small hand in each of his, and they clung close to his side as they passed the two detectives, eyes wide with both fear and fascination. "Second door on the left," the pastor said, then he led the children down the stairs and out of sight.

* * *

Peter's room was in a front corner of the house, with windows on two walls. It was a typical boy's room, painted blue, with a simple wooden bedstead covered by a plain white chenille spread and a wooden dresser that had been stained a dark oak. Three airplane models hung from the ceiling near a battered student's desk, and a couple of battleships roamed the seas of shelves that climbed the wall above it. A cheerful braided rug covered the carpeting between bed and windows.

Sam took the closet and Kate took the desk. The back side of the desk against the wall was lined with stacks of books and notebooks. A supplemental textbook on World War II lay to one side of the plain blotter, with strips of white paper marking various places extruding from the top. Index cards filled with notes and looseleaf sheets of lined paper covered by a large, loopy scrawl indicated a term paper in progress. An old portable typewriter, an Olivetti, stood upright in its case on the floor nearby. Obviously, he wasn't far enough along to start the typing yet. A plain water glass operated as a pen and pencil holder.

A small assignment notebook was carefully placed in a back corner of the blotter. Kate picked it up and leafed through it. Each week had its own double spread of pages, and homework assignments were entered as they were accumulated, then checked off with a red mark when completed. An occasional line-out traded one assignment for another, otherwise all had been checked off since the beginning of the school year. A very organized young man, she thought.

The organization ended, though, at this past week. Monday's, Tuesday's, and Wednesday's assignments were the same as the rest . . . marked down and checked off. The previous day, however, was written helter-skelter, with heavily drawn boxes beside it, and the word *Sarah* printed in bold, thick capital block letters across Thursday's space. A series of blackened crosses trailed down the page margins. Schoolwork had suddenly lost its importance. There was no entry for Friday yet. And he'd left the notebook home, she thought. Had he known he wouldn't be needing it? Thoughtfully, she set it to one side.

Sam had finished with the closet and was searching the dresser drawers. Kate looked over at him. "Anything?" she asked.

He shook his head, frustrated. "Not even a dirty magazine."

"That'd be under the mattress, wouldn't it?" she said, lightly. "Isn't that where you guys stash stuff like that?"

"There you go with your stereotypes again. That's the first place mothers check."

"So where? Secret panels, like in the Hardy Boys?"

"The rug's a possibility."

She eyed it doubtfully. "I'll let you have the pleasure." She started in on the desk drawers.

Nothing. Paper supplies. A box of number two pencils. Rulers, a stapler, paper clips, a manual pencil sharpener, an assortment of erasers. One drawer held all the Bible school information from Northwest College . . . the student handbook, the college bulletin, a copy of his application and his letter of acceptance. The bottom drawer held a pile of used notebooks from past years, and underneath were a couple of simple drawings of airplanes made during grammar school art, washed with watercolor.

She closed the drawer and sat back to think. She'd found nothing personal. No letters, no Christmas cards, no nostalgic reminders of dances or other school affairs. Nothing beyond the airplanes and the battleship models on the shelves to indicate any personal interests beyond school. This kid had to be an honor student, she decided, he was so neat and tidy. Which was what every parent dreamed of, but was of no help to a cop.

She eyed the bedside table, an old square wooden one up on high legs with a lamp and an alarm clock on top, and a single drawer in the center. Maybe . . . She pushed back from the desk, opened the drawer and riffled through the junk. A Bible, with a soft, leatherlike cover; a small, slender softcover book, *The New Teen's Topical Bible*; an old sheet of assembly instructions for a model airplane; a bookseller's ad clipped from a newspaper, with a title on early planes circled in red; a peeling, wooden yo-yo that looked older than she was, with pocked edges that a puppy might've chewed. She thumbed through the Bible, but there were no margin notes, nothing marked. The wrinkles running the length of the spine indicated long-term use, and the gold cloth place holder was tucked into the Book of Revelation. One line in Verse Seventeen, Chapter Seven was marked by a penciled asterisk in the margin: *. . . and God shall wipe away all tears from their eyes.* Sadly, she replaced it in the drawer.

She picked up the Topical Bible next. It had no place holder, but again, the spine was well broken in. The cover leaf was inscribed by Pastor Barnes as a gift to one Peter Dickerson on the occasion of his thirteenth birthday. The table of contents was divided into chapter headings, with specific topics listed under each. They all dealt with some aspect of a teen's life, from building a relationship with God and your parents, to overcoming adversity, both inner as well as outward. Love, guilt, lust, sin, grief, even the subjects of masturbation and homosexuality were dealt with through Bible verses appropriate to each topic. She leafed through the book, scanning some of the verses as she went. The ones selected for inclusion reiterated the same theme—avoid temptation at the cost of your eternal soul. Still, she was impressed in spite of herself. Woodhaven Church undertook the education and training of the whole person, leaving nothing to chance.

Which made the likelihood of Sarah's pregnancy all the more impossible to understand. How, with the strict controls imposed by home, school and church, had the two of them found any chance at all to be alone together? Never mind going against a lifetime of conditioning against all sin to indulge in the sexual act?

Sure enough, Sam was rolling up the braided rug. Kate moved to the side window, out of his way. She watched him a moment or two, struggling with the soft, awkward weight of the rug, then swung around to stare out the window. From the road, the ground sloped sharply up from the curb to reach its apex at the window before dropping off at a steep pitch to the backyard, level with the walk-out basement. A rhododendron in a deep shade of pink similar to the one she'd planted a year ago was riotously in bloom. She stared at it a moment before the import of what she was seeing hit her.

The plant was set to one side of the window, close to the corner where it would be a showpiece of the front landscaping. The window itself was a broad slider, and while the fixed half of it hovered above the huge rhodie, the part that slid out of the way had nothing below it but a garden space between plants. That section was screened, but the screen had the little tabs inside for removal for easy cleaning of the outside of the windowpane. It was no more than a couple of feet from windowsill to ground. "Sam? Come here a minute. Look at this."

He missed it, too, at first glance. He saw the rhodie and nodded. "Just about the same shade as the one you planted last year."

"Now look straight down."

He got it then, and gave a soundless whistle. "So. A few stolen midnight hours, you think?"

"Could be." She leaned against the window frame. "He was tall, long-legged and slender. A good athletic build. It wouldn't have been that hard for him to climb in and out, would it?"

"I shouldn't think so. Either of us could probably do it." He returned to rolling up the rug. Nothing there. He replaced it and surveyed the room. Everything was as they'd found it. They'd both been careful not to leave the room looking as if it had been tossed. "Did you come up with anything at all?" he asked.

"Nothing much. His school assignment notebook's here on his desk. As far as I can tell, it's the first time he's missed taking it to school. Unless he kept it at home full-time and recopied assignment notes in it each night. But I don't think so. They were too random, written at different times, sometimes pen and sometimes pencil. So why didn't he take it with him today?"

"You think he planned to play hooky?"

She was silent a moment, trying to think it through. "He was basically an obedient kid, Sam. He knew he shouldn't be skipping school and going to the park. So which would he do, show up late and hope to explain it away, or not show up at all, figuring that by Monday he'd come up with some excuse to cover his absence? Which would you do?"

Sam joined her at the window, leaning against the opposite frame, facing her. "I can't answer that," he said with a slight smile. "I was never an obedient kid."

She looked at him curiously. "Did you ever skip school?"

"Now and then. Especially the last couple of years. I didn't have a lot of patience with school by then. It was obvious some of the teachers didn't care, so I didn't either."

She smiled at him. She believed it. Sam wasn't the type to suffer fools gracefully. Then her smile faded as she turned and looked back at the room. Nothing. Not a note, not a name, not an initial, not a doodle. "Seen enough?"

He nodded. "Let's go."

In the basement, they stopped at the door to the rec room. Pastor Barnes was reading to the tear-streaked family from the Bible, his voice deep, sonorous, but muted. It was hypnotic, Kate thought, the way his rich voice carried them along in quiet waves of emphasis. There was assurance in it, comfort in it, a lulling of concerns in it. And faith. The faith came clear. As did the sorrow. But somehow, he made it seem bearable.

She waited until he'd finished, then as the parents bowed their head in prayer together with the two young children, she beckoned the pastor to the doorway. "Please tell the Dickersons we're through. And thank them for their cooperation."

The little girl had started weeping again in her father's arms. Kate turned away and followed Sam out to their cars.

Chapter Eighteen

They returned to headquarters and were called immediately into a meeting by the Captain. Hatch sat back in his chair at his weary worst, fingers steepled beneath his chin, black brows dipped in a deep frown, as he listened to Kate's report all the way through.

Her investigation to date had been based on the theory that Sarah's death had been caused by a father-to-be panicked by an unwelcome pregnancy. Now, no matter how she argued it, Peter's death had destroyed that theory. If he was the baby's father, who killed them both? And if he wasn't, that meant the pregnancy was coincidental to the murder, and if it was coincidental, then why did these particular two kids have to die?

When she'd finished, Hatch grunted and summed it up it one sentence. "In other words, you lost the boyfriend and blew the motive all to hell."

There was nothing to say to that. Kate and Sam both stayed silent.

Hatch expelled a heavy sigh. "All right. What's next?"

"We look for a new motive," she said tiredly. Hatch's weariness was catching.

"Outraged parents." Hatch made it a statement.

"They're alibied," she responded.

"Outraged pastors."

She stayed silent.

"Outraged congregation."

She stayed silent on that one, too. He was goading her now.

His eyes bored into hers. "In other words, you don't have a clue."

Kate stirred restlessly in the hard side chair. There was nowhere to go with this. What was she supposed to do, identify the killer by serendipity?

Sam spoke up then. "Look, it's only been forty-eight hours since Sarah was found," he said in a reasonable tone. "The church has several hundred members. And Katie hasn't had a great deal of help and assistance on the case. From any quarter. Either church or bullpen."

Hatch let his gaze move slowly from Kate to Sam, then fixed him with a long stare. "Well, that's not *my* fault," he drawled in a mild tone. His eyes were pure muck. "*You're* the one who wanted a desk job."

Sam's mouth tightened at the rebuke. "If you're upset with me, deal with me directly. Don't take it out on Kate."

"Now, why would I be upset?" The mildness was still there in his voice, but his look grew harder with each word. "Just because one of my detectives spends all her days doing God knows what without bothering to check in? Just because another of my detectives decides he wants a nice cushy job with banker's hours? Just because yet another of my detectives spreads himself over every newspaper and television station in town? What, me upset?" Hatch's eyes were slits now and he spread his hands in a mockery of helpless wonder. "Naw."

So that was it, Kate thought. Goddard had hit the media again. God *damn* that man! But at the same time as an instant fury raced hotly through her, there was an underneath feeling of relief. Hatch wasn't angry just with her. He was thoroughly pissed off at the lot of them. And Goddard most of all. She noticed Hatch didn't mention Goddard's appearance on the promotion list.

For all her insight, though, there was no point in continuing this. All Hatch was doing now was letting off steam, and it was getting Sam mad. He had gone rigid in his chair next to her, and his face had taken on the look of stone. None of that did her investigation any good at all.

"If we could get back to the case a minute," she said quietly, drawing Hatch's attention away from Sam. "I have a couple of ideas I want to try out. If these don't pan out, then I'll have to start over again. At that point, I'll need some help. Up until then, I can handle it." She gave Hatch a slight smile. "And yes, I'll report in more often."

Hatch grunted. "And Goddard?"

"I can direct the media inquiries to me," she suggested.

Hatch snorted. "That's all I need is some radical little sob sister doing a feature article on the one token female in my homicide division."

It was pure bait. Hatch really was looking for a fight. Ignoring the provocation, she said calmly, "Goddard's next up in rotation. Something should break this weekend. A tavern fight, if nothing else. So he'll be around, but he won't be, if you know what I mean."

Hatch jerked upright in his chair. "Good. It'll be a real pleasure not seeing him every time I turn on my goddamned television set." He began to paw through the ever present stacks of papers on his desk.

The interview was at an end.

Sam had been sizzling when they'd come out of the Captain's office, but as he cleaned off his desktop, he gradually calmed down. When all was put away, he came over and perched on the far edge of her desk. "He was just touchy tonight, Katie," he said quietly. "He didn't mean any of it."

"I know, Sam." She filed the last of a miscellaneous clutter of papers away and slammed the bottom desk drawer shut. She sat back then and sighed. "I know he doesn't mean it. It's just so damned hard to face him sometimes. It seems like he tries to always keep me on edge."

"Maybe that's his way of controlling you."

She gave him a quizzical look. "You really think I need controlling?"

A smile began. That special, warm smile of his that came from inside. "Perish the thought." But before the smile could worm its way into her heart, he turned away and started getting ready to check out for the weekend.

Exasperated, Kate didn't say anything. Visitation for Sarah was just getting under way and she wanted to be there. Written reports still had to be done. And she had to get her files purged. She'd have to work all weekend playing catch-up while Sam lounged around on his second honeymoon. She rose and grabbed her purse from the back of the chair.

As she started walking out, he fell into step beside her, turning serious. "Are you going to be all right going home tonight?"

He'd brought up the subject she'd been trying to avoid thinking about for the last hour. Going home. Goddard didn't know she'd discovered he was her own private burglar. Would he have another little surprise planned for her homecoming?

Then, irrationally, she was instantly furious with Sam. Why? she wanted to snap at him. Are you suddenly available for escort service? Do you have a minute or two to spare from your wife? "I'll be fine, Sam," she said in a level voice.

As if sensing her anger and divining the reason behind it, he didn't respond right away. They were outside by then and they crossed the parking lot in silence toward the back where she'd parked beneath some overhanging trees. Just short of her driver's door, he caught her arm and swung her around to face him, clearly worried. "If you went home now, I could follow you and make sure everything's all right."

It occurred to her then that Sam didn't know what Goddard and Fry had done, either. She hadn't had a chance to tell him. As suddenly as it had come, the anger was gone and she was touched by his concern. "I'll be just fine, Sam, honest." On impulse, she stood up on tiptoes and kissed his cheek. "Thanks," she whispered. "I really mean that. Thanks."

Before she could back away, his hands were gripping both her arms, his near-black eyes dark with heat. "No," he growled in a low voice. "This is how it's done." He took her in his arms, pulled her close to his body with one arm and raised her chin with his free hand. His lips came down on hers. Hard.

She gave in to it for a long, delicious moment. It felt so damned good.

Then she came to her senses and pushed herself away. Without a word, she unlocked her car and climbed in behind the wheel. Only when the engine was running and the car was in gear did she finally glance up at him. He hadn't moved, and she gave him one small, regretful smile before she backed out of the slot.

As she slowed for the exit from the parking lot, she saw him still standing in place, looking after her. For a brief second, her foot hovered over the brake. Then, with a motion born of firmness, she stamped it down on the accelerator and roared away.

The body of Sarah Taft had been moved from the mortuary into the church building in preparation for the funeral in the morning, and placed in a small anteroom of the church social hall. The parents had chosen a simple birch coffin, adorned by a single rose carved into the top. The lid was closed. The Tafts stood next to it, accepting expressions of sympathy with a quiet, touching dignity. Pastor Barnes stood in silent attendance nearby, the tall, gaunt figure of Pastor Ellsworth next to him. The younger daughter, Lizzie, was not in the room.

Martha Taft was closest to the coffin, clutching a small black prayer book in one hand. Sorrow was carved deep in her face, but resignation and strength and dignity were chiseled there, too. She had the worn look of a stolid prairie woman suffering yet another blow in a life filled with many of them. Some women were born like that, Kate thought, born with an old-age weariness in their soul, knowing ahead of time that trouble was bound to come, sooner or later, one way or another.

As Kate approached the Tafts, Daniel moved closer to Martha and hovered protectively at her side, his eyes fierce within the sorrow that webbed his face. He was like a bull elephant ready to go on the rampage to prevent any more harm to his mate.

Pastor Barnes watched with a slightly worried cast in his eyes, as if concerned that Kate would let something slip, but she merely murmured a few words of sympathy to the parents and moved on. This was neither the time nor the place to break the news of Peter Dickerson's death. Pastor Ellsworth watched her with open dislike, staring down his humped beak of a nose at her as if she were some specimen of distasteful bug, his eyes cold in the gaunt face. Kate gave him a simple nod.

She returned to the main room where the church members had gathered. The women were dressed in somber dresses and the men in black suits. The young people wore their cheerless school uniforms. The only touch of color in the room was the large framed picture of Sarah set on a table in a corner, and the two home-cut sprays of deep red rhododendron blossoms that pillared it.

The food had been set out on long tables at the kitchen end and there was a milling of people around it, filling plates. Couples, she noticed, stayed fairly well together until they'd gotten their food, then they drifted apart to join friends talking in quiet groups, segregated by age and sex, their voices hushed, their faces subdued.

Mrs. Hickman, Denise's mother, was standing silent with a group of middle-aged women, wearing a black rayon dress shiny with age, her thick, heavy features dour as she followed the conversation from person to person. Evelyn Dietz, Kate's onion-chopping neighbor at the potato-peeling session, had joined a group of younger wives, and the school secretary was over in one corner, huddled with the church secretary, deep in talk.

Denise Hickman was off in a group of girls her own age. Tears streamed down the cheeks of more than a few of the girls, including hers. Nancy Wells, the English teacher, was in their midst, holding what looked like an impromptu counseling session. She seemed to be directing her comments to Denise more than the others, but the rest were listening closely, nodding now and then as she spoke. Nancy's face was filled with natural, warm sympathy as she spoke to Denise, her eyes steady as they occasionally roamed the whole circle, including everyone in her glance. The combination of steady eyes and overwhelming compassion gave her a look of tough love. Kate watched her, speculatively. There was a lot of backbone in that woman. She'd do what had to be done, and wouldn't shy away from it. A very pragmatic lady.

Nearby, standing like a sentinel in the midst of a flock of geese, Pastor Bob was encircled by a bunch of grade-school boys who didn't quite know how to act. They twitched and jerked and tapped their feet, their natural energy wanting to take flight and be free. But the intensity of the evening kept them all more or less in one spot, and their faces were as sober as any grownup's. Pastor Bob was addressing the group as a whole, his boyish face set in determinedly serious lines. When he finished with his little talk, Billy Hickman asked a question, and the pastor squatted down to eye level with the youngster to answer it. His face shone with pure love for the kids encircling him.

Her gaze wandered on, skimming the crowd again for the one person she'd come here to find. Finally she saw him.

Norm Overholtz had just arrived, long after his parents had gotten there, and was standing among a group of guys that looked to be of college age. He'd dressed in a white shirt, tie and dark slacks, clothes that were loose enough to hide his pudginess, and he'd slicked his hair back. From a distance, he looked quite presentable, almost attractive.

But the social awkwardness that always seemed to mark him was even more apparent here. He was constantly adjusting his glasses upward on his nose, and his acne-scarred face was filled with a deep misery he took no trouble to hide. His friends were talking amongst themselves and he stared at them as if they were aliens from another planet. He wasn't connecting at all.

She watched him for a good long while, studying him, analyzing him, trying to penetrate the surface of the social awkwardness. Troubled, she finally gave it up and her gaze moved on.

As her glance idly passed over a far wall, she noticed Pastor Matt standing back, doing what she was doing, watching and observing. Tension etched his features with lines that weren't there two days ago. He had a remote, almost studious look on his face as his gaze roamed the room, stopping here and there for a brief questioning second before moving on, as if he'd crawled deep into himself and was peering out at a world he didn't know, trying to divine the truth of it. He looked—Kate fumbled for the right expression—he looked like a cop.

A quick swing of his eyes caught her watching him, and their eyes met and held for a moment. He nodded to her once, face inscrutable now, then his eyes moved on. He stiffened suddenly, and Kate swiveled her head to follow the beam of his gaze. His wife had arrived.

Patty Jacobson stood in the basement entryway at the foot of the stairs, posed much as she had been earlier that day, and looked vaguely at the crowd. She'd changed again, this time into a navy blue suit of a neat, trim cut. The conservative effect was spoiled, though, by the white silk blouse with its froufrou of ruffles cascading down her chest. Her hair was still fluffed around the cheekbones, and there was a stronger sheen of pink on her lips. She looked like an aging cheerleader trying to relive the high school glory days.

A few silences fell at her appearance, but there were far too many people in the room for her entrance to make that much of an impact. Although a couple of the men did give her secret, speculative glances. Even the Ten Commandments couldn't eradicate lust, Kate thought.

She took it in all in one swift glance, then instantly switched back to watch Matt. His face had gone cold and rigid, his lips thinned to a narrow angry line. Then the look was gone. He composed his expression into inscrutable neutrality, drew himself up straight and headed for his wife's side.

Patty had been scanning the crowd and saw him finally. The large blue eyes fastened on him as he worked his way through the crowd. She stood demurely in place, waiting for him to reach her, and when he was finally by her side, she gave him a sweet smile and slipped her hand through his arm. She said something and he shook his head in response, eyes cold. She started pouting, and with a firm pull of her arm, he led her into the anteroom where Sarah's parents sat.

The ever present Emma Barnes had seen all this. She withdrew from her own group where she'd been talking and made her way to the anteroom door. When Matt emerged, Patty's arm still firmly gripped in one hand, Emma took over and led her back to her own group. She elbowed room for two, and keeping Patty glued next to her, she picked up the conversation where she'd left off. Matt watched his wife a moment or two, his face closed down again, then worked his way to the basement stairs and was gone.

Since Patty's back was to the anteroom, she'd missed seeing Matt's exit from the basement and she kept craning her head toward the anteroom door, looking for him. But Emma Barnes was firmly planted in the circle and, by default, courtesy of the hand gripping her arm, so was Patty. Finally Patty subsided into a pouting sulk that changed into a sweet smile whenever she caught someone looking at her, then fell back into the pout when the person looked away.

The buzz of the many conversations going on mixed, blended and blurred into one loud drone, and it was impossible for Kate to overhear anything but a single word here and there. She stayed put for a long while, noting faces, postures and body language, looking for that odd note that makes a cop's antennae go on alert. But except for the little drama between Matt and his wife, nothing at all struck her as out of the way. It was a normal gathering of normal people behaving in the same manner as any other group would at a somber event like this.

Finally she left the safety of the little harbor she'd carved out for herself and began to wander. Moving between groups, she was able to pick up phrases and comments more easily than she had standing back against the wall. Almost all of it concerned Sarah, what the Tafts would do now, and parents' worry for their own children's safety. Fear was abroad in the night, she thought, and had taken up firm residence in this room. And they didn't even know about Peter's death yet. Once that news got out, then fear would escalate into terror.

Lizzie Taft was off standing in a corner with a group of eight-year-old girls, staring down at the floor, a part of them while not a part of them, separated by her sister's tragedy. There were pitchers of orange juice set out amid stacks of small paper cups, and Kate poured some into two cups and carried them over to the corner. She smiled down at the bunch, excused her way through, and moved to Lizzie's side. "Want one?" she asked softly, holding out a cup.

Lizzie looked up, recognized who she was, then looked back down, shaking her head.

Kate sipped from one of them. "You eaten anything today at all?" She pointed to the opposite end of the room. "There's a lot of food over there."

Lizzie started to nod, then looked up and shook her head. "I'm just not hungry." Her eyes were puffed and swollen from tears.

She'd been so brave that first night, Kate thought. "That's what I thought," she said, cheerfully. She held the untouched cup out again. "Drink up. And no excuses."

With reluctant obedience, Lizzie accepted the cup and stared down at the orange liquid.

"Drink up," Kate repeated.

The girl wrinkled her nose. "Do I have to?"

"Yep. It's the law."

One of the girls watching giggled once, then caught herself and clapped a hand over her mouth, remembering the situation.

Under Kate's stern gaze, Lizzie took a swallow of the juice, then made a face. She shoved the cup back at Kate. "I'd rather have a Coke," she said, firmly.

It wasn't Kate's idea of great nutrition, but she said, "Got a Coke machine around here?"

All the girls shook their heads now, their eyes wide. "That's not allowed," one said.

But one of the girls tugged at Kate's sleeve, motioned her to bend down and whispered in her ear, "Pastor Bob keeps some in a special place he's got."

"Really." Kate smiled. "Well, we'll just have to go ask Pastor Bob, won't we."

Another helpful little girl stuck out an arm, pointing across the room. "He's over there."

Kate followed the direction of the point. Pastor Bob was standing now in the midst of a group of male teenagers, speaking seriously to one of the boys. "Right." She emptied her cup of juice and slipped it under the rejected one, then held out her free hand. "Come on, Lizzie, old girl, let's go hunt up that Coke for you."

Shyly, Lizzie took her hand and allowed Kate to lead her through the crowds across the room to where Bob was standing. Lizzie held back at the edge of the group, swamped by the tall male bodies blocking her way. Kate had no such niceties. Grasping the child firmly by the hand, she excused her way through and approached the pastor. "I'm sorry to interrupt, Pastor Bob, but could we talk to you privately?"

His face suffused with instant concern. "Of course. Later," he said to the guys, and he led Kate and Lizzie to a quiet space against one wall. "What can I do for you?"

"This young lady here is suffering from a severe thirst," Kate said gravely. "And I understand that there is a secret stash of soft drinks buried in this church somewhere."

He flashed his open grin. "Well, now, there just might be. But only for the most grievous of calamities."

"I do believe this qualifies."

He grinned down at Lizzie. "That true?"

She nodded, her eyes wide at the adult conspiracy taking shape here.

People were beginning to notice them. Bob seemed to pick up on the questioning stares, too, and quickly beckoned Kate to follow him.

He led them upstairs to a small utility room behind the main office that held a copy machine and paper supplies. A small under-counter refrigerator had been slid beneath a worktable set in front of a window. He dug out three cans of Pepsi, popped the lids and handed them around. "Let's take these in my office," he said. "We'll be more comfortable there."

Kate hesitated. "I don't suppose there's any snacks around to go with these," she said.

He caught the implication instantly. "Had a little problem eating today?" he said to Lizzie.

She hung her head as Kate nodded an emphatic yes.

"I don't think there's a thing," he said slowly. He glanced at his watch. "There's still an hour of visitation left and there's plenty of food downstairs."

Lizzie still looked downcast.

"I've got a better idea," Kate said. "Can I borrow your phone?"

Bob led them into the outer office, turned on the desk lamp for her and motioned to the phone. Kate called Dispatch and asked to be patched through to the patrol car closest to the church. When the Blues came on the line, she explained what she wanted. She took a little needling from them but won agreement. Food on the way. Mother MacLean, she thought as she hung up. This would make the rounds.

Lizzie watched her throughout the call, her eyes big and round. "Can you really do stuff like that? Just make a phone call and get a hamburger brought to you?"

"Sometimes." Kate grinned at her. "Impressive, hunh."

"Boy, I'll say."

Over the girl's head, Kate exchanged a grin with Bob and rose. "I need to wait outside for the squad car."

He nodded and rose, too. "We'll come with you." He held out a hand for Lizzie to take.

The evening light was turning into the darkness of night as they settled on the front steps of the church. Pepsi can in hand, Lizzie snuggled up close to Kate's side and she reached out and put an arm around the girl, pulling her close in, giving her a tight squeeze.

Pastor Bob had watched this from where he sat on Lizzie's far side. "Do you have children of your own?" he asked.

"No." Kate smiled down fondly at Lizzie's head. "No, I don't," she said softly. "Someday, maybe." Then she looked up at him. "And you?"

Bob's eyes drifted away and he stared at the first star just beginning to shine in the night sky. "I'd like to make a home for some of the refugee children abroad. Maybe adopt a couple. We have so much and they have nothing. I'd like to share something of mine."

"Why don't you?" Kate asked softly. At her side, Lizzie contentedly sipped her drink.

His face saddened and he just shrugged, not answering.

She drew a few conclusions about the state of his love life, but said nothing more in that direction. Lizzie seemed content, glued to her side. The woods across the street were quiet and still, their ragged treetops rising up into the star-filled sky like a forest of cathedral spires. It was serene, calming and peaceful.

The burgers finally arrived, Kate reimbursed the Blues, let them get away with some bad jokes as a tip, and assured them she owed them one. And she'd be happy to owe them ten, if they'd keep this quiet. "Yeah, right, MacLean, you bet," one of them answered. They drove off, laughing.

Lizzie had never eaten a Big Mac. She took a tiny bite, not sure about this whole thing, and tentatively chewed it into a million pieces before cautiously swallowing it down. Then her eyes lit up, and she lunged for the next bite, demolishing a major part of it in three or four swift gulps. The French fries went down as well, though she did mention through a mouthful of food that her mom made better ones. Thicker and crisper, she said, spraying crumbs of food as she talked.

Kate and Bob ate theirs, too, legs stretched out in front of them, the night air growing chill around them. They had to get back inside, Kate knew, before Lizzie was missed and someone panicked. But it was pleasant to sit in the stillness of the night and enjoy the peace for the moment.

As he ate, Pastor Bob talked about the children's needs, the programs that he'd put into place to help meet those needs, and the ones he was trying to get established. Time, he said again and again, time was his biggest enemy. There was so much to be done, and he couldn't get everything in place fast enough. If only he didn't require sleep, he said humorously. It cost him eight hours a night he could be working otherwise.

Kate swallowed the last French fry, crumpled her papers and slid them into the bag. She sipped some of her soft drink. She had some questions she wanted to ask him, but she didn't want to ask them in front of Lizzie. She waited until the girl had finished eating, then crumpled up her papers to toss. "Think that'll last you for a while?" she asked Lizzie.

The answering nod was enthusiastic and heartfelt. "Could we do this again?"

Kate grinned. "You bet. But for now, you probably should get back downstairs. If your folks discover you're gone, they'll be most upset."

Lizzie nodded and obediently hopped up. "Okay. Are you coming, too?"

Kate shook her head. "Not yet. There's a couple of things I

need to talk to Pastor Bob about. But we'll see you back to the door."

"Okay." Lizzie was a hell of a lot more chipper, Kate noted, than when she'd first seen her. And she'd eaten her whole meal. Kate smiled to herself. Mission accomplished.

They walked the girl to the church steps and watched to make sure she made it safely down the basement stairs, then Pastor Bob turned to her. "You wanted to talk to me?" He was obviously worried.

They were alone in the night, the darkness quiet around them. It was about as much privacy as they were going to get. Kate nodded. "About Sarah. Did you spend much time with her?"

"Mmmm, yes and no. I saw her often in the course of a week, simply because of the activities going on at the church here. But I didn't have a lot of quality contact with her. Not the one-on-one that I do with a lot of the teenagers."

"How odd," she murmured. "I was told that you and she spent a couple of hours alone together in your office just last week."

He stared at her with shock. "Good grief, no! Why would someone say something like that?"

"Then you didn't meet with her in your office?"

But his eyes were already narrowing in thought. "Well, now, hold on a sec. She was at the summer counseling meeting we held. That was last week. But we certainly weren't alone."

"What was that about?"

"Early in the school year, we have interested eleventh- and twelfth-graders fill out applications for summer camp counseling positions up at the retreat. Over the winter, I go through them and cull out the best, then I bring them together for a preliminary meeting before I make my final decision. That meeting was held last week and Sarah was there."

"But with her pregnancy," Kate pointed out, "she wouldn't have been able to do that, would she? Why would she attend, then?"

The young pastor seemed troubled. "Maybe she didn't know about it then."

"Possibly. Did she seem any different at the meeting?"

"Well, on thinking about it, maybe she was a little quiet. But then, Sarah was always quiet."

Kate nodded agreement with that. "How many kids were at this meeting?"

"About twenty."

"Peter Dickerson?"

"Yes, Peter was there."

"Norm Overholtz?"

"Yes."

Norm again. "What about Denise Hickman? Was she there?"

Bob shook his head. "No. I'd love to have her, she'd make a wonderful counselor, but her mother holds a tight leash. As much as I've tried, I just can't get Mrs. Hickman to loosen the reins. It's caused quite a problem, I'm afraid."

Kate ignored that for the moment and studied him quizzically. "And that was the meeting with Sarah? The whole of the meeting?"

He gave a sober nod. "Yes."

"And you never met with her alone."

He shook his head. "Nope. You're free to check my calendar. I was tied up every day after school in one group meeting or another. The last few weeks of a school year's a crazy time for me."

She almost believed him. It was too easily checked. A two-hour gap in his schedule would show up like a pothole in a freeway. Patty Jacobson had made up the story and told it to Kate with a straight face. And it had been a lie. The whole thing. Just an outright lie. Why? Just to make trouble? Or were there deeper motives here?

But caution dictated just a bit of care. She studied him. "Where were you Monday afternoon after the budget meeting broke up?"

His answer was prompt. "Coaching the softball team." He

flashed his irrepressible grin and spread his arms wide. "I'm clean, copper, honest."

She believed him then. He'd had no meeting alone with Sarah. Patty Jacobson had lied.

She returned to the subject of Denise and asked a few questions about her situation and what the problem had been. It was a lengthy tale, but the long and the short of it was simply that Denise had counted on going to Northwest Bible College, but her folks had refused to sign their permission last year when applications were due, and a major uproar had resulted.

"I spoke with them," Bob said, "Pastor Ellsworth spoke with them, even Pastor Barnes got involved. Her dad was okay, he could see how much it meant to her, but her mother absolutely refused to give an inch. Her father—Denise's grandfather—was fighting cancer and the mother was adamant that after graduation, Denise stay home and help out. If she put her foot down like that about a college education, she wasn't about to consider letting Denise do any camp counseling."

"How was she able to go on retreat then?"

"It's a school activity, it's required. Her mother couldn't stop it."

"Denise was pretty broken up by Sarah's death," Kate said slowly. "How is she going to take Peter's death when she finally hears about it?"

"Just as hard." There was no flashing grin this time, only concern. "She was nuts about him."

Kate stared. "Really," she murmured.

A sudden scenario unrolled itself. It started with a boy in love with one girl, and that girl's best friend in love with the boy, and the reel played out from there.

Except that Denise had been on retreat when Sarah was killed.

Pastor Bob was just going in when Matt came plowing out the doorway, carrying a cardboard carton with the flaps loosely folded over. "Oops," he said, doing a quick jog to avoid knocking the other pastor over. "Sorry."

"Run down by a man of God," Pastor Bob said. "Knew it would happen sooner or later if I didn't mind my *p*'s and *q*'s." With a quick flash of smile and a jaunty wave, he was gone.

Matt watched him disappear down the basement stairs, then turned to Kate, brooding down on her for a long moment, face remote once more. The confident, outgoing, compassionate man she'd first met had turned into another Sam. Moody, withdrawn, seriously troubled about something.

Finally, he opened a flap on the carton. "I've been hunting for you. I dug these materials up for you. They're everything I've got on the church and the history of the church. I don't know if they'll help you or not, but I felt you should have them."

She stared, first at him, then at the carton, then back at him again. "Why?" she asked, surprised. "Why now?"

"This has to stop." His eyes were level on hers, his voice even and determined.

She nodded. The deaths, he meant. The killings.

"Where's your car? I'll tote these out there for you."

"In the parking lot."

"Then let's go."

They walked around the outside of the office wing in silence, his swift stride carrying them quickly along the paths and walkways in the darkness. In the parking lot, she led him to her Honda and opened the trunk. He didn't relax until everything was safely stowed among the other stuff she had there. Then a flash of the old Matt came back as he looked down. "Paint cans?"

"My laundry room." She slammed the lid shut. "Buttermilk yellow. It's my weekend project."

He looked at her then. "I know so little about you, really."

She gave a half-smile. "That's because of what I do. I concentrate on everyone else."

The return walk was a slow amble along the pathway leading to the rear church office door. They walked in silence for a few steps, out of shadow, into starlight, back into shadow again. The night was quiet around them, the stillness building a quiet intimacy. The time for confidences. "I'd still like to know why you've done this for me," she said softly.

In the darker shadow of one fir in the black night, he stopped. "I'm afraid," he said simply. "There are some things going on within the church that I don't understand, Kate. I can't make sense out of any of it."

"What things?" she asked mildly.

He shook his head. "Just minor stuff, I guess, compared to everything else. Ansel Lang's suddenly ordered us to cut our budgets way back. And he's delaying the opening of the campgrounds for a few weeks. It's little stuff, picky stuff. Still, it's strange. The timing's strange."

"Sounds like he's expecting a serious cash flow problem. Or unexpected expenses."

"I guess. A twenty percent shortfall, if my budget's an example."

"Why is he delaying the opening of the campgrounds?"

"Money, he says. To cut down operating costs."

Kate's eyes narrowed. This retreat or campgrounds or whatever the church cared to call it was becoming a damned nuisance. It had played a background role in this case from the beginning, starting with Sarah missing retreat, Denise going on retreat, not being able to question Nancy Wells until she got back from retreat, Alice Dickerson being on retreat, and last, but not least, the existence of the retreat itself.

What Donna Wilhelm had said was beginning to echo ominously. The retreat had been closed down before, and now, suddenly, again. What the hell was going on up there anyway?

"Matt, exactly where are the campgrounds?"

"On a little cove at the head of Hood Canal."

"Which county?"

"Jefferson," he said. "Why?"

That would be the Port Townsend area. "Just curious."

Before she could phrase another question, a voice behind Kate rang out. "There you are!"

They both swung toward the voice.

Patty Jacobson stood, halfway down the sidewalk. She had on high heels, Kate knew, yet she'd made no sound. There'd been no click of the heels on the walkway, and no sounds of the church office door closing. And Kate was well aware of how the scene could be interpreted. She and Matt were standing mere paces apart, his head bent down in quiet conversation with her as she looked up at him. In the intimacy of the quiet dark surrounding them, they could be taken as two lovers caught in a clandestine meeting.

Patty came up to them, her eyes fixed on Kate in a ferocious stare. Then her face smoothed out and she aimed her sweet smile at her husband. "I'm ready to leave, Matthew," she said in a girlishly soft voice.

"It's too soon, Patty," he said evenly.

"Not for me."

"I'll have to stay, then."

"Of course." The smile was still there, but her tone was dead flat. "I don't, though. I have my own car. As usual." She gave Kate a withering glance, turned on her heel and started to move around her husband toward the parking lot in the back. This time her heels clicked with loud anger. Matt made no effort to follow.

From the distant parking lot, a car door slammed, an engine roared to life, and tires crunched over gravel. In a second, headlights swept across the black wall of woods and on down the private road. The car stopped at the intersection to the main road, then made a right and sped off into the night.

Matt said nothing. He looked up overhead, his eyes roaming the stars as the car receded into the distance. When the sound had faded completely away and the silence of the night had returned, he let his gaze finish its meandering journey, then drew in a deep, steadying breath and turned his attention to Kate again, back under control. "Sorry. It's been a week."

It was said with quiet dignity, and Kate merely nodded.

He gave a ragged half-smile. "I need to get back inside now."

"I'm through for the night," Kate said. "You go on ahead." Then she hesitated and gave him a measuring glance. "If you ever need someone to talk to . . ." she said softly. "Outside of the church, I mean."

There was enough starglow to see the sardonic smile cross his face. "But only if I'm innocent, right?"

"Oh, no," she said with a quiet smile. "Cops love it when the guilty talk to them, too. It's always such a challenge."

He nodded, as if some assessment he'd made of her was true. "You're a dangerous lady, Detective MacLean. With that soft way about you, you could lead a person down the garden path real fast. Right to where the noose is swinging."

She grinned. "You know what they say. Satan has a seven-day workweek, while God only has a six. I figure He needs all the help He can get on that day off of His."

After Matt had reentered the church, she gave the night a few moments to go back to sleep, then quietly moved down the walkway to the parking lot. Except for Patty Jacobson, no one had left the visitation yet.

She moved up and down the aisles of cars until she found the Overholtz station wagon that Norm had been washing that morning. She wrote down the make, model and license number, then headed for the bike racks set to one side of the walkway near the back door. Several bikes were parked there, Norm's green one among them. Nodding with satisfaction, Kate walked to the back of the parking lot where her own car was parked.

Mentally, she traced out the most logical route home for him, then chose her spot, a corner two blocks from his house. She parked where she had a good view of the street, then hunched back in the seat and waited.

The Overholtz's car passed her first, driven at a sedate speed by

Norm's father. The mother sat beside him in the front seat, staring stoically straight ahead. Neither one noticed Kate.

A few minutes later, a single headlamp rounded a far corner and came gliding down the sidewalk. Kate got out of the car and started walking toward it. She jammed her fists in the jacket she'd put on against the evening chill, stopped beneath a streetlight where she'd be seen, and leaned back against the post. The progress of the bike down the sidewalk slowed considerably. She waited patiently until he was near enough to hear her easily.

"Hello, Norman." She gave a friendly smile. "Got a moment?"

The bike suddenly wobbled to a stop. Norm climbed off and walked it into the cone of light, squinting at her through his thick glasses. "What're you doing here?"

"Taking a stroll." She looked up at the star-jammed sky. "Nice night out."

He nodded warily. "Yeah. I guess."

"I saw you at Sarah's visitation tonight. You were standing with a group of guys. I have to say, you looked a little lost."

He stared glumly down at the handlebars and nodded. "That's kind of how I felt. The guys were all talking about their summer plans. It didn't seem right, you know? It was as if Sarah didn't mean anything to them. I mean, she dies, you get her buried, and go on about your business. It's so—so *heartless*."

Kate nodded. "That's the ruthless part of death. The world keeps on turning when it feels like it shouldn't."

Her response obviously disappointed him, for his face turned bleak. "That's what Pastor Matt says," he said in a low, dejected tone.

"You really loved her, didn't you," Kate said softly.

Shamefaced, he hung his head. "Yeah," he muttered, "I guess I did."

"How much?"

He lifted his head up slightly. "What do you mean?"

"I mean, how much did you love her?" Kate said, her voice patient. "Supposing she fell in love with someone else. Not you, but someone else. Did you love her enough to let her go? To wish her every happiness, then to give her freely to another man, knowing she could never be yours now? Did you love her that much, Norman?"

He seemed to grow up in an instant. His shoulders straightened and he stared off into the distance, pondering her question. And suddenly, Kate saw the man he would be. The pudginess would thin down, the acne scars would fade into a typical man's coarse skin, and the clear gray eyes, somewhat lost now in the baby-fat cheeks, would become a compelling, dominating fixture.

Finally, he nodded. "Yeah. It'd have been hard, but I would've let her go."

She eyed him skeptically, but let his answer pass. "I enjoyed our little chat this morning," she said casually. "And I see you got your bike washed. What time did you finally make it to school?"

"Eleven o'clock class."

Bingo. Kate had left him shortly after nine. Within Len Franklin's time frame for Peter's death, that gave him over an hour for a stop at Bridle Trails.

"I wasn't going to go at all, but my mom made me. Said it was better to go than to sit around, moping." He shrugged. "I guess she was right. It made the day go by a little faster. Maybe."

"What time did you leave for school?"

"I don't know. Right after I finished washing the bike, I guess."

"What did you do when you first got there? Talk to any buddies or anything?"

"No, I didn't feel much like talking. I just went and sat on the footbridge awhile, just watching the creek run under."

"Nice day for it," Kate observed. "Anybody else out watching the water run?"

He shook his head. "Just me. It was so silent and peaceful, I—I kept losing myself . . . like I go off into a trance, or something. Except it's heavier than that, blacker than that." He drifted away into sorrow again, his face wracked with misery.

She gave him a moment, then asked a few more questions. Had he ever taken Sarah on a walk in the woods? Had they ever gone on a picnic, or explored the area? Was he one of those Northwest students who wandered over to Bridle Trails to eat lunch or read his Bible now and again?

No, he answered in a disinterested tone. He'd never been alone with Sarah, he never took walks in the woods, alone or with anyone else, and he never left the Northwest campus to go to the state park. The import of her questions seemed to pass him by.

"Do you have a driver's license, Norman?" she asked.

No, he rode his bike to school every day.

She added it up in her mind. Opportunity, plenty. Motive, jealousy and revenge. Slay the fallen angel, then slay the one who'd caused the fall. Method. She thought of the old-fashioned wire basket hanging from the handlebars. Could he have carted off the branch in that? Laying it across the basket top, possibly?

She considered taking him in now for some formal questioning, but finally decided against it. There was more work to be done before that. They had to trace the various routes he might've used riding to the park and search out anyone who might've seen him. And fine-comb the route for the branch or branches that had been used on the two victims. She wanted to make sure all her *i*'s were dotted and the *t*'s crossed.

But logically, it was looking good and she looked at him with pity. By committing murder, the boy had short-circuited the life the man could've led. And it would make the third young person with a life wasted—two by murder, one by execution. What a tragedy. Damn it all to hell, Kate thought, why did smart people do stupid things anyway?

Suddenly, he shook his head with a fierce motion, as if to fling away the grief that had encompassed him again, and slammed a foot down on a pedal. "I gotta go," he muttered.

She let him go, watching him swoop around the corner and zip out of sight.

Yes. Jealousy and revenge made a hell of a motive. It all added up.

In theory.

Troubled, she retraced her steps to her car and climbed in behind the wheel.

It certainly would help if she didn't feel quite as sorry for him as she did.

Chapter Nineteen

Friday night in downtown Kirkland was like spring break in Daytona. The streets were jammed with the young and the desperate, staggering with elbows linked from bar to bar, feeling invincible. Hails, shouts and shrieks were the call of the wild, and it was all friendly and harmless. Until drunken highs turned into ugly lows and the brawls began.

Kate had no interest in stopping at the tavern. On Friday nights, Smokie Jo's was the same as Hector's, Anthony's Home Port and all the other bars and taverns in town. Too many people jammed into too little space, with the jukebox blaring like a rock band and the overflowing crowd using the edges of the pool tables as bar stools. Besides, she was tired. All she wanted now was her slippers and robe, and a little quiet time to think.

Coming from the church, Kate crossed the freeway on Redmond Way heading into downtown Kirkland and was instantly engulfed by the traffic mess. She sat at one light for two turns of the red, sat at the next one through three turns, only to come to another standstill as drivers tried to make the left turn across oncoming traffic into Lakeside Park. The last car blocking her finally got its break and she was free. She gunned up Market Street into a relatively open stretch at the top of the hill and made the left onto her street. There were a few darkened cars parked along the curbs up and down the street, otherwise it was empty and quiet, a balm to her soul.

She approached her house slowly. She hadn't thought to leave a couple of lights burning when she'd left that afternoon. The idea of entering a dark house made her nerves twang. She was prepared to drive past if anything looked out of the way. But the small Cape Cod sat peaceful and still in the starglow, its facade serene.

The garage wasn't a problem for her. She had an automatic opener. Once the door was up, the sweep of her headlights fully illuminated the interior and there were no dark, hidden corners for anyone to use as a hiding spot. Inside, she kept her car lights on as the garage door slid back down, watching in her rearview mirror to make sure no one slipped around the corner and up behind her before it was fully closed. Then she exited through the side door and walked up the lawn, sticking to the center of the yard away from any shrubs and trees that could hide an attacker.

She recognized that kind of extreme caution as being totally irrational. Never, at any time the previous night, had she been in any physical danger. There'd been no one in the house when she'd gotten there, no one with a knife or a gun hiding in a closet or the shower waiting to jump out at her. Yet she couldn't shake the feeling of having lost a prized sanctuary, her personal safe harbor. Paranoia was developing swiftly.

She climbed the front porch, collected her mail, then hesitated at the door. Suddenly impatient with her own fears, she shoved the key in the new locks, heard the deadbolt slide back with a satisfying click, and shoved the door open. A quick glance showed everything in place where it should be.

She swept through the house, ending up in her bedroom. No ghosts behind the doors, no ghouls in the shower. Laughing silently at herself, she dumped the mail on the desk in her den, then went back to the laundry. The grim, dingy laundry. She didn't like even looking at it. Tomorrow, she promised.

She scrounged for a flashlight, grabbed her keys, crossed the backyard into the garage and unlocked the trunk of her car. The carton of materials from the church was heavy and awkward. She dumped keys and flashlight through the loose flaps on top of the materials, lifted the carton free and slammed the trunk shut. The paint cans could stay put for now.

She made the safety of her laundry room, carried the carton into the living room, then returned to lock the back door, shoving the deadbolt into place. The click of it sliding home felt as good to her ears as the click of a cue ball knocking the eight ball home. She leaned back against the solid wood of the door and took a deep breath. Then she went to change clothes.

She checked out her bedroom thoroughly. It looked undisturbed. She relaxed then. The house hadn't been touched. And if she were going to turn as paranoid as this, she thought, she'd better start thinking about leaving little traps in sensitive places. Like threads stuck on drawer fronts that would fall unseen to the carpet if they were opened. Or buckets of water on top of a partially opened door.

Yeah, right.

She stripped off her work clothes and holster, and pulled on a nightie and the ragged terry cloth robe. As she was moving back and forth in the bedroom, exchanging shoes for slippers, she caught sight of herself in the mirror and came to a sudden stop. Her cheeks were sunken in from cheekbone to jaw, small fine lines splayed from the corners of her eyes, and the sockets were smeared with dark circles of weariness. She sank onto the vanity bench. She looked ten years older than she had two days ago. The stress and strain of the way she was living was taking its toll.

For the first time, she wondered how all this was going to play out. Sam, the Captain, Goddard, the promotion, the continual manpower shortages . . . Added together, they made one hell of a long list of negatives.

But it was more than the work, she knew. It was the whole Eastside. She thought of the traffic battles she'd fought just to reach her street. The beauty was gone, the charm was gone, the comfortable, small-town feel was gone. All destroyed by a bunch of self-serving creeps selling the Eastside, tract by tract. What was there left for her here anymore? Again the vision of the wide-open spaces of Montana etched itself deep into her mind.

She should move on while she was still young, she thought, as she picked up her hairbrush and idly started pulling tangles free. Find her spot on earth and settle in. She could waitress if she needed to. Or open a detective agency. Or work for an attorney. Or, heaven forbid, do it her mother's way, go to law school, meet a nice man, settle down and have children.

Yale Law Review. Yeah, right.

She set the brush back down, rose from the dressing table and moved into the kitchen to pour herself a glass of wine. Then she lit a fire, settled on the couch, and instantly, the carton caught her eye. She took a sip of wine, pondering it a moment. Would it be worth pawing through tonight?

Why not? she answered. What else did she have to do?

Not a damned thing.

She sat on the edge of the couch, dragged the carton to her knees and skimmed through the church information. Bulletins, announcements, brochures and pamphlets, all homemade, gave a written and pictorial history of the church, from a simple cedar building in a small wooded clearing to the sprawling complex it was today. It was all out of order, mixed up as any random shuffling of the cards could be. She hunted up pen and paper for notes, then sat cross-legged on the rug and started unloading handfuls, putting them into chronological order. Once they were organized, she started at the beginning, Day One.

At first, the growth of the church had been steady, starting with a few people meeting in a modest residential living room service, then a few dozen hardy souls sitting on folding chairs organized into formal rows in what looked like a storefront. Then came a reproduced picture of a forest wilderness, with a youthful Pastor Barnes standing to one side, face rapturous, a visionary even then. The next shots showed the bulldozers and backhoes at work, carving out a clearing, then digging the foundation for the church. An equally youthful Pastor Lang stood next to the senior pastor in that shot.

She studied the pictures of both men. They'd been good-looking in their youth. Thomas Barnes was slimmer then, and was half turned to the construction site with a look close to ecstasy on his face. Ansel Lang hadn't worn glasses in those days, and was really quite attractive in his slight, wiry way. There was a quiet pride and look of ownership on his face as he stood next to the senior pastor looking at the work being done, as if he'd personally brought this development to pass.

The pictorial progress of the construction continued until on a bright sunny day, Pastor Barnes in a flowing black robe raised his hand in a Pope-like gesture and blessed the newly completed church. More than two hundred people were watching him, dressed in their best Sunday clothes, their faces aglow with smiles of pride. Some of the people in the photograph were younger versions of parishioners she'd been dealing with. Others were unfamiliar and unknown to her.

Four years later, the backhoes and bulldozers were back, more clearing occurred and the office wing began to take shape. The group shot at its dedication showed a congregation that had easily doubled in numbers. Pastor Barnes was slightly heavier in these pictures. But Ansel Lang seemed the same, small and slight. And still smiling.

Then came the hiatus.

The congregation didn't seem to grow much, the complex certainly didn't grow, everything remained at a standstill. Then after several years of quiet, there was an explosive growth in buildings. Every year or so, it seemed, more buildings were being added. Slowly, church memberships began to increase. The group pictures of the congregation grew more distant and indistinct until they showed simply a blur of people, the camera too far back from them to reproduce any one face and still fit everyone into the shot. Even so, there didn't seem to be enough of an increase to justify the building.

Pastor Lang, however, was no longer smiling. The tension keynoting his present-day demeanor was even then being written on his face.

She arranged the pictures in a collage around her, and began to pore through the written materials. Religious festivals, Christmas pageants, Bible study groups, quilting bees and church suppers. Activities common to any church. The only unusual note was a prayer of thanks for the generosity of one Earl Haverness who'd donated a section of land on the Olympic Peninsula to use as church campgrounds. A small work party was formed to clear enough land to allow a few tents to be pitched there, and eventually an announcement was made that the campgrounds could now accommodate six different family tents at once. A couple of years after that, the clearing had been doubled to allow a dozen camping sites and the campfire ring had been added.

That was it. The whole sum and total of the church. Until, after a few years of absolute stability and steadiness, it was suddenly announced that the church would be starting its own private school in the basement of the church. Within a year, the explosive growth of buildings had begun.

What exactly had fueled that explosion of construction? There was nothing to account for it that she could see. From the activity pictures taken year by year, there didn't seem to be any kind of a startling increase in membership that would account for suddenly having barrels of money to spend on one building project after another. Yet if the church had saved up for each one, there'd have been a lag-time between them while the coffers were refilled again. But there'd been none of that. They'd gone from building to building to building without a break. It was like a big-time lottery winner who'd been living paycheck to paycheck suddenly able to go on a millionaire-style buying spree.

Kate tapped her pen on the rug in unconscious rhythm, staring down at the semicircular collage she'd arranged around her. There'd been something about this church that had bothered her from the beginning. The modest, unassuming lifestyle of the congregation she'd met didn't fit with the wealthy kind of complex they worshipped in. It took more than donated nails and volunteer carpenters to build the kind of setup they had. There was something dreadfully out of kilter with the picture and her nose fairly tingled with the scent of it.

Then she viewed it as the Captain would if she were arguing it in front of him. There were two possible explanations for this appearance of subtle wealth . . .

She glanced at the clock. It was after eleven. A bit on the late side for civilians. But by cop time, still early. She looked up Matt's home number on the church bulletin, went to the phone and dialed. He wasn't home yet, she was told by his wife, in a petulant-sounding voice. And it was Pastor *Jacobson,* not *Matt.* Kate hung up, gritting her teeth. Patty Jacobson really got off on her husband's position in life.

She dialed the church and the phone was picked up on the first ring by Matt himself. "I've gone over the materials you gave me tonight," Kate said. "Thanks much, they were helpful. But I've got a couple of questions. Did the church take out mortgages on any of their building projects?"

"No, they used a process called a building fund. That built the church, then the office wing."

"And the rest?"

Silence. "Income from investments," he said finally.

"What kind of investments?"

More silence. Then he said softly, "You're asking some of the same things I've started wondering about. Ansel Lang plays that sort of thing pretty close to the chest. We simply get the annual result in dollars and cents. Exactly what investments are entailed only he knows."

"What about Pastor Barnes? As senior pastor, wouldn't he be in on that part of it?"

"I'd like to think so." His tone, though, indicated a strong doubt.

"You don't sound too sure." Again there was a lengthy silence.

Kate could picture the distress he was feeling. It was there in his voice, and it would certainly be there in his manner. "What's wrong, Matt?" she asked softly.

He exhaled a long, slow breath. "I've just been told to cut my budget another ten percent. That's on top of the twenty percent I mentioned earlier tonight. And the summer retreat and camping program hasn't just been postponed, it's been cancelled for the whole season. So I don't know what's going on, but something sure is wrong."

"Who's authorized this, the budget cuts and the camp closing? Pastor Barnes?"

"No. It's direct from Ansel."

She chewed on that one silently for a long moment, then said, "Matt, does the church earn enough from camping fees to affect thirty percent of the church's budget?"

"No. All the camping fees do is make the campgrounds self-supporting, so that it pays its own way. But no, there's no extra money to help out with our church expenses down here."

"Then let me reverse the question. If the campground supports itself, why is it being closed? Closed or open, either way, it wouldn't affect your budget. Why are the two being linked like that?"

His tone grew heavier. "That's what I'd like to know."

They were both silent then. Finally Kate said, "Okay, thanks, Matt." She hung up, then headed back to the materials. She pawed through them until she found what she'd thought she'd seen there. A map of the campgrounds, and the route to get there. She'd made a decision finally. She was going to donate her Saturday to the case. She was going to find that damned retreat.

She rose before dawn, slipped into jeans, a dark T-shirt and a denim jacket, then dug around in her den closet for the camera equipment she hadn't used in a while. It was all contained in a hard-sided case, and she checked to make sure she had lenses and film, then slid her gun down behind the camera body. She fixed up an insulated tote bag with a couple of cans of soft drinks and some trail food and loaded her car. The front seat was a mess of yearbooks, plat maps, and other bits and scraps of the investigation, but she'd tackle that when she got back later today, she promised herself. She backed out of the garage, and headed toward the Sound.

The Washington State ferries were beautiful boats, large, sleek, white and clean. Kate caught an early one at Edmonds, climbed up to the cafeteria deck and bought a bagel and a cup of coffee. She carried them out of the main dining area toward the bow of the boat and took a seat facing forward on one of the comfortable padded benches next to the broad bank of windows that gave an unrestricted view of Puget Sound. It was too early for the heavy weekend tourist traffic to the peninsula to have started yet and the cabin was sparsely populated. She ate her bagel, the peace of the early morning seeping into her as she felt the quiet throb of the diesels far below and the smooth glide of the ferry cutting through the water.

A seagull landed on the deck railing and stared in at her. She unearthed her camera, swapped the telephoto lens for a wide-angled 35–80 zoom, and shot a scenic through the clean window, the soft gray and white body of the gull poised against a background of blue waters merging with a cobalt blue sky. Shot made, she lowered the camera, then simply watched the bird as he rode the rail. When he tired of fighting the boat-generated wind to maintain his perch, he rose with a long leisurely flap of wings, found an air current, spread his wings and let it carry him up in graceful whorls and circles until he had soared out of sight. Was that what the afterlife was like? she wondered. The human soul taking wing with the grace and freedom of a seagull, shed of the weighted, awkward body that kept a person earthbound?

Through with her bagel, she tossed the paper plate into a trash can, carried her coffee onto the deck and leaned against the rail, the wind ruffling her hair as she watched the Kitsap Peninsula come ever closer. The air was clean and crisp, filled with the tang of salty brine that stirred her blood whenever she got near the sea. Courtesy of all those New England whaling captains in her bloodline. Born to the sea, they'd claimed. Maybe that was the cause of her continual, underlying restlessness. She was born to the sea, but lived a land-bound life.

She studied the tiny port of Kingston as the ferry maneuvered into Appletree Cove and lined itself up with the ferry dock. A small town, a couple of thousand people, maybe. Just her kind of place. Wonder if they needed a cop? The ferry horn blasted, alerting the world to its arrival. Reluctantly, she turned away from the rail and her own thoughts and joined the line of passengers going down the inner stairwell back to their cars.

Route 104, a narrow two-lane road, ran north out of Kingston along the edge of the Sound, then curved west through the tiny town of Port Gamble, with its post office, museum and streets of company housing, and on through twisting miles of dense forest. Once across the Hood Canal Bridge, the road broadened into a full-fledged highway edged by evergreens, with the thick ropy flanks of the wild, uninhabited Olympic Mountain Range dead ahead. Only one car had traveled this far with her, and when the road opened up it quickly passed her and sped off into the distance. Then she had the whole world, mountain, forest and road, to herself.

She followed the road west to 101, the main highway running down the entire western length of Hood Canal to Olympia, and turned south. A few miles north of Quilcene, she turned east onto the first of a series of backcountry roads, and wound through a maze of twists and turns and more back roads cut through miles of deep forest. The church map was clear and well detailed, thank God, otherwise she'd have ended up like the poor babes in the woods, stranded, without a clue as to the way home.

The area was veined with logging roads. Stopping at one point before negotiating a mean twist in the road, she lowered her window and listened. The only sound she heard was the quiet idle of her car engine. The woods ranged around her in dark silence. How in the world could a church bus make it through here? How could the congregation possibly *find* it in order to make use of it? For that matter, how had Pastor Barnes found it originally? Shivering in the dank coolness, beginning to question the wisdom of coming here alone, she double-checked the church map to make sure she'd made no wrong turns. Taking it on faith that she hadn't, she put the little car in gear and inched forward around the turn, the undergrowth scraping car fenders on both sides.

A wooden swing gate stretched across the church's access road. She pulled the nose of the Honda up to it, hopped out and swung it open, drove through, then closed the gate behind her. She drove slowly along a hard-packed mix of dirt and gravel, on the lookout for potholes and trenches carved by winter melt. The trees stretched up high overhead, blocking the sun, and the forest extended in an unending canyon ahead of her.

The road led through an old section of wood that had been logged years ago and was covered with a scraggly second growth. Still cautious of the jarring bumps and dips, she moved forward at a snail's pace until, mercifully, the cut-through widened and smoothed out into a passable road once more. A small, hand-carved wooden sign posted low on a tree to her right proclaimed Camp Woodhaven. Just beyond, a narrow driveway cut off from the dirt road and curved away down a hill.

At the top of the hill, to one side of the driveway, a broad clearing had been leveled and graveled and encircled with logs to form a rudimentary parking area. Past this upper parking area, the access road twisted away again into deep woods. She drove the length of it until it widened into a spacious graveled parking lot, surrounded by a solid wall of forest. She'd reached the end of the road.

She pulled off to the side into a dense shade of a tangle of firs, switched off the engine and, window down, listened. Birdsong, and a breeze rustling through the trees. That's all she could hear. The whole area was deserted. She dug her camera case out of her trunk and slung it over one shoulder, then locked the car door, pocketed the car keys, and headed back down the road.

The camp driveway curving down into the lower forest was a

car-width wide. Wheel tracks made at some point when the ground had been wet and soggy had petrified into a pair of deep ruts that twisted and turned down the hillside. Walking the hump was easier than trying to maintain footing in the uneven ruts, and she strolled down the hill like it was a sidewalk in Seattle. She'd walked a quarter-mile or better when she rounded a bend in the woods and the land opened up and broadened, the camp suddenly spread out in front of her.

The campgrounds were vast, one long stretch of crescent curving like opened arms around an isolated private cove. Clusters of log cabins were scattered in and amongst several small groves of pines, and an enormous lodge built of logs stood in the center of a spruce-studded clearing overlooking the shoreline. Along the shore, a row of canoes and rowboats had been pulled high and overturned along one bank above a series of interconnected piers that ran out into a private cove. The water lapped gently against their pilings, its mirrored surface reflecting the exquisite blue of a clear morning sky, and the warm spring sun poured down over it all like a blessing from God.

Kate stood still, completely astonished, then broke the trance enough to wander through the compound with the awe of a child. A series of needle-carpeted pathways led from cabin to cabin, winding through trees that had been thinned to a few solitary stands of majestic spruce and fir. The pathways were immaculately raked, the pine needles evenly spread to cushion the foot. Cabin porches were swept clean of any debris, the windows shone from a recent polishing and bright checkered curtains hung at every window. The clearing, mostly open to the sky and sun except for the wall of forest around the perimeter of the campgrounds, boasted a thick and lush coat of the needles.

The lodge was as well groomed as the rest of the compound. It was huge, a good hundred feet long and half that deep, with a sharply pitched roof lined with dormers that promised a full second story. She circled the building, peering through large windows that opened onto the wraparound verandas. A huge center lounging area, with a massive stone fireplace climbing up an end wall, was furnished with several clusters of sofas and deep easy chairs. An open stairwell ran up one side wall, then turned for a long gallery-style balcony with rooms that opened off the rear. Beneath the stairwell on the ground floor, an archway led into a large combination dining hall/meeting room taking up one whole end of the building, running its full depth from front to back. The opposite end of the building was divided into smaller meeting rooms. The commercial-sized kitchen and service areas were in the center rear, behind the lounging area.

She walked full circle back to the massive, double front doors. Nailed to the siding above the doors was a large cedar sign with hand-carved letters set into three neat lines:

Behold, how good and how pleasant it is
for brethren to dwell together in unity.
Psalms 133:1

She read it, then reread it. The passage was apt. From the beginning, she had felt a strong sense of community among the members, a sense of commitment, caring and concern for one another that was far too rare in a world that could care less about the other guy. And a setting like this would only enhance and cement those feelings. How on earth had people like this gotten mixed up with murder? And why?

Deep in thought, she moved down the broad veranda stairs and continued on. Further down the shoreline was another clearing with a large campfire circle, where the slope of the ground dipped and formed a natural amphitheater. Scattered around the clearing were barbecue pits, picnic tables and hefty, seat-high logs. Through the cleared underbrush further up the hill, she could spot more enclaves of log cabins. The place was huge, completely encircled by forest.

She continued walking west along the waterline until the wilderness reclaimed the slope and the shore became an impenetrable barrier, then she made a U-turn, retracing her steps until her forward progress was brought to a halt again by the same wild and tangled forest.

She followed the edge of the woods up the hill until its arch passed the center and it curved back down to the shoreline, looking for a trail, a path, a deer path, or a break of any kind. Nothing. No way in or out except by the driveway. Clogged with body-blocking salal bushes and tangles of blackberry vines winding in a jungle madness around the trunks of stunted scrub trees growing in the shade of the parent trees, the whole compound was as secure as a prison yard.

She moved toward the piers then, and walked out to the far end of the longest one, looking around at the surrounding waterfront. No houses, no cottages, no piers, no boats were in sight. Just forest coming down to the waterfront as far as she could see. The place was completely isolated and private.

She turned her back then to the water, sat cross-legged on the end of the pier in the hot mid-morning sun, and surveyed the entire complex from cabin enclave at one end to cabin enclave at the other. She was stunned. Stunned by the beauty of it, stunned by the vastness of it, stunned by the simplicity. She tried to absorb it all, toting up the overall worth of the place. While she couldn't put a dollar amount on the cost, for she had no familiarity with construction costs, she was sure she was looking at a layout easily worth a few million dollars in today's real estate market. At that realization, she gave a soundless whistle and began trying to figure out how this all tied in with the deaths of two teenagers clear over on the other side of the Sound.

Then her eyes rose to the wild forest above the campgrounds.

In her studies of Matt's material the night before, she'd discovered a discrepancy between the early crowing about the amount of land the church had acquired and the years-later hand-drawn maps directing church campers to the site. The early reports and map had described and shown a full section of land, one square mile of it, six hundred and forty acres, about the size of

Bridle Trails State Park. The land had been bordered to the east and north by state forests, and on the west, by the timber company lands she'd driven through. The southern edge, of course, was the campgrounds and the cove.

But after the church's growth hiatus had ended, the maps began to indicate just the access road she'd driven in on and the campground below. There was a whole tract of land, hundreds of acres of it, above the access road that was unaccounted for.

Several explanations were possible. The church had no use for it and deeded it to the state for more forest land. Or they'd sold it, to the timber company, for instance, to raise money. Or they'd merely simplified the map and the driving directions to guard against losing a few church members to the wilds of the Olympic Peninsula, truncating the property to create less confusion for the church members.

She felt that those were all good and valid theories, and she was half tempted to just let that puzzle go. She'd seen the campgrounds now. They were certainly more substantial than the basic, raw tent sites she'd thought they'd be, but everything looked at peace here, and what they had to do with the killings was beyond her.

But she had this need to dot the *i*'s and cross the *t*'s. It was genetic, she was beginning to suspect. Her curiosity was definitely getting the better of her.

She packed up her camera and hiked back up the lane to her car. Listening one last time to the hum of the forests, she felt the human emptiness of the area. It was almost frightening, this terrible sense of being absolutely alone in the world.

So, she promised herself, just a quick look-see then. She slid her camera case into the front seat of the car and climbed in behind the wheel.

Chapter Twenty

The large parking circle where she'd left her car was at the edge of the state forest. According to the early maps, she'd be partway up the slope, crossing the bottom third of the church's original section. Driving slowly along the private road, she kept her eyes peeled on the upside of the slope, looking for any break in the forest wall that would lead to the rest of the church's land. There was none.

She reached the swing gate that marked the end of the church lands and crossed into the timber company's forests marbled with logging trails. She explored any trail leading up the mountainside. Some offshoots were car width, with deep ruts worn in over years by heavy logging trucks, and she was able to drive the length of them. Others could just barely be called a path, and she left the Honda and hiked them to the end. They all dead-ended at solid forest walls.

By early afternoon, she'd explored every trail coming in from the south, west and north. There was a vast tract of forest she was circling that she just couldn't penetrate; every small inroad into the woods ended with a solid wall of the wilderness blocking her way. She drove along the northern border for a few miles, finally found a county road heading south back down toward the bay, took it and headed along the eastern edge of the forest.

She was curving around a tight bend when she spotted a hard-packed dirt road leading back into the woods. She turned onto it and crept along as it twisted and wound into the interior. At one point, it climbed uphill for a few hundred yards before it crested and began a gentle downhill slope. The forest allowed no view of the water, but from a dead-reckoning perspective, she figured she was only a mile or so above the church campgrounds. There was no doubt it was contiguous to the church property. It had to have been part of the original parcel.

She rounded a curve and came into a parking bay that had been built up to road level with logs and dirt fill. There was room for about four vehicles to park, nose-in, but at the moment the short parking strip was empty. There were no buildings in view, only the forest, with a bulldozed driveway leading off to the south downhill through the trees.

She slowed to a halt, looking the situation over, unsure of how to approach this. With no cars parked there, with no buildings in sight and no one around, and with only the usual noises of forest birds and animals drifting in through her lowered windows, she had no way to assess what was ahead. She decided to play it safe.

She passed up the parking bay and kept on the access road until she found a wide spot a few hundred yards beyond. She pulled her car far enough into the shrubby undergrowth so that it was hidden from the driveway, then dug out her hard-sided camera case. She tugged the camera free from its compartment, rearranged the rest of the contents so her gun was on top, strapped the camera securely around her neck by its tight leather holder, then slung the large case over one shoulder. Over her other shoulder went the insulated picnic bag, and she headed off. If anyone discovered her, she was just another shutterbug roaming the earth, happily snapping away.

Walking along the roadside, she examined the wall of underbrush blocking access to the interior of the woods until she found the remnants of an old deer trail. With a last glance around at the empty—and safe, she reminded herself—openness of the road, she slipped into the deep cover of the forest.

The woods were moist and cool and dark. Terribly dark. The firs grew thick, with branches that touched fingertips at the base. Huckleberry thickets and salal bushes clogged any opening the trees left. The ground below was littered with dead branches and rotting logs. She let her eyes adjust to the dimness, then picked her way from tree to tree and shrub to shrub, working her way through the twists and turns of the deer path.

She ducked and dodged stray branches that could snap and scratch, tripping now and then over humped roots or rotting logs covered by dead forest debris, barely avoiding a couple of nasty falls. Obviously, the deer knew something about maneuvering through the woods that she didn't.

One spot was particularly treacherous. A deep, sheer-sided gully carved by winter runoff twisted across the deer path. A ropy tangle of tree roots arched out over the gully bed of flat granite rock and wild sweet grass, creating a toe trap for the unwary. One particular root snaked directly across the path, hidden by needles, dead leaves and deep shadows. Picking her way along, Kate caught sight of it just in time to avoid a knee-breaking fall on the granite bedrock. Once past it, though, the path ran level for a pace or two before bending around a thick stand of blue spruce and snaking out of sight. Finally, the undergrowth began to thin and she could pick up the pace a little.

A distant sound of girlish giggles drifting in over the chirrups of birdsong brought her to a dead halt. She cocked an ear, seeking its direction. The giggles seemed to come from directly ahead. Then they died away and she could hear nothing more. She inched ahead. Stronger daylight worked its way in as trees thinned. Another few steps and she was at the edge of a clearing. She positioned herself carefully behind one spruce, then gently lowered a face-high branch out of her way and peered out, squinting against the sudden bright glare of a southern sun bearing straight in on her.

In the center of a large clearing was a lodge similar to the one down at the campgrounds. Long, deep verandas. A steep gabled roof, with a row of dormers lining the front downslope. A massive fieldstone chimney rising to the ridgepole. In front of the lodge, two vans and an old Oldsmobile station wagon she'd seen parked at the church before were pulled up in a driveway turnaround.

A couple of more giggles sounded. On the near side of the veranda, two teenaged girls sat on the rail, backs to Kate, dressed in slacks and loose, lightweight tops. One of the girls, her hair in braids tossed forward over her shoulders, was talking. The other, hair pulled back in a ponytail, tilted her head, listening.

Kate dropped the front flap of the leather case, swung her camera into place, zoomed the telephoto in for close-ups and began shooting. She ran off a roll of film, focusing on the girls, then switched lenses for some wide-angled shots of the lodge and grounds. As she reloaded her camera and changed once again to the telephoto, the girl who'd been talking ended her tale with an extravagant gesture, and both girls broke into a battery of fresh giggles.

The open screen door of the lodge swung outward and a third teenager came onto the veranda, holding a large suitcase in one hand. She sat it down at the top of the veranda steps. She said something to the other two, they slid off their perch, and all three began moving what apparently was a good-sized pile of luggage hidden by the railing down the front steps to the parking area.

All three girls wore maternity smocks. All were in the advanced stages of their pregnancies.

And one of them was Josie Hendrix.

Kate sucked in a sharp breath. So *that's* what was being hidden from the church. A group home for unwed mothers. Which wasn't illegal in itself. Group homes for the unfortunate had been a legitimate part of society since the days of the first orphanage. So what they were doing was in no way against the law.

In fact, given the church's stance against abortion, it was rather honorable.

Then why were they hiding it from the church?

She frowned and swung her camera lens around to follow the girls as they made trip after trip to carry the luggage to the vans. She took care to stay well concealed, shoving the camera through the tree branches, taking as many shots as her finger could fire.

While the other two made the trek back and forth, Josie Hendrix had taken charge of loading the luggage into the back of the van. She was a pretty girl, far prettier than the yearbook pictures showed, with light blond hair, large blue eyes and a sprinkling of freckles across her cheeks and nose. Kate took a dozen shots of her, some close-ups, some with a wider angle to show the large bulge of her belly.

After a bit, Kate lowered her camera. So far she'd counted thirteen suitcases, with more to come. That was far too much luggage for just three girls. Either they were young Imelda Marcoses in training, or there were a lot more girls around. Kate focused her camera lens once more on the front porch, hunkered down and waited.

Within a minute or two, the screen door swung open and a man and two women emerged into the dusky shadows of the veranda. Using her telephoto lens as binoculars to penetrate the depth of the shadows, she zoomed in for a close-up look. Well, well, well, she thought. Nancy Wells. With Pastor Ansel Lang at her side. The second woman was a plump, motherly looking woman she'd never seen before.

There was some disagreement going among the three of them, for Nancy Wells was doing some heavy talking to them both. Ansel Lang stood there, shaking his head, chin set at a stubborn angle, protesting whatever she was saying. The motherly woman nodded agreement at each argument Ansel made.

Kate's shutter finger started firing shot after shot. The argument continued for another couple of minutes until Nancy put both hands on her hips in a pose of utter frustration, gave Pastor

Lang an exasperated stare and said something short and sharp to him. His protests withered away and he turned and stared into the distance. Straight at the trees shielding Kate. His back went suddenly rigid.

Kate's reaction was instant. She dropped to the ground and scrunched down behind the thick protective screen of the lower spruce branches. He could've stiffened at something Nancy said. Or he could've stiffened at seeing a glint of sunlight off the lens of the camera. Whichever, she was taking no more chances.

After a moment, when no alarm sounded, still bent low, she cautiously pushed one end of a bottom branch down to create a small slit of vision. All three were still on the porch, back in conversation. Without her telephoto lens, she couldn't make out their facial expressions, but there was nothing in their posture to indicate alarm. And it appeared Pastor Lang had gotten over his little pout enough to turn back and join in the discussion again.

The three girls finished loading the van, climbed the veranda stairs and joined them for a moment, then the whole group went back into the lodge.

Kate backed away from the spruce and stopped to consider her situation. She'd shot several rolls of film that neither Pastor Lang nor Nancy Wells would be happy about. She needed to get the hell out of there. But if Pastor Lang indeed had seen her and she were caught, they'd be sure to examine her camera bag and they'd destroy any used rolls that were there.

She dumped her camera bag on the ground, withdrew the used film canisters, then rummaged in the picnic bag for the sack of trail food that she'd bagged up at home in a food storage bag with a twist tie. She went a little deeper into the woods and dumped all the trail food out, scattering it over a wide area of thicket, went back to her camera, rewound the partially used roll in her camera, and loaded all the film canisters into the sack. She made a hole beneath the needles underneath the spruce, pushed the tied bag deep into it and smoothed the needles back in place. A rummage through the camera case produced an old lens wiper and she twisted it into a tight coil and wound it around a twig to mark the tree.

She stood up and roamed the area, looking for any signs of her presence. The trail food had sifted well into the thicket. Some hungry squirrel might find it, but it was doubtful any human would. And the needle carpet beneath the spruce looked its normal humped and undisturbed self. There was one last thing to do. She loaded a fresh roll of film into her camera, then ran off a series of quick shots of the woods behind her. If by chance she was caught and the film was developed, all they'd show would be a series of close-up studies of some not very interesting fir branches.

She'd done what she could. She started heading out.

She tried to glide along the deer path as silently as she'd come. Think deer, she thought. Pretend you're a deer. The gully was less treacherous returning than it had been going, and knowing what was there now, she crossed the grass-covered bedrock and took the tripping root in stride.

As she made her way back, she kept track of the forest noises. A rustle of leaves here, another over there. Each one brought her to a dead halt. But the chittering of coons and the songs of the birds continued on undisturbed.

The closer she got to the road and her car, the safer she felt, and her thoughts began to wander. Her mind was clicking now, putting the story into chronological order. It all added up like a cash register tape. The closing of the campgrounds many years back—so this place could be built, of course. Then the sudden wealth of the church, the explosion of money and buildings. The one or two girls each school year who'd suddenly disappeared. Even the rumor of the harems fit. What was a collection of young women if not a harem?

But this place dealt with more than just the local Woodhaven unwed mothers, Kate surmised, threading her way through the treacheries of the deer path. Though the words of the girls on the veranda had been indistinct, she had picked up a lilt in the murmur of one of them that was odd for the Pacific Northwest.

There'd been almost a Southern slur in the phrasing, a certain drawling rhythm that westerners don't have. She'd have bet all her comp time that this home for unwed mothers was being filled with a pool of pregnant girls from throughout the country.

She made it safely past the last loop of root, rounded a bend without any more trips and broke free of the woods.

Pastor Lang stood on the road with a hunting rifle aimed at her breast, his glasses glittering with reflected light glare.

She came to a sudden standstill. Her eyes flicked from man to gun. Neither look was encouraging. Behind the sun-glazed lenses, the man had face and eyes as cold as the rifle barrel. Very un-pastor like. As for the gun, it was a Winchester thirty-ought-six, like Daniel Taft's, except scratched and worn, an easy gun to carry in the woods, yet plenty big enough to hold the size of slug that would crash a deer. Worse, it carried five of those little hummers, just in case the shooter's aim was lousy. And the hammer on this one was cocked and ready to go. It was nothing to argue with, for it could bring any cop to an instant dead halt. Literally.

Kate took it all in with one glance, then gave him a sad smile. "Oh Ansel," she chided gently, indicating the gun pointed straight at her. "What do you want to go and do something really dumb like this for?"

Ansel Lang motioned for her to start walking but Kate didn't budge.

"You haven't done a lot of this, have you, Ansel? Capturing a cop at gunpoint, I mean." She shook her head sadly. "The first thing you should do is make me put my camera case in the car. I have a gun in there. Then you should frisk me to make sure I don't have another one taped to me someplace. Really, Ansel, when you've got a cop in your sights, you've got to take a few precautions here and there."

Not giving him a chance to respond, she marched off down the road in the direction of her car. Lang had no choice but to follow her. Or to shoot her.

She tramped up to the back of her car, dug her keys out,

opened the trunk and dumped her case in. Then she stalled a bit. She added the picnic tote and made a big deal of shoving the paint cans around to make room. But he was smart enough to stand well back from striking range.

When everything was arranged just the way she wanted it, she straightened and slammed the lid shut. "At your service, Pastor Lang. Lead on."

He marched her back along the road and down the main driveway to the lodge. He stayed several paces behind her, within easy shooting distance, but too far back for her to make a sudden swing and grapple for the rifle. Compared to the deer path, the driveway was a Sunday stroll in the park, and though she tripped and stumbled on purpose a couple of times trying to draw him closer, he simply paused and waited for her to right herself. He was cold, deliberate in his motions, and grim. Very grim. Resigned, she led the way into the parking area and headed for the front veranda steps.

"Around to the back," he ordered. She obeyed.

The rear door to the lodge was in the center of a long wall, with a row of windows spreading out on either side. She kept watch for any place she could hide, anything she could use as a duck blind, anything she could grab as a weapon. But the rear veranda was bare, with not even a garbage can in sight.

The door led into a utility hall, with a large kitchen off to the right that held a six-burner restaurant-sized cooking range and a commercial-sized refrigerator and freezer. Off to the left was a laundry with two pairs of commercial-sized washers and dryers. Her suspicions that the lodge housed more than three girls were right. Being right, though, didn't provide her with a whole lot of satisfaction at the moment. Again, her quick scan showed nothing she could snatch as a weapon.

He ordered her into a back hallway just beyond the laundry room, then on down into an office at the back corner of the house. The room was fairly large, fully carpeted, and comfortably furnished with a couple of deep, soft chairs, some bookcases and an old rolltop desk and swivel chair. Dusky daylight seeping in from windows shaded by the veranda gave it a dim, peaceful look. It was a combination office and adult retreat, Kate surmised, for when a houseful of giggling teenagers got too much for—whom? The unknown woman on the porch?

Lang gestured with the rifle barrel to one of the deep chairs, waited until she was seated, then turned the wooden swivel desk chair around to face her and took it himself. He switched the rifle to a one-handed grip, the stock tucked back under his arm, the barrel still aimed at her, his forefinger firmly inside the trigger guard. With his free hand, he swung the phone from the top of the rolltop down into his lap and punched an intercom button. "Nancy, I'm in the office. I need you in here immediately." He set the phone down without waiting for a response, then sat and stared at Kate, face clearly worried.

Catlike, jungle senses crackling, eyes hooded to blank her thoughts from view, Kate tucked her feet under her as if settling in for the duration, curled deep in the chair, appearing at ease.

A racket of noise was coming from overhead. The thumps and thuds of several pairs of feet pounding back and forth across the floorboards above mixed in with a lot of chatter and giggles. An occasional friendly yell punctuated the sounds. Now and then, a deep-throated, more mature voice interspersed a comment.

She glanced up at the ceiling once, then back at the pastor. "How many girls do you house here at one time?"

He motioned her to silence, but his glance jumped from the noises overhead, down to his wristwatch, over to the door, then back to her.

Kate pushed him a bit. "Does Pastor Barnes know about this little setup?"

Before he could answer, Nancy Wells shoved the door open. She paused in the doorway, hand on the knob, mouth open to say something, face filled with irritation. At the sight of Kate, though, she went rigid. "I should've figured." Her eyes flicked to

Ansel, then to the rifle. Hands on hips, she snapped at him, "What on earth have you done?"

"That's what I asked him," Kate said mildly.

"She was snooping around," Ansel said.

Nancy gave an exasperated sigh. "But a rifle? For heaven's sakes, Ansel!"

The pastor wilted a bit.

Nancy turned away from him and aimed a hard stare at Kate. The silence stretched out and Kate was beginning not to like that stare. It had the cold, impersonal look of a cattle rancher selecting a prime heifer for slaughter. Finally Nancy said to Ansel, "What have you told her? How much does she know?"

There were two ways Kate could play it. She could sit there and play the innocent, hoping they'd let her go. If there hadn't been a weapon involved, she might've tried that ploy.

The rifle, though, changed all that. Bringing her into the lodge under rifle point confirmed that something was badly out of kilter here, and Nancy would no more buy the innocent act than Kate would've if the situation had been reversed.

Kate spoke up before Ansel could. "I already know most of it," she said calmly. "You didn't ride the bus up to retreat with the girls. You drove up later on at suppertime. After you killed Sarah."

Nancy's eyes turned amused and Ansel's face drained of color.

Kate waited, giving Nancy plenty of time to respond. Inside, she was all cat, light-footed, aloof, her mind icy cold, leaping from connection to connection to connection. Nancy remained silent and she pushed on. "When Sarah got sick that morning, you made a pretty shrewd guess as to what was wrong. You talked with her when you took her home, got her to admit she was pregnant, then you went back to the school to talk to Pastor Lang about bringing Sarah up here. But he was tied up in budget meetings until after three, and you had to wait for him to get free. The two of you agreed to make the pitch to Sarah, so you went back to her house and using some excuse, got her out of there.

You and Pastor Lang took her to an out-of-the-way place, Bridle Trails, where no one you knew would stumble on you. You took her for a stroll in the woods and explained your program here. But Sarah surprised you. She planned to keep her baby. And so she turned you down. Flat."

Kate paused. So far it all fit. The key to Sarah's murder lay in Sarah's character. It always had.

"Her refusal left you in a terrible quandary," Kate went on. "You had exposed your whole scheme up here and she'd rejected it. There was no way you could count on her silence, and so she had to die. One of you picked up a branch that was lying around and swung.

"Once she was dead, then it was a matter of pure logistics. One of you carried the branch away and dumped it somewhere. I'm going to guess you, Nancy. You'd have to drive up here for retreat anyway. It'd be easy enough to toss it along any of the miles of woods along the route here. And you, Pastor Lang, while Nancy came on up to retreat, you went back to the church and got on with the rest of your day."

He'd long since dropped his gaze to the center of the rug. Now he raised up, face drawn and old. "I wasn't there," he said dully.

Poker-faced, Kate absorbed the confirmation of her story. She believed him. There was that flat sound to it that made it a statement of truth. Nancy was her killer.

Nancy didn't react to the pastor's statement. In fact, she did none of the things partners-in-crime did when one turned on the other. No snapping at him to shut up, no finger-pointing, none of the verbal tricks that were so typically pulled in front of cops and that were such a giveaway when they were.

Instead, she watched Kate with thoughtful eyes. "Why would I do any of that?" she asked coolly. "It's not illegal to run a group home like this. There'd be no need to kill Sarah."

"You're right," Kate agreed. "It's not illegal to run a group home." Adrenaline fueled her mind now, that superhuman rush of pure intellect that leapt the chasms and gaps of her thinking,

canyons that couldn't be crossed by even the most plodding trail of thought. Her synapses fired like a nest of machine guns and the answer fairly leaped out at her, blindingly clear. Money and unwed mothers. She let the silence build a moment, then added, "Unless, of course, you're selling the babies."

She'd connected. Nancy didn't react, but Lang did.

He kept the rifle aimed at Kate, but his spine sagged and his shoulders slumped and slowly he collapsed back in his chair. A look of despair and defeat crept into the lines of his face. He seemed like some papier-mâché caricature of a man, stiff-surfaced but hollow inside, collapsing in on itself from sheer weakness. The rifle sagged in his arm.

Nancy saw this. Cool as always, she held out her hand to Ansel for the rifle. "I'll take over now, Ansel. You go round up the girls and get going."

He looked up at her blankly for a moment, then reluctance and worry edged in. He tightened his grip on the rifle stock. "What are you going to do?"

Nancy held out her hand for the rifle and snapped her fingers, like a teacher standing over a student, snapping her fingers to be handed an overdue homework assignment. "Don't worry about it. Just get going, will you?"

Kate gave the pastor an appraising look, wondering if he would protest, but the rifle barrel wavered even though he still hesitated in handing it over.

"You know," Kate said to him, working at keeping her voice easy and level, not wanting to risk challenging him and getting his back up. "If you had nothing to do with Sarah's death, you're not in half the trouble you would be otherwise."

His look quickened with hope for an instant, but Nancy's quick mind had divined where Kate was headed with this, and she was already reacting. She grabbed the rifle from the pastor and, keeping her distance, swung the business end into place, aimed directly at the center of Kate's chest. "Go, Ansel," she commanded. "You're running out of time."

Kate had no trouble deciphering that order. Suitcases, girls dressed to leave. Train, bus or plane. Plane, she'd bet. It would be a three-hour drive between here and Sea-Tac, at least, depending on ferries. She stole a glance at her watch. Two-thirty now. Say, six o'clock arrival at the airport. Seven o'clock flight, then?

Ansel wavered a full second longer, then nodded. With a last worried glance at the two of them, he left the room.

Nancy took over the swivel chair that Ansel had occupied, rifle held properly in both hands, finger in place, and was frowning at Kate again, a problem to be solved. Getting rid of her was obviously next on Nancy's priority list. Kate shifted gears from travel schedules to survival.

She sat silently, tracking the noises in the house. The steady steps of Pastor Lang as he climbed some kind of bare-wooded staircase up to the second story. The murmur of voices up there, his deep male one, a throaty female one, the lighter ones of the girls. The trample of footsteps down the stairs and a milling about in the front part of the house, then another trooping across the front veranda. Two engines came to life with a throaty roar. The vans, Kate thought, listening sharply. There was a shift of gears, a powerful surge, a second shift and another powerful surge, and the engine sounds droned off into the distance and slowly faded away to silence.

Now there was heavy stillness. Just an occasional creak of the log walls, or the slight groan of floorboards settling back onto their crossties. The sounds of a house that was empty.

Nancy stayed put in the swivel chair for a long moment after the drone of the last van died away in the distance, then rose. "All right, we take a walk now." She backed up to a corner of the room and gestured with the rifle barrel. "You first. Out the door, along the hallway, then out the back door."

Kate didn't move. "You know, I took pictures of everything," she said conversationally. "I took shots of you, and him, and the pregnant girls. And the other woman you were talking to. That's

what Pastor Lang saw, the sun reflecting off my camera lens. That's how he knew I was in the woods. And when he found me, he made me put the camera case in the trunk of my car before he brought me in here. You'll want to get the film out of there."

Nancy's eyes narrowed. Lang was gone now. There was no way to prove or disprove what Kate had said.

Kate pushed harder. "Of course, that's only one roll. I hid the others in the woods. And those have shots of the girls loading the suitcases in the van. I used a telephoto lens on those. I just bet those shots turn out clear enough to capture the license plates of the two vans. And of course, once I'm pronounced missing at headquarters and my partner and his buddies start tracking back my movements and find this place, they'll search the woods for some trace of me. So I've left a little marker to help them." She nodded vigorously. "Yes, you'll want to destroy those, too. I took several rolls of pictures out there."

Nancy had no idea whether to believe her or not, and for the first time, doubt showed on her face. "What kind of a marker?"

Kate smiled and shook her head in a sad way. "No, I don't think so. You're going to have a hard time making me tell. What're you going to do, shoot me? You kill me, you'll never find the film."

Nancy's gaze locked with hers. "I'm a crackerjack shot." It was the calm statement of truth. "I can wing a rat on the run. Your kneecaps would be a bigger target. And slower. As easy as shooting a tin can."

Kate stared right back at her, keeping the amusement alive in her face. "But then," she said softly, "you'd have to drag me out of here, and that'd leave traces, too. You have to think this through, Nancy. You're not in a helter-skelter situation like you were with Sarah. You got lucky down at the state park. You can't keep counting on luck, though. There are just too many details involved."

They stared at each other, locked now in psychological battle.

"If it were me," Kate continued on, "I'd make me get the film out of the car, then I'd make me lead you back into the woods to where the buried film is, have me dig it up and hand it over, then gun me down on the spot and leave me there. The old hunting accident setup. In murder, Nancy, the simpler, the better."

Nancy thought it over with suspicion plain on her face, looking for the traps. Finally, she gave a slow nod. "Let's go."

They made a silent parade of two down the hallway and out the back door into the blazing sunlight. Outdoors, Nancy made a prodding motion with the rifle. Kate didn't bother trying to talk to her as they walked up the driveway to the road. First, she wanted to keep the situation defused. To keep Nancy as relaxed and at ease as possible, persuaded this was all going her way. Second, she didn't believe it would do any good. The woman was too cool and shrewd to volunteer anything.

They made the walk down the road in silence. Stopping several paces back from her car, Kate spread her hands and with great care slowly turned around. She pointed to her jeans pocket. "My car keys." Taking care not to make any sudden movements, she slid thumb and forefinger into the pocket and slowly withdrew the key chain. "The camera's in my trunk. Do you want to open it, or shall I?"

Nancy made an impatient gesture for Kate to toss the keys to her. Then she motioned Kate back a few paces, moved to the trunk, opened it and looked in. The paint cans, the camera case, the picnic tote. Nothing else was there. Satisfied, Nancy backed away and motioned Kate forward.

The camera case was on the right side of the trunk, facing sideways. The paint cans were in the middle, one beside the other, and the soft-sided tote was to the left. Without moving the camera case out of position, Kate undid its leather catch. With the rifle aimed at her, there was no time to pluck the gun free and swing it into position. She'd be dead before the gun cleared the trunk. She carefully lifted the leather-cased camera from the bag so that Nancy could follow every move and see clearly what it was.

She rewound the film, then turned the camera face-down in her hand and fumbled to unsnap the flap of the leather case. She finally got the back of the camera opened and removed the spool of film. Now she was juggling camera, case flap and film spool above the opened trunk. The spool slid out of her hands. "Damn."

"What?" Nancy snapped.

Kate turned, closing the leather flap around the camera as she did. "Dropped the film." She turned back to the trunk and began feeling the trunk floor for the film. Her fingers closed on it instantly and she palmed it in her right hand, then transferred the camera to that hand so its body hid the spool. "It's rolled someplace. Let me get this camera out of the way . . ." She lifted the lid of the big case and placed the camera inside, dropping the film in and pushing it down out of sight. She pulled her hands free and let the lid flop back down.

Halfway there, she thought. Keep your cool.

Now she used both hands to scrabble around in the depths of the trunk. Off to one side, Nancy began to make impatient noises. Kate felt around a couple of more times, then straightened and sighed. "I'll be damned if I can find it. I think I'm light-dazzled, I can't see a thing. You try." Her right hand trailed listlessly over the top of the paint can.

"Back off to the side," Nancy ordered as she started to move forward. Kate counted. One, two, three paces that Nancy took. She herself backed up only one, her hand now trailing over the second paint can, catching the wire bucket handle this time. One more step, she urged. Come on, Nancy, take just one more step.

Nancy took the step. In one smooth move, Kate grasped the bucket handle, swiveled and let the paint can fly. It cleared the lip of the trunk with an inch to spare and caught Nancy on the side of the temple before she could duck. She cried out with sudden pain. The rifle dropped as her hands flew to her head, and she staggered a step or two before her knees folded and she sank to the ground. The rifle crashed to the ground, off to one side.

It was a split-second dip into the camera bag for the gun. Kate shoved the safety off and took aim.

Nancy pressed her hands against her temples until the pain eased enough for her to raise up a little. She shook her head and blinked a few times to clear her vision, then looked up at Kate. Her glance, still slightly glazed, flicked from Kate to the automatic aimed at her chest. One hand began to creep out toward the dropped rifle.

"Don't even think it," Kate said easily.

Nancy jerked her hand back.

The lid of the can had been popped by the blow, and paint was pouring out in a thick, glutinous pale yellow mass. A splash of paint had hit Nancy's cheek and splattered like freckles over her skin.

As Nancy became aware of something wet on her cheeks and reached up with a finger to test what it was, Kate lounged against the trunk, gun still aimed at Nancy's chest. "You know, I just knew I was going to like that shade of yellow."

When she got Nancy back to the corner room under gunpoint, Kate made two phone calls. The first was to the local emergency number for some help, then she called the Captain and completely filled him in on her situation. She refused to bother Sam at home.

After she and Hatch had agreed on procedures and manpower and she'd hung up, there was a brief period of quiet during which she and Nancy stared at each other. Nancy's face was set in taut, righteous lines and she was staring at Kate with the distaste and loathing of a Calvinist viewing the devil in person. But there was a smugness underneath the loathing that, after a while, Kate began to wonder about.

Mentally, she began to squirm a little. She already had one doubt about her theory. Why had Peter been killed? He'd played no part in the scenario she'd sketched out.

But more than that, the look on Nancy's face clearly said she was off-base on the whole thing. Finally, she glared at the woman and said, "What?"

Nancy's cool amusement grew. "Don't the police usually check out alibis before making accusations of murder?"

That rocked her.

Then the first emergency vehicle arrived, local official personnel began showing up, and the jurisdictional dances began. There were the county fire trucks with paramedics aboard, followed immediately by some state forestry types checking to make sure a fire wasn't really involved. An ambulance and a couple of Jefferson County deputy sheriff's cars pulled in next, followed in quick order by the Port Townsend police, who'd heard the radio traffic, then the sheriff himself, who'd come to see what the ruckus was about. The Port Townsend police chief, hearing the uproar on the emergency band, decided to join the fun. Then the feds arrived. Three cold-eyed suited types, who were inclined to take charge because of the possibility of an interstate baby-selling racket.

As each unit arrived, its personnel took their turn staring from the doorway into the small corner room, gawking at the two women sitting quietly there, their eyebrows raised in not-so-polite disbelief. All this for that? their expressions said.

As the crowds increased and the chatter ranged from who should take charge to what was needed to be done next, Kate grew increasingly concerned about the preservation of the scene and evidence there. Finally, when it appeared chaos would win over order, she stepped in and took charge.

She borrowed a pair of handcuffs, locked them around Nancy's wrists, then snapped out order after order, eyes blazing, daring anyone to challenge her. The sheriff had jurisdiction over the lodge. She set a couple of his deputies to guarding Nancy, had another couple of them retrieve the buried film, then made the rest mark off the entire clearing with crime scene tape. When the first of it was in place, she pointed beyond the tape and ordered, "Out. Everyone out."

Finally a measure of calm descended on the clearing, with

grumbling men milling around behind the yellow tape. She began then to sort through the conflicting needs and jurisdictions. There was evidence she needed, such as Nancy's car being impounded. There was evidence the feds would need in their racketeering investigation, such as the records from the group home. And they both needed to interrogate Nancy. Next was the problem of where the Jefferson County Sheriff's Department stood, now involved in both a homicide case centered in King County and a federal racketeering investigation about to get underway.

The Captain, Sam, and two more detective teams arrived. By then, it was late afternoon and it felt like the heat of the entire world had gathered in this one spot to pour a concentrated fire down upon the clearing. Wiping perspiration from her forehead as she stood in the hot sun, she outlined the situation to Hatch, explaining the state and federal jurisdictions involved. Firemen, ambulance attendants, state forestry officials, deputy sheriffs and the Port Townsend police department watched. The sheriff hovered nearby. The feds stood off by themselves, cold-faced, aloof, and remote.

Kate finished her report and waited for the Captain's response.

Hatch slowly rotated his gaze around the clearing, toting up the equipment and personnel there from six different jurisdictions, then turned muddy eyes onto Kate. "Just couldn't keep it simple, could you, MacLean."

Chapter Twenty-one

Ansel Lang was caught at the Kingston ferry dock, with seventeen pregnant girls, a woman named Betty Howard, and eighteen airline tickets to Memphis, Tennessee. Upon her original call and briefing to Hatch early in the afternoon, the Captain had relayed a message to the Kingston law enforcement people to pick them up. They'd been rounded up like meek little lambs just as they were about to board the ferry.

While they waited for the group to get there, one of Hatch's teams, two of the federal agents and a unit from the sheriff's department went to rouse a local judge to get some warrants signed. More feds choppered in, with briefcases and calculators, ready to go over the financial records of the home as soon as the paperwork showed up.

It was early evening when the caravan of police, vans, girls, woman and Lang returned to the lodge. The girls were taken to Port Townsend Hospital as a precaution against unexpected baby arrivals, and the three adults were kept separated in different bedrooms with deputies guarding the locked doors.

The Captain had worked out all the jurisdictional disputes between the sheriff, the federal agents and his own people. Kate and Sam had all three prisoners until the warrants showed up, Hatch informed her, at which point the feds would take over. It was the best he could work out with the agents. While Hatch conferred with the sheriff about making video cameras and tape recorders available for the interviews, Kate and Sam organized their interrogation. They'd question Betty Howard first, the girls second, then Pastor Lang, saving Nancy Wells for last. Nancy was still playing the wronged, righteous soul. She was one tough broad in every definition of the term, and they needed every ounce of ammunition they could get before tackling her.

Because of the number of people who'd be watching the interviews, they decided to set up the recording machines in the living room, where there'd be room for everyone. They moved a small table and some straight chairs from the kitchen into the center of the room and surrounded it with a bank of lights for the video recorder. As Kate organized the setup, the remaining FBI agent, a man named Al Jenkins, looked on, watching her speculatively. She ignored him. She was in charge of this aspect of the case. He'd have his shot later. When everything was set up and the cameras were in place, she had the Howard woman brought in.

Betty Howard turned out to be the quasi director of the group home. As far as she knew, the lodge was simply a home for unwed mothers and she'd been hired to supervise the girls and oversee the place. The girls did all the work, the cleaning, the laundry and the cooking, earning their room and board. As for the actual running of the home itself, Nancy Wells selected the girls who'd be coming there and Ansel Lang paid all the bills.

She didn't know exactly what happened after the births occurred. She thought the babies were simply put up for adoption after birth. Yes, a full-time nurse had lived on the premises, but she'd been let go the day before. No, they'd never run into any caesarean births, and no, there had never been any other medical emergencies that couldn't be handled right there. They had, after all, a fully equipped delivery room in the basement of the lodge, and the nurse was also a trained midwife skilled in dealing with most births, even long, protracted ones. A local doctor in Quilcene signed the birth certificates.

As for the flight to Tennessee, all she'd been told was that the home was being closed for renovations for the next few months, and she was to deliver the girls to Memphis, turn them over to a representative from an attorney's office there, then she was to turn around and catch the next flight back to Seattle. She'd been given an extra three months' pay, and if she were free when this place reopened, she could have her old job back. In the meantime, she'd be looking for work elsewhere.

She claimed innocence of any other knowledge about the Tennessee connection. She dealt solely with Ansel Lang and Nancy Wells and reported to either one of them. No, she'd never seen anyone else from the church up there, she didn't even know a church had been involved. As far as she was concerned, she worked strictly for the group home. And no, she'd never spoken to the attorney from Memphis, or anyone else from Tennessee. That part had all been arranged by Ansel Lang.

Kate spent as much time with her as she dared, but the woman's story remained steadfast, and at last she gave up. It was fairly obvious she had no connection to the church or to the murders, which left it up to the federal agents to examine her exact role in the baby-selling affair.

By then, patrol units had brought the girls from the hospital back to the lodge for their interviews. They were from all over the country, mainly from the Midwest and deep South, but some were from the mountain states, Colorado in particular, and a couple were from the East Coast. All they knew was that when they'd been picked up at the ferryboat, they'd been headed for Tennessee, where they were to be met by someone and dispersed to other places. Aside from the assurances they'd received from Nancy Wells that nothing had changed except locations, that they'd be well cared for and that their babies' adoptive parents still waited, they knew nothing else. And no, except for transportation costs home and a hundred-dollar bill for traveling expenses after the birth had occurred, they received no money for putting their babies up for adoption. They knew absolutely nothing about any church in Kirkland, or even about the church campgrounds just south of the group home. They weren't allowed to go beyond their own yard while they were up there.

There was no reason to hold them for the homicide investigation at the moment. Again, the federal agents would have to determine the depth of their involvement. Kate sent them back to the hospital for a twenty-four-hour watch and had Ansel Lang brought in.

Pastor Lang came into the room resigned and beaten. He'd had a good long time to think his thoughts, an epiphany where the meaning of all previous life choices become crystal clear and the future stretching out ahead of him was simply one long continuum of pain and penance. Any fight that had been in him was gone for the moment. Defeated, he spoke in a weary voice with no life or fight in it.

Hatch stood against one wall, out of the pastor's line of sight, merely observing and listening. Sam sat two chairs down from Kate on her side of the table, lounging back, taking it all in. Kate, in charge, also appeared relaxed and at ease, quiet in her questions, asking just enough to get him started, then content to sit back and let him tell it in his own way. The inquisition would come later.

It had started, he said, innocently enough. When the church was young, it had embarked on a building program, constructing first the church, then the office wing. But in doing so, the church had become desperately short of money. They'd overextended themselves, counting on an increase of memberships and tithes to pay for the program, an increase that simply didn't happen. Thomas Barnes had not been aware of the seriousness of the problem, Pastor Lang said, he'd just waved away any concerns about money by saying God will provide. And he was right in a way. Through the skills of Ansel Lang, monies were juggled and the church managed to make it from one month to the next. God did provide.

Then the senior pastor had received the donation of a vast tract of land over on the Olympic Peninsula. He'd envisioned a combination study center and retreat, a place where love for the Christian life and the moral climate he saw as so necessary to everyday life could be deepened and strengthened for his congregation. This, he felt, would not only be good for his church members, it also would be an added incentive for new prospects to join the church. By then, the lines of staff responsibility had been clearly delineated. Pastor Barnes was in charge of the visions. Pastor Lang was in charge of paying for them. And that was a constant juggling act for him, robbing Peter to pay Paul.

During that same time period, Nancy Wells, a fairly new church member, had been teaching in a public high school, and was beginning to see a severe decline in moral values among the teenagers she taught. Sexual promiscuity was rampant. Abortion, even more so. Worse was the brazen openness of these girls, who'd brag about having to take a couple of days off to get rid of their "little" problem. Disturbed, she did some investigating and learned through church affiliations about a lawyer in Tennessee specializing in Christian adoptions and got in touch with him. His group, he'd explained, brought together babies available for adoption and prospective parents ready to provide loving, Christian homes for the unwanted babies. He said that all the expenses of the unwed mother were paid for by the prospective parents, including a little "extra" to cover her "pain and suffering." Nancy tucked that information away, and when she discovered some more girls about to undergo abortions, she managed to persuade one of them to move in with her for the duration of the pregnancy, giving the baby up for adoption after the birth rather than killing the fetus.

When she'd nurtured the girl through the pregnancy, Nancy had added up the total monies she'd received from Tennessee and had been surprised at the amount involved. Prospective adoptive parents were willing to shell out many thousands of dollars in order to get a baby. Plus medical expenses. Plus other miscellaneous expenses for housing, feeding and clothing the mother-to-be during her pregnancy. Nancy began what Pastor Lang termed a cottage industry in her home. She saw the first one through delivery, then took in a second, then another and another.

After several adoptions had gone through without a hitch, mainly due to Nancy's counseling and encouragement whenever the girls threatened to change their minds, the lawyer had approached her with the idea of establishing a home for these girls. He had access to girls in trouble throughout the country and he'd have no trouble filling a home with young unwed mothers needing to hide their pregnancies and willing to give their babies up for adoption.

Nancy, aware of the church's difficult financial situation, had taken the idea to Ansel Lang. They could use the upper church property on the Peninsula for the facility, she suggested, which would be private and remote, yet near enough to the community hospital in Port Townsend if something went medically wrong. Ansel saw the proposal as a financial savior, the answer to the church's money problems. At that point, he took over negotiations with the lawyer and the ante per baby increased dramatically. The attorney would also see to the construction money for the facility. A foundation that kept everyone involved once removed from the paperwork was formed and the campgrounds were closed for one season to allow the construction of the facilities without any danger of discovery.

Once the home was in operation and the first of the monies had started flowing in, Ansel funneled it into the church coffers through the old "foundation grant" accounting technique. Pastor Barnes accepted these monetary gifts as bounty from God; thus he never questioned the source of the funds. He simply accepted them as a symbol of God's blessing upon his ministry.

As the years had passed, both Nancy and Pastor Lang had grown increasingly comfortable with the idea that the exchange of money was for the *care* of the girls, not for the babies, and had done a thorough job of rationalizing their project as good for everyone. Adoptive parents got healthy children they could love, unfortunate girls got safely past their predicament, and the church received a lush influx of moneys to fund their continuing battle against an immoral society. Most important of all to Nancy, the abominable practice of abortion was averted with every baby they saved and she became even more convinced of the righteousness of what they were doing. "That's all she thought about," Ansel told the three detectives, "saving those babies from the abortionist's knife. If she could've, she would've taken in every pregnant girl in the country."

The moneys allowed the church to expand and bring to fruition some of the other visions Pastor Barnes had, including his own school system. While the group home was mainly filled through the Tennessee attorney with girls from other parts of the country, once the church began their own school and Nancy took a teaching position there, she kept a close watch on the older girls for any in trouble. Which did happen now and again in spite of all the precautions the church and school took. One or two a year, Pastor Lang said. So he was not completely shocked when Sarah came up with her problem.

Nancy had properly diagnosed the situation, gotten Sarah to admit it, then approached Lang after the budget meeting on Monday afternoon to discuss whether or not Sarah should be offered the opportunity to move into the group home. After some debate, they'd decided that, in spite of the anomaly of her getting pregnant, Sarah's basic tendency toward responsible behavior would lead her to accept a responsible solution to her problem, which was concealing her pregnancy and putting the baby up for adoption. Thus the risk of revealing the existence of the home was outweighed by the benefit to everyone. Nancy returned to the Taft home to have a further discussion with Sarah.

They'd been dead wrong, though. Sarah turned them down flat.

Nancy returned to the church about three-thirty and caught Lang in his office. According to the report she gave him, Sarah had listened to the proposition all the way through. She'd been somewhat surprised at the existence of such a home, though Nancy had been careful not to tell her where it was located, and doubly careful not to imply that it was connected with the church in any way at all.

But after all of that had been discussed, Sarah simply said no. She was going to keep her child, she said. She categorically refused to name the father of the child, and simply said they were deeply in love and were planning on getting married. Nothing Nancy could say, no argument she mustered, no hard sell she gave, could sway Sarah in the slightest. She had a youth's typical confidence in the glowing future that lay ahead for her, her husband-to-be and their child, and she was equally as confident that together they could weather the ensuing scandal within the church community. She refused to even consider the idea of giving her baby up for adoption.

Ansel and Nancy talked the situation over. They couldn't make Sarah give her baby up if she didn't want to do it, they couldn't force her into the home. They concluded that Sarah would have to be left to fend for herself, to make her way through the mess she was in as best as she could, unaware of exactly how harsh the church's retaliation would be. At that point, Nancy left the church, headed for the campgrounds. He finished up his normal workday in his office, then went on home.

Kate had sat studying him throughout his story, trying to key in on the core of the man. He'd started off quiet and meek, humbled by the situation he found himself in. The sharp creases of his suit had long ago given way to baggy sags, and his shirt was limp from the heat of the day. At first, he'd kept looking around the room with confusion, at the cops, at the video camera, running an absent hand over the top of his head, smoothing down the few separate strands of hair left up there. There was clear bewilderment in his eyes, as if he couldn't quite take it all in. How could a virtuous man of God find himself in a place like this? he seemed to be asking himself.

That didn't last long, though. Ansel Lang was not an emotional man. Not in the positive sense of the word. He would never be the caring, supportive, compassionate person that Pastor Matt was, for instance. He would view problems as though they were a column of figures to be totaled. Run the calculator, get the answer and move on.

But he was not without emotions altogether, and he didn't bother hiding those that surfaced. Most notable was his impatience. Impatience with the questions, impatience with the personnel there, impatience with the process. Anger followed next. Anger that he couldn't just end it when it suited him. Anger that he had no control in this room. Anger that he had to sit and endure this interview whether he wanted to or not.

And with the anger came the truculence. By the time he reached the part of the story about setting up the home, his voice was hard-edged, testy and quarrelsome. "There was nothing improper in what we've done," he contended. "We were being paid to feed and house these girls, that's all. How the adoptions were handled was none of our concern. We aren't any different than any other short-term care facility. The girls came, they stayed, they gave birth, then they went back to their lives. A little wiser, one would hope. As for the babies, they were picked up by a nurse with impeccable credentials and taken away. What happened after that was not our concern."

As if the official personnel sitting there were arguing with him, he exploded in anger. "We saved those babies, damn it!" He pounded the table with his fist. "We saved them from being murdered by their own mothers. How dare you sit here and insinuate we were doing something wrong!" He went on and on about the abortionist's knife, the fate of those poor little souls, the moral evil involved in the whole process, and again and again proclaimed the virtue of what the group home did.

Kate and Sam watched him from behind impassive faces.

When his outrage finally sputtered to a standstill and he'd quieted down to simple righteous indignation, Kate asked mildly, "Well, just how much money *did* you take in for the care of these girls?"

He had the numbers down to the decimal point. Four and a half million dollars and change. Now he turned comfortable, back on familiar ground, proud of his financial acumen. Some of it had been invested as the start of an endowment fund. Every year, he saw to it that the principal grew, yielding ever increasing amounts of income. He talked of percentages and rates of return, the value of one investment over another, the course of the financial markets, present and past, and predicted a financial future where inflation would slowly creep upward again, as would interest rates, and what he hoped the church would gain in increased yields during the coming year. There were no signs of any of the moral complexities involved. This was simply good asset management. How those assets came to be accumulated was immaterial. Cold hard cash was neither moral nor immoral. It simply was.

"And exactly how much," she asked in the same gently curious tone, "did you and Nancy keep for yourselves?"

His indignation was a sight to see. Suddenly, the Pastor Lang she'd seen before tonight, the unremorseful and undefeated Pastor Lang who'd looked at her so coldly through those thick glasses of his all through the investigation, was back. "Absolutely none," he said in a cold, sharp tone. "We wouldn't do something like that."

Kate smothered her reaction to that. Selling babies, yes. Embezzlement, no. How strange the lines are drawn within some people, she thought. "You mentioned the money problems the church was having. I was told the original church building only cost something like twelve thousand dollars. Everything else was done through volunteer help or donations. Time, labor, building materials . . ."

He frowned. "I don't know where you heard that. Twelve thousand was the original estimate. The actual costs ran triple that. That was a great deal of money, twenty years ago. It could pay for a pretty nice home in full."

"So this income you took in, that wasn't pure profit, was it?"

"Of course not, that was gross income. Naturally there were operating costs to be figured in. Net was considerably less."

"What about the legalities of building on church-owned land? Weren't you skirting a fine line there?"

"I have authority to handle all business transactions on behalf of the church. I split away the upper section of land and deeded it over to the foundation. It became a separate entity."

"And there were no squawks about that?" Kate asked.

"It didn't affect the campgrounds. And the church had no need of it. Why would there be?"

"And Pastor Barnes knew nothing of this?" she said with polite disbelief. "You gave away half his church's property and he didn't know?"

"No."

"I imagine he'd be pretty upset if he found out, wouldn't he?"

Pastor Lang shook his head. "He'd understand."

"Then if he'd understand," Kate said softly, "why didn't you simply bring him in on the plan?"

"He doesn't concern himself with those kinds of details."

It was a dire indictment of Thomas Barnes's ministry, Kate thought. He'd worked so hard to create a perfect world for his flock, but like all perfect worlds, it was an unattainable goal. People turned out to be all too human. They betrayed and they lied and they killed and yes, they probably even coveted their neighbor's wife. They committed every sin on earth, just like real people do. Pastor Barnes was in for a soul-wrenching shock.

Kate began to focus in on Monday afternoon. "When Nancy came to talk to you the second time that afternoon, what time did she leave?"

"We only talked a couple of minutes. She was late leaving for the campgrounds and I was busy, so we didn't spend a lot of time discussing it. Sarah had said no, and that was it. I'm going to guess it would've been a little after three-thirty when she left. Twenty to four at the latest."

Kate played with that. Plenty of time for Nancy to stop by the Taft house, pick up Sarah, take her to the clearing in the park and swing a branch. "When you said she was headed directly for the retreat from your office, you're *assuming* that's what she did."

"No. That's what she told me she did, later."

"Oh, so you did talk about it some more."

"Naturally. The timing of Sarah's death was rather a shock."

"But you don't *know* for a fact that she went straight to the campgrounds, do you."

Pastor Lang looked down at the tabletop and repeated the exact words he'd used before. "I wasn't there."

Kate just looked at him. He'd neatly separated himself from the murder. And Nancy. In fact, he'd separated himself from the whole mess, not taking responsibility for any of it. During the whole time he talked, he had not taken an ounce of responsibility for any of this. It was Pastor Barnes who'd gotten the church into financial trouble. Pastor Lang was just a little innocent left to clean up the mess. It was Nancy Wells who found the attorney, who took in the unwed mothers, who came up with the idea of the group home, of building it on church property. Again, Pastor Lang was simply the poor little dupe, forced to go along with it all to save the church. The only things he'd taken credit for were the financial investments, and he was actually proud of those.

She hid the distaste she felt. "You weren't there," she repeated. "At the state park, you mean."

He glanced up. "That's right. The church secretary will tell you that. There was a stack of phone messages waiting for me when I came out of the budget meetings. I spent the rest of the afternoon returning calls."

"But you and Nancy had a lot to protect, didn't you," Kate said softly.

He gave her a hard stare. "I don't know what you're trying to imply here—"

"Well, just look at it from our viewpoint, Pastor Lang. You and Nancy offer to help Sarah through her pregnancy, so you tell her about the home and how the baby can be adopted out. And she rejects the whole idea outright. But now she knows about the home. If she really was planning to keep her baby and marry the dad, then the whole church was going to know about her pregnancy anyway. How could you trust her not to say something to someone? Even a casual comment would be your undoing. So both of you had some pretty strong reasons to not want Sarah around."

"That's absolutely preposterous! I quizzed Nancy thoroughly about what she said to Sarah. It was all generalities. We *know* of this home, she told her, not we *have* this home. It could've been anywhere in the world, for all Sarah knew. There was absolutely no danger in the home being tracked back to the church. None. As for the adoption, Nancy simply said she knew someone who could help her. That's all. If challenged by anyone in the church, she'd merely have explained that there were lots of agencies out there, ready to help. That's what we told the Hendrixes when Josie turned up in her mess, and it's the same story we would've told the Tafts. So any other thought you might have is ludicrous, ludicrous and unjust."

"And Peter?" she asked softly.

She caught him off guard and he looked confused a moment. "What about Peter?"

"Where were you from seven to about ten on Friday morning?"

He looked thoroughly shocked at the question. "You mean when Peter was killed?"

"I mean exactly that, yes."

His gaze was hard. "I was in Seattle. From eight until ten or so. I had a breakfast meeting with our accounting firm."

Her only physical reaction was a brief quirk of the eyebrows. She dutifully wrote down the names of the people the pastor said were in on the meeting. And Nancy Wells had been teaching class. Both alibied. Damn. "If you're as innocent of the murders as you claim to be," she said calmly, "why were you closing down the group home?"

"We didn't right away," he snapped. "Sarah's death was a shock, but there was really no connection between her and the home. It didn't seem like there was anything to worry about. But when Peter was killed, too, that was too much. I figured it was safer to close it down for a while."

"Safer?" Kate echoed softly.

He made no response.

"Did you stop by to see the Tafts Thursday night?"

"No."

"Then when did you talk to Peter after Sarah's death?"

"I didn't."

The old truculent Pastor Lang was back, impatient, brusque, wanting to get on with it. He even glanced at his watch once, as if he had someplace important to be. Then awareness of where he was came over him and he slumped back in his chair once more, glaring at her.

"Then who else in the church knew about the group home?" she asked.

"No one."

"No one," she echoed with polite disbelief.

He took umbrage at that. "Who in the world would we tell? Thomas Barnes lives too much in his private visions to be concerned with the actual day-to-day details of running the church. Charles Ellsworth is more concerned with his precious zero pregnancy rate than seeing what's going on around him. Matt Jacobson would've acted high and mighty about the whole thing, and you can't trust Bob Garrett with anything unless you want it blabbed all over the place. And it's unthinkable to let any of the general congregation in on such a project. It was none of their business, anyway. So who would we tell?"

And that, she thought, was his real opinion of his church and the other pastors he worked with. Contempt and derision.

Kate brought the interview to an end.

They broke for something to eat. One of the deputies had scrounged around the kitchen, fixed some coffee and made a batch of sandwiches. Kate took her food out onto the back veranda, sat on a top step and stared at the forest darkening with the oncoming night. She had finished her sandwich and was drinking her coffee when she heard footsteps come out on the porch. She figured it was Sam and ignored them.

Al Jenkins, the FBI agent who'd been watching her, climbed down the top few steps, coffee cup in hand. "Mind if I join you a minute?"

She looked up at him and shrugged.

"I'll take that for a yes." He sat down a distance away and sat silent a minute, sipping his coffee. Then he turned his body so he could lean back against the railing post and watch her. "That was a good session in there. You do nice work. But I get the feeling it didn't help solve your case."

She thought over his question. "Do I look that worried?"

"Troubled. Not worried, troubled. It's how I get when I feel something's out of whack with a case."

Kate looked at him then. He was thirtyish, tall, neatly put together, trim waisted, slender hipped. Dancer's hips, she thought. The moon hadn't risen yet; his face was hidden in shadow. Yet he hadn't seemed as arrogant as the rest of the feds, his demeanor was friendlier, showing more interest and curiosity than the others. Somehow he'd just seemed more involved.

"What do you do about it?" she asked.

He gave her a half-smile. "What every other dick in the country does. I go back to the beginning and start poking around all over again. You have no choice, you know. You have to follow the scent where it takes you, and when it turns into a dead end, you have to go back. I've spent years on some cases. Reaching dead ends and going back to square one again and again, ad infinitum."

That made her feel a bit better. Even those she considered the "real" pros, the feds with all their resources, facilities, fundings and training, went astray now and then. Back to square one, then. She thought of Norman Overholtz, and nodded sadly.

Behind her, Sam swung the door open and called out, "We're ready with Wells."

Kate smiled a quiet thank-you to Jenkins, then bounced up from the steps. Nancy Wells. She was going to enjoy this one.

Nancy Wells's turn on the hot seat was short and sweet. She let them bring her into the room, let them get the video camera adjusted on her, let them announce day, date and time for the audio, let them read her her rights. She let them do all that without a murmur. Then, when it was all done and everything was in readiness for the interrogation, she looked the camera straight in the eye and said coolly, "I'm not saying a word. I want legal counsel."

The interview was over.

Sizzling inside, Kate had her taken back to the guarded bedroom. She was damned if Nancy was going to get her phone call just yet.

Hatch pulled Sam and her into the kitchen and closed the door on the curious faces in the other room. He stood on feet planted firmly apart, muddy eyes fixed on Kate. He looked grubby, with a stubble of black beard already shadowing his chin, and his clothes were well rumpled. "Well?"

Weary and drained, Kate leaned back against the solid wall behind her and stared off into space for a long moment. Sam stood a few paces away, waiting quietly. She went through it all again in her mind, the motives, the opportunity, the alibis. After a moment, her gaze drifted down to meet the Captain's. "They're not involved in the murders," she said wearily. "Let the feds have them. They'll fry them like a side of bacon."

Chapter Twenty-two

They caught the last ferry out of Kingston late that night, a caravan of them. Al Jenkins led a parade of federal vehicles, with Nancy Wells and Ansel Lang handcuffed in the back of separate cars, sandwiched between agents on either side. Sam and the Captain had each driven their own cars up to the lodge, and they followed Kate's in the ferry line. Once aboard, they all stayed put. Hatch was parked just behind her, leaning back against the headrest, listening to a melancholy country-western tape that drifted through his opened windows. In the car behind him, Sam sank low into his seat and slept. The feds were in the next lane over.

Kate's was the first car in her lane, and she stared at the miles of night-black water spreading ahead of the bow. The boat-generated wind carried a bite in it and after a few moments, it penetrated her denim jacket. She rolled up her window against the cold, then stared out at the water again. Finally, sick of her own thoughts, she leaned back in her seat and closed her eyes for the rest of the ride across the Sound.

It was well after one A.M. when she drove into the driveway and pushed the button on the garage door opener. She was too tired to be nervous about coming home. Exhaustion—the cure for paranoia, she thought. Though she did scan the interior of the garage to make sure she was alone, and she deliberately crossed the yard in the center of the lawn.

She'd climbed up to the front porch and had just collected her mail when a car without lights on glided toward the curb in front of her house. Door keys in hand, she froze. Then she made out the low-slung profile of a Camaro. Black. There was no mistaking that car. Goddard. He'd been waiting for her.

Again, she'd forgotten to leave her front light on. The porch was dark and shadowy, the street deserted and empty. The whole world was asleep. Except for one coasting car. And she was acutely aware of how alone she was.

She'd grabbed the camera case with her gun repacked inside it from the trunk of the car and hung it from her right shoulder, out of the way. Casually she slid the mail back into the box and slipped her key chain into her left hand, then opened the case lid and worked her gun to the top of the camera equipment. She waited, hand inside the case gripping the gun handle tightly.

But the car continued to glide on past. Down the block, its lights came on, the motor revved a couple of times like a bull pawing a warning, then the car sped away, peeling rubber.

In spite of a sudden case of the shakes, she managed to insert the key and get her door open. She slipped inside, slammed the door shut and shoved the new deadbolt home, then she turned and leaned against the door, head tilted back, and stared at the ceiling.

She tried to dismiss the incident as a rather juvenile prank designed to frighten her. Inwardly, though, her stomach pitched and fluttered in rhythm to the pounding of her heartbeat, and she had to admit Goddard's little fright-provoking stunt had worked. The man was, at best, psychotic. Having to deal with him as a colleague had been bad enough, but the thought of having him in charge of their division—and her—was terrifying.

She stood there until the last sound of the car died away. Then she recouped some of her spirit, dug her gun out of the camera case and unlocked the front door to bring in her mail.

If he came anywhere near her, she'd shoot the son of a bitch.

* * *

The Captain had ordered her to take the next day off, and she'd planned to sleep away her exhaustion. But in the predawn darkness of Sunday, the ringing of the phone slowly brought her out of a deep sleep. It took her a good couple of moments to crawl her way to the surface. She fumbled with the receiver and muttered a thick-tongued hello.

"Good morning." Len Franklin's deep, cheerful voice rumbled across the line. Obviously he'd had his first cup of coffee, Kate thought. She should introduce him to Lucy Gray.

"I wanted to catch you before you headed in," his cheerful rumble continued on.

"I'm off today," she mumbled in a thickened, sleep-slurred voice. "I thought I'd sleep in."

That didn't faze him in the least. "I've got Peter Dickerson done and, guess what, surprise, surprise, he wasn't the daddy to Sarah's baby. Wrong blood type."

Her eyes flashed open at that and she shoved the last of sleep away from her. "You're sure?"

"Positive. Sarah was O-positive, the fetus was A-negative, and Peter's B-positive. There's no match there."

Her mind flew, trying to assimilate new bits and pieces. Peter *wasn't* the baby's father. Then who was, and why was Peter killed then? "What about the time of death, Len?"

"If you know when he ate his Cheerios, I've got it for you."

Her notes were in the other room. What had Alice Dickerson said? She replayed her mental tape of the conversation. "Six forty-five," she said finally. "His mother said he ate breakfast at six forty-five. And yes, it was Cheerios." She didn't want to even think how he could tell. Not at this hour in the morning.

"Okay, then. That sets the time of death between eight forty-five and nine-fifteen yesterday morning."

"Good." Instantly, her mind went back to Norm. Now she could zoom in on him, track his movements—

Then the frown came. "Are you sure about that?" she asked.

"Positive. It's correlated both ways, Katie. First, by the condition of the body when I examined it at the park yesterday. Some things set in a certain number of hours after death, and not before. And second, working the other way forward, he died between two and two-and-a-half hours after he ate last. If he ate at six forty-five, then he died between eight forty-five and nine-fifteen, like I said. Does this create a problem for you?"

An image of a freshly washed and waxed car and bike came to mind, the cement driveway still wet under both. "A little one," she said in a small voice. "I think my only suspect just got alibied."

The day dawned hot and still. From the looks of the huge orange orb sidling upward in the clear, cloudless sky, it was only going to get hotter. Kate slipped on a pair of shorts and a T-shirt, poured her coffee and took it barefooted out onto the back porch where she could sit on the steps and watch the flaming colors spread their vivid stripes across the lower heavens.

A serious depression was nibbling at the edges of her consciousness. Her case had gone to hell in a handbasket. It had just plain fallen apart on her. She felt like she was fighting an octopus, with tentacles here and tentacles there, holding her at bay, stopping her from getting near the brain center, and every time she managed to bypass one tentacle, another would rise up and wrap itself around her like some thick, obscene growth. If only she could wrestle the octopus into submission, get a handle on the case. Her fear was that once it did break, it would be all of a sudden, all at once, with a vicious thrashing of the waters and a clutch fight to the death.

Glumly, she buried her chin in a palm supported by an elbow planted on top of her thigh and stared straight ahead at nothing. What next? She could devote the day to going back over all the materials and develop some new questions to ask. Obviously, she'd been concentrating on the wrong ones. Or she could go into headquarters and do some of the paperwork piling up. Or she could purge her files, a job to be done sooner rather than later. Or, she could simply forget it all for now and go back to bed.

She stared back up at the heavens. The dawn colors had blurred and waned, and now a summery blue sky stretched from the Cascades to the Olympics. Her sunrise had faded on her. Just like her case.

She went back to bed.

She slept until noon. Over a fresh pot of coffee at her snack bar, she got out her notebook and the church roster. She went over the names of every person she'd met since the case began and came up with a list of people whose whereabouts were unaccounted for during the two murders. Then she began making some calls.

Alice Dickerson had been up at retreat on Monday afternoon and at the church, working on the food, on Friday morning. Her husband had been at work at those times. Yes, Denise Hickman had been at retreat with her.

Emma's voice was pure ice on the phone when Katie called the Barnes home for the pastor. Pastor wasn't home. He'd been called down to some federal offices in Seattle by Ansel Lang. Her tone of voice said it was all Kate's fault. But in response to Kate's questions, she said that Pastor had come home shortly after three on Monday, and left for the church on Friday around ten. Up until then, he'd locked himself in his study at home to work on his sermon for Sarah's funeral. And yes, she said icily in response to Kate's last question, she knew exactly where Patty Jacobson had been on Monday afternoon from three until five. Sitting right beside Emma Barnes at a needlepoint workshop. Along with Terry White and Kate's potato-peeling neighbor, Evelyn Dietz.

That one phone call knocked out most of Kate's candidates for villain of the piece. With a strong sense of foreboding that it would be no more productive, she made the next call.

Pastor Ellsworth's voice was about as cold as that of Emma Barnes. He'd gone into a curriculum planning meeting with some of his teachers after the budget session on Monday. At her request, and in glacial tones, he listed the people in the meeting with him. Friday morning he was at the dentist. "I suppose you want their phone numbers," he said sarcastically.

"That would be helpful," she responded in mild tones, and, taking down the numbers, created a second list.

Since it was Sunday, and with an edge of self-importance clearly in his voice that he was privy to such privileged information, he included his dentist's home number. Kate made the calls. The pastor was well alibied.

That left the last name on her original list and she dialed the by now familiar number.

Pastor Matt had had a doctor's appointment Friday morning, he told her.

She took down the doctor's office number, then said to him, "By the way, blood tests have proved that Peter Dickerson wasn't the father of Sarah's baby after all."

There was a moment's silence, then he said, "All right, I'll tell the Tafts. From their point of view, I don't know if that's good news or bad news."

She hung up and looked at her list again. Everyone there was clear. That left approximately seven hundred and sixty-three people she hadn't personally met yet, to be questioned.

She slid off the barstool and went to Smokie Jo's and shot some pool. Then she went to dinner with Pearl, where they dissected Sam as well as their pizza. She was home and locked in behind her deadbolts before dark.

She was up early on Monday and stopped for some breakfast at Papa's Diner, but ended up barely touching her bacon and eggs. She finally pushed her plate away and was on her way to headquarters as the sun came up over the Cascades. She was too deep in thought to even notice the sunrise.

Peter's funeral was scheduled that morning at ten. She could go and watch and observe some more, but she'd done that at Sarah's visitation Friday night and so far no one had accommodated her by wearing a sign proclaiming *Guilty* across its front. There was no reason to suspect anything different would occur at Peter's funeral. She gave brief thought to going anyway, but she didn't have the heart. Instead she spent the morning doing all the reports that had piled up since Friday morning.

She did call and check on Ansel Lang's Friday morning when Peter was killed. Three reputable men from a top-line accounting firm swore he was at breakfast with them during the critical time period. She thanked them and went back to the reports.

Throughout the morning, Goddard had taken to wandering around on the loose, a major pain in the ass. With the word out about his upcoming promotion, he strutted around the bullpen like an emperor at a peasant's gathering. Fry was a slight, dark shadow behind him. In between his struts, Goddard kept watch on her, eyes narrowed, arms crossed, but she refused to react. She also refused to give him the satisfaction of mentioning seeing his car drift past her house Saturday night. Instead, she concentrated on her desk work, and under the guise of doing her reports, she began to purge her files.

It seemed to take forever. When you finally became aware of what someone else might read into things, it seemed most everything she'd written down outside of her formal reports could be misinterpreted and turned into a weapon against her. Lord, she thought at one point, I really am getting paranoid.

Then the phone call from Homer came. He'd had the analysis done on her signature on the safety-deposit box bank form. He went into a detailed report of the various tests they'd run, but the long and the short of it was that someone had cut her signature out of some other document, and had taped it into place on this one. They'd then run it through a copy machine, whited out any signs of the tape, and recopied it, ending up with a clean form which, from the bank's point of view, she'd clearly signed. And no, there was no way to track down who had done this.

Paranoia justified, Kate thought, and went back to purging the files.

When she'd finally finished, she stuffed the purged papers in a manila envelope to take with her and shoved her cleaned desk drawers closed and locked them. It wouldn't keep Goddard out, not after his little tricks with her house and her safety-deposit box, but it made her feel better.

It was late, well after two when she broke for lunch. She hurt Sam's feelings by going off alone. He gave her his most sorrowful basset hound look, but she needed to get out of this zoo that passed for a workplace and be alone with her melancholy thoughts.

She grabbed the I-90 and drove all the way up to Snoqualmie Pass simply to get some of her misery out of her system. Just shy of the summit, she pulled into the Swiss Hutte, a mountain chalet serving an outstanding cheese fondue. She placed her order, but skipped the wine she'd normally have with it and had iced tea instead.

When the fondue came, though, she simply swirled a cube of bread in it, watching the trail it made in the melted cheese. Tired, glum, discouraged, she stared down at the thickly coated cube, feeling her stomach heave at the sight of it, trying to figure out where she'd gone wrong.

Slowly she circled in on it. She'd made a basic assumption—that only Lang and Wells and the baby's father had known of Sarah's pregnancy. Who else could have known?

Her eyes began to narrow in concentration. As she stirred the same bread cube over and over in the fondue pot, she began to focus in on how to find out. After a few minutes, an idea came to her. The thought of it made her grit her teeth. She fished for some other solution, but found none.

She stirred the abused cube a bit longer, but in the end gave in to the inevitable. It had to be done. Sighing, she paid the bill for the food she hadn't eaten and left.

Maisie was grazing in the pasture again under the hot blazing sun as Kate turned into the long driveway leading up to Lucy Gray's place. Puget Sound had yet another hot, sunny day and automatically Kate glanced over at the mountains and searched the western sky for some cooling rain clouds. But the sun beamed down from a perfect umbrella of untainted blue that stretched from the Cascades to the Olympics. She pulled her blazer loose from the sweat spots spreading underneath her shoulder holster. Nature's furnace going at a full roar was hell on someone who had to disguise wearing a gun. She'd be glad when the heat wave broke.

Lucy was in the barn, mucking out Maisie's stall. She took one look at Kate's heat-flushed face and grim look, and set the shovel aside. "Let's go inside. Looks like you're in desperate need of a shot of lemonade."

Kate followed the woman into the cooler dimness of the kitchen and sank gratefully into a chair at the small round table. She watched Lucy dart from cupboard to refrigerator, then accepted the glass of ice-cold lemonade with gratefulness and downed half of it, nonstop. She set the glass down and sat back with a sigh. Her gaze focused then on the old woman sitting across from her.

Lucy had sat quietly sipping her own cold drink, waiting patiently for Kate to speak.

At last, Kate gave her a wry half-smile, acknowledging within herself the irony of coming to the woman for help after ordering her to stay out of her case. "Lucy," she said finally, "when you were telling me how you found Peter's body, you mentioned making some phone calls that morning. That would've been Friday morning. Exactly when, to whom, and why?"

Like many people, Lucy had a wall phone hanging over the end of one kitchen counter, with pens and notepads and a telephone book piled beneath. Without a word, she got up and went to the stack, pulled the large phone book loose, then pawed through the notepads until she found what she wanted. She carried the armful back to the table and attacked the telephone directory first. "This is the new one issued at the beginning of the year," she said, pointing to the bright yellow cover with the year printed in huge black type. She searched through the white pages until she found the listing she wanted, then she turned the book so Kate could read it and pointed to one line. "Supposedly, Josie Hendrix left school in November because her parents were transferred out of state. But as of January one they were still listed in the phone book. Different address, but same first name and initial. So I made a few calls around to see what was what."

"And how did you make those calls?" Kate asked. "Who did you call and what did you say?"

"I went straight to the source. I called the Hendrix home and reached Mrs. Hendrix." Lucy grinned. "For some reason, she thought I was some kind of research telephone-survey person asking about church affiliations. Then I inquired about family members, and she listed two kids, both in grade school, both attending a private Christian grade school. Not Woodhaven, though. When I persisted, she said her oldest daughter was attending a private school in Tennessee, Oakcrest Academy in Memphis. When I started asking about it, though, she turned skittish on me and wouldn't give me the phone number or address and finally hung up on me. A helpful long-distance operator assured me that there were no listings in Memphis or any of the neighboring suburbs for an Oakcrest Academy. Then I called the Tennessee Board of Education and another helpful lady searched all the private-school listings they had. She looked under every variation of Oakcrest she could think of. Oakcrest Academy, Oakcrest School, Oakcrest Christian, Oakcrest High, Oakcrest Christian Academy, even just plain Oak and Crest schools, with just the one word in the name. There was nothing that even came close."

Lucy was enjoying this display of her detecting skills, and Kate had to smile a bit at the show. The old woman hadn't done badly for herself. But still, the disappointment was sharp. Though Lucy couldn't know it, the Josie Hendrix disappearance was solved. She'd been hoping for something different, much different. "And so you concluded what?" she said.

"That Josie Hendrix was nowhere near the state of Tennessee."

To Lucy's credit, she skipped the crow of triumph and made it a flat, quiet statement of fact.

"And those were all the calls you made?" Kate asked.

Lucy's face filled with sharp humor. "Good gracious, no. It's not enough to prove where a girl isn't, you need to prove where she is." She nodded in the direction of the road. "Donna Wilhelm across the way had given me an old church roster from Woodhaven. So I started making some local calls, trying to find a friend of the Hendrix family. Someone with a girl Josie's age, who might've kept in touch with her through letters or something."

Kate felt a sudden stab of hope. "What time was this?"

"Oh, I started in my phoning about eight in the morning. I must've been on the phone with the Tennessee people a good thirty or forty minutes, so I'd guess it was close to quarter to nine our time before I started on the local ones."

Kate's hope blossomed. "Okay," she said calmly, not daring to get too excited yet. She nodded at the notepad with name after name neatly printed down the page. "I gather you made a list."

"Yep. Sure did." Lucy held up the pad. "Everyone I tried, and everyone I reached, and notes of what they said." She handed the pad to Kate.

Kate scanned the list, then took it a name at a time. Most of them were unfamiliar. But three of them were startlingly familiar. The Hickmans, the Dickersons, and the Tafts.

Mrs. Hickman and Alice Dickerson had both answered when Lucy called. Martha Taft hadn't been home. "What reason did you give for your call?"

"Just that I was trying to track down an address for Josie Hendrix, that I had a little gift to send her." Lucy shrugged. "They didn't ask me how come or anything. I guess since I sound like I am, a dotty old lady, they took me for being an aunt or something. But neither of them could help me. Mrs. Hickman said her daughter, Denise, hadn't heard from Josie since she left. And Mrs. Dickerson said she didn't have a girl that age, just a son. And he wouldn't have been in touch with her for any reason."

"Your note says that Martha Taft wasn't home. Who did you talk to there?"

"Mr. Taft."

"And what did he say?"

"Nothing much. Just that Sarah's visitation was that night, and Martha had gone out to bring in some food for the crowd. And that he wouldn't have known if Josie and Sarah had kept in touch or not, I'd have to talk to his wife about that."

"And did you?" Kate asked softly.

"Sure. I called back later in the morning. She was home then and said the same thing Mrs. Hickman said, that the girls hadn't kept in touch. She was about the last call on the list, and after that I had some lunch, then I took Maisie over to the park for our ride. The rest you know."

Finding Peter's body, she meant.

Kate nodded and fell silent. Could it be?

As she sipped her lemonade, she stared out at the sun-washed pasture, Lucy forgotten, and wandered back over the case. She started from that first moment of viewing Sarah's body in the glen, and moved forward from there, scene by scene, statement by statement. She drained each moment of its nuances, reliving tones of voices, expressions, eye contact or lack of it, body language, gestures, milking even the smallest mannerisms for clues as to the state of the inner soul. She turned these memories over and over in her mind, like separate pieces of wood, examining the tops, the sides, the undersides, the grains, the irregularities, measuring the strengths, looking for the weaknesses.

But there were no weaknesses in the wood, she thought. None. None at all. And a great sorrow welled up within her. Pastor Barnes's perfect world was going to take yet another blow.

Chapter Twenty-three

She left Lucy's shortly before four with a growing sense of urgency. Sarah had been killed exactly one week ago, almost to the minute. To Kate, the symbolism in that fueled a growing sense of dread. Instinctively, she knew who the next victim would be. Not wanting to use Lucy's phone, she raced to the nearest gas station and dialed the Overholtz house. No answer.

A flutter of panic hit. Stay calm, stay calm. Norm could be anywhere. At school, working on his term paper, studying in a dorm room, lounging on the college lawn, sitting on the footbridge over the creek, on his way home, on his way to church, anywhere. It was senseless to try and track him down. She'd have to come from the other end.

She jumped back in the car and thumbed through her notebook for the original notes she'd made on the case. Yes. Right there. She knew where the street was, about a five-minute drive south of here. Even though Peter's funeral had been held this morning, it was still a Monday, and she had a suspicion that with the kind of schedule those well organized church folk set up, some routines would be strictly adhered to. Particularly in this case.

Then, because she couldn't just let it go without one more attempt, she tried the Overholtz house again. No answer.

She called the Duty sergeant then, looking for backup. Sam had gone home. "Patch me through to Brillo, will you?" she demanded. But no, Brillo wasn't there either. Goddard and Fry were around, though. She snorted with disgust and hung up on him. *Damn* it.

That was it then. No backup. She didn't even know where she'd be to tell a team where to meet her. She took ten seconds to weigh the risk of waiting versus the risk of not waiting. Not waiting won. At exactly three-fifty, she backed her car out of the gas station and sped away.

The street was in an old section of Kirkland, south of town off of State Street. She had to go through downtown gridlock to get there. She hit every red light there was.

The house was an old, small frame building, no more than four rooms, she judged, set behind a picket fence that had recently been freshly painted. More of the church's work, she guessed. The street was full of parked cars, but not the one she was hoping to see. And there was none in the driveway nor in front of the house.

She almost kept going, but knowing a little of the situation, she decided she'd better stop and check. There was no answer to her light knock on the front door. She hadn't expected one. She pulled open the screen and tried the door. It was unlocked, and she stepped inside, calling out a soft hello.

The inside was tidy and clean, the old furniture gleaming with a fresh coat of polish, the threadbare carpet freshly vacuumed. The kitchen counters were spotless.

Ellis Dixon lay in a big four-poster bed in the back corner bedroom, dimmed to twilight by the heavy, drawn shades. The old man was curled on his side in a fetal position, his breathing ragged and weak, but regular. His face was an unhealthy scarlet-tinged yellow and his flesh had been shrunken by the cancer eating up his liver so that the paper-thin skin seemed glued directly to his bones. She laid a light hand against his cheek. He felt feverish, and his breathing had a slight, wet, whistle sound to it. A day or two at the most, she judged.

On one wall near his dresser hung an old framed photograph of a young bridal couple from at least fifty years ago, the groom proud, the bride small and pert. The large round table next to his bed held a smaller photo of the bride some decades after. Her hair had turned gray by then and her face was plump, but behind the bifocals, the eyes were still pert and perky. There were no other signs of the woman's presence. Gone, long ago.

She stood by the bedside for a few seconds more, watching the rise and fall of his chest with a professional eye, doing an automatic respiratory count. You could read the progress of the disease from the medicine bottles lined up on the dresser. Mild pain prescriptions gave way to stronger ones. Those were now pushed back against the mirror, and an array of hypodermic needles and small bottles of morphine rested on a snow-white towel folded neatly beneath them. He was in no more pain now, drifting out there somewhere awaiting his final release. Godspeed, old man, she thought. She's waiting for you.

The phone was in the kitchen. She reached Pastor Barnes at the church, explained the old man was alone, and was assured someone would be there in minutes. She glanced at her watch. Four-oh-eight. She couldn't hang around and wait.

She didn't bother driving past the other two houses that interested her. That would be a waste of time now. Instead, she headed straight for Bridle Trails State Park.

The old gray Ford sedan was parked at the rear of the parking lot, the only vehicle there, barely noticeable in a patch of shade created by the slant of the late-afternoon sun. The dull green bike had been pulled well off to one side, as close to the forest wall as possible without scratching the paint. The parking lot was empty of horse trailers. The day riders were gone, the evening ones hadn't arrived yet. There was no sign of Barb Denton, the ranger.

Kate didn't bother pulling her car out of the way of later incoming traffic. As soon as she saw the Ford and the bike, she braked hard, grabbed her keys from the ignition, and ran.

She halted at the opening to the southern trail and listened. She could hear nothing but muted traffic sounds from the distant freeway. She reached inside her blazer and drew her gun.

The path ahead was in dimness. She moved a stealthy pace or two forward, so that she got her face out of the direct sun and held up for a moment or two while her eyes adjusted to the difference in light. Once she could make out the fine small details of the woods, she crept soundlessly down the packed-down path, pausing every other step to listen. Not even a bird chirped. Something had made them fall silent.

She was still a bend or two away from the clearing when she heard the faint murmur of a soft voice.

". . . Yea, though I walk through the valley of the shadow of death, I will fear no evil, for thou art with me . . ."

Kate moved then. On cat-light feet, she raced around the last two bends, gun held out straight ahead of her, gripped in both hands.

". . . thy rod and thy staff they comfort me . . ."

Already facing the clearing, she burst into the opening and dropped into a shooting crouch and froze.

". . . thou preparest a table before me in the presence of mine enemies . . ."

The body of Norm Overholtz lay crumpled in the center of the clearing. He looked like he'd been kneeling and had simply rolled over sideways onto the ground, except the back of his head was caved in, matted with blood, bone and tissue. He was in the same sprawled position as Peter had been. It was impossible to tell if he was still breathing or not.

Martha Taft knelt over him, head bowed, a small prayer book open across the palm of her hand, a short, thick, bloodstained branch at her side. ". . . thou anointest my head with oil; my cup runneth over . . ."

Keeping her gun barrel firmly fixed on the praying woman, Kate slowly rose from her crouch.

". . . Surely goodness and mercy shall follow me all the days of my life, and I will dwell in the house of the Lord forever."

Her head remained bowed in silent prayer another moment or two, then she raised her face toward Kate. A serene smile turned the planes of her face into ones of celestial beauty lit with a radiance from deep within. "Amen," she said, softly.

Norm Overholtz was dead. Keeping her gun firmly aimed at Martha, Kate had the woman back up to the far side of the clearing and probed the boy's carotid artery for a pulse. Nothing.

The other woman smiled as she watched. She waited until Kate had finished testing for any signs of life and said, "My work is done now."

Keeping a wary eye on her, Kate said softly, "Yes."

Martha nodded. "I think I'd like to sit down for a minute. There's a nice picnic area on the other side of the park entrance," Martha said. She had a wistful look on her face. "Could we sit there awhile? I'd like that."

Kate was stymied. She had no car radio, there was no handy wall phone hanging from a nearby tree, and the park was deserted. She had two choices. Walk the woman at gunpoint to the nearest house, a good quarter mile away, or hold her at the park until someone arrived who could go and call for help for her. There was no hurry now; Norm was beyond help. She nodded at the woman. "Yes, we can sit there. You lead, I'll follow."

Kate settled the older woman at one of the tables, then took the seat opposite. The picnic area was in heavy shadow now, and the air had taken on the damp chill of deep woods. From distant trees, the birds began their evening song, melding and blending into a single joyous chorus.

Martha wore only a simple dark dress of light broadcloth, and Kate said, "Are you cold? You could slip my blazer on."

"No," she said softly. "I'm not cold." Her face lit up once again with that strange, radiant smile.

She was not your typically beautiful woman. The gray-streaked bun of hair was pulled back taut from her face, emphasizing the heavy broadness of the cheekbones. The forearms were solid and well muscled, as if from kneading heavy weights of bread dough. Her breasts were heavy, and her trunk was thick at the waist.

Yet the incandescent look of glowing serenity gave her a saintly kind of beauty, the same kind of beauty a woman like Mother Teresa had, that strange, indefinable beauty of one who lives in a realm far beyond the earthly planet they currently inhabit. That otherworldly quality bothered Kate greatly. It was as if Martha Taft had seen heaven and was patiently awaiting her passage there. No, Kate corrected, it was as if the woman's soul was already there, and now she was merely awaiting the final passage from the body that would follow. Kate kept a tight grip on her gun, as if the escape from earth would be a physical jog away from the park that could be halted with a bullet through the kneecap.

Martha seemed content to sit quietly with hands folded on the table, staring into some private vision with that same strange smile on her face.

When it was obvious that she would volunteer nothing, Kate prompted, "We have to talk about it, you know."

Martha gave a serene nod.

"Then we'll start with Sarah. You knew about the baby, didn't you."

Another serene nod.

"From the kitchen, you can hear all the bathroom sounds, and you heard her being sick in the mornings, didn't you. When she acted like nothing was wrong, and carried on with school and all her other activities, you suspected what her problem was."

Another nod.

"Then when she couldn't go on retreat because she was sick,

she called you at Ellis Dixon's. Probably after she talked to Nancy Wells. And you brought her here to talk."

The same nod.

"Did you try to talk to her about the baby and her plans at all?"

Martha shook her head, no.

"Did you ask her about the baby's father, who he was?"

Another shake of the head, no. "It wasn't important at first. Not till later, when I got to thinking about it."

"You simply killed her."

Martha looked up at Kate. "I sent her to live with the Lord."

"Just because she was pregnant?"

"She'd been a bad girl. '. . . yet will I slay even the beloved fruit of their womb,' " Martha quoted. She smiled shyly. "Hosea Nine, Verse Sixteen."

Kate kept her voice even. "And Peter. When you did start to think about it, you thought he was the father."

Back to the nods again.

"And so you killed him."

Nod.

"How did you get him here?"

The shy smile returned. "I invited him to come here with me to pray for her soul."

"Is that how you got Sarah here?"

She shook her head, no. "I told her we needed to spend some time together in prayer with God," she whispered. "But in a place where God walked alone."

"And then?"

"And then, when she went to the Lord, I laid her out and smoothed down her hair, and made sure her dress was neat and tidy. Like you do with a child. I laid her out with love."

And that's the clue I should've picked up from the beginning, Kate thought. Actually, she had. The difference in how the bodies lay when found. Sarah had been killed with love. Peter had been killed with rage. She simply hadn't attached enough significance to it to make it count. Instead, she'd gotten waylaid by peripheral mysteries, like Josie Hendrix and a baby-selling ring.

"Then when you learned Peter wasn't the father," Kate went on, "you figured it had to be Norm. And he had to die, too."

The eyes suddenly blazed. "They shall be consigned to the flames of hell for their sins." For a moment, the fire of madness burned scorching hot, then the blaze died down and the eerie radiance returned.

"Doesn't it also say in the Bible, 'vengeance is mine, saith the Lord'?" Kate asked.

The quote had no effect on the woman's serenity.

Kate pressed on, trying to reach the human inside. "I've always been taught that revenge is best left to God."

It was like rain off a duck's back. It made no impact whatsoever. Martha simply said, "I'd like to pray now," and she closed her eyes and bowed her head, effectively removing herself from any more questions.

Frustrated, Kate sat silent, staring for a moment at the thick strands of hair pulled taut across the top of the woman's bowed head. She wanted to reach across and yank some sense into the woman, make her sit up straight and take part in the real world. When had Martha Taft gone over the edge anyway? Had it been a precipitous fall, initiated by the crisis of her daughter's pregnancy? Or had she been gradually slipping down that steep slope of madness for a long while now, and had the pregnancy merely finished the slide, propelling her to the bottom?

Still keeping a firm grip on the gun, Kate sighed, feeling the first stirrings of pity for everyone involved in this. The repercussions would live on a good long while. As for the woman's sanity, that would be for the shrinks to battle out in court.

A movement in the trees caught her peripheral vision. Kate stilled, seeking the source. As the sun lowered into an evening sky and a false twilight fell over them, the trees had merged with the undergrowth into one mass of deep shadow, without distinction, without detail. She hadn't heard anyone arrive. But then she wouldn't have. The traffic noises all blurred into a dull background rumble that merged into a whole. But something was in there, the birds had stopped singing again. A rider?

She caught a glint of metal through the branches just before she heard a loud crack. It sounded like a tree branch breaking with a vicious snap.

Across from her, Martha exhaled a soft "poof," and slowly slumped forward.

Kate froze a moment with disbelief. Then she shouted *"No!"* She leaped up and fired toward the dark spot of the woods where the glint of metal had showed. Her automatic was woefully inadequate at that distance. She fired twice more in pure frustration, then she fired again. *"God damn it, NO!"*

"Hold fire!" a deep male voice rang out. "I'm coming out."

The limbs of the firs dipped like fronds caught in a typhoon, and the figure of Daniel Taft pushed through, holding his rifle above his head with one raised arm. The other hand was stretched out at the side to show it was empty.

Kate trained the gun on his heart. "Stop!"

He stopped in mid-step.

"Drop the rifle!"

The rifle clunked to the ground.

In a quieter voice still filled with command, she said, "Now kick the rifle ahead of you and step backward three paces!"

His face impassive, Taft kicked and backed up. The rifle spiraled clear of the underbrush.

"Now step to the side. To your right. Keep going."

She left the table and began circling the picnic area to her own right, her gun barrel tracking with him. When he was close to the riding ring, she ordered him to halt again. Never letting the gun waver from that point center left on his chest, she moved to the rifle, squatted down and picked it up by feel.

Keeping her distance, she commanded him to a nearby table. When he was sitting down and no longer a threat, she glanced over at Martha Taft. The woman's head had landed on the prayer book. A red stain spread slowly over the back of her dress. She didn't seem to be breathing.

Kate edged toward the woman and probed the neck. No pulse. The blood flowing from the small neat hole in her back had stopped. She'd gone to her Lord, Kate thought. She patted the dead woman's shoulder once in parting, then moved toward Daniel Taft.

Daniel watched her approach with calm eyes overrunning with sadness. "I'd like to go to her, if I may," he said, quietly.

Kate neared him and stopped. "Why?" she said, her voice hoarse. "For God's sake, why did you shoot her?"

He gave her a quizzical look as if she were mighty dense to have to ask. "She couldn't have stood a trial."

"You *knew* she killed your daughter?"

He considered that. "No, I wasn't sure. Not until today. Though I kind of wondered about it, off and on. She was so strange about Sarah dying and all. All she'd do is rock in her rocking chair, and read her Bible, and tell me that Sarah had gone to live with the Lord. It was as if Elizabeth and I didn't exist anymore. Everything was Sarah. She'd talk about Sarah being up in heaven, how happy Sarah was now that she was with the Lord, how Sarah would understand everything now. At first, I thought it was shock. Grief and shock. That she was stricken by Sarah's death and that was the only way she could deal with it. But then when Peter was killed, she was as cold as ice. Every time his name was mentioned, she'd sit in her rocking chair, quoting all kinds of Bible verses that dealt with vengeance and revenge. I couldn't even get her to go to his funeral."

He sat easily, with his feet apart, hands held out at his side in plain view. "Then once I started thinking about it, it grew more and more worrisome. I knew Ellis Dixon was on such strong pain medicine that it would be easy to leave him alone for an hour or so without anyone knowing. He'd sleep right through it. And she'd been taking care of him Monday afternoons. So when Pastor Barnes called me at work this afternoon from Ellis's place, trying to find out what happened to her, why she'd left the old man alone, then I knew. And I worried that she'd found someone else to kill."

Kate nodded. "She did. Norm Overholtz. He's down in the same clearing where Peter and Sarah were found." She found herself suddenly close to weeping. "Oh, God, Mr. Taft, do you know what you've done to yourself?" She nodded toward his wife's body. "Do you know the price you'll pay for this?"

His face was reflective as he nodded. "Yes. You're going to be putting me away for a long time. But you see, if I didn't stop her, she'd have either gone on killing, or gone to trial. And I just couldn't let that happen to poor Martha. I couldn't let either happen to her." He ran a shaky hand over his face to keep from weeping. "She was such a good wife . . ." Then the tears came anyway, and slid silently down his face.

Kate kept him at gunpoint until the first suppertime rider finally came by.

Lucy Gray, of course.

A squad car was first on the scene, and not until the uniformed patrolmen had Daniel Taft securely handcuffed and the rifle in their possession, did Kate lower her gun hand. Then her arm trembled as if it were frozen to a jackhammer.

Sam arrived far too soon to have responded to the call. He just suddenly appeared from the trail and stopped to take in the whole scene, patrolmen, body, Kate, Lucy Gray, Daniel Taft. He was dressed in jeans and a windbreaker, the casual clothes of a guy through with his shift, and Kate was so damned glad to see him, she could've hugged him. She thought she'd never seen anyone look as good as he did at the moment.

She was off sitting by herself at the table farthest back from the riding ring, hunched over and miserable, still trying to recover from a bad case of the sudden shakes. She watched him as he followed the old routine—scan the scene for danger first. Satisfied everything was under control, his eyes sought and found hers. A slight smile twitched at his lips and a look of relief filled his eyes, but he merely nodded at her, then walked over to Martha Taft. He did what she had done, what the Blues had, what they all did, he sought a sign of life. After some fruitless searching, he straightened and shook his head. He turned and studied Daniel Taft for a moment, then approached one of the patrolmen.

He listened intently as the patrolman talked and gestured first toward the parking lot, then the clearing beyond it where Norm's body still lay crumpled, then to Martha and Kate, and finally to the trees and the section of the woods where Daniel had stood. Sam asked a question or two, listened with his head cocked to the answer, then nodded. Finally he headed Kate's way.

He put a casual foot up on the bench across from her and leaned on his knee and grinned slightly. "It's almost the Memorial Day weekend. Should be the Fourth of July instead, the way you celebrate."

"You mean with a bang?"

"You got it." His eyes warmed with concern. "You okay?"

"Yeah, I'm okay." From her huddle, she peered up at him. "How'd you get here so fast? The Blues just called it in."

He kept his face impassive. "Oh, seems this certain Duty sergeant started worrying about this certain Homicide dick who called in asking curious questions about some backup before hanging up on him, so he called me and reported it. I've been hunting you ever since."

"But how'd you know how to find me here?"

"Where else would a certain Homicide dick asking curious

questions about some backup go, but to the scene of the crime, eh?"

She straightened up a bit from her miserable huddle and glared at him. "Sometimes, Morrison, I think I underestimate you."

His gaze was steady and serious, but the corners of his mouth twitched in that maddening touch of humor. "Sometimes, MacLean, I think you do."

Epilogue

The hot spell kept on. A scorching sun sent the temperature into the high nineties and kept it there, day after day. Daily papers used big, black headlines to announce each day's high, prophets of doom proclaimed a return of the drought and editorials began to call for strict water conservation measures. It was only May, they said, and look at the heat already, what would the summer bring? People grew testy, their tempers razor-edged, their faces flushed and their clothes limp and wilted. Traffic grew worse as everyone sought relief down by the lakefronts or up in the cooler air of the mountains. The taverns were crammed, beer orders jumped off the scale, and fights to the death broke out over a simple thing like a parking space. Homicide was busy.

Kate wasn't, though. She'd been taken off the streets until Internal Affairs cleared her in the shooting of Martha Taft, and had spent the days catching up with the paperwork. Lacking a computer, she pulled a rolling typewriter table over to her desk, and began on the backlog of forms.

She'd broken the case into two parts, the case against Daniel Taft, and the postmortem case built against Martha Taft. They had Daniel Taft cold. It was a slam-bam, thank-you-ma'am, straightforward bang-bang case with a cop as an eyewitness. They didn't get any better than that. Kate made a brief plea with the

D.A.'s office for a reduced charge of murder, admitting that while yes, the man had killed his wife, he'd also killed a killer. The D.A., as hot and testy as anyone else from the heat wave broiling Puget Sound, didn't buy it. Daniel was booked for Murder One. Kate left that meeting shaking her head once more at the tragedy of this whole thing, then placed a call to Pastor Barnes to ask what would happen to Lizzie. Several church families wanted her, she was assured. She'd be well-loved and well taken care of. They were working on the legalities now. Satisfied, she hung up and went back to winding up the postmortem case against Martha Taft.

There was no question of Martha's guilt. Homer's lab crew had worked their miracles on Martha's car, and had matched scrapings there to the debris removed from both Sarah's and Peter's skulls. With each victim, she'd swung a killing branch, then placed it in the trunk of her car and tossed it away someplace else. They'd never find either of the branches, but they didn't need to. The trace evidence alone convicted her. Kate thanked Homer and added another report to her paperwork on the case.

Phone company records provided the final link. A call had been made from the Taft house to the Ellis Dixon residence at three thirty-seven the afternoon Sarah was killed. The timing fit. Nancy Wells had had her little talk with Sarah, offering the group home and adoption as the solution to her problems. Sarah had rejected it. She was keeping her baby. When Nancy left, Sarah wasted no time in following through on her decision. People had to be told, and among the first would have to be her mother. So she'd called the Dixon house and broken the news. The tragedies followed as if preordained. Martha had definitely done all three killings. There were no more loose ends.

Word of the shootings had gotten around the bullpen and detectives drifted by her desk in ones and twos. She'd replayed the scene of the shooting in her mind, over and over, catching the glint of metal in the trees, hearing the crack like a breaking tree-limb, seeing the body of Martha Taft slowly slumping onto the table. In the replay, there was plenty of time to react. To prevent. To forestall. In the replay, she aimed better, shot sooner, nicked the rifle hand, deflected the tragedy. In her replay, no one died.

But it couldn't be replayed, and she had this need to tell the story again and again to anyone who'd listen. Sam explained that this was a common reaction. Every time you told it, you grew a little closer to acceptance. Everyone who stopped took a few moments to perch on the corner of her desk and listen, letting her talk it out. Each of them had his own story of cases gone south, and when she was through, had said all she could say, they told her their own stories. It was their way of offering comfort, of telling her, Hey, shit happens. Whatever chasm existed between herself and the rest of the Homicide squad was bridged for a little while. She welcomed their efforts. It made her feel less alone for the moment.

Except for Goddard, of course. He wandered over at one point, a cold, uncaring look in his eyes, a thick sheaf of papers in his hand. "I need some typing done."

Without missing a beat, she rolled the current sheet out of the typewriter, scooped up all her files and rose. "Help yourself," she said with a sweet smile. Then she walked off, leaving him standing there.

The phone call she'd been waiting for came late that day. It was almost quitting time when it came in, and she was relieved that it did. She'd been hoping she wouldn't have to be the one to make it. She listened, then said, "Yes, I can meet you tonight, what time? . . . Okay, I'll see you then."

Sam looked over at her. "What was that about?"

"Personal business," she said. It wasn't quite true, but close enough so her conscience was clear, if not quite pure.

Leaning back in his chair, Sam stared at her silently for a moment, a long, reflective stare. He'd been pretty self-absorbed all day, she'd noticed. He was still doing paperwork for the Captain, so he'd spent his shift at his desk, too, but it seemed that whenever she'd glance over at him, he'd be leaning back in his chair, staring off into some private vision, face dark, remote and closed. Now, after that reflective stare, he suddenly jerked upward in his chair and grinned over at her. There was a mischievous warmth to that grin that sent her heart scudding out of rhythm. She put the brakes on it and adopted a matter-of-fact tone. "What's the matter?"

"Not a damned thing. Gotta go. Personal business." His grin broadened, carving deep ruts down his sad basset-hound face. A slight dimple indented one cheek. Beguiled, she found herself watching it for a bit too long. Then she came back to reality, flushed, watched him leave, then swung back to finish out her shift.

After checking out for the day, she had time to kill. She stopped for a long leisurely dinner at George's, hunched over the newspaper, catching up with news, editorials, and the comics. Then she went next door and shot some pool at Smokie Jo's until it was time to leave. She drank Coke, not wine.

The night was damned near as hot as the day, and the streets were still full of traffic as people drove around, seeking a place to chill out for real. It was a relief to be able to turn onto the church's secluded back road and be rid of the last of the tailgaters.

The church's parking lot was empty except for one car, the nighttime activities over, the complex put to bed for another day. She parked next to the car and followed the pathways to the rear entrance of the church office wing. The night offered no coolness, no breath of air. It promised another day of scorching heat in the morning. She scanned the western sky, but stars glittered against the black velvet of the night sky. There wasn't a rain cloud in sight, nothing to indicate a break in the heat wave.

A lone light burned in the entranceway to the office wing. The door was unlocked. She entered the foyer with a cop's caution, coming to an immediate halt to listen, all her senses alive and alert. The building felt empty, but a rectangular box of yellow light spilled out of the open doorway of Pastor Matt's office. She took one more listen, then moved with catlike quiet down the hall and came to a halt in the open doorway.

The room was total chaos. Wall photos were down and the bookshelves were cleared off. The desk was heaped with books, file folders and framed photographs. Cartons were scattered everywhere, their flaps open, fully half of them already filled. There was barely room to maneuver from box to box to box. But Matt wasn't in the room; he wasn't anywhere in sight.

She looked up and down the hall. No light showed around the cracks of any of the doors. Then inspiration came and she moved down the deserted corridor to the counseling room at the far corner and tapped on the door.

There was a long silence, then Matt's voice gave a weary, "Who is it?"

"Kate MacLean."

"The door's open."

He was standing in the dark in front of a large picture window, framed against the lighter night sky, staring into a private walled garden. He turned at her entrance and leaned back against the frame to watch her approach.

She left the door open, moved through the dimness of the room to the other side of the window and leaned against it, too. The night lights illuminating the hallway cast a web of shadows over his cheekbones and eyes, but it clearly outlined his mouth, curved down at the corners under the weight of a deep sorrow. He looked both so young and so old all at once. Her heart went out to him. "How are you doing?" she asked.

He shook his head, blinking hard. "It's been a hell of a week."

It was the first time she'd ever heard him swear. She gave him a moment, and when he said nothing more, she went on. "I saw the cartons. You're leaving the church, aren't you."

He gave a rueful nod of the head. "I have to."

"Does Pastor Barnes know?"

"Not yet," he said evenly.

She kept silent. This was his show. But he said nothing. "I was grateful you called," she said, finally. "Otherwise I'd have had to call you."

His face took on a weariness beyond his years. "You know."

She nodded, then turned her head slightly to look out into the garden. "Yes, I figured it out. You were very much in love with her, weren't you."

The silence was lengthy.

She kept her gaze fixed on the garden. The shrubs planted there were mere black humps against the lighter tones of the wood fence. Her gaze traced the outline of each one, idly trying to separate one from the other. Like suspects in a murder case, she thought. Sort them out and view them as individuals.

Finally he stirred. "Yes," he said in a low voice. "God help me, yes."

"And you were the father of her baby."

"Yes."

She turned her head and looked at him now. The room side of his face was in total darkness, the other half was lit by the starglow. The two halves of man, she thought. Half-devil, half-saint. "It was right here in this room, wasn't it. After choir practice. Or during the activity nights on Saturdays. Slipping out during a movie, for instance. Or during the Saturday work parties. She'd leave a little early from the day-care center and report a little late to her parents, and there'd be some stolen time for the two of you here."

His eyes were fixed on her now, the side of his head sagged against the window frame, all resistance gone from his body. He said nothing. He was simply listening.

"I imagine at first," she continued on, "there were excuses made. You needed to talk to her about something, she needed to see you about something else. Then it began to grow into something more, and you just wanted to spend time together. And eventually the inevitable happened."

He'd been silent so long he needed to clear his voice to get the word out. "Yes."

The word hung in the air a moment as she turned back to the garden. "The pain of your dilemma must have been excruciating." She waited, but there was no response to that. "Did you know before she was killed that she was pregnant?"

"No. Not until you told us about the autopsy report."

That's why he'd been so shocked, she thought. She would've suspected sooner except for that shock. It had been real and blinding. "I have to ask you," she said as tactfully as she could, "why you didn't take precautions. You're married, without children, surely you know how to protect yourself."

"I didn't know I could father children," he said simply. "Not until I visited a doctor Friday morning and had myself tested." So that had been the burr under his saddle, she thought, remembering back to the angry young pastor she'd run into that morning.

He chose a spot in the garden just outside the window and stared at it for long moments before speaking again. "My wife—" He stopped, then tried again. "It was agreed before we married that we would have children. But when the first year went by without a child, then the second, she claimed there had to be something wrong and had us both tested. Later, she said the problem was with me. I was sterile." He still stared at the garden, but his body had slowly stiffened with anger and there was a bitter note in his voice. "After I received the doctor's report Friday morning, that's all I thought about, that some horrible mistake had been made years ago, and she was the one who was sterile. But somehow, it didn't ring true, something there didn't make sense. I waited until she arrived at the church to help out in the kitchen, then I went on home and did some looking around. I found some pills in a little compact case hidden in one of her dresser drawers. They were birth control pills. There was nothing wrong with either of us. She had deliberately prevented us from having children."

He faced Kate directly now. "It explained so much, so much that had puzzled me over the years. Her insistence whenever we talked that yes, absolutely, she wanted children, would love to have children. And yet, her distaste of them was obvious. She waved that away by saying having your own would be different. I believed her. From laziness, I think now. It was easier to believe her than not believe her. If I didn't believe her, it would be a crisis point in the marriage. So I let it go. But there were other things. Her extreme concentration on furnishing the house just so, spending far more than we could afford, really. Creating the perfect home for me, she said. Being the perfect wife for a minister of God, creating the perfect surroundings that befitted the minister of God she'd married. But there was also her reluctance to become involved with the church, or even make friends within it. Yet she had almost a pathological need to be hanging on my arm in public as if we were the perfect couple. Then at home, at night, every night, she slept in a separate room." He gave a slight bitter laugh. "I can't imagine why she thought she needed the pills. We hadn't had a relationship in years."

"And so you came to love Sarah," she said gently. "Warm, and kind, and gentle, and compassionate. With a heart filled with love."

He laid the side of his head back against the window frame, his body slumped, the anger suddenly gone. "Yes," he said simply. "I came to love Sarah."

In the starglow bathing one cheek, Kate could see the glisten of a tear trail down his cheek. She wanted to go and hold him, just take him in her arms like a child and hold him close until the pain swamping him eased. She stared out at the night-black shrubs, once again trying to separate and trace back to the parents the intertwining branches and outlines. "I guess I have to ask," she said slowly, trying to use some delicate phrasing, "what there was about Patty that drew you to her in the first place."

The silence went on so long that she began to think he hadn't heard the question. But then he said softly, "She seemed—sweet, I guess. Sweet and dedicated and very, very committed to what I believed in. We were young and idealistic, a whole shining world stretched out at our feet." His voice turned somber. "Then reality set in. My work was very different than she'd envisioned it. She thought it would be Sunday sermons and handshakes afterwards, then I'd be hers for the week. She also thought there'd be more prestige to being a pastor's wife than there was. She wasn't accorded the kind of respect that she thought she deserved, the kind of respect Emma Barnes received. That Emma spent years earning. From then on, Patty pitted herself against the church in a battle for possession of me. My time, my energy, my attention. And there wasn't enough of me to go around. Or I didn't make available enough of me to go around. Whichever, it started a downward spiral that I couldn't seem to reverse. And she wouldn't consider counseling, ever, she said, whenever I suggested it. Counseling was for people with problems, and the church was creating the problems, not her. So there was no need for her to go, was her thinking."

"What will you do?" she asked him.

There was another lengthy silence. When he did speak, finally, his voice was heavy with weariness. "I don't know. I simply don't know. I can't see myself leaving her. I honestly don't know what she'd do if I did. It just doesn't seem like she could manage on her own. But I can't see myself staying, either, participating in the farce that's been created."

"Have you said anything to her about the pills?"

"Not yet."

"Will you?"

"I'll have to, sooner or later." He drew himself up straighter and turned back to her. "I'm at a total loss, Katie, just at a total loss. It's been too much. Sarah's death. Peter's death. Norm's death. The tragedy of Sarah's parents. The mockery of my marriage. I don't even begin to know what to do. I don't have a handle on any of this at all."

"So your answer is to leave the church."

"I have to. I'm taking the whole story about Sarah and me to Thomas in the morning. I won't be able to stay after that."

Kate gave some thought. "I'm not so sure, Matt. A few days ago, I'd have agreed, there'd be no room in this church for this kind of—human problem, if you will. But Pastor Barnes has been through one soul-wrenching week here. It could be it's humanized him a little, brought him down from that lofty perch of his a bit. He may be more forgiving than you think."

Matt gave a sorrowful shake of the head. "It isn't his forgiveness I need. It's God's. By keeping my silence about Sarah, I am directly responsible for two lives being destroyed. No, three. No, make that four. If I had spoken out in the very beginning, neither Peter nor Norm would've died, and maybe Martha would still be alive, too. Then Daniel wouldn't be in the mess he's in. Four lives destroyed because of me, because of my silence. That's one hell of a burden for the soul to carry. It's God's forgiveness I need. Not Thomas's."

She could've played it down, she could've cited mitigating circumstances to ease his burden a little, she could've said no, he was being too hard on himself, she could've pointed out that he'd had to wait until he was sure he was responsible for Sarah's pregnancy, she could've made excuses, all sorts of excuses.

But the bald truth was that Matt was right. If he'd spoken out from the beginning, the story would've taken a different turn, and that would've ordained a much different ending. Married or divorced, he was going to have to carry the guilt from this one to his grave.

They stared at each other through the dimness of the room, acknowledging the truth of his words with bleak honesty, neither saying anything.

God's punishment, she thought sadly. So much heavier than man's could ever be.

As late as it was, after ten, traffic still slowed her down and it took a good forty minutes to make the ten-minute drive to headquarters. The parking lot had emptied out and she circled, checking the cars that were still there. Sam's was parked in the shade at the rear. Goddard's was gone. She pulled in next to Sam's and crossed the lot.

Sam was bent over her desk, composing a note, when she rounded the last curve of the filing-cabinet maze. Her footsteps startled him and he jerked up like a puppet on a string and swung her way.

"Hi," she called out. "What's up?"

The note was in his hand and he simply held it out.

She took it from him and looked at it. It was just a piece of scratch paper with an address and phone number written on it. She read the address. An apartment over in Juanita. A mile or so from her house. She looked up quizzically.

He lounged against his desk. "New address. Mine."

Their eyes locked and held until a slow flush climbed her face. She dropped her gaze back to the slip of paper in her hand and thought of margaritas and enchiladas and evenings with Sam again. Especially evenings with Sam. She looked back up at him.

He nodded, then swung away and went to his desk. He didn't look her way again.

Her phone rang and she dropped into her desk chair to take the call. It was Len Franklin. He was homesick, lonely, and sick of communing with corpses. Would she go out for a late dinner with him tonight?

She peered over at Sam's desk. Even though it was late, he was still busy working. Their old pattern was back. Was that good, or not so good?

"Hold on a minute," she said quietly into the phone, "I'm thinking."

She swiveled her chair around, lounged as far back in it as it would go, propped her feet on her bottom drawer and had a long internal dialogue with herself.

When she'd argued everything both ways to Sunday, she nodded once, then straightened in her chair with a sudden clunk of ball bearing. "You know what, Len?" she murmured into the phone. "I'd like to help, I really would, but it's just not going to work out for a while." She made a few soothing comments, stroked his ego some, because she still had to work with him, then hung up. She rose then and walked over to Sam's desk.

He glanced up from his paperwork as she paused in front of him.

She perched casually on the corner of his desk. "That was Franklin. Wanted to take me out for a late dinner."

The moment hung between them as his eyes searched hers.

"I told him no."

Relief flooded his face, and he lounged back then, folding his arms across his chest. He wore the happiest grin she'd ever seen.

Honestly, she thought, crossing her own arms, watching him. Talk about your self-satisfied smirk. And he really was a homely old thing. Like the old family basset hound, with that long face and those big, warm, brown eyes. And the dewlaps. Don't forget the dewlaps. He was really nothing special at all. You could run down any street in town and pass a dozen men that were better looking, that were much more attractive than he was. And that probably made a hell of a lot more money than he did . . . *and* worked normal hours to boot.

Of course, he did have cute buns. She'd have to tell him that sometime, he had really cute buns. And then there was that maddening twitch of the lips when he was trying to bite back a smile. And there were the margaritas he enjoyed, and the enchiladas he loved, and the way his eyes had made sure she was all right after the shooting, and the card game after the break-in, and . . .

Her pulse did a jig. "Mexican tonight?" she asked, casually.

He replied, equally as casual. "Why not?"

He shoved his papers together into one stack and locked them away in his top drawer. Then he grabbed his jacket from the top of the filing cabinet he used as a coatrack and they walked out into the still hot night air together.

	DATE DUE		